I0637275

The Case of the Reincarnated Lover

By Juli Monroe

Special thanks to Dannelle Shugart. When friends say they'll "die for you," I'm not sure this is exactly what they meant.

Chapter 1

Saturday, May 1, 2010.
Not Quite Midnight

DO THE WORDS "VAMPIRE" and "camping" go together for you?

Yeah, not for me either, so I was surprised when Paul suggested we go down to Prince William Forest State Park for an overnight trip. He said there was something he wanted to show me, and who was I to turn him down when he was so excited?

Now you should know that I am a city boy all the way. Bugs and dirt are not my idea of a good time. I'm more inclined to spend my weekends dancing the night away at gay dance clubs with Stephen, my boyfriend. And today was Beltane, traditionally celebrated with…well, let's just say it's a fertility rite, and I'm more than willing to continue the tradition, even though I'm not intending to be a father anytime soon.

I stumbled over yet another root and swore softly. "Why did I let you talk me into this again?"

Paul turned to look at me. His eyes gleamed in reflected moonlight. "Because we're friends?"

I paused to take a drink from my water bottle. "Yeah, I guess that's a good reason. How much farther are we anyway?"

"Almost there. It'll be worth it. Trust me."

I grumbled wordlessly under my breath but followed him. Yeah, the funny thing is I did trust him. I'm not sure my parents raised me to have a vampire as one of my closest friends, but they got over it when I told them.

We walked for maybe another ten minutes, and I tripped over yet another root just as Paul reached out a hand to stop me. "Quiet. We're almost there. We'll have to crawl from here."

I shook my head, sure he was kidding. Crawl? As in along the ground? Putting me in contact with even more bugs and dirt?

He dropped easily to the ground and started slithering along, making absolutely no noise. I sighed and got down on my hands and knees and followed him, with considerably less grace and somewhat more noise. He looked back at me over his shoulder, the reproof evident in his eyes, and I tried to move more quietly.

After a few moments, he stopped me again and turned to whisper in my ear. "Just another foot or two. Very quietly now."

I slid forward, barely breathing. I had no idea what I was supposed to see, but I heard the suppressed excitement in his voice, and I was pretty sure it would be good. As long as it wasn't some weird kind of bug.

Nope, not a bug, although at first I wasn't sure. As I slowly lifted my head, the clouds parted, and the moon, just a few days past full, shone silver on a small ring of stones in the exact center of a tiny clearing.

Small forms danced in the air over the circle. There must have been close to a dozen of them, and they darted here and there. Their movements looked random at first. As I watched, however, I noticed some pattern to their dance, though the meaning eluded me.

"What do you think?" Paul's whisper was barely audible.

I tore my eyes from the marvel in front of me to look at him. His eyes gleamed a shade just slightly darker than the stones in the clearing. His expression was a mixture of hope and awe.

"A fairy ring?"

He nodded.

"I thought they were just legends."

His lips twitched. "Just like vampires."

He had me there. "Yeah, I guess."

"No, they are real. And right in front of us. Look!"

I glanced back just in time to see a larger fairy fly into the middle of the ring. Don't get the wrong idea. When I say "larger" I mean maybe twelve inches instead of six or eight. I wished I had one of my vision enhancement potions.

Just then, Paul put something in my hand. I looked down to see a small sport bottle.

"You're kidding me."

He chuckled. "No. I figured you'd need it."

"When'd you get it?"

"I swiped it while you were trying to coax Gimble out from under the couch."

Gimble, one of my two ferrets, is the feistier of the

two. She knows the rules perfectly well, but mostly chooses to ignore them. When she wants my attention (like when she knows I'm about to leave), diving under the couch is one of her favorite tricks.

I checked the label in the moonlight. Sure, I trusted Paul, but my father drilled me endlessly as a kid. Never, ever, swallow a potion unless you've checked the label at least twice. Drinking the wrong potion can have...unfortunate...consequences. It only took one mistake to teach the lesson forever.

It read "Vision Enhancement" in my neat calligraphy. (Hey, I'm a warlock. Gotta learn the fancy writing for potions and scrolls.) I gave Paul a grateful smile, popped the top and drank it down.

A moment later, the potion started working. Moonlight suddenly illuminated almost as well as the midday sun. Details were starkly sharp, and I could see at least twice as far. I looked again at the fairies.

Pre-potion, they had been little more than glowing shapes. Now I could see tiny humanoid forms in the sparks of light. Gossamer wings buzzed from their shoulders, moving at speeds that would impress a hummingbird.

The fairies were naked. And quite anatomically correct, I noted, blushing. They were about evenly split between males and females, and their miniature faces were aglow with delight and rapture.

What about the larger fairy? I guessed he must be their king, and, other than his size, he was kingly in every way. Yes, even that way if your mind must sink into the gutter. His arms and shoulders were muscular, and his tiny face was perfectly chiseled. He was just as naked as his followers, with the exception of a simple circlet on his brow.

Just then he raised his arms, and all the fairies stopped, hovering in place in a blur of wings. He spoke. I couldn't hear his words, but from the expressions of his followers, it must have been inspirational. Reading body language, I started to suspect that he was more priest than king.

"Is it some sort of religious service?" I asked, keeping my voice as low as possible. I knew Paul would have no trouble hearing me.

Paul shot me a look of amused puzzlement. "Of course. It *is* May Day after all."

Right. Why wouldn't fairies celebrate it too? Which led to an uncomfortable thought. "Umm, they aren't going to…you know…right in front of us, are they?"

Paul's eyes danced with mirth. "Not right in front of us, no. As soon as this part of the ceremony is completed, they'll fly back into the wood and…you know…"

Yeah, I have a hard time saying the word "sex" around him. So sue me. He's one of the hottest guys I've ever known, and, unfortunately, he's straight, which doesn't stop me from thinking, but does make it quite embarrassing to talk about it.

I tried to play it cool. "That's good. I'd hate to think you brought me out here to watch woodland porn."

He started to say something, probably to continue the teasing, when I caught a blur of movement from the circle and turned just in time to see the entire group flitter off into the woods. In their absence, the circle seemed to shrink, still magical and mysterious, but lessened somehow by their departure.

"That's it then?"

Paul nodded. "Pretty much. Fairies aren't into long rituals. They're not the brightest supernatural creatures ever, and that's about as long as their attention span can manage." He stood up, extending a hand to help me up. "What did you think?"

I grinned at him. "It was amazing. Thank you!"

"Worth the bugs and dirt?"

"Well," I said. "I don't know about that." But I was still smiling, so I knew he wouldn't take me seriously. "How'd you know they were here?"

He shrugged. "Runner mentioned it a couple of months ago…"

Runner was the leader of a pack of werewolves living in the D.C. area.

"… after some of his people discovered the ring," he continued. "We think they are recent arrivals since they'd never seen the ring before. I'd seen their Beltane ritual before, years ago, and I thought you'd like to see it too."

I do a lot of ritual magic as a warlock, so he's right. I'm always interested in new ones, though maybe I'll skip the flying and naked parts. Not really my thing.

I said as much, and he smiled, a look of quiet satisfaction on his face. "Anything else interesting here?"

Paul shook his head. "No, the show's over for to-day. Want to head back to the campsite?"

"Sure. I think you promised me marshmallows."

He smiled. "I did at that. And if we are lucky, I might have even packed some chocolate."

"If you have chocolate, I am your man."

He laughed and threw a casual arm around my shoulders as we turned to walk back to our campsite.

As we drew near to the tent, I was reminded that "camping" means different things to Paul and to me. My parents had a small RV when I was a kid, and they occasionally convinced me to accompany them on trips to the Grand Canyon or other cool places. It was fun, but hardly what anyone would call "roughing" it.

Paul, however, was of the old school of camping thought. Think "tent." And not one of those high-tech tents that folds down into a bag the size of a big paperback. No, this tent looks like it might remember the Battle of Gettysburg. It was made of heavy canvas and used actual wooden poles and stakes. I'd teased Paul about spending the night surrounded by stuff that could kill him, but he'd just shrugged and said, "It's what I'm used to."

While the tent looked like it could give a convinc-ing history lesson, Paul assured me it was solid, and the sleeping bags and other camping equipment were modern. Paul's sleeping bag was cool. It was made of thick material that was almost light proof, and it had a hood that covered his head. When he was in it, he was completely covered. Good thing. If I were a vampire, I'd want more than a bit of ancient canvas between me and certain death.

You've probably got all sorts of wrong ideas about vampires. Paul doesn't sparkle. He doesn't hate his "immortal, undead existence." He does use the subway to get around, but not in the tunnels. Nope, he rides the trains just like the rest of us. Sunlight will kill him, but crosses don't affect him. Wooden stakes yes. Does he need to sleep on his native earth? I don't think so, but I can't speak for certain. I've been to his house, but I've never seen the inside of his bedroom.

I eyed my sleeping bag. It wasn't quite as fancy, but it looked like it would work. Paul had been thoughtful enough to provide me with a fold-up ground mat. It wasn't going to replace my comfy mattress at home, but it would do for one night.

He started building a fire. "Want to help me out with a quick spell?"

I shook my head. "Am I ever going to convince you that 'boom' spells are only in the books?"

He grinned at me over the intricate pile of kindling and logs. "But don't you believe everything you read?"

"Sure." I picked up two small sticks and crossed them. "Which is why I'm completely certain you will now run howling into the woods."

"Touche." He struck a match and lit the tinder. In moments, he had a roaring fire.

I love fire. Always have. When the flames curl around the logs and pop little sparks into the air, it looks as if something's living in there, just waiting for me use my magic to pull it forth.

"What're you thinking?"

"Not much. Just that fire always seems alive."

"Yes."

We settled back and just watched for a while. Paul and I haven't been friends for long, but we've moved into that stage where we can just be together, not needing conversation. He's solid. I've viewed his aura, and to someone with my magical senses, he feels good to be near.

Although something about him seemed a bit off, especially considering the awesomeness we'd just seen.

"Something wrong?" I asked.

Paul shook his head. "Not really. Why?"

I shrugged. "Dunno. My warlock senses are tingling."

I got the grin I was hoping for, but it was strained enough to let me know I was onto something.

"All right. Yes. There is something."

I just waited. Trust me. You do not push vampires. Not if you want to stay healthy.

Finally, he sighed. (Yes, vampires do that, even though they don't need to breathe. My best guess is it's a left-over habit. Or the only way to properly express certain emotions. I haven't decided which yet.) "You know how I was gone for a week or so recently?"

I remembered. About a month ago, he'd left suddenly, with no warning beyond a vague text message. "Yeah," I said, hoping my voice sounded like I wanted to hear more.

"I'd heard about a serial killer in New York, and I went to investigate."

"Did you find him."

He nodded, the motion slow and pensive. "I did. And I killed him."

I cocked an eyebrow at him. "So what's the problem? Bad guy's gone. He can't hurt anyone anymore."

And before you get all over me about taking this so calmly, it's what Paul does. He rarely kills humans, saving it for killers and other folks who are truly evil. And yes, I do trust him to know the difference. Well, mostly. It's complicated being friends with a vampire.

So I was pretty surprised at what came out of his mouth next.

"I'm beginning to question even those kills, Dafydd. I've taken so many lives since I was turned. I swore off non-evil doers, but I have to wonder. Am I just using 'ends justifies the means' thinking here?"

Okay, heavy stuff for camping. What happened to ghost stories? However, I gave it the thought it deserved and finally said, "Look, I can't make these decisions for you. It's your life … or undeath, and right and wrong aren't nearly as clear as we'd like them to be. I guess what I'm trying to say is follow your instincts. You've lived a long time. If your gut's telling you killing even bad dudes is wrong, then don't do it. Find 'em and turn them into the cops, or something."

I paused again, wanting to make sure he really got the next part. "But make sure good people aren't at risk when you do it. If someone's bad enough that he needs to go *now*, then do it. Don't hesitate. 'Good of the many instead of the few' kind of thinking."

Paul chuckled at that, although he frowned. "I didn't think you'd read Jeremy Bentham."

I frowned right back at him. "Dude, I have no idea who that is. I was quoting Spock."

He got that pretentious I'm-way-older-than-you-look that I really hate sometimes. "Of course. My mistake."

No way I was letting him get away with that. "And the fact that you just pulled that face on me tells me you have never seen *Wrath of Khan*, which we will rectify as soon as we get back."

I don't get full-out belly laughs from him very often, but that did it. I just grinned at him, which made him laugh harder.

"You're right. I was otherwise occupied when that one came out. And *The Motion Picture* was so bad, I just never got around to it."

Still chuckling, Paul got up to check the fire. The bed of coals was glowing nicely, and he rummaged in his pack for chocolate, marshmallows and, of course, graham crackers. I grinned as he came back, juggling the s'mores makings, and I got up to help him.

"I think it's been almost a decade since I had these."

Paul handed me the chocolate, put down everything else and then went back to his pack for metal skewers. I raised an eyebrow at them. "So modern? I thought you'd go for the sharpened stick approach."

He cocked an eyebrow in my direction. "Vampire, remember? Sharpened wood is not my favorite."

I nodded at the tent. "Uh huh. I think you're just spoiled by all the modern conveniences."

"That too."

We settled happily around the fire to roast marshmallows. Of course, my first one slid off the skewer into the fire. We both had a good laugh at that, but eventually, I got one to the perfect shade of golden brown, and we munched toasty goodness and got our hands completely sticky.

Before you tell me that vampires can't eat anything but blood, let me remind you that TV and Bram Stoker got a lot of it wrong. Paul can eat, for recreation. It doesn't nourish him, but it doesn't hurt him either, and, although it makes no logical sense, he still has taste buds. Or their supernatural equivalent. He once told me that his enhanced sense of smell also affected his ability to taste. In a good way, he assured me.

I was licking the last bit of chocolate off my fingers when Paul's phone rang. We both frowned at it, as he got up to grab it before it vibrated its way off his sleeping bag.

"Who could that be?" I asked as he answered.

Immediately, I knew it wasn't good. Paul's expression went from confusion to concern and then to anger. He didn't say much, just asked "Where?" "When?" and "How soon should we meet?"

I sighed and began to gather up our stuff. Obviously this camping trip was over.

When he hung up, he began taking down the tent.

"Who was it?"

"Damien."

"What now?" I asked.

"The rogue has killed again. This time, more spectacularly."

Late last year, we'd learned about a rogue vampire killing people in D.C. He (or she) has been particularly difficult to stop, especially since the local vampire community couldn't figure out who it was. You may be wondering "What's a rogue?" "Don't all vampires kill?" While it's true that most vampires do kill humans, they are usually careful about who and how. This one on the other hand has been overt about it, enough so that the local vampire community was getting worried humans would start to notice.

Paul's been eager to join the hunt, but because of intricate vampire politics, he's been sidelined. Damien, another vampire and a friend to Paul, had been keeping him in the loop.

"What do you mean by 'spectacular?'"

The tent came slithering down, and Paul quickly gathered up the canvas, jamming it into a rough bundle. "I'm not sure yet. Damien didn't have all the details, but he's killed more than one person this time. And left them in Lucius' front yard."

I winced. That took balls. Lucius is the oldest vampire in D.C., so to mess with him was either suicidal or making one hell of a statement.

"I assume you're going to the scene."

"Of course." He tossed the wadded-up tent into the back of his car, a red Toyota Prius.

"Good. I'm coming along."

Paul turned to face me, his expression set. "No."

"Yes." I rolled up my sleeping bag, willing my hands to remain steady. I haven't pushed Paul very often, and I wasn't certain how he'd react.

"This is none of your business."

Oh, so he was going to play that card, was he?

"I'm the most powerful practicing warlock in the city. Supernatural dangers are my business. And last I checked, vampires are supernatural. And dangerous."

Since he was the one who had pushed me to take my responsibilities as the city's defender more seriously, I didn't think he could say much to that.

"It will be very dangerous."

I refrained from rolling my eyes at that. "Like facing down a pack of infected werewolves was a walk in the park?"

He walked over to his sleeping bag and knelt down. His movements were stiff, lacking most of his usual grace. "Is there anything I can say to make you change your mind?"

"Nope." I stood up and tossed my sleeping bag into the trunk. Then I grabbed my pack. I was ready to go. I looked at him expectantly.

"All right. Do we have everything?" Paul managed to sound exasperated and fond at the same time.

I glanced around the campsite. "Looks like it. Let

me gather up the trash, and we'll toss it in the dumpster on the way out. Do we have to do anything to check out?"

He shook his head. "No, I paid on the way in, and that covered it."

He threw his sleeping bag and pack into the car while I gathered up all the trash into a plastic bag and tied it closed.

"I'm ready."

He motioned me to the passenger side, and we both got in. So much for our first camping trip. The fairies had been great. At least the world had left us alone long enough to eat s'mores.

I'M NOT SURE I'd ever been in this part of town. You know how almost every city has someplace only the rich and privileged can live? In D.C. area, Potomac Manors is the premier of those areas, with the highest median income in the region. However, it's considered a "new money" region, so I was surprised to learn that Lucius, the oldest local vampire lived here. I was expecting something in Georgetown: you know, smaller, less gaudy houses, but much older money.

I said as much to Paul, and he responded with, "Lucius is old, yes. But he's considered a bit gauche by the older of our kind. The New York and Chicago families will barely speak to him."

"Families?"

He glanced at me. "Of course. You know that we

call those we create 'children.' Naturally, we extend that to a family structure."

"So vampires are kind of in an extended family kind of thing?"

He nodded. "Yes. We get some of our power and prestige by age and ability. But a large amount of it comes from your sire and his or her family line."

I had to ask. "What about your sire and line?"

I've never seen someone's face close down that fast. "I'd rather not speak of it, thank you."

Okay, ending that line of questioning now. "So is Lucius' line considered prestigious?"

He nodded, and his expression lightened at the change of topic. "One of the best actually. Though not really because of him. He gets his status from his sire."

"Anyone I might have heard of?"

He smiled, the expression lacking humor and sharpening the lines of his cheekbones in the reflected street light. "More than likely. I presume you have read *Dracula*?"

I choked and coughed to clear it. "You mean *the* Dracula?"

Humor tinged Paul's tone. "Of course. Nasty fellow. I met him once, and I'd prefer to leave it at that."

I nearly choked again. "You mean he's alive...or whatever. You know what I mean. He's still around?"

Paul nodded. "Yes, although he rarely leaves Romania now." He shook his head. "*Dracula* is a delightful piece of fiction. I've read it many times, and I've always suspected Stoker might have met a real vampire. Likely not Dracula, but perhaps one of his line. Typical of you humans, though, he got most of it wrong. Especially the death part. A vampire like Dracula is very difficult to kill. Once you've gotten past, oh, 400 or so, it takes more than just a stake to the heart."

He didn't elaborate, and I didn't ask him to. Paul wasn't that old, somewhat shy of two hundred, and I'd seen him in action several times. I didn't want to think about what he'd be like a few hundred years from now.

"How old is Lucius then? Was he one of Dracula's first?"

Paul snorted. "Hardly." He pulled to the side of the road and parked. "We'll walk from here. No, Lucius is, let me think, close to three hundred." He smiled at me. "You may think this is a marvelous city, and it is, but to vampires, this is little better than Podunk Nowhere. My kind prefers Europe. If they must stoop to visiting the Americas, they prefer New York, Boston, or Chicago."

I frowned. "Why Chicago? It's not as old as D.C."

"True. But it's in the middle of a huge nexus of power."

I nodded. You've heard of the Lake Michigan Triangle? No? Well, it's not as well-known as the one in Bermuda, but it's been responsible for a number of disappearances over the years. I've never been to Chicago, but it's on my list of "must visit" places, just to experience the power that is supposed to pervade the very air.

"I didn't know vampires were attracted to magical power."

He shrugged and started to get out of the car. "We're attracted to power of any kind. Why not magical too?" His voice was bleak, and I wanted to ask more, but he was already walking away. I scrambled out of the car and hurried to catch up to him. As soon as my door closed, I saw him flash his keys behind him to remotely lock the doors.

I couldn't help gawking at the homes we passed. Huge didn't even begin to describe them. Most of them were elegant, with long drives leading to houses with multiple wings. My family, all nine siblings, their spouses and kids, could have lived in one with room left over to entertain friends.

"They're all right," Paul said. He has an odd way of guessing my thoughts.

"I'd say!"

He shook his head. "They're too gaudy. Too large. I prefer my house."

Truth to be told, I preferred his too, but I didn't have a chance to say anything. Ahead of us was another of the huge houses, with lights lit and people bustling over the yard. We'd arrived.

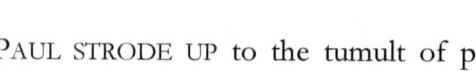

PAUL STRODE UP to the tumult of people, vampires, lights and cameras as if he belonged. As we approached, a vampire broke off from a crowd to approach us. As he came closer, I saw it was Damien. He looked relieved to see Paul, although he frowned when he saw me. I kept my expression neutral. It would be a long time, if ever, before I'd be accepted in the vampire community, and I was okay with it. Perversely, I did have a bit of status. When Paul had taken me to Lounge 201 to aura read the vampires, they were naturally curious about me. Although I hadn't understood what I was doing at the time, I managed to leave them with the impression that Paul was bonded to me. Apparently, it was not unheard of for powerful warlocks and witches to establish ongoing relationships with vampires. As a result, they didn't have to like me, but they did accept that I had the right to accompany Paul. And they knew to leave me alone.

Bonded warlock was much better than the alternative. Food.

"Paul," Damien greeted us as he approached. He nodded in my direction, and I nodded back. I wished I were wearing something more impressive than cargo pants, a ratty black t-shirt and GMU hoodie. I looked like a displaced camper, not a powerful magical practitioner.

Damien made no comment on my attire, and I said nothing, letting Paul take the lead with his people.

"Damien. What can you tell me?"

The other vampire sighed. Yes, it seems to be universal among them. "More than I'd prefer, and not as much as you'd like."

Paul raised an eyebrow. "That's cryptic."

He nodded. "I know. I think that's the way he wants it."

"How many?"

"Three. And we're not sure what to make of it." That got my attention. From his voice, I suspected he knew exactly what to make of it. Which left the question. Had he shared his suspicions with the other vampires?

Paul looked around the bustle. "Can you get me to the scene?"

Damien glanced around also. "I think so. Lucius isn't here right now. He left to gather the Families." Yes, you could hear the capital "F" in his voice. That was interesting, but I didn't know what it meant.

"They're taking it that seriously then?"

Ah, Paul knew. He'd explain it to me later, I was sure.

"Yes. This is the tenth incident in two months. Lucius can't afford to handle it alone."

Paul nodded. "I knew that. I'm just surprised he took so long to figure it out. Take me."

Damien started walking but paused to look at me. "What about him?"

"He's with me." Paul's voice left no room for argument, but Damien looked like he wanted to anyway. Paul gave him a sharp look, and Damien bowed his head and continued on without protesting.

If you're getting the idea that vampire society is all about position, power and posturing, you're right. My impression is that Paul is old enough and powerful enough to make most of the vampires in D.C. jump. I've only met one so far, Lucius, who can make Paul jump.

As we approached the front yard, I was able to get a better look at the people. The chaos looked more controlled as we got closer. Most of the people were vampires, but there were a few humans in the throng. Interestingly, one of them wore a police ID badge on his belt. Paul had said the vampires had influence in the police department, but this was the first time I'd seen proof of that.

One of the humans was kneeling, examining something on the ground, but as we approached, she stiffened and looked up. She saw me, and her eyes widened.

She opened her mouth but before she could say anything, Paul spoke. "Yes, we know. Say nothing about it here."

The woman bowed her head slightly and resumed her examinations.

I looked at Paul, who shook his head and mouthed, "Witch."

My eyes widened, and I took a closer look at the woman. Like me, she didn't look like anything special, though she was better dressed in a dark suit with trousers. Sensible for someone who had to kneel down and check out dead bodies regularly. I thought she'd be about average height (and therefore just a bit shorter than me), and I guessed her age at around 40.

I itched to bring up my aura sight to check her out, but it's very distracting. When active, I have a sort of doubled vision, seeing both the regular world and the magical world at the same time. I'd experienced that distraction around vampires before, and it's dangerous. Vampires will do almost anything to get an advantage. Besides, I didn't need my sight to sense the tension in the air here.

As I watched the witch examine the scene, I noticed she was very pointedly not looking at me, and I suppressed a grin. Obviously she had her sight active. My calling is obvious to someone who knows what to look for. As is my power level.

"What can you tell?" Paul was asking the witch. He'd obviously been examining the area near the bodies, which were covered by a large tarp.

"This was intended as a message." Her voice was low and deferential, confirming my suspicion about her relative status in the group.

"How can you tell?"

"The energies surrounding both the bodies and the whole area. They weren't killed here. This was the dumping ground. The vampire was sated while he was here, and I sense amusement. No rage, anger or bloodlust. Just amusement. He expected this to shock someone."

I found myself nodding. She might not match my power, but she was very good at reading to get all that, normal for a witch. I'm unusually good at aura reading for a warlock. It's traditionally a strength for women. Assuming what she sensed was correct, I concurred with her assessment.

Paul was looking at me, and he saw my nod. He gave me a nod of his own, his eyes expressing satisfaction. "Any idea who the message was for?"

"No, sir." The woman waved at the tarp. "But look for yourself. Perhaps you'll understand it."

Paul leaned down and pulled back the tarp. Damien stiffened beside me, and I looked at him. He ignored me. All his attention was on the tarp and what was beneath it. I had the feeling he knew who was intended to receive this message, and I stepped forward to see what Paul had revealed.

As soon as Paul exposed the bodies, he hissed and stepped back. His eyes glowed yellow, and his fangs dropped.

I looked, and muttered curses under my breath.

The witch looked at Paul and then at me. Her eyes held none of the distraction of aura sight, and I guessed she had dropped it. "You understand the message?"

"Oh yes," Paul answered. "It's aimed at me."

I nodded. As Damien had said, there were three bodies. A man and a woman, both young. Their bodies were locked into a mockery of a passionate embrace. The third body was a young girl, perhaps eight or so. She had been positioned on her side, as if she were watching.

All three of their throats had been torn out, and they were pale. There was little blood on the ground, however.

I looked at Paul, and saw both anger and pain in his eyes.

Damien spoke. "It's what it looks like then, Paul?"

Paul nodded. "I think so."

When Paul and I met, he'd been haunted by the ghost of a former lover, whom he'd killed, along with her husband, in a jealous rage. They'd had a child, though Paul hadn't known about her, and their child had been eight when he'd killed her parents. Her mother had haunted Paul until he'd returned her ring to her daughter.

While I'd never seen the husband, I had seen the ghost and the grown-up version of the daughter. The bodies of the two females were eerily close, and I assumed the man was as well.

"They are supposed to represent one of my kills, from many years ago." He frowned. "Though I never killed the daughter."

I finally spoke. "I think he wanted the message to be very clear. Not only why they were killed, but probably also to tell you that the daughter isn't safe. He knows who she is. And probably where."

The police detective perked up at that. "Can you give me her address?"

I nodded. "I don't have it on me, but if you'll give me your card, I'll make sure you get it as soon as I get home."

"Can you arrange protection for her?" Paul asked.

The detective nodded. "I think so. We'll need a good cover story, but that shouldn't be a problem."

Paul nodded. "Good." The word came out almost as a growl. He turned to leave. "Dafydd, come on. We've seen what we need here."

Damien looked at me, his expression curious and

weighing. Uh oh.

"Paul." I spoke the word clearly, just loud enough to be heard.

The vampire stopped and turned, his expression darkening. I shook my head and flicked my eyes quickly to Damien, hoping the other vampire wouldn't notice. Paul's eyes widened, and he bowed his head. "I'm sorry. Was there more you wanted to see?" His voice was respectful without crossing the line to subservient.

Actually, there wasn't, but I thought quickly. I needed to follow this charade through. "Do you have any idea how long they've been dead? Or how long they've been here?"

The witch nodded. "Yes, sir. Based on aura decay, I estimate time of death as about seven or eight hours ago." She frowned. "As for how long they've been here, that is harder. As I'm sure you know, I need the baseline strength of the aura of the person who left the bodies. I could estimate, perhaps, based on what we can surmise from the other killings?"

I did my best to maintain an even expression. "*As I'm sure you know*? Heck, I didn't know any of that. I'd never tried to estimate time of death from 'aura decay.' I'm not even sure I knew auras decayed, although it made sense as soon as she said it. As for the other?"

However, I simply said, "Did you view any of the sites of the other killings?"

"Yes, three of them."

I nodded. "Excellent. Then your estimation would be better than mine."

I heard Paul choking back a laugh behind me. Guess I wasn't fooling him.

The witch's eyes … changed. That's the best way I can describe it. It's subtle, and you probably wouldn't notice the difference unless you actually saw them in the process of shifting. However, our eye color becomes sharper and more vibrant. I'm told it's particularly noticeable in someone, like me, who has blue eyes. Hers were brown, so I noticed more that her expression grew distracted, like she was looking at a world that existed next to, but not quite touching ours.

I smiled to myself. She might know things about aura reading that I didn't, but I was better at concealing the exterior manifestation. I couldn't do anything about my eye color, but my father worked hard to teach me to shift into aura sight with no corresponding change in my expression. Served me well that time at Lounge 201. I hadn't realized at the time that vampires were familiar with practitioners, and if I'd been less good at it, they might have realized I'd been reading them.

Her sight shifted, she turned to the scene, scanning slowly back and forth. After a moment, she looked back at me. Her eyes were still altered, and I assumed she was reading me. I carefully controlled my emotions and expression. No point now in letting on that she knew something I didn't.

When she spoke, her voice was flat and emotionless. "The rogue felt little rage or anger. The predominant emotions I'm seeing are satisfaction and satiation." She frowned. "Also fear. But fear like fear of superior. Not fear of anything or anyone nearby."

Out of the corner of my eye, I noticed Paul nodding, but I kept my attention on the witch. "How long, do you think?"

She shrugged. "No longer than three hours. Perhaps as little as two?"

The detective spoke up. "Assuming your time of death is correct, that would make sense. Rigor would just be setting in, making it possible for him to pose the bodies. It's a tight timeframe, but just possible."

"Then that means the bodies were found soon after they were dumped. It took Paul and me almost an hour to drive here." I neglected to mention that it would have taken somewhat longer if he had bothered to obey the speed limit. I'm not sure how he does it. Perhaps vampires have the same aura as TV heroes. You know, the one that allows them to break the limit and never have a cop around unless it's important to the plot.

Damien nodded. "That's correct. One of Lucius' servants heard a noise outside, and when he investigated, he found the bodies. Lucius called me before leaving to call the Family meeting. I called everyone else, including Paul."

One of the other vampires, who had been silent until now, said, "And Lucius'll have your head for it. You know he doesn't want that one involved."

Damien turned to him. "Enough, Jason. He put me in charge of the investigation, and I'll run it my way until he tells me otherwise. The rogue is sending a message, so Paul is involved whether we like it or not."

The other vampire backed down, but it was obviously he planned to have words with Damien later. That, however, wasn't my concern. "I'm guessing the rogue made the noise deliberately. He wouldn't have wanted his tableau to go un-noticed for too long."

"Agreed," Paul said.

"What's security like on the grounds?"

"None of your business, warlock," Jason said.

Paul growled, low and deep in his throat.

Jason's eyes flashed amber for a moment. "You may be older, but you don't scare me, Paul. I'm in charge of Lucius' security, and when I say it's none of his business, I mean it."

Paul's eyes flashed right back, but I put my hand on his arm. His muscles were tensed, but he relaxed slightly under my touch. "Understood, Jason." I kept my voice smooth, soothing without patronizing. "I don't need specifics. I assume it's secure enough that someone shouldn't be able to just waltz up and take as much time as he needed to set this up without being seen."

Okay, I admit I was making this up as I went, this sort of investigation not being my thing. Fortunately, I watch a lot of cop shows.

Jason nodded, the gesture short, like he was making it in spite of himself.

"Then we're looking at an inside job or someone who is very, very good at getting places without being seen."

"Or magic," Paul added.

"Or magic," I agreed. "Did you see anything to indicate that?" I asked the witch.

She shook her head. Based on everything else she'd said, I figured she knew what she was talking about.

"No magic then. That leaves the other two." I faced Jason. "I suggest you check your staff, equipment and procedures."

Sure, baiting a vampire was a really bad idea, but I was kind of enjoying the look of frustrated rage on Jason's face.

"He's right," the detective said.

Jason snarled, turned and stalked back to the house.

"Thank you," I said to the witch. "You've been very helpful." Which was true. I needed to confirm and then learn the stuff she was talking about. Something told me this wasn't going to be my last crime scene.

"You're welcome," she said.

I motioned to Paul, and we left.

WE WALKED BACK to the car in silence. In this neighborhood, we couldn't be certain who else might be listening.

Paul unlocked the doors to his Prius with a happy little "chirp" from his key fob, and we got in. He pulled away from the curb, and we started back for less fancy parts of town.

When we were out of the neighborhood and back on the highway, Paul turned to me with a grin. "You had no idea about that 'aura decay' stuff, did you?"

I shot him a worried look. "Was it that obvious?"

He shook his head, still smiling. "Only to me. I figured you would have mentioned it earlier if you had known about it. And I noticed you tense when she mentioned it. I doubt the others knew you well enough to recognize why you reacted."

I nodded. "Good. Keeping up this charade of you being bonded to me is not easy."

His smile faded. "Yes. Well done back there, by the way. I was so angry I completely forgot about that."

"Did I do it right?"

"Just about. A touch less arrogance perhaps. It's more a bond of equals than anything else. But I shouldn't have sounded like I was commanding you, so I think it worked this time."

"That's what I thought. Which is why I backed off as soon as you asked if there was anything else I wanted to see." I grinned. "Of course, that put me in a bind. I didn't actually have anything else to look at."

"Good thing, though. We learned more than if I had just stalked off." He glanced at me, eyes wicked with amusement. "And now you know more about your own ability."

I waved him off. "Yeah, yeah. Never gonna let me live that down, are you?"

"Probably not."

Bantering with Paul was fun, but it was ignoring the bigger issue. "Paul. Why is the rogue sending you a message?"

His hands tightened on the wheel, and I could hear

the leather creaking under his grip. From his expression, I thought he was going to try to brush me off, and I was ready to push it, but then he relaxed.

"It's a long story, and it has everything to do with how I became a vampire. I guess...I guess it's time to finally tell you that story."

My heart beat faster. I'd been wanting to hear this almost from the moment I met him. I knew how old he was. He'd told me that after the fight with the werewolves, and he'd given me enough information to figure out who he really was. Although he'd never said, because he refused to tell me his full name, I'd figured he was a recognizable historical figure. I hadn't looked though. I wanted him to trust me enough to tell me on his own, so I'd decided to give him time to tell me the story when he was ready.

"I'd like that."

He looked at me. "I'm not sure 'liking' is a part of it. It's not a pretty story."

I shrugged. "I figured. Remember that I know you were a killer for a long time. I assumed you'd done some terrible things."

"Did you? But you can't really know the extent."

"No, I can't. Not until you tell me."

He sighed. "I...I don't know how to say this."

I smiled at him. "I do. You're afraid I won't stay your friend if I know what you've done."

He looked at me, eyes widening. "How?"

I shrugged. "Because I think that's how I'd feel if I were you." I reached out to touch his arm and realized as I did so that I almost never touched him. He frequently places a hand on my arm or shoulder, but I almost never do the same to him. I wondered why and decided I'd have to figure that out.

From the way he looked down at my hand, I realized he'd noticed it too.

"It's okay," I said. "Who you were is less important than who you are now. And I like you now. What you did can stay in the past, as far as I'm concerned."

He shook his head. "No, it can't. I need your help with this, I think. And you need to know why he's sending me love letters."

"All right then, let's go to your place, and you can fill me in."

He glanced at the clock on his dash. "It's late. You still okay?"

I nodded. "Yeah, I took a long nap this afternoon. We were planning the camping thing, remember? If I was going to spend time with you, it was going to have to be at night. Not much fun to watch you combust during the day."

He chuckled. "Right. Camping. Seems like that was weeks ago now."

"Yeah."

Paul drove in silence for a moment, and I thought about everything we'd just seen. "About it maybe being an inside job? Think that's possible?"

Paul nodded. "Possible and likely. You've seen my kind. They posture and position. If someone thought they could get an edge over Lucius, they'd try it.

Damien will look into it."

"And if they find him."

My friend chuckled. "Don't be so sure about it being a 'him.' Female vampires are just as status conscious. And even more likely to back stab."

We rode in silence the rest of the way to his house. I did want to know about Paul's background. I'd been waiting long enough, but I couldn't quite shake the feeling that my world was about to be rocked. And not in a good way.

Chapter 2

Sunday, May 2, 2010.
Too Damn Early

WE GOT TO his house, a beautiful row house in the Mt. Vernon Square area. For those of you who don't live here, that's actually a part of the District and is nowhere near the home of George Washington. It's a heavily gay area, and I've always wondered why Paul lived here, but I figured he wanted to be where people are more accepting of differences.

His house is cream-colored and with an almost turret at the top. The window surrounds are ornate and sort of gothic. The first time I saw it, I believed it was the sort of place an urban vampire would like. Much nicer than the semi-mansion we'd just come from.

Paul let us in, and asked, "Want something to drink?"

"A Coke would be great. I'd better not have anything alcoholic. Don't want me nodding off in the middle of your story."

He nodded and headed back to the kitchen, while I settled in my usual chair, a comfy wing-back thing that looked like it would fit in a Colonial home. Most of the room was neat, but his dining area, as always, was a mess. He used it as his computer station, and papers, books and bits of computer hardware were randomly scattered around. I was always strangely reassured that even vampires could be messy.

I idly scanned Paul's book shelves to see if he'd bought anything new. I did a double-take when I saw the new Jeffery Deaver novel.

"Hey, how'd you get *The Burning Wire*? It's not supposed to be out for another week or so."

He came back with my Coke and what I'd started calling a "blood cocktail," a vile mix of animal blood and some sort of spirit, usually scotch but sometimes wine, and even once, I saw him mix it with a dark ale. Yuck!

"A friend got me a reviewer's copy."

"Lucky you. Is it any good?"

He handed me my Coke and shook his head. "It's not my favorite. I didn't finish it."

I took a long gulp. It felt good going down, and I fancied I felt the sugar and caffeine start to pick me up. Long nap or not, it was almost 2:00 in the morning, and that's awfully late. Or early. I'd been trying to shift my sleep cycle to be closer to Paul's, but I can't manage a completely nocturnal lifestyle. I grew up in California, and I still like my sunshine.

"Good to know. I won't waste my money."

He stretched out on the couch, which is an odd sight. Paul is always well dressed, and acts like a gentleman. When you know he was born in the 19th century, his manner makes perfect sense. But in the last month, he's started to relax around me. And he is the master of sprawling on the couch. He took a long drink from his glass and sighed.

"Guess it's time to start."

I took another drink and put my glass on the side table, on the coaster, of course. Most of Paul's furniture qualifies for antique status. "I'm ready."

"All right. As I told you already, I was born in 1832. My full name is Paul Joseph Revere."

I blinked. "You mean, as in…"

He nodded. "Yes, I'm the grandson of Paul Revere."

Well that explained why he didn't like to give his full name. "Okay. I guess I should have seen that coming."

"You mean to tell me you really didn't look me up? I thought when I gave you my date of birth, you wouldn't be able to resist."

I shook my head. "No, I didn't look. I wanted to wait until you trusted me enough to tell me yourself."

He abruptly took another drink, and I gave him a moment.

"Thank you," he finally said.

"You're welcome. But I still probably should have figured it out. All the famous Americans seem to be Johns, James and the like. I don't know any famous 'Pauls.'"

He chuckled. "You're right. There aren't many."

I shifted to get more comfortable. "So I don't know anything about you. I mean, naturally I studied your grandfather, but I don't remember studying about you."

He got up and went to his shelves. Reaching up, he pulled down a book and gave it to me. *Harvard's Civil War* by Richard F. Miller. "If you really want to know, read that. It's mostly right, and it talks about most of the significant stuff I did."

He sat back down. "All you really need to know now is that I was pretty much a wastrel as a young man. I graduated dead last in my class at Harvard and drifted for several years until a boating accident woke me up and put me back on track. When the war broke out, it was just logical for me to join the cause."

"Union side, right?"

He nodded. "Of course. I was all Northern in my attitude and thinking. I served in the 20th Massachusetts." He paused and looked off, his expression absent. "It's difficult to describe war to someone who hasn't been through it." His eyes came back and focused on me. "That's not to say I think less of anyone who hasn't been in a war."

I shook my head. "No, I get it. I can only imagine, and I can't know how close, or far off my imaginings are."

"Exactly. Like I know some magical theory but have no idea what it feels like to actually cast a spell."

I smiled. "Yeah, that's something I wish I could make you feel." I feel sorry for non-magical people. The rush of power flowing through you, completely under your control, is a rush better than any drug. Or so I assume since I've never done drugs. When you handle the forces I do, you don't want your mind impaired in any way. I don't even drink much.

"So I get that I can't fully understand it," I continued. "But tell me as best you can. I'm guessing your experiences as a human affected the vampire you've become."

"To some extent. I've never talked about this with anyone, so pardon me if I'm not exactly direct."

I shrugged. "Ramble away." I was eager to get any glimpses into Paul as a person. I'd sort it out and make sense of it later.

"I was captured early in the war and almost executed in retaliation for the Federal handling of Confederate prisoners. Prison leaves its mark. It also cemented my loyalties to my fellow prisoners. I was raised a gentleman, and I was determined to bear the experience, and if necessary, die like a gentleman."

"But you were released?"

He nodded. "Yes, eventually. And I rejoined my unit and fought until Gettysburg." He laughed, short and with little humor. "Probably the most famous battle of the war, and it's where I died. Or rather, where I should have died." He paused, and his eyes went away again. "I was shot in through the lung and into the gut. There was never any question that I would die. The only question was when. The surgeons made me as comfortable as they could, but medicine was always in short supply, and I refused when I could. Better that they should go to men who had a chance of survival."

I couldn't imagine what it might have been like. You see pictures and movies of the horrors. Men missing limbs. Blood and flies everywhere. But Paul had actually lived it. What does that do to a man? Especially one who has lived as long as he and seen war and the same mistakes over and over again?

"I lay there in the medical tent and had time to look back over my life. What I had done. What I hadn't. That I'd never see my wife or children again. What they would think when they heard I was dead. The course of the war and the future of the nation. I'd never see those things, or so I thought."

Paul broke off suddenly, frustration all over his face.

"What?" I asked.

He shook his head. "I don't know the words to describe it. I'm not a storyteller. Never have been. If only I could somehow show you."

I probably should have thought it through before speaking, but the words were out before I could stop them. "There is a way. Do you trust me?"

Paul's gaze was intense. "What do you mean?"

Now I had to see this through. "Do you trust me?"

"Of course. Surely you know that by now."

He was right. I did know it. He was trying to tell me about when he'd become a vampire. If that didn't imply trust, then I couldn't imagine what would. I nodded. "All right then. There is a way. It's a spell." I broke off. I trusted him. He trusted me, and I still couldn't say this without hesitating.

Paul put a hand on my leg. "It's okay. Tell me about the spell."

I sighed. I'd started this. "It's in a gray area of magic. Not many people know how to do it or that it's even possible. I can basically create a link between us, and then I can project your memories onto something. A mirror. A scrying bowl. Anything like that." I chuckled. "I could probably display it on a TV, if we could get one into a circle."

Paul sat back. "I've never heard of that before. Why is it gray?"

"Because it involves a link to your mind. Any magic affecting the mind is at least gray, if not black."

Paul's expression was still confused. I understood what he was probably thinking. It's an image. Where's the harm in that?

I continued. "It's gray because what can be seen can also be altered. If you know what you're doing and are powerful enough."

His eyes widened. "So you could alter my memories?"

"Yes."

"You are powerful enough? And know how?"

I looked down, unable to meet his eyes as I answered. "Yes."

Paul's hand squeezed firmly. "But you wouldn't. I know you. And I trust you. You'd never do anything to hurt me."

I finally looked up. I had to make him understand

this. "You're right. I wouldn't. But can't you see the fine line I'd be walking here. These memories are painful to you. The temptation to…ease them."

At that moment I knew I loved him. Pure, simple, honest love. I'd never thought about it before. Sure, I was attracted to him, and we were friends. I knew I'd die for him, and he for me. But I'd never taken the next logical step and examined what that meant.

I'd have to deal with this later. If I was going to do this spell, I needed to remain focused. Because there was danger here. Because I loved him, I didn't want to see him in pain. Not when I could ease it. Fix it. But that would be unspeakably wrong. We are defined by our memories. To change them would make him someone different, and I didn't want that either.

He nodded. "I see why you might be tempted. But you won't, Dafydd. It's not in you to do that to me. I understand the danger, but I want you to do it."

I took a deep breath. "All right. I will." I still felt nervous, but now that the decision was made, I also wanted to show him my greatest talent, one that I had never had a legitimate reason to use.

Paul cocked his head and asked, "But I'm curious. If it's so gray and you say it's not well known, who taught you?"

"No one."

He blinked. "Then how?"

I sat back in my chair and thought back to a warm summer day when I was, I guess, around ten. "It was an accident, actually. It's not uncommon for witches and warlocks to spontaneously manifest powers, especially if they are strong in a particular talent. As you know, divination is my strength, and this falls into that family. I was hanging out with a friend, right after I'd seen a movie. He'd wanted to see it too, but his family couldn't afford to go the theatre."

"What was the movie?"

I laughed. "*Jurassic Park*. Seen it?"

"Of course! One of the best movies ever."

I nodded.

"So what happened?"

"We were outside, near the pond where we spent most of the summer swimming. I was describing the movie to him, and all of a sudden, he yelled and pointed to the water. The movie was playing there, in absolute detail."

"He didn't freak?"

"Are you kidding? We were still at the age where you didn't question stuff like that. Besides, we'd been friends most of our lives, and Samuel knew weird stuff happened around me. He was okay with it. Anyway, we sat there and watched the movie. I could feel the energy draining from me, but I didn't care. It was too cool.

"Until my dad found us."

Paul chuckled. "I can only imagine."

I winced at the memory of both the whipping and the lecture I got from my grandfather. Of the two, the lecture had definitely been the more painful.

"PopPop and I had a long talk after that. He explained to me exactly what I'd done. What I could do, and what it meant. It was my first lesson on magical ethics, and it was the first of many. Not many warlocks that age get ethics lessons. Kids aren't really old enough to understand until they are teens, but my father and grandfather knew if I had a supremely gift, I needed to understand why I had to control it."

I smiled sadly at one last memory from that time.

"What?" Paul asked.

"Samuel never quite forgave me, or my father for showing up when he did."

Paul's eyes danced in amusement. "You hadn't finished the movie?"

I shook my head. "Nope. Dad found us right in the middle of the kitchen scene."

"Ouch!"

"Was it ever. He had to wait a couple of years until it came on TV to finally finish it."

Paul amusement broke out into a laugh. I'd not realized before then how beautiful was his laugh. I just watched him until he stopped.

"What now?"

I shook my head. Time to stay focused. Now was the wrong time to be distracted by emotion. "Nothing, just remembering."

"Have you ever done it since?"

"Just once. Dad and the coven took down a powerful summoner. He'd done terrible things, and they wanted a record, to use as an example of why summoning is so dangerous. I linked with PopPop to play the memory, and Dad recorded it."

Paul shook his head. "Magic and technology in action."

"Yep." I shrugged. "If it works. But I was 'rewarded…'" I made quote marks in the air as I said it. "…with another couple of weeks of ethics review. Just to impress upon me that this wasn't something I was ever to repeat."

"Are you sure, then?"

I was and said so. "Yes. I'm an adult now. I know right from wrong, and I know how to use the power."

"It might not be important enough for…"

I held up a finger to stop him. Oh, he was right. It wasn't on the same scale as showing the horrors of an uncontrolled summoner, but this was my chance to share some of Paul's past. And that made it important enough for me to try it. "It's important. I'll be careful."

He nodded. "All right then." He glanced around his house. "I guess we'll need to go to your place. You'll need stuff to prepare, right?"

I shook my head. "Not for this one. All I need is a circle and a mirror." I shot him a grin. Mirrors and vampires were another thing the legends had wrong.

"You don't need…I don't know…incense, ingredients or something?"

"No, that's part of why this is dangerous. I'm strong enough to do this without preparation. Just like I did when I was a kid. I just need the circle to be sure the energy stays where it's supposed to and to help me focus. That's all."

His expression was sober, and I knew I'd impressed upon him the gravity of what we were doing. But he looked as determined as I felt.

"Got any chalk?"

He shook his head. "Yes, I probably do, but we won't need chalk. I think I have something better."

My ears perked up at that. "What?"

He stood up. "Follow me."

I did, and he started to lead me upstairs. I'd never been anywhere except his living room and the downstairs bathroom (eerily clean and bare). I was definitely interested. I knew he did something that resembled sleep, and I was curious about his bedroom. I mean. Who wouldn't be, right?

The upstairs was as neat as most of the downstairs. Paintings marched up the stairwell, old things that looked like they had been painted a century, or more, ago. I guessed they might be family. Then at the top of the stairs, a movie poster for *X-Men*.

He chuckled when he saw me look at the poster. "Good movie."

"I agree. Just not sure it quite goes with the family portraits."

He shrugged and led me on, passing a couple of doors. We stepped into his bedroom, and I stopped, my mouth dropping open. "Wow! Just wow!"

The master bedroom was huge, as in like practically the size of the entire upper level. More shelves lined the walls, jammed with books. A comfortable chair under a lamp made a cozy reading alcove in one corner, and several free-standing clothes presses occupied walls that weren't covered by shelves.

But the room was dominated by a huge sleigh bed. At least king sized and made of richly polished cherry wood, it was piled high with comforters and pillows.

Paul smiled at my reaction. "I'm a vampire, not a monk." He strode over and lifted the bed skirt. "And no earth."

I flushed. He must have guessed I'd been curious. "So the legends had that one wrong too."

"Yes."

As fascinating as was the bed, I saw the real reason he'd brought me here. Several rugs covered the polished hard-wood floor, and one of them was woven with concentric circles. The outer circle was easily large enough for my spell.

"Will that work?"

"Definitely," I answered. "Now all we need is a mirror or the like."

He grinned. "Well, you said you could use a TV." He walked over to the other side of the room and opened a door that led onto the biggest closet I'd ever seen. He vanished inside and emerged a minute later with a small TV, about 14". "How's this?"

I laughed. "You've got everything." I waved a hand at the room. "I've never seen a bedroom this big in a house this size."

"You won't. When I moved in, I remodeled the upstairs. There used to be three smallish bedrooms up here. I knocked down the walls and turned it into one big room." He shrugged. "Not like I'm going to start a family or anything."

"Or if you do, your type of family doesn't involved children who live with you for years."

He nodded. "Truth."

I took the TV from him and placed it in the center of the rug. "I'll use the outermost circle for this. That'll give us enough space to be comfortable." I looked out the window, trying to remember which direction I was facing. "Where's north?"

Paul pointed.

"Right." I adjusted the TV, so we would be facing north while I did the spell.

"Does direction matter?" His voice had more life in it now.

"Not exactly, but divination spells often work better when facing north. PopPop taught me that, although he never gave me a good reason why. As long as it works, I don't argue." As I spoke, I walked over to the large windows, covered by heavy curtains, drawn tight. "Mind if I open these?" I pulled out my phone and glanced at the time. "We've got plenty of time to be done before dawn."

"Fine by me. I usually open them up at night. I like to look out on the lights of the street."

I opened the curtains and tied them back. I worked better when I had some connection to the outdoors, and I was glad his windows faced the right way.

I turned and made a slow circuit of the room. Everything looked right, and the energy balance in the room felt good. I was sure this would work. I stepped into the circle and motioned to Paul. "Okay, let's get started."

In a moment, he stood beside me. Sometimes he moved like a human, and then other times he moved too fast, reminding me of his true nature.

"Do we do this standing or sitting?"

I dropped down in a half-Lotus position. "Sitting. We'll be more comfortable if this takes a while."

He sat down, legs crossed. I hesitantly reached out, remembering my early observation that I rarely touched him, and lightly gripped his arm. "Shift just a bit to your right, please."

He did so. "How does this work, exactly?"

As he shifted, I felt the energies snap into place, and I nodded. We were ready. "I cast the circle. That blocks out energies from the outside that might disrupt the working. Then I make the link with your mind, and you start to remember."

"That's all there is to it?"

I chuckled. "Well, I'm going to be messing with a lot of energy, which is why I'm setting this up carefully. But if I'd needed to, I could have just formed the link with your mind and started projecting."

He shook his head. "I'm used to things taking longer, that's all."

I cocked my head. "You watch magic frequently?"

"Not what you'd call frequently, I guess, but as long as I've been around, yes, I've seen it done a fair bit."

"Well, let's see what you think of this."

I closed my eyes, focusing my attention on my center, which lay just a bit left of my belly, just above my waist. A warlock's center varies slightly from person to person, but it's generally in the middle of the body. Finding it is the first thing we learn because all the energy flows from there. You can do magic if you're not completely centered, but it will never be as effective, and you can waste a lot of energy. What's the point in that when you can take just a moment to do it right?

Centered, I reached within and without. If you've never done it, that probably sounds impossible, but energy comes both from within the body and from the world surrounding us. At that moment, I felt the trees outside, energy in the air surrounding us, and even a trickle from Paul. I left that alone for now. I'd use it later to form the link to his memories.

Most of the energy for casting the circle came from me, but I supplemented it with what was around me. I opened my eyes and visualized a glowing light surrounding us. You wouldn't have seen anything if you'd been watching. I could have made it visible, but that would have taken more energy, and it was a waste. I knew it was there. That was enough.

As soon as I had the glowing sphere firmly in my mind's eye, I gathered power and willed it in place around us. I told it to make a boundary around us, conforming to the circle on the rug, and the magic obeyed me, snapping into place.

Can I cast a circle without having an actual circle to use as a guide? Well, yes, but it's harder, and again, why waste energy when I don't need to?

I closed my eyes again, feeling the pulse of magic around me. It was good. I still had plenty of energy within me, but I couldn't feel anything from outside. It's easier to control the flow of power when dealing with a particular, finite pool. Everything within the circle was predictable, and I didn't have to worry about ebbs and flows from whatever might be outside.

I nodded my head and opened my eyes to look at Paul. "Circle's cast. Are you ready for the next part?"

His eyebrows went up. "That was fast."

"I didn't need a full ritual circle for this. When I cast those, it takes longer, and I have to walk the perimeter with my knife and all. That's probably what you've seen in the past."

"Yes."

"For this, I just need something to block out anything that might interfere. For a ritual circle, you actually imbue the circle with an element of the ritual you're going to perform. No need for that here."

"Then I guess I'm ready."

"Good." I considered for a moment. "I'm going to draw on your energy to help form the link and fuel the spell."

He frowned. "I didn't think I had energy you could use. Technically, I'm dead."

"True, but something animates you, and that something contains energy. Plus there's the blood you consumed earlier. It's not much, but it's enough for me to use to make the link. I can do it without tapping you, but we'll get a clearer image if I can link your energy into the spell."

He shrugged. "As long as you don't take enough to de-animate me."

I shook my head, comfortable with what I was doing. The amount I'd need for this was small, and I'd never do anything to risk harming him. "No worries about that. I won't take much, and almost everything I use will be from the blood. However, you'll probably feel a bit weak, and you'll want to feed afterwards."

"I can do that. I just stocked up, so I've plenty of pig's blood in the fridge."

"Good. Okay, then, just relax and don't worry if it feels a bit weird. You might experience the sensation of having something drawn from you. I don't think I can harm you, but if you should feel pain or anything alarming, let me know."

He nodded. I closed my eyes again and reached out. This time I grabbed a bit of energy from Paul and shaped it to my will. Here's the part I can't properly explain since I never actually learned how to do this. I took his energy and, the best I can say is I stuck it to my aura. As soon as I did so, I could feel Paul. I couldn't read his thoughts or anything that specific, but I was aware of him, his presence, and I had a dim awareness of what he was feeling. Apprehension mostly, not surprisingly.

Then I twisted his energy and mine together and

"tossed" them toward the television.

A gasp from Paul told me it had worked. I opened my eyes, and saw images flickering over the screen. They were going by too quickly for me to get anything other than impressions. War, definitely. Blood. Fangs puncturing the neck of a woman. An image of me, just a hint, and it went away faster than any of the others. I had no idea the context of that image, but I was absurdly pleased that I rated highly enough to be in his thoughts.

"How?" he asked, his voice barely above a whisper.

"Magic," I said. "Concentrate now. Cast your mind back to the memory you want to share. Focus on it and ignore the other memories. Once you've got it firmly in mind, I can hold onto it, and you'll be able to relax and let it play out."

He nodded, effort written all over his face. The wild flow of images slowed and finally stabilized on the dim interior of a tent.

"This is it. This is where it all began."

Chapter 3

July 3, 1863.
Around Midnight

G ROANS AND HARSH panting filled the air in the tent. Lamps burned nearby but did little to illuminate the scene of horror.

Flies buzzed, a constant drone in the background. Blood was everywhere. On the dirt floor of the tent. Covering the orderly moving about, checking each man in turn. Blood-caked bandages lay abandoned in a corner, and the dim light shone on operating instruments that would have felt at home in a medieval torture chamber.

Although the memory projection couldn't include smells or physical sensation, I could feel the coppery memory scent of blood in the back of my throat, and all my limbs ached in sympathetic pain.

The orderly moved out of view and nothing remained but the anguished sounds. I wanted to close my eyes, but I couldn't.

Then a figure moved. Menace followed him out of the shadows. He was tall and broad shouldered, wearing a gentleman's outfit: dapper vest, waistcoat, gabardine trousers and a jaunty bow-tie. The look should have been comic to my 21st century clothing taste, but the overall effect was alien. His long black hair was pulled back in a neat tail, and his brown eyes caught a glint of yellow in the diffuse lantern light.

He smiled, but there was no humor in it.

A voice spoke. It was unmistakably Paul's but it sounded…old, and it held a definite Boston accent. I finally realized what about Paul's voice had bugged me since our first meeting. His accent was faint now, but I knew now it used to be from the Northeast.

"I told you before. My answer hasn't changed."

Pain, deep agonizing pain resonated in that voice, and I felt my heart clench. I'd seen Paul wounded, even badly, but he'd never sounded like that.

The other man spoke. His voice was smooth and low. "How can you prefer *this*…" The scorn in his voice was plain. "…to what I can offer you?"

"I am a gentleman. Let me die the way I lived."

He laughed, his smooth voice growing harsher. "You, a gentleman? You don't know the meaning of the word. Do you really think that dying, in pain, covered in blood and your own filth makes you a gentleman?"

A pained swallow. "I chose this, knowing I might die. Nothing has changed my resolve."

The man pulled something from his pocket, a small hand mirror. He held it in front of him, and I could see Paul's face.

I gasped. My friend's gray eyes were clouded and his features drawn. He had a neat beard, trimmed short though a bit scraggly at the moment. His cheekbones were prominent, and his lips were cracked and bleeding.

"Look at yourself. You've been shot in the lung. You can barely breathe. You know there isn't much time."

The face in the mirror shook his head.

The man's smooth voice evened, growing almost hypnotic. "And even if you did, by some miracle, live, what do you have to look forward to? A few more years of dubious health, followed by the inevitability of death. Why, Paul? Why do you choose this?"

"Because what you offer is horror beyond imagination. Blood to live? Killing without compassion or thought? No, that I can never accept."

The man shook his head. "Then we have come to this. I had hoped to convince you of your own will, but I will have you, Paul Joseph Revere. I have longed to have a disciple from one of the famous families. Yours isn't quite at the top of my list, but you'll have to do."

"No!" Paul's voice was faint, but firm.

The man smiled, fangs extending from his gums, gleaming bright in the dim light. The faint yellow in his eyes deepened until they glowed.

"What are you going to do?"

His smile broadened. "I allowed you to believe that you had a choice, but you do not." He lowered his head, fangs looming in the vision.

All I could see next was the top of his head, but I could hear Paul's anguished moan, and the vampire's head moved in a small, rhythmic motion. With growing horror, I realized the motions were caused by his drinking. After a few moments, the vampire pulled back and neatly caught a drop of blood with his tongue. I watched in stunned fascination as he lifted a talon to neatly slice open his wrist. He held his arm away from his body, spilling not a drop onto his clothes. He lowered his wrist.

"Drink."

"No." Paul's voice was faint, nearly lifeless.

"You will drink. You can't help it. No one's will to die is that strong."

He pressed his arm down, and I heard small sucking sounds.

The vision broke, and Paul doubled up on himself, his arms around his body as he rocked back and forth. I put a hand on his shoulder and waited.

Chapter 4

Sunday, May 2, 2010.
Almost 3:00 AM

P AUL RECOVERED QUICKLY and sat up. "I hadn't realized I remembered it that clearly. Or that it would affect me like that."

I willed away my anger at the long-ago event. "Of course it would affect you. You died and were…reborn into something else." While I liked Paul as he was and wouldn't want him to change, I couldn't help feeling fury at the long-ago vampire and his actions.

Paul shook his head. "I didn't quite die then. It doesn't always happen instantly. I lingered until the next morning, just long enough to learn that we had won a decisive victory at Gettysburg. I died to the sound of fireworks, celebrating both the 4th and our victory."

I blinked. "You died on the 4th of July?"

He nodded. "Yes, ironic isn't it that I became a slave on Independence Day?" He paused, eyes growing flat before continuing. "There was no time or place to bury the bodies there, so I was placed in a coffin, and, I supposed, piled with the rest of the men who had died. I never saw my coffin. By the time I roused the next evening, my master had already recovered my body, and we were in a carriage, bound for his estate in Maryland."

"Wouldn't it have been burned, or confiscated or something?"

He shook his head. "No, money can buy much privilege, even in time of war." He sighed and leaned back, supporting himself of his arms. "He didn't trust me, of course, even though he was able, to some degree, to compel me through the bond created between a vampire and his creator. He locked me into a rich suite of rooms and sent me a young girl. My first kill."

"Couldn't you have…"

Paul's voice was firm. "No, not when I was that young. Hunger was all I was. Mindless hunger and the need to kill. To drink. Fledglings are like that, sometimes as long as a year." I heard coldness in his voice. "Some never come out of that state. The Families kill them when they find them because they are a danger to us. It is they who are the origin of most of your kind's vampire stories."

His voice was flat. I'd never heard him like this. I've seen him angry. I've seen him happy. I've seen him in pain. I've seen him kill. But he's always worn his remaining humanity, holding it close like the precious thing it is. Now, however, he was all vampire. The faint link forged by my spell remained, and I could feel him. Cold and alien.

I feared him then as I had not feared him when I first met him, fangs deep in the neck of a serial killer.

Paul blinked, and his gray eyes were warm again. "I'm sorry, Dafydd. I didn't mean to get lost in my past."

This was the Paul I knew. And loved.

I shivered but kept my voice even. "I understand. I know I don't always know what it means to be a vampire, but I might have a better idea now. But I'm still not sure what this has to do with the rogue."

Paul sighed. "It has everything to do with the rogue. You see, the rogue doesn't act alone. He, or she, is merely a tool of the one who created him or her, though, in this case, I think the rogue is male. It usually is."

My eyes widened, and I thought I knew where this was going. I wished with all my heart, however, that I was wrong. "What do you mean, usually? And who created the rogue?"

He looked at me. "You mean you haven't figured it out by now?" His eyes searched mine. "Ah, I see that you have, but you don't want it to be true." He nodded. "Yes, what you have guessed is correct. The rogues are created by my former Master."

I swallowed. "And you…"

He nodded. "Oh, yes. I was one of them for a very, very long time. In fact, I was one of the best he'd ever created."

I quickly did some math. He was created in 1864, and I knew he'd renounced killing in 1977. Did that mean? "You mean you were a rogue for over 100 years?"

He shook his head. "No, not that long. And I suppose we can't properly call them rogues since they do act at the direction of another. It's what we've always called them, though, both his creations and the ones who go feral on their own."

"How long then?"

"Only about 30 years."

That was still a long time. "Why? Why does he create you?"

He sighed. "That is the question no one has been able to answer. If we, his creations, don't know, I doubt anyone does."

"Okay then. Wrong question. Exactly what does…did he have you do?"

"Slaughter."

The word hung between us, flat and definite. I can't begin to say how much I didn't want to know more, but this thing had hurt my friend years ago. And was still hurting him now. I needed to know everything, so I could help. Altering his memories would be wrong. Justice, or vengeance, maybe, against the master vampire? Those I didn't have a problem with.

"Tell me. Give me the details."

Paul shook his head, sudden and hard.

I made my voice firm. "I will help you with this. But I need to know exactly what we are up against. Only you can tell me that."

His shoulders relaxed. "All right. I'll tell you."

I shook my head and motioned toward the television. "No. Don't tell me. Show me."

I could see that he wanted to protest, but he knows me well enough now to see when I'm not going to back down.

"All right. Is the spell still active?"

I nodded.

"Then I will show you a representative sample."

Chapter 5

Mid-summer, 1873, Boston,
Massachusetts.
Just after midnight

PAUL WALKED ALONG a narrow street, lit by gaslights. I'd read about them in stories, but I'd never actually seen them until now. The quality of light was different from electric lights, softer, warmer and yet not safer. They left larger, darker shadows in the night.

He strode along, head moving from side to side. His vision was…odd. He would look at a person, and it was as if he briefly stopped time.

Shift.
Stop.

A beggar, blind and filthy, hand outstretched.

Shift.
Stop.

A woman, dressed in red, also with a hand outstretched, but a different kind of entreaty.

Shift.

Stop.

A gentleman in a long black cloak, striding with measured steps, silver-handled walking stick striking the pavement in precise taps.

You get the idea. It was odd to see how he focused all his attention for a moment on each person before rejecting and moving on to the next. And that's when I got it. Paul was hunting. This was the world to a vampire on the hunt. I couldn't stop the shiver that went through me.

He weighed and rejected several others before he found his prey. I couldn't tell what set him apart from the others, but Paul's attention stayed on him for several seconds. As he watched, the normal sounds of the street faded away until all I could hear were a steady heartbeat and the regular flow of his breathing. From Paul there was absolutely no sound.

The man, hardly more than a boy, was dressed in patched, but clean, trousers and a loose shirt. He wore no shoes, and he looked thin, as if he never quite got enough to eat. He looked up, saw Paul and froze.

Prey recognizing predator.

The boy started walking away, fast, just shy of a run. Paul followed, his steps smooth and sure. I could tell by the way the vision moved that he was not running, but was easily keeping pace with the boy at a steady walk. After several moments, the boy turned a corner. Paul's pace increased, and he turned the corner just a few paces behind the boy.

He was running now, maybe 20 yards down the deserted street. Paul's head moved left, right, up and down. No one in sight. No open windows. No sounds other than the boy's racing heart and quickened breathing.

Now Paul ran. But not like a human runs. There was little up and down motion. Instead, he seemed to glide along the ground. He overtook the boy, who had increased his pace, in seconds. The boy turned, flung up his hands to try to protect himself, but he had no chance. Paul grabbed him.

"Scream if you want, boy. It will do you no good. I can drain you before anyone will come."

The boy's heart beat faster. His eyes were wide, all pupil with no iris visible.

"Please, mister," he said, his voice high. "Please don't kill me."

My stomach clenched at the fear in his voice.

"Are you frightened, boy? Am I the monster in the night that your mother warned you of?"

"Yes, mister."

"Good."

And with that, he tore open the boy's throat and fed. True to his word, it took only a moment. One second the boy was alive, terrified but alive. The next he was slumping to the ground, motionless.

Paul glanced down at himself. He was wearing a black suit, trousers neatly pressed, waistcoat richly embroidered, white shirt gleaming in the dim light. He ran his hands down his shirt, which was still spotless, not a drop of blood visible.

From the motion of the vision, he nodded, I guessed in satisfaction. Then he turned.

"Well, master. Did that please you?"

A shadow moved in the alley, resolving into the vampire I had seen in the previous vision. This time he was more formally dressed, long coat with tails, snow-white shirt and trousers pressed into severe creases.

"It was over too fast."

"You wanted me to take someone nearly in public. I did not think you would approve of my taking my time and being discovered by a passer-by. Mobs with torches and pitchforks do not increase your pleasure, master."

"True. But next time I want you to make it last." He glanced down at the body. "More pain and blood. I want them to feel horror when they discover the body."

"As you wish, my master."

"And now, my former gentleman. Abase yourself."

Paul turned to walk toward the wall. As he walked, he unfastened his trousers. He pushed them down. I heard the rustling of cloth behind us, and I realized what was to come.

Paul spread his legs and braced himself against the wall.

Mercifully, it was over quickly, and Paul refastened his clothes, running his hands down them as he had after killing the boy. He did not turn to look at his master.

"You may have the rest of the night for yourself. Return before dawn."

"Yes, master." The tone was respectful, but there was another emotion there, buried deep.

Rage.

Chapter 6

Sunday, May 2, 2010.
Close to 4:00 AM

I LEANED FORWARD and closed my eyes. I wanted to throw up, but I wasn't going to do that on Paul's rug.

A hand hesitantly touched my shoulder. "I'm sorry. I never...never wanted you to know of that."

I shook my head, controlling my stomach by force of will. As soon as I felt that I could look up without losing the s'mores from earlier, I sat up. "No. Now I have an idea of what we are up against. I needed that."

I also needed to know exactly who and what Paul was. Would it change my feelings toward him? No, they had not changed. I still loved him. Which didn't answer the question of what to do about it, but the question was still worth considering.

Finally, I was able to ask, "Then he had you kill to...I don't know...get him off?"

Paul's hand remained on my shoulder. "I think that is part of it. But it's not all. As I said, I don't think I will ever understand his motivations."

"Did he always..." I swallowed hard, not wanting to say the word. "Did he always rape you afterwards?

He shook his head. "No, not always. Not even

most times. But you wanted to know him, and that was a good representative example."

I felt drained, and I noticed Paul's face was pale, even for him. "I think that had better be the end of show and tell for tonight. You need blood, and I need a drink."

He nodded. "You said it would drain me. I hadn't realized how much."

"Too much emotion."

I reached out a hand to the woven circle and covered the line. Immediately, I felt the energy disrupt and drain away. "All right. We can move now."

I got up as fast as I could and ran for the nearest bathroom to throw up.

Mercifully, Paul stayed away. I heard him moving around his bedroom, opening and then closing the closet door, presumably to put away the television.

After several minutes, I felt better and got up to wipe my mouth and wash my hands. I emerged from the bathroom. Paul was gone, and I went downstairs to find him.

He was in the kitchen, taking a bag of blood out of the fridge. As I approached, he handed me a shot glass.

"It's the good stuff."

I took a sip. He was right. It was good and burned pleasantly going down. The warmth settled both my stomach and my emotions. "Um, sorry…about…well in your bathroom." My face reddened, and I couldn't make myself say, "threw up."

A small smile played around his lips. "No need to

apologize. I probably would have reacted the same if I had been you." He held up the bag in his hand. "Do you mind?"

I shook my head, understanding the question. Could I stand to watch him drink blood after what I'd seen? "I don't mind."

He opened the bag, poured the contents into a large glass and we walked to the living room, sipping our respective drinks as we went.

As we settled into our respective chairs, I said, "You called him 'master.' Was that literal, or…?"

He took a long swallow before answering. "It was and it wasn't. There is a link between a vampire and his progeny. He could compel my behavior to a point." He paused. "As I said earlier, a fledgling vampire is basically a creature of hunger and need. He provided for those needs and taught me to kill in the manner that pleased him. But he couldn't change my essential nature or make me do something I was completely unwilling to do."

That didn't sit well with me. "But you've rejected killing. Well, mostly. How does that work?"

He sighed and finished his blood. I took another swallow of my drink, feeling the burn go all the way down. Something told me I was going to need the fortification.

"This is where it gets hard to explain. I haven't even worked it all out for myself, and I've spent a lot of time thinking about it. I was a good man. I cared about my men, my family and others. I didn't want to become a vampire. I wasn't lying to him when I said that. But once I was a vampire, I found I liked still being…alive. Well, you know what I mean."

I nodded. He's always referred to himself as "alive," even though it's not strictly true. Sounds better and rolls off the tongue easier than "undead," I guess.

"When I came out of the madness of being a fledgling, I discovered I was very good at the hunt, stalk and kill. I enjoyed it, although when I allowed myself to think about it, which wasn't often, it didn't jive with the man I had been. I finally decided that what I liked, both as a man and as a vampire, is being good at what I do. As a man, I was a good leader. As a vampire, I'm a good killer."

"Then why did you turn away from it?" My head was starting to hurt. It was late; I was tired, and none of this was making sense. Who was Paul, and was he someone I could still call "friend?"

"Ah, that is the question." He stood up, went across the room and plucked his bayonet off the wall. Turning, he handed it to me. "What is this?"

I frowned. "A bayonet."

"That is what it is called, but what is it?"

I wasn't sure what he was getting at, and I just looked at him, a blank stare on my face.

"It's a weapon." His voice held that tone I knew well. The one that said he desperately wanted me to get his meaning. And I thought maybe I did.

I nodded, the motion slow and thoughtful. "And you don't blame a weapon for what it is. Is that what you mean?"

He nodded, his expression guarded, but I thought I saw a hint of entreaty in his eyes. He didn't want this to ruin our friendship either. I thought carefully before I spoke next.

"But a weapon has no intelligence or will. It is something you wield. And it can be melted down and turned into something else."

Hope began to fade in his eyes, and he reached for the bayonet. I put my hand on it and resisted him taking it. "But," I said.

Paul pulled back, brow furrowing.

"But you are intelligent. You can change your nature, to a degree, if you want to. You may be good at the hunt, but you can choose."

"Yes." His tone gave nothing away.

"So tell me why you chose to leave your master." My instincts told me there was more to this than the abuse and killing. Something fundamental to Paul and who he was.

He closed his eyes briefly. "I left my master because I didn't want to be a slave. During the war, when I was held in a prison camp, I saw a Negro woman whipped. For no reason other than that she was a slave and her master could. I'd never been so angry in my life. My Colonel worried that I was going to lash out in my rage, but I managed to control myself. Barely. I swore then I would never tolerate slavery."

I nodded. "But that's not all, is it?"

He shook his head, and continued, heat in his

voice. "No. I wanted to do more than leave him. I wanted to kill him. He kills most of his creations within ten years or so. By then most vampires can resist the mild domination from their masters. I had asked questions when we saw other vampires, rare though that was, and I learned what my fate was likely to be.

The anger faded from his voice, shifting to disgust. "So I pretended to be like him. To serve him willingly. So he would keep me alive, and I might have my chance."

This was starting to make sense. This was the Paul I'd thought I knew. "So what happened? You obviously got away, but you didn't manage to kill him."

He took another long drink of blood. "No, I never had a chance. And after about thirty years, I realized he was too old and wary. I was never going to get a chance. I wasn't strong enough to kill him, but I was strong enough to get away. He'd grown to trust me, somewhat, and he gave me a bit of freedom. One day I saw a chance, and I took it. I ran and placed myself under the protection of another Family."

He must have seen the surprise in my face because he added, "It's not usually the vampire way, but I was strong. My bloodline was good, and…" He paused. "Some people adapt well to the change. Others do not. I adapted very well. I'm stronger than most my age, even those from good lines. Lucius was glad to have me."

My eyes widened. "Lucius? He is your protector?"

He laughed. "No, not any longer. I'm old enough

and strong enough now that my master doesn't dare come after me directly. But I still feel some gratitude toward Lucius for his help then. Which is why I put up with him now. Occasionally."

"So hooking up with him was enough to keep your master from trying to kill you?"

"Yes. I've always known it was never finished with us, but I admit I never thought he'd come after me this way."

"Why now?"

He shrugged. "Why does he do anything? It will be difficult to stop him without knowing his motivations." He paused. "I need to visit Lounge 201 this evening to see what I can learn. Would you be available to accompany me?"

I hadn't been back since last year, when we were researching the werewolves, and honestly, I was a bit apprehensive about it. Imagine how a rabbit would feel hanging around a group of wolves and you'll have a pretty good idea of what being at the vampire bar is like for me.

But Paul is my friend.

My thoughts froze. I hadn't hesitated. With everything I had learned about him, he was still my friend.

He was watching me, his expression blank, but I knew him well enough to see the apprehension he was trying to hide. I smiled, full and easy. "Sure, I'll go with you. I assume you'll want me to read people."

Relief flashed in his eyes. "I'm not sure. Something is telling me that it would be a good idea for you to be there."

Intuition is a fundamental piece of magic. I'm not going to argue with it. Suddenly, I yawned. "Sorry about that. It is awfully late for me."

He nodded, got up and took my glass from me. "Of course. I shouldn't have kept you out so late." He grabbed his keys and glanced outside. "I've got time to drive you home and get back before sunrise."

"Thanks."

We drove to my place in silence. I had a lot to think about. I'd learned a lot this evening about Paul. Some of it I had suspected. Other things I had not. But I was grateful that in spite of it all, we were still friends.

He dropped me off, and I staggered into my apartment. The ferrets were delighted to see me and wanted out of their cage to play, but all I had the energy for was to top off their food and water, promise to make it up to them later and stagger for bed.

I didn't even bother to take off my clothes. Within moments, I was asleep.

Chapter 7

Sunday, May 2, 2010.
Late afternoon

WHY DO I never remember to turn off the ringer on my phone before going to sleep?

The opening bars of "All I Need Is Love" went off right by my ear. Great. Left the ringer on and dropped it right by my ear when I crashed.

I yawned and fumbled for the phone. From the ringtone, I already knew who it was. Stephen, my boyfriend.

"Hey."

"Hey, yourself." A pause. "Did I wake you?"

"Yeah." I tried to make my brain work, but it resisted my best efforts.

"Out really late last night?"

Uh oh. I know that tone. "Sort of. Remember I had that camping trip I told you about. We stayed up kind of late. You know. Roasting marshmallows, telling ghost stories, and the like."

Yes, I can lie even while half asleep. It's part of being a warlock in a world that doesn't believe in magic.

"Oh. Have a good time?"

My brain was starting to function, and I sat up, leaning against the headboard. "It was good, yeah. They dropped me off early this morning, and I just crashed. I glanced at the clock on my phone. 4:23. It was about time for me to get up anyway if I was going to be ready for Paul to pick me up on his way to the bar.

"Want to get together tonight?"

I groaned inwardly. Did I ever. With everything going on, losing myself in Stephen's company sounded really good. I paused for a moment. Interesting that discovering my feelings for Paul didn't affect wanting to be with Stephen. Not sure what that says about me and not sure I want to know.

"I can't." Damn. What excuse to use this time? Maybe it was time to come clean about Paul. "It's a friend's birthday, and I need to go to the party."

"Oh. An old friend?"

I suppressed a snort. "Yeah, you could say that."

"A good, old friend?" His voice held a note of suspicion.

"Yes, but not that kind of friend. Just the friend kind."

"Then why can't I come along?"

Damn. Why didn't I think about that before I started down this story? The last place I wanted Stephen was surrounded by hungry vampires. "It's kind of a private event." True enough.

"Okay." He drew out the word, and I knew he wasn't mollified. "But you'll have to make it up to me later."

"Definitely." I said it with the little growl I knew drove him crazy.

"That's more like it." He used the deep, husky voice that drove me crazy. "Promise me that you'll keep next weekend open."

I shifted, my body waking to his tone. "You bet. No plans. I promise."

"Good. Call me later, okay?"

"Okay."

Just as I was about to hang up, he asked, "Where's the party anyway?"

I didn't see any harm in telling him. "Lounge 201. Near Union Station."

"Oh. Not my type of place anyway. Have fun."

"I will."

We hung up. We'd been dating for about half a year, and it was good. Honestly, it was very good. The sex was hot. We had a lot in common and could talk for hours, but neither of us has used the "love" word yet. Was it because we didn't love each other? Or were my feelings for Paul getting in the way? I knew I'd have to sort all this out soon. It wasn't fair to Stephen for my heart to be divided. But nothing Paul had said this morning had led to me to believe he was interested in men. In fact, considering what his master had done to him, he might be turned off men forever as anything other than friends.

Very frustrating.

I took a very cold shower. Purely to wake up, of course.

Clean and dressed, I wandered into my living area. My apartment isn't much to look at. I select furniture based on price (cheap) and utility (comfy or practical) rather than style. Yes, I know. The perception is that all gay men are closet decorators. Sorry to disappoint. I can concoct a potion to make you faster. But I can't decorate my way out of a paper bag.

A large cage dominated one side of my living room, and four beady eyes were giving me "the look." Gyre and Gimble are my ferrets. I call them my familiars, but truthfully they don't help me with magic at all. Other than making me laugh, which is just as good for warlocks as for the rest of you.

Gyre is the typical sable color that you probably think of when you visualize a ferret. Her fur is particularly glossy, and she's won a couple of ferret shows. Yes, there are ferret shows, just like for dogs and cats. She's from a champion line, though I've only entered her for fun. The "Best in Show" trophy she won at her first show still has a place on honor on top of my entertainment center.

Gimble is white with streaks of black. Technically, her color scheme is known as "silver," but she doesn't have enough black in any of the right places to win any shows. Plus, she nips. Hard. I entered her in one show (the same one where Gyre won), and the judges made it clear she wasn't welcome back.

Oh, well, she makes up for everything with spirit and a joy in life that always makes me smile.

I let them out, and they danced around the living room. Gimble nipped my toes and promptly ran under the couch. Gyre followed me to the kitchen, hoping for a raisin or two. Since she was being good, I gave her two.

Gimble immediately ran into the kitchen for her share. I only gave her one. She rewarded me with another nip. I grabbed the scruff of her neck and dragged her around the floor a few times. When I let go, she danced back into the living room, Gyre following her closely. Happy sounds of ferret mayhem ensued.

I knew that gave me a few minutes to grab some food and brew a pot of coffee. How did humans survive before coffee?

While the coffee brewed and some leftover stew warmed in the microwave, I checked email on my phone and discovered that Stephen's call hadn't been the first that day. It had just been the first one to penetrate my exhaustion.

The earlier two calls had been business related. I listened to the messages. Pretty much what I had expected.

You probably figured that magic was my business, right? That maybe I made potions for star-crossed lovers or tracked down lost family heirlooms? Let me be clear. I don't make love potions. Like memory projections, they are a very gray area, and I avoid them. I am good at tracking down lost jewelry and the like, but it doesn't pay well.

No, I pay my rent by selling vitamins and other nutritional supplements for a multi-level marketing company. Direct sales runs in the family. Mom is a fantastic Mary Kay Director. She tried to get me interested in the business (gay men can do really well in Mary Kay), but make-up is so not my thing. I like to stay healthy though, so I went that route.

One of the two calls was from someone in my downline. She usually calls me some time on Sunday to get focused for the coming week. I'd be more inclined to return her call if her attempts at focus actually accomplished something.

The other call was from Bob, my upline. Apparently there's going to be a big meeting next weekend for all the distributors in the area, and he wanted my help getting set up. Him, I decided to call back. Luckily, I got through without playing voice mail tag.

"Hey, Bob, got your message."

"I hope you didn't answer because you were up to something with that lovely boy."

Honest, it wasn't as creepy as it sounded. Bob had introduced me to Stephen, and he was watching the progress of the relationship with much interest. Probably because Bob is currently between boyfriends. And if I say "drag queen with no fashion sense at all," you'll probably understand why.

"No, I was napping. Long night."

He chuckled, and I allowed him his assumptions. No need to make this conversation any longer than it needed to be. "Nice. Very nice."

I grinned. "Yeah, Bob. So what do you need from me next weekend?"

His voice went to businesses-like immediately.

That's what's so odd about him. On his own time, he's a disastrous dresser and as big a queen as you'll ever see. But when it comes to business, he dresses well and is as professional as you'd want. His income reflects that as well. If I could do half as well, I'd be set for the rest of my life. "The usual. Help setting up the equipment, greeting people and making them comfortable. And if you've ever figured out how to clean up with magic, that'd be nice too."

Yes, Bob knows about me. And the magic clean-up thing is a running joke between us. He just doesn't see the point if magic can't keep his house cleaner, and I have to keep telling him it doesn't work that way.

"Sure thing, well except for the cleaning part. But I'm willing to help clean up the old fashioned way."

"With your tongue?"

"Yeah, right Bob. That's a good way to tidy up. I'll keep it in mind."

"You do that. See you Saturday around eleven then? The program officially starts at 1:00, but I think people'll arrive early."

"Will do." I hoped this thing with the rogue vampire would be done by the weekend. I doubted a big distributor meeting would be improved by the addition of blood and screaming.

We said our good-byes, and I messed about online, checking how my team had done last week. I was pleasantly surprised to see we'd had a very good week. My check would be a little larger than usual, which meant I'd be treating Stephen very well when we met.

I was in the middle of viewing a new training video when someone knocked at the door. I figured it was Paul, but I still checked the peep hole. I was starting to get a reputation in the supernatural community, and while I doubted any of the bad guys would knock first, caution seemed in order.

It was Paul, and I let him in. The ferrets immediately ran over to him, dancing, spinning and nipping at his feet. He laughed and wrestled with them for a minute while I shut down my computer.

"They must have missed you last night."

I checked my desk for anything the ferrets could steal. Clear. "Yeah, they were really not happy when all I did was crash. I'm amazed Gimble didn't bang her food bowl all day." Then again, considering I had slept through two phone calls, maybe she did.

Paul gave both of them a good ear scratching and then put them in their cage. Gyre promptly curled up to go to sleep. Gimble gave him a tiny, but baleful, glare. "I'll come by later and give you a long romp," he said. That seemed to mollify her, and she curled up next to her cousin. Within moments, they were both asleep.

I checked food and water. Both good. "Okay, I'm ready."

Paul checked me out, running his eyes first up and then down. "Nice."

I smiled. "Thanks. I thought I might as well keep up the image." The last time I'd visited Lounge 201, I'd inadvertently portrayed myself as a bonded warlock

Companion to Paul. Apparently, I'd left the impression that I was first among equals in the relationship. This time I dressed to reinforce the image. I'd dug out my best tight black leather pants and paired them with a high-collared white silk shirt. A close-cut black blazer and highly polished loafers completed the image.

His eyes twinkling, he said, "It's an interesting mix of leather bar and business."

I punched him in the shoulder, and he grinned. "But I think it will give the right impression. I considered a cape, but I thought that might be just a bit over the top."

"Yes, I think it would have been." His tone was dry, with just a hint of amusement. "Ready?"

I nodded. "Let's go meet the vampires."

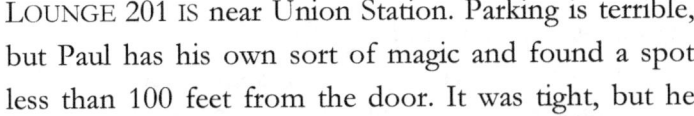

LOUNGE 201 IS near Union Station. Parking is terrible, but Paul has his own sort of magic and found a spot less than 100 feet from the door. It was tight, but he makes parallel parking look as easy as driving down an empty highway.

As we stepped out, I glanced around. The sun was down, but there was still a faint hint of light on the horizon. I figured it was still early for the vampire crowd, and I wondered if we'd find the right people to talk to.

As I finished my quick survey of the area, a group of young women walked by, did double-takes and smiled at us. It might have been me, but was more likely Paul, who was dressed in a white linen suit that probably cost as much as my entire wardrobe. His navy silk shirt was half-unbuttoned, and showed his chest to good advantage. There's something about a hot guy in white that draws attention.

We smiled and nodded at the girls but walked briskly to the Lounge. I started to pull out my ID, but Paul stopped me with a gentle hand on my shoulder. "They won't card you now. You're clearly with me."

I nodded and put away my wallet. We walked down the short flight of stairs to the lounge and entered.

It just looked like what you might imagine in a vampire bar. The decor ran heavily to red and black. Beautiful people wandered around, drinks in hand. Some of the drinks were clearly alcohol. Others? Well, let's just say you might want to be careful which drinks you steal a sip from. Like the decor, most of the outfits were shades of red and black. It's kind of a theme for vampires, as you might guess.

The patrons weren't just vampires. Plenty of humans circulated as well. Some of them prowled, although to my eye, they looked silly, trying to imitate real predators. Others clung to their vampire of choice and scowled at any of the prowlers who came too close. The vampires who noticed the jockeying for position seemed amused by the antics of their "pets."

As with the last time I was here, I wondered how anyone could think hanging out at a predator's watering hole was a good idea. I know we are drawn by danger, but seriously? This was just insane. And no, my friendship with Paul is something completely different. Honest.

Paul glanced around. "I don't see Damien. That's odd. He left a message earlier that he planned to meet me here."

"Maybe he's just fashionably late?"

"Maybe." His tone said "not bloody likely," but I didn't comment on it.

"Who else can we talk to who might know something? What about Darlene?" Darlene was another vampire who hung around with Damien. I wasn't sure about the exact nature of their relationship, but they seemed to be friends of a sort.

Paul shook his head. "I doubt it. She's too much of a bearcat, and Damien tries to keep her out of his investigative work. Darlene's liable to blow her top at the wrong moment."

Bearcat? Sometimes Paul's slang is so out of date I can't even identify the century it's from. That one sounded like it might be from the 20's, and I made a mental note to look it up on Wikipedia later. It's kind of a game I've started playing, although I haven't clued Paul in yet.

Suddenly, the hairs on the back of my neck stood up, and I turned around, forcing myself to do it slowly. Fear is the last emotion you want to show in a vampire bar.

A short vampire approached us. He was maybe an inch or two shorter than my five feet, seven inches (okay, six and half), but his presence made him seem much taller. His hair was black and cut loose, falling straight down to the middle of his back, almost giving the impression of a cape.

His features were even, and some might find him attractive, if they could get past the air of menace surrounding him. His gray eyes held no hint of warmth, though they didn't seem particularly unfriendly either. It was hard to put any emotion to them.

The last time I had seen him, he'd been wearing gray and blue, but tonight he was following the trend of black and red. His suit was well-tailored and probably even more expensive than Paul's. His only jewelry was an intricate silver Celtic cross around his neck.

That was just his physical appearance. If my aura sight had been active, I'd have seen mostly black. Little of humanity remained in him.

Of course, the last time I'd seen Lucius, the oldest vampire in D.C., he'd been in a good mood. This time, his aura was almost visible without the benefit of my Sight, and I took an involuntary step backwards, conducting a quick inventory of the potions I had secreted about my person, ready in case this ended in a fight.

"Paulus! How dare you invade my home uninvited!" He didn't yell, but nearby conversation faltered.

Paul straightened. I stepped to the side a few inches, trying to send the message that I was there to support him but leaving him room to deal with the master vampire in his own way.

"Good evening, Lucius." His voice was calm without being soothing. He projected confidence. "I believe you are misinformed, and I apologize for any confusion that may have caused."

Lucius stopped, his body still tight with anger, but I saw a flash in his eyes that made me frown to myself. Perhaps this was merely a show for the underlings?

"Misinformed? I think not."

Paul inclined his head a few inches. "I was not un-invited."

Lucius straightened, his nostrils flaring. "Who had the gall to invite you to the scene?"

"Why, it was Damien, whom I believe you put in charge of the investigation. He suspected Malachai was sending a message, and he wanted me to interpret it."

Malachai? I realized this was the first time Paul had used his name.

All conversation ceased, except for a few humans seated in the small alcoves scattered around the bar. Lucius glanced around him, and, like a wave, conversation began again, starting near us and moving to all corners of the room.

"You dare much to speak that name in my territory."

Paul's shoulders relaxed as he answered, and I stopped counting my potions. "Refusing to speak his name won't make him leave, Lucius. He is challenging your authority more plainly each time."

Lucius' shoulders tensed again. "I thought this last one was a message to you."

"True, but am I not a member of this community

and so messages to me are, by extension, a challenge to you?"

The elder vampire snorted. "Depends on the message, I suppose."

I caught motion at the edge of my vision, and I turned to see Damien approach. The door was still closing, and he must have just arrived. I frowned when I looked at his face. Vampires are always pale, but he was practically white.

"Pardon my interruption, sir, but I believe this latest message was aimed at all of us, including you, Lucius."

Both Paul and the elder vampire frowned. "What now?" Lucius asked at the same time Paul said, in a voice little more than a whisper, "No, he didn't."

Lucius nodded. "Darlene is dead."

I took a step back. I wasn't certain of the exact relationship between Damien and Darlene, but Paul had said earlier that they had been close. From the expression on the younger vampire's face, I wondered if Paul had understated it.

Paul put a hand on Damien's shoulder. I would have expected his pride to shrug it off, but it seemed to calm the distraught vampire.

"How was she killed?" Lucius asked.

"Staked, raped, throat torn out and left in our living room for me to find."

I wasn't fond of most vampires, but I winced. I hadn't known her well, having only met her the one time, but I didn't like to think about anyone I knew dying like that.

Lucius' gray eyes flashed, but his voice was calm. "You have my word, Damien, that he will not get away with this." He turned to Paul. "You are correct. This challenge to my territory and authority cannot go unanswered. I had thought he was baiting only you. I was...incorrect."

I wouldn't exactly characterize his voice as apologetic, but I guess it was the closest he could come to it.

He glanced at me. "This does not concern you, warlock. You are, of course, welcome to remain in the Lounge, but I must ask you to absent yourself from our discussions." His tone was respectful but left no room for argument.

Paul answered before I had a chance to put my foot in my mouth. "Respectfully, elder, I prefer he stays. Malachai has used magic before. Dafydd can be an asset."

Lucius waved a hand. "We have a tame warlock to do our bidding."

"But Dafydd is not tame, and he has considerably more power than the other. He has abilities I've not heard of before."

Lucius' eyes shot to me, faint interest gleaming in them. "Is that so?" He paused, expression considering, before nodding. "Very well then. I am not so proud that I will deny us resources that may prove useful." He motioned to someone behind the bar, who nodded back and motioned to the short hallway that led to the restrooms, and, I guessed, to an office. "Come with me. We can share information and perhaps devise a plan." He began to walk in the indicated direction, and the three of us followed.

Before we had moved more than a few feet, threading our way through the crowd, which opened up before Lucius, a female voice said, "Paul? Is that really you?"

Paul froze, and when I say "froze," I mean that he became still in the way only a creature whose heart didn't beat and who had no need to breathe could freeze.

I glanced around and watched a young woman approach us. She was short, just over five feet and plump. Long brown hair hung neatly down her back, and she was dressed in a simple pastel sundress and sandals. Her appearance stood out from the rest of the patrons. There was a lightness and sunniness about her at odds with the danger-seeking vampire junkies surrounding us.

"What is this?" Lucius asked as he turned. He must have seen the look on Paul's face because he stopped and looked at the young woman.

"Paul?" I asked. My friend's expression was blank, showing no emotion at all, and he only did that when he was badly shaken. I couldn't see anything about the girl to trigger that extreme a reaction, and I resisted the temptation to active my aura sight to learn more.

"Paul?" Lucius said, his tone commanding.

Paul blinked suddenly, and his body relaxed. "My apologies." He still didn't turn to look at the girl, who was standing nearby, a confused expression on her face. He bowed to Lucius. "I believe I need to speak to this girl. The situation might be more...complicated than we realized."

The rest of us looked at her. I didn't see anything unusual about her, and I could hardly wait to learn what was so significant about her.

Lucius frowned. "Explain."

Paul shook his head. "I will, sir. But allow me a bit of time first."

Lucius looked from Paul to the girl and then to me. "Warlock, do you know what this is about?"

I shook my head. "I do not."

"Very well." He nodded to Damien. "You, though. Come with me. I need to hear everything you know about the latest kill." His words were business-like, but his tone held the faintest hint of sympathy.

Damien nodded, and the two of them left.

"Paul? I don't understand." The girl's voice was lost and confused. "How do I know you? And why are things complicated?"

I blinked. Huh? She knew him but she didn't? What was up?

Paul finally turned to face her, his motion slow and reluctant. "What's your name?"

"Nicola."

Paul closed his eyes briefly, and I watched the spasm of pain cross his features. "Of course. It would be." He reached out to touch her. "Come with me. I think I have some explaining to do."

He gently gripped her arm and began to move toward one of the alcoves. It was occupied, but the vampire and two humans quietly got up and left at a glance from Paul. I followed, eager to learn who she was.

The three of us sat down at the round table, the girl between us. She still looked confused, and Paul's expression was mostly stunned, so I decided it was up to me to start the conversation.

"Paul, you obviously know her. Want to start?"

He shook his head. "Nicola, if I may ask you first, how did you come to be here this evening?"

She frowned. "First, who are you?" She nodded at me.

"Sorry," I said. "This all happened very suddenly. I'm Dafydd Smith, a friend of Paul's."

She nodded, her expression still confused, but her voice strengthening. "Okay then. I'd really like to know why I know you, but if you insist." She paused for a moment before saying, "I was sitting out on my porch, just enjoying a glass of iced tea when a young man came by and said there was someone I'd want to meet at Lounge 201."

"And you just got up and came here?" I asked.

She frowned again. "Well, when you put it that way, yes, it does sound odd, doesn't it? It made perfect sense at the time, though."

"What time was this?" Paul asked.

"I'm not sure. About 6:00 or 6:30, I guess."

Paul and I looked at each other and nodded. "Before sunset," he said at the same time I said, "Not a vampire then."

"Vampire?" Nicola said, her voice filled with disbelief.

Paul looked at her. "Then you don't know what I am. Only who I am?"

She put her hands on her hips. "I don't know much of anything about this. And I'd like some answers." Her voice grew shrill with both anger and fear.

I moved my hands in a calming motion. "One more question, and then I'm sure Paul will be happy to answer your questions."

She calmed down. "All right. What is it?"

"Did you come over right away, or wait a while?"

Her expression became puzzled. "Well, I came over right away." She looked at her watch. "And I've been here quite a while, haven't I?"

I nodded. "And none of this seemed odd to you?"

"No, but it sure does now."

I was liking her more by the minute. Sure, she'd gotten mixed up in something weird, but she wasn't letting it phase her.

Paul looked at me. "Any ideas?"

I frowned. "Maybe. Let me puzzle on it for a while. It certainly sounds like magic."

She glanced at both of us in turn. "Magic and vampires? Are you two crazy?"

Paul sighed. "Unfortunately, not. And now I think it is my turn."

I'll say.

The vampire motioned to the bar, and a moment later, a young woman came over to us.

"Yes? What can I get you?"

"House special for me, thank you," Paul replied. He glanced at me.

"Coke, please."

Nicola shook her head. "Just water's fine for me, thanks."

The woman nodded and hurried away. Paul waited until she returned with our drinks. Nicola didn't look happy about it, but she said nothing.

The woman returned, handing Paul a wine glass filled with something very dark. I guessed what the "house special" probably was. She put down my Coke and Nicola's water before hurrying away. I wondered exactly what the vampires did to ensure such excellent service.

Paul took a long swallow and then said, "Nicola, you're going to find most of what I say hard to believe at first, but hear me out. By the end, you'll be surprised at how much of it makes sense."

"All right," she said, voice doubtful.

"First, do you believe in reincarnation?"

My eyes widened at the question, and I had an inkling where this might be going. You see, belief has nothing to do with it. Reincarnation is a fact all witches and warlocks know. I'm aware of at least four past lives, and there's probably more. Not that I've spent a lot of time pondering it, but it's helpful to have some idea of where our souls have been. It probably won't surprise you to learn that all four of my past lives were warlocks. Well, three of them at least. One of them was a witch. Nope, gender swapping isn't uncommon.

"Not really, no? Why?"

He sighed and took another drink. "Because reincarnation is true, and you and I have known each other before. Several times."

She shook her head. "No, that's crazy. Impossible."

"Any more impossible than you knowing him without knowing why?" I asked. "Or coming here tonight without knowing why?"

"Well, no. But I'm sure there's a rational explanation."

"There is," Paul said. "You and I have known each other before." His voice dropped, and his eyes glowed faintly amber. "Nicholas, listen to me."

I blinked. Nicholas? That wasn't the name I'd been expecting. I'd thought... Wait a minute. What I'd thought didn't make any sense either. Now I was just confused.

"Paul," I started to say, but he shook his head and motioned at Nicola.

She was staring at Paul, a curious look on her face, like she'd just awoken and didn't know where she, or he, was. "Paul?"

The vampire nodded. "Yes, Nicholas. It is I."

A different person looked out of Nicola's eyes. I can't explain the difference, but I didn't have any doubt that "she" was now a "he."

"It's happened again, then?"

"Yes." Paul answered.

"He" looked down at himself and gasped. "But I'm a bit different this time."

A small smile played across Paul's face. "Just a bit."

I held up a hand. "Um. Confused here. What just happened?"

Nicola glanced at Paul. "I think you'd better answer. I know some of what happened, but not enough to explain."

Paul nodded. "Dafydd, meet Nicholas. He…used to be my lover."

I blinked. Paul? With a male lover? Who was now a female? I took a long swallow of Coke but in my haste, I wasn't careful, and some of it went down wrong. I coughed, and Paul reached over to pat me between my shoulder blades until I got my coughing under control.

When I was able to speak again, I said, "Okay, now I'm even more confused. Leaving aside the male lover part, how is he…or she…or whatever able to be consciously aware of past lives. I mean, you did some sort of Vampire Mind Whammy thing?"

Paul shook his head. "No. Sorry. I'm not explaining well. This took me by surprise. Let me start again." He glanced at Nicola/Nicholas. "This should help you out too."

Nicola nodded. "I'm all ears."

Paul took a deep breath. "Dafydd, I told you about my master and what he turned me into. Nicholas, do you remember that?"

He nodded. Even though the body was female, he

was so clearly male that I had to think of him that way. "I think so. Rape, pillage, plunder, all that at his command. Something like that."

"That's close enough. After I left my master, I continued to kill, though less often and with more care in selecting my victims. I was able to indulge myself in the hunt and stalk for days, sometimes weeks at a time. I grew adept at making my victims fall in love with me. When I finally killed, it was sweeter for the emotion."

This was more what I'd thought vampires were like, though I wasn't happy to hear that my friend had been like that.

Nicholas spoke. "He'd selected me as one of his victims, and he wooed me for weeks."

Paul nodded. "This was just before the turn of the century, I think."

Nicholas nodded. "Yes, 1899 in New Orleans. I remember it was summer."

Paul smiled in memory. "Yes, the nights were so short. It made it all the sweeter."

They shared the look common between old lovers. I felt sort of left out, and I was surprised at how much it hurt.

"The problem that time," Paul said, "was that he wasn't the only one who fell in love."

"You too?" I asked.

"Yes, vampires can love." He glanced down, averting his eyes from mine. "I haven't been entirely forthcoming on that subject, I realize."

Nicholas was looking from him to me, his eyes

considering. He smiled. "He's a vampire. Don't take offense. They keep secrets like you and I keep collectables."

Paul raised his eyes again. "I had decided to make Nicholas my companion, for as long he would have me. You've probably also wondered if vampires can make love to humans. Yes, we can, but it is dangerous, especially when we are young. The bloodlust can overcome us during passion, and we can't restrain the impulse to kill."

Nicholas spoke, his voice sad. "I was willing to take the chance. I loved him that much. But he was too young, and one day... Well, you can figure out how it probably ended."

I nodded. I wasn't sure what to think. So much had been revealed and answered in the last few minutes, but I still had more questions.

Before I could ask any of mine, however, Paul asked Nicholas. "Do you have the ring?"

Nicholas nodded and pulled a chain from under his shirt. On it was a simple silver ring in the shape of a running Celtic knot. It practically glowed, even though I hadn't activated my aura sight. When I saw it, my mouth dropped open, and I looked at Paul. "How is that possible? I mean, we returned it, didn't we?"

The ring Nicholas wore on a chain around his neck was the same one Paul and I had given to a young woman almost a year ago to settle the restless spirit of her mother.

Paul ignored my question. "How did you get it?"

Nicholas paused, eyes growing vacant for a moment. Then he nodded. "Good thing I have her memories in addition to my own. About a month ago, a young man came up to me on the street with the ring. He said I must have dropped it. I said it wasn't mine, but something about it pulled at me, and I kept it."

Paul frowned. "Describe the young man."

He blinked once but answered. "Nothing special. About six feet tall, long brown hair in a ponytail, lean. Looks like he exercises, but a swimmer or biker, not a weight lifter."

I must have reacted because Paul looked at me. "Someone you know?"

I shook my head. "It's probably nothing, but that's an excellent description of Stephen."

Paul frowned. "Not likely."

"Who's Stephen?" Nicholas asked.

"My boyfriend."

"Oh." Nicholas frowned.

"What?" I asked.

His eyes went distant again, and I guessed he was searching memories. It must be distracting to have so many memories in one body. Finally, he said, "I think the man who gave me the ring was the same man who told me to come here this evening."

Paul nodded. "That doesn't surprise me. I think you have been deliberately aimed at me."

Fear shot through me. "We need to check on Natasha then." I said.

Paul's eyes widened as I looked at Nicholas and

said, "That's the woman who was supposed to have your ring. If this is a message aimed at Paul, she might be in trouble."

"Or it's too late," Paul said.

"Possible, but just in case…" I got out my phone and sent a quick text to Laura McCall, a good friend of mine who was a white-hat hacker. She'd be able to track down Natasha in a matter of minutes.

Paul watched me and when I was done, he said, "Laura?"

I nodded. "Assuming she's not too busy, she should get back to us in a few minutes. So, I'm guessing the ring has some significance."

Nicholas looked confused at our exchange but shrugged and said, "Yes, Paul gave it to me back then. It shows up every time I come back."

"And how many times have you come back since then?"

Nicholas shook his head. "I'm not sure. Still a little fuzzy on that."

Paul answered. "This would be the third time. 1933. 1977 and now 2010. This time was a bit fast."

I did the math. "You never lived very long then."

"No, Paul has killed me every time." You would have expected some emotion, but he said it the same way you might have said, "The sky is blue."

I looked at Paul, whose expression was full of pain. "Why?"

The vampire shook his head. "In 1933, it was an accident. I didn't know who he was until I saw the ring.

He was just another victim. I saw the ring and tried to stop, but it was too late. And you know about 1977."

I nodded. "Yeah, except that you told me you killed Natalie because you were in love with her and didn't want her to be with Nick."

When we'd settled the ghost of Natalie by giving the ring to her daughter, she'd spoken to me right before moving on to tell me that Paul had lied. I guessed I now knew what he'd lied about.

I shook my head. "I'd ask why, but that can wait. I'm guessing you think Malachai had something to do with all this?"

Nicholas gasped. "Malachai? Your old master is behind this?"

Paul nodded. "I think so. Dafydd, you asked about the 'Vampire Mind Whammy.' Yes, vampires do have the ability to influence the thoughts and emotions of humans."

"And obviously bring up memories of past lives. I didn't think anyone could do that. How can you?"

Paul shook his head. "No, I can't do that. My strengths lie in the physical. I'm very weak in mental influence."

"Then how…"

"Malachai," Paul answered. "He is one of the best of my kind. He can bring past memories to the surface." He turned to Nicholas. "My guess is that he found you and worked on you, perhaps using the ring as a focus. He probably left the memories just buried behind the thinnest of veils. The man who told you to come here might have given you some word or signal to break down most of the veils."

I got where he was going. "And then you used your ability to bring them all the way forward. When you told him to listen to you."

"Yes. That's about the limit of my abilities, but I can do that much. And Malachai would know I could. He probably set his trigger taking that into account."

"So I'm a pawn in Malachai's game?" Nicholas asked. "How would he even know about me?"

Paul looked grim. "Malachai has made it his business to keep on top of my doings over the years. I don't know how he found you this time, but it doesn't surprise me."

I had a sudden, nasty suspicion. "Is Malachai a warlock?"

Paul nodded. "Yes."

Great. Vampire and warlock. Why couldn't we be up against an easy master boss? I nodded, though. Things were finally starting to make sense. "A divination would explain how he could find you. I've never heard of it being done, but I suppose you could create a spell to track down an incarnation, especially if he had a focus like the ring." I turned to Nicholas. "That ring almost glows with power if you know what to look for. It's been tied to your soul for almost a century, so I think he could use it for that purpose."

Paul nodded. "I didn't know that could be done, but it does make sense."

Nicholas was shaking his head. "It doesn't make

much sense to me, but you two seem to know more about it than I do. Okay, so your old master is playing games, with me as his pawn. Why, and what can we do about this?"

I had to ask. "You seem awfully calm about all this. I mean, I know reincarnation exists. I even know about some of my past lives, but I've never been forced to remember them like you have. In your shoes, I'd be a gibbering idiot."

Paul snorted. "I doubt that. I've seen you in action."

Nicholas arched an eyebrow at Paul.

"Not that kind of action," Paul said with a small smile.

Nicholas grinned and looked at me. "I guess I can't explain it. I mean, I know I should be terrified. Paul has killed me three times, but…" He examined the vampire, his expression thoughtful. "He's different this time. I know he won't kill me again. I don't know how I know it, but I do."

I hadn't been aware how tense Paul had been until he suddenly relaxed. "I am different. The last time I killed you changed me. I seldom kill now, and only if the person is a danger to society."

Nicholas chuckled. "The vampire version of Dexter."

He and I shared a grin. I'd thought the same thing the first time I'd met Paul.

Paul sighed, the sound showing frustration. "I'd like to get Malachai out of my life for good. He's been this constant weight, with me never knowing when he'll show up next."

"Then Nicholas has asked a good question. What can we do about it?" I asked.

"Do we know what he wants this time?" Nicholas asked.

Paul shook his head. "I never know what he wants. This time is no different. Just to make me miserable."

Nicholas and I both frowned. "That can't be it," Nicholas said. "No one does stuff just to make someone miserable. There's got to be more to it than that."

I was starting to like this guy, in spite of myself. He thought like I did. "I agree. Maybe you're too close to it, Paul. Walk us through some of what he's done in the past. Maybe we can find a pattern."

His expression was doubtful, but he shrugged. "All right." He glanced around. "Maybe not here, though. He probably has ears here."

I glanced at Nicholas. "Umm, not to put too fine a point on it, but maybe you should bring Nicola back? I mean, this is her life."

Nicholas nodded. "You're right. Do you suppose she'd remember all of this?"

Paul considered for a moment. "I suspect so. Let's try." His eyes went intense for a moment as he looked at Nicholas. When he spoke, his voice was low and hypnotic. I would have rolled my eyes at the cliché if I hadn't seen it work.

"Nicola. Come back to me and remember all that has gone before."

Nicholas closed his eyes, and when they opened, someone else looked out of them. She blinked. "What just happened?"

"Do you remember?" Paul asked.

She nodded, her motion slow, as if she were just waking up. "I think so." Suddenly her eyes widened and she looked back and forth between me and Paul. "I do remember. I remember...past lives. Is that right?"

Paul smiled. "Yes, that's right, Nicola."

She frowned. "And someone's trying to do something to you? And I'm in the middle of it?"

Paul and I both nodded. This was incredible. I've only seen one other person so completely in touch with his past selves, and that was my grandfather, after a focused meditation session. Even then, he was only able to pull up one past self, and he forgot the specifics within a few days. Something told me Nicola might remember longer than that. I wasn't sure what effect that would have on her, but for now it was fascinating to see.

Her expression cleared. "Yes, I do remember. At least bits of it. I don't like that someone's been messing with my mind, and I want to stop him."

"All right then," Paul said. "Let's go." He glanced at me. "My place, do you think?"

"Probably. I assume you'd know if Malachai had bugged it?"

His eyes widened. "I hadn't thought about that. I'm not sure I would."

I shrugged. "Don't worry about it. I can check for

that, assuming he'd use magical means."

Just then my phone beeped, and I jerked. I'd forgotten about the text I'd sent to Laura. I pulled out my phone. "Hang on a sec."

It wasn't much, just

She's fine. But she did report a stolen ring to the police. Want me to check that out?

I texted back:

No, but can you check Paul's house remotely to look for bugs?

Her answer came back almost immediately.

No problem, as long as it's not super high-tech. What's the address?

I looked at Paul. "Laura says Natasha is fine and she can check for tech bugs, as long as they aren't like state of the art."

"He wouldn't use anything that good. He's never been that modern."

"Good. Okay if I give her your address?"

He nodded. "Yeah, I trust her."

"Who's Laura,?" Nicola asked.

I answered as I sent the address. "A friend of mine. Hacker, and a good one."

"Oh. You have odd friends."

I grinned. "What can I say? I'm an odd kind of guy."

"I'll say," Paul said, also grinning. Then he turned to Nicola. "How did you come? Want to follow me?"

She shook her head. "I took Metro."

"Ah, then allow me to offer you the comforts of my carriage, lady."

She giggled, and I rolled my eyes. "Yeah, don't let him fool you. It's just a Prius. Nice wheels, but hardly a carriage."

She gave me a stern look. "Never diss a man when he's trying to be a gentleman."

She excused herself to visit the restroom before leaving, and I took the moment to ask, "How are you doing?"

As soon as she left, Paul's shoulders slumped. As I suspected, he'd been forcing himself to stay strong. "I'm not sure. Seeing him again. But as a 'her.' I guess I should have expected it eventually."

"You really loved him, didn't you?" I didn't really want to know the answer, but it was the right thing to ask, under the circumstances.

He nodded. "I did. Now, though? I don't know. I'm not sure what I feel right now."

I put a hand on his shoulder. "Take it slow then. I don't think she'll be putting any pressure on you."

"Agreed. And now would not be the best time for a relationship anyway." He looked at me, his eyes concerned. "You don't really think Stephen is involved, do you?"

I shook my head. I'd been successfully ignoring that suspicion until now. "I don't know."

"He didn't know we'd be here tonight, so he couldn't have told her."

"That's the thing." I heard the frustration, anger and betrayal in my voice, and I forced myself to calm down. "He did know."

"How?"

"I told him." My voice came out in an almost growl. "He called this afternoon and wanted to know if I'd be available. I told him I had a party to attend." I gave him a small smile. "I said it was your birthday."

He snorted. "Only half a year late."

I shrugged. "I was sleepy, and it was the first thing that came to mind."

Paul waved a hand. "No problem. Go on."

"Anyway, right before we hung up, he asked me where I was going. I didn't see any reason not to tell him, so I said."

"What was his reaction?"

I shrugged. "Just that it wasn't his type of place and to have fun."

"What time was this?"

I thought for a moment. "Fourish, maybe? It was just after I woke up."

I could see him doing the same math I'd just done. "Assuming he knew where she lived, he had time to get over there."

I nodded. "Yeah, I'd figured that."

"But," Paul's voice was firm. "It doesn't mean it was him."

I blew out a breath. "Yeah, I know that too. But my

instincts are screaming at me, and I've learned over the years to pay attention to them."

His expression was grave. "And I've learned to trust them too. We'll be careful."

Nicola came back just then. She must have noticed our expressions. "What?"

I shook my head. "Nothing. When I figure it out for sure, I'll let you know."

She gave me a curious look. "Okay. Ready to go then?"

We both nodded and got up. Lucius had reappeared in the main room and was holding court in one corner. It looked like they were having some sort of strategy session. "Do you need to join them?" I asked as we walked past. "He had wanted you earlier."

Paul nodded to Lucius as we left, and the master vampire gave a small nod of acknowledgement. Paul shook his head and took Nicola and my arms to nudge us along. "I'll have to tell him something, but I think I can hold off until tomorrow."

I wasn't in any hurry to see that conversation.

We went outside and started for Paul's car. The sun was completely gone, no hint of sunset left in the darkened sky.

Paul had just pulled out his keys to remotely unlock the door when I heard a low growl from the shadows to our right. I turned.

Amber eyes gleamed in the darkness, and I stepped back just in time to avoid a sudden charge. However, I wasn't the target. Fangs flashed, and Nicola dropped with a cry, blood spurting from a long gash on her arm.

Before I could react, Paul snarled next to me and leaped to stand over Nicola. His eyes had shifted, and both his claws and fangs were extended. "Dafydd! Get out of here!"

Heck with that. I wasn't going anywhere, but I did need a moment to gather myself. I ducked behind Paul's car and pulled out a speed potion. If I needed to run, I preferred to do it really fast.

I peered out from behind the car to take in the situation. Paul was still hovering protectively over Nicola, who wasn't moving. I could see the blood spreading from her injury.

The other vampire stared at Paul. He was shorter than Paul, maybe just an inch or two taller than me, and slight of build. Paul was fast, but I suspected this vampire was faster. My friend might have the advantage in strength, however.

The strange vampire was blond and would have been attractive, if not for the glowing eyes and fangs. Plus the arrogant expression and tilt to his head.

I don't generally go for the bad-boy type.

His tongue darted out to lick away a smear of blood, and he smiled, though there was nothing of humor in the expression. "Two humans to protect, Paulus? I can take you easily."

Why wasn't he attacking? He was right. He had Paul at a disadvantage. Paul was fast, but if the other vampire lured him off, like by attacking me, he could probably kill Nicola before Paul could react.

At that moment, the vampire darted in, aiming for Paul's throat. Paul snarled and struck with his claws, never moving from his position over Nicola.

"You're fast, but I can take you on strength," Paul said, his voice steady.

The other vampire sneered. "What good is your strength if I kill both your humans before you can even react?"

I had no idea of his real name, but I decided "Cocky" would fit.

Okay, the best thing for me to do was to even the playing field. I was no match for a vampire, but if I could free up Paul to move as he wanted, I figured he could handle one vampire. I shot a quick glance at the door to Lounge 201. Better do it before reinforcements showed up. I wasn't sure which side the other vampires would take if any came out.

I pulled out another potion. Strength this time. I don't usually like to mix potions. They are hard on the body, but I didn't think I was strong enough to lift Nicola without magical aid. I downed both and felt a surge of energy course through me. I felt like I could run forever, lift buildings and maybe have energy left over to make love all night.

I shook my head. Definitely did not need to be distracted by those thoughts, but it was an unfortunate effect of the potion mix.

My time was short. The potions wouldn't last more than a minute or two. I looked back at Paul and the other vampire. Lucky me. They were involved in some sort of alpha male stare down, and no one was looking my way. Paul had shifted to stand in front of Nicola instead of on top of her. Good, that gave me room to maneuver.

I ran as fast as I could, which under the effect of the potion was faster than an Olympic sprinter. I was halfway to Nicola before either vampire noticed me. Paul attacked, attempting to use his superior strength to knock the other vampire off balance. Cocky dodged, making the movement look effortless, and he reversed direction to charge me.

Good thing I wasn't where he was expecting. I guess he'd never dealt with magically enhanced speed before.

I darted past him and grabbed Nicola. Damn! She was heavy, even with my potion strength, but I lifted her to my shoulder. As soon as I had her, Paul shot past me to engage Cocky, who was looking around almost comically, trying to figure out where I'd gone.

Paul hit him hard, shoulder blocking him and knocking him off balance.

I settled Nicola into a rough approximation of a fireman carry and ran. Well, moved as quickly as I could, which was something more like a trot. I turned a corner and passed a patrolling police officer, who blinked as I approached.

"Evening, officer," I panted as I approached. "Could I get you to call an ambulance? She's hurt pretty bad."

"What happened?" he asked, as his hand moved for

his radio.

This was one of those times when the truth just wouldn't do. I gently lowered Nicola to the ground.

"Dog attacked us. Big one. Maybe a pit bull. A couple of guys distracted it while I got her away."

He nodded as he radioed for both an ambulance and animal control.

A crash sounded around the corner, from the direction of Paul and the other vampire. Uh oh. I really didn't want the officer to see that, but there wasn't much I could do. Distract him? Nothing came to mind, and I watched him jog to the corner.

I stayed by Nicola. For all I knew, Cocky had defeated Paul and was coming for me. I still had a few more seconds on my potions, but I didn't want to push it.

Before the officer could round the corner, Paul appeared. His face was back to normal, and he looked unhurt. He did have a slash down one sleeve, but I didn't see any blood.

"What happened?" the officer asked.

"Big dog," Paul answered.

I almost collapsed in relief. I had no idea how he knew, but so far our stories matched up.

The officer motioned to me. "He said a couple of guys distracted the dog. You one of them?" He was looking at Paul's sleeve.

"Yes, officer." Paul answered, tone smooth but with a hint of agitation. Not bad, but I couldn't help but think he should have sounded a bit more worried.

After all, he had supposedly just tussled with a big dog.

The officer nodded. "I called an ambulance. And animal control. They should be here soon."

I could already hear sirens, and I willed them to hurry. Nicola looked awful. Her face was pale, and the wound on her arm continued to bleed. I struggled to remember what little I knew of first aid and put my hands over the wound, hoping the pressure would stop the bleeding.

A moment later, Paul and the officer were beside me.

"How is she?" Paul asked.

"Bleeding bad." My hands felt slippery, and I was having a hard time keeping a grip on her arm. And of course, that was the exact moment my speed potion ran out. The strength wouldn't be far behind.

Paul stripped off his shirt and made it into a pad to place over the wound. "Try holding that. Help will be here in a minute."

"Can you describe the dog, sir?" the officer asked as soon as it looked like we had the bleeding under control.

Paul stood up, muscles rippling in the street light. I split my attention between Nicola and him, reassuring myself that he hadn't been injured. His chest was unmarked. My strength potion ran out, and I fought to stay upright. Every muscle in my body wanted to collapse. I hate potion aftereffects.

Paul was speaking. "It was dark, and the dog was moving fast, so I didn't get a good look at it. Brown or maybe black. Big." He turned to me. "Would you agree, Dafydd?"

I nodded, trying to hide my weariness. "Sounds right. Maybe a pit bull or a mastiff? It's jaws were big."

Paul gave me a sharp look, and I didn't think my act was fooling him. However, before he could do or say anything, the ambulance pulled up, and medics jumped out to take over. I let them, grateful to have experts in charge.

We answered the officer's questions, Paul smoothly directing most of the questions toward me, so we wouldn't get caught in conflicting stories. He might not be good at the Vampire Mind Whammy, but almost two hundred years had taught him how to manipulate a conversation. I couldn't quite keep the tremble out of my voice, and the officer, who had identified himself as Jack, asked if I was all right.

I nodded. "It's not every day I have a run-in with a big dog."

The paramedics rushed by with Nicola. One of them stopped long enough to say, "I think she'll be fine. She's lost some blood, but the wound is clean. You did well to stop the bleeding."

"Where are you taking her?" Paul asked.

"Howard University. Either of you family?"

We both shook our heads. "Friends only," I said.

"I can't let you ride with her, then, but ask at the desk. They'll let you know how she is."

With that, he rushed for the ambulance, and they took off, siren wailing.

The officer took our names and a bit more information before letting us go. Animal control was just pulling up as we started walking away.

Halfway to Paul's car, I swayed and almost collapsed. Paul grabbed my waist and held me upright. "You okay? Did he get you too?"

I shook my head. "No. Aftereffects of taking two potions."

Everything hurt. The best I can describe it was like running a marathon and then going twelve rounds with a heavyweight boxer. Magic can do marvelous things, but the body pays for it later, especially after two potions. One I can usually manage fine, with little more than sore muscles the next morning. Two, however? That's something else entirely.

"You took two?"

I nodded, the motion taking more effort than usual. "I figured I needed speed and strength. She's no light weight."

He supported me to his car and practically lifted me into the seat. "Take you home?" he asked as he climbed in the driver's side.

I shook my head. "No, let's stop by the hospital and see how she's doing."

The look he gave me was pure gratitude. I smiled at him. "What? You think I'm not going to be concerned about one of your friends?"

He started the car. "No, I should have known, but...I fear I have put you through some hell these last couple of days."

I shrugged, trying not to wince as the motion made me discover another set of muscles that hurt. "I can handle it. Like I said, I knew what I was getting into. You are a vampire, not a priest."

He snorted and pulled onto the street. "Definitely not that."

"So what happened back there? When I heard the crash, I thought Cocky'd killed you and was coming after me."

"Cocky?"

"Sorry. That's what I was calling him. Not like we'd been introduced."

Paul nodded. "Ah. I don't know his name either. He's fairly young. I'd guess no more than five years turned."

"He seemed pretty tough."

"He was fast. Fortunately, I was stronger. After you grabbed Nicola, I was free to maneuver. I know a few more tricks than he did, and he broke off."

"Part of the message then," I said. "He never intended to kill any of us."

Paul was a moment before replying. "I hadn't thought of that, but I think you are correct. If he could have killed Nicola, I think he would have. He obviously hadn't expected you to react as you did."

I grinned. "Never count the warlock out."

He nodded. "Good work back there. It was the best thing you could do, getting her out of the way."

"I figured. Let you do what you do best while I get rid of the distractions."

Howard University Hospital was just a few blocks from Lounge 201, and Paul pulled into their parking lot. I pointed to the big "Emergency Room" sign, and he parked nearby.

"You up for this?"

I took inventory of the muscle aches and joint pain. It wouldn't be fun, but I'd live. I nodded. "Yeah. A couple Advil wouldn't go amiss, though."

He got out of the car and came around to help me out. I could get used to his chivalry. "I saw a gas station on the way in. They won't have much information for us yet. How about I get you settled and go get you something?"

Part of me thought I should tough it out. On the other hand, if he was offering? "Sure. I'd appreciate that."

I forced myself to walk as normally as possible into the building. I didn't want anyone thinking I was a patient when I knew I'd be fine after I had a few hours' sleep.

Paul settled me in the waiting area and went to the desk to check on Nicola. I hoped no one else noticed how the fluorescent lights made him look even more dead.

He came back a minute later. "They just admitted her and can't tell us anything yet."

"Pretty much what we expected."

He nodded. "Yes. I'll be back in a few minutes with Advil for you."

"Thanks. See you in a bit." I waved him off and

leaned back to close my eyes. I hurt, and I had a lot of thinking to do.

The obvious thing that I should be thinking about was what to do with Nicola and what to do about Malachai and his rogue. They were the real danger right now, and part of me wanted to ponder them.

But a bigger part of me couldn't get away from the fact that Paul was interested in and had been in relationships with men. Why hadn't he told me? More importantly, why hadn't I picked up on something earlier? My gaydar is usually very good, and it consistently told me that Paul was straight.

I suppose I could be right about him not being into me, but I had been totally wrong about him being straight. In hindsight, he'd even as much as told me that when he'd said that vampires didn't view sexuality the same as humans. He'd strongly implied that vampires didn't worry about gender, either in their victims or those they chose to associate with.

I groaned and threw an arm over my face. All the signs had been there, and I'd looked past them. Why? Did it mean I wasn't interested in him? Was I afraid of approaching him that way?

I was crap at this. Give me a situation I can solve, either with a spell or something else. This introspective stuff has never been my strong point. I suck at meditation too. I learned just enough to be able to focus my will for a ritual or spell, but sitting around clearing my mind and contemplating the Universe? Nah. Not for me.

And now the doubts I had about Stephen. He couldn't have been the one to send Nicola to Lounge 201. Or could he? As far as I knew, he was the only one who knew where Paul and I were going to be.

A shadow fell over me, and I jolted upright, ready to defend myself.

"Easy. It's just me."

Oh, Paul. Right. The vampire stood in front of me, a couple of tablets in one hand and a glass of water in the other.

"Thanks," I said as I took them. Quickly, I swallowed the pills, hoping they'd work fast.

"Any word yet?"

I shook my head. "No. I've just been sitting here thinking."

He smiled and sat down beside me. "I could tell."

"That brow-furrowed thing was a dead give-away, huh?"

"Yes. What were you thinking about?"

Great. How to answer that one. Sitting in a hospital emergency room, waiting to hear about the condition of the reincarnation of Paul's former lover was not the time to ask, "Why didn't you tell me you liked guys?"

Hospital personnel bustled around us. They weren't listening, but I didn't want to talk too much about weird stuff until we'd had a chance to get somewhere private. So I opted for the safer topic. "I've been trying to figure out if Stephen was the one who lured Nicola to Lounge 201."

He frowned. "Seems unlikely. From what little

you've said about him, he doesn't sound like the type."

"But how can I really know? It's not like I've known him that long. And he did know where I was going to be."

"Have you told him about me?" His tone was unreadable.

I shook my head. "No. He knows about my magic, but I haven't told him anything else. I was thinking it was about time to tell him more, but how do you start that conversation? 'Hey, Stephen. When I'm not seeing you, I hang out with this hot vampire and beat up bad guys.'"

I searched Paul's face for some reaction when I described him as "hot," but he knew how to make poker players look expressive.

"I can see how that would be awkward," was all he said.

Not helpful. "So I agree. He's not likely, but I think he's more likely than some mysterious bad guy following me around. Definitely more likely than someone following you around. You'd know, right?"

Paul nodded. "Probably. Although another vampire might be able to slip by me."

"Like that guy you just sent packing?"

He shook his head. "No. I would have noticed him if he'd been following me. Malachai, though?"

"But he's not likely to be following you himself. Doesn't sound like his style."

"Magic?"

I had to think about that. Tracking rituals are

straightforward. If Malachai had even minimal talent, he could pull that off. But that would tell him where Paul *was*. Not where he *would be*.

I said as much, and Paul looked thoughtful. "What about precognition? You can do that."

I snorted. "Yeah, in my dreams. Literally. And I have no control over what I sense. The visions come to me. I can't even offer topical suggestions."

"So you're not going to win the lottery?"

"Hardly. The only way that'd happen is if I needed the money to fulfill something else. And since I haven't had a lottery winning dream yet, I'm guessing I'd better not hold my breath."

"As far as I know, Malachai's talents aren't precognitive anyway."

I suddenly realized he'd given me the answer to something I'd been wondering about for a while. "Malachai is why you know so much about magic."

He nodded. "Yes. He didn't share much, but I know how to keep my eyes open, and I was with him long enough to pick up some of what magic could do. And what it couldn't."

"That makes sense." And realized I'd been stupid. "I know how to check if Stephen is involved with Malachai."

Paul's eyes brightened. "Yes?"

"Yeah, I've obviously been distracted because I should have seen it before now. If Stephen has been associating with a warlock, it'll show up in his aura."

"Will it? I didn't know that."

I nodded. "Oh, yeah. We rub off on the people we hang out with."

Paul looked somewhat alarmed. "So my aura will show that I've been with you?"

"Yeah. Is that a problem?"

He shrugged. "Probably not. I don't think I get my aura read very often."

"And since we've sort of let it be known that you and I are...well magically bonded in some way, any of the warlocks who work with the vampires would be expecting to see it."

"True." I could almost watch the thoughts go across his face. He hadn't expected that. And he was working out if it made him vulnerable. That thought made me sad. If associating with me made him vulnerable, then a romantic relationship was not likely. I sure hoped Stephen wasn't involved with Malachai. I'd been enjoying regular sex.

Paul shook himself. "So you'll check Stephen's aura?"

I nodded. "Yeah. I'm supposed to call him soon anyway. I'll see if he's available for coffee, and I can check him then."

"Will he know what you're doing?"

Good question. "I don't think so. If he's clean, definitely not. If he's been working with a warlock, he might recognize it, but I know how to keep the signs minimal."

Unlike that tame witch I met last night, I couldn't help thinking.

"Have you read him before?"

Now that was an interesting question. No, I hadn't. And in hindsight, that was weird. I don't go around reading just everyone I meet, but you'd think I'd have checked out boyfriend material before now. "Now that you mention it, no, I haven't."

He frowned. "I thought you would have."

I nodded, slowly. "Yeah, that's just what I was thinking. Now I'm suspicious."

"Of what?"

"I'm wondering if someone has used magic on me. Subtle stuff. Just enough to stop me from reading Stephen."

Paul leaned forward. "That would be mind magic, correct? What you said was forbidden?"

I heard my voice harden. "Oh yeah, and if someone's using mind magic in my town, I intend to put a stop to it."

"Can you tell if someone's used magic on you?"

"Yes, I can. I intend to check on that as soon as I get home."

Just then a young doctor started walking our way. She looked tired, and I guessed it had been a long night in the ER. Her hair was sweaty and looked like it had spent most of the night under a cap. She pushed it back in what looked like a tired gesture as she approached. Her brown eyes, however, were steady as she spoke.

"I'm Doctor Grisham. You're here with Nicola Shugart?"

I realized that was the first I'd heard her last name.

"Yes," Paul said. "How is she?"

The doctor smiled. "She's fine. We needed stitches to close the wound, and we'd like to keep her overnight for observation. She lost a lot of blood. I don't think she needs a transfusion, but I want to keep an eye on her, just in case. By morning, however, she should be ready to go."

Relief washed over me. Nicola was an innocent, caught up in something for no better reason than who she'd been in a past life. I was glad she hadn't had to pay too high a price for her involvement.

Paul's shoulders relaxed, and he smiled. "That's good to hear. Can we see her?"

The doctor nodded. "For a minute. We're going to move her into a room, but you can have a few minutes with her before then."

She motioned us down the hallway and back into an area that had lots of little alcoves created by curtains. I could see people on examining tables in most of them.

After a moment, we arrived at Nicola's area, and the doctor left with "They'll be here in about five minutes to take you to your room."

Nicola didn't look too bad. She had several tubes hooked to her arms, and she looked pale. Her face was particularly drawn, but she gave us a smile when she saw us.

"Thanks for getting me away from the vampire, Dafydd."

I blinked. I'd been half expecting her to be upset

with us for getting her involved. Gratitude was the last thing I'd expected.

"Uh, you're welcome."

"How are you feeling?" Paul asked.

She shrugged. "Not too bad. They bandaged me up and gave me some good drugs. I feel pretty good now, but I'm guessing that'll change when they wear off." Her speech was slightly slurred, and her eyes not fully focused. "Did you get him, Paul?"

The vampire shook his head. "No, he ran off soon after Dafydd got you away."

"Too bad. What next?"

"We've got a few things to track down," Paul said. "But don't worry. You should be safe in the hospital, and I'm going to ask some friends of mine to keep an eye on you when you get out. Assuming you don't mind giving me your address."

She thought for a moment. "I guess not. Malachai already has it. I don't see much point in keeping it from you. What friends?"

I figured he meant the werewolves, and I wasn't wrong.

"Are you sure about that? Aren't they dangerous too?"

"They're okay," I said, thinking it might be more reassuring coming from a fellow human. "Runner's pack are good people. They patrol the city, keeping an eye on the weird stuff."

A nurse showed up and gave us pointed looks. We hastily said our goodbyes, and Nicola gave Paul her address and cell phone number. He promised to check in with her later in the day, and we left.

The Advil was starting to work. Now everything ached instead of stabbing.

We walked to his car, Paul putting a companionable arm around my waist. I might have used it for support, but don't ask me to admit to it under oath.

When we got to his car, he opened my door and steadied me as I stiffly climbed in. "Home?" he asked.

"Yeah, if you don't mind. I need a hot shower and some sleep before I check out what's going on in my mind."

"Can you get rid of it if he has influenced you?"

I fastened my seatbelt and said, "I think so. I need to call my dad in the morning. He taught me how to check for outside influences, and he covered the basics of how to get rid of them, but I need a refresher. One question?"

"Sure."

Paul had been more open lately about vampire abilities, but I wasn't sure this question wouldn't cross a line. "Can you tell me about how vampires use their mind control abilities? I need to know more about what he might have done."

He frowned and changed lanes. "Like what?"

"Does he need to be in physical proximity or can he do it from a distance? The only vampires I've talked to lately have been you and a few at Lounge 201. That makes me worried that he can affect people at a distance."

He shook his head. "No, we need to be close. It requires eye contact. I don't like to think this, but my guess is that he met you on the street, pulled you aside, did what he needed and then wiped your memory of the incident."

I smiled.

"What?"

"I'm not smiling at the part about him doing his thing up close and in person. That part scares the crap out of me. But, if you're right, there will be a memory that I can access."

Paul blinked. "I just said he probably wiped it."

I nodded. "Right, but memories are virtually impossible to wipe completely. It's there. I just need to get at it, and I think I know how to do that. If I can bring back the memory, then I'll know exactly what he did, making it easy to counter."

Assuming, of course, that he had done something and that we weren't jumping at shadows.

"All right. I'll leave this one to the experts. I'm better at gathering intelligence and punching things."

We drove in silence for a minute before I realized I'd forgotten something. "Hey, sorry, but I never said anything about Darlene getting killed. I sort of got the impression she was something of a friend."

He shook his head. "Not exactly a friend. More an acquaintance. I'm closer to Damien. However, he and Darlene were all but inseparable. You see, they were brother and sister and turned together. I'll have to drop by his place later and offer my support."

I could only imagine what it would be like to have one of my sisters killed like that, and I'm not especially close to them. "Yeah. If there's anything I can do, let me know."

"Thank you, Dafydd."

We arrived at my house, and I climbed slowly out of the car.

"You need a hand inside?"

I waved him off. "No, I'm fine. Thanks for the offer, and for the Advil earlier. They're helping."

"Hold on a second."

I turned in time to see him lean over into the passenger seat and toss out something small. I fumbled, dropped it and leaned down to pick it up. My back protested, but I ignored it. I chuckled when I picked up the bottle of Advil.

"Thanks."

He gave me a smile. "Call me when you know anything. Leave me a message if I'm still asleep."

I nodded. "Yeah, okay."

"Besides," he added. "You might like the new message."

Now I'd have to call him.

"Right, talk later."

He waited until I was in my apartment before pulling away. It's nice sometimes having someone look out for you.

I doubted anyone would really be inside, but I still did a quick circuit of the place before I fully relaxed. The ferrets were asleep, and I knew they'd be agitated if anyone had been there, but I was deciding I couldn't really be too careful these days. I made a mental note to study up on protective spells as soon as possible.

I took a long shower and felt better. The aches had subsided to general stiffness, and I could live with that. I checked the ferrets' food and water, opened their cage so they could get out to play if they wanted and, yawning, headed for my bed and a few hours' sleep.

Chapter 8

Monday, May 3, 2010.
Mid-morning

I WOKE UP curled into a small ball, warm ferret bodies pressed close to me, cuddled in the crook of my legs. As soon as I stirred, they jumped up and began dancing around the bed. Gimble gave my arm a "good-morning" nip, and I groaned.

"Ease up, girls. Dad had a rough night."

No sympathy. Gimble started chasing her cousin all around me. I made a good home base and place to hide behind. They were cute to watch, but after the third time Gimble used my stomach as a launching pad, I shooed them off me and staggered into the kitchen for coffee and more Tylenol, in that order.

Thirty minutes, two cups of coffee and a heaping bowl of Cap'n Crunch later (shared with the ferrets, of course), I was starting to feel semi-functional. Time to look for influences in my mind.

I poured one more cup of coffee and headed for my magical work room. As always, Gimble tried to follow me in, but I blocked her with one bare foot (which she nipped) and closed the door in her exasperated face.

Ferrets and magic don't mix, but I've never been

able to convince Gimble of that. I think she figures there's the mother lode of raisins hidden in here.

No raisins, but I do have a small altar, a couple of boxes of stuff, two shelves with books, a work table and a small rug.

The rug is amazing. In movies, you've seen wizards laboriously draw circles, right? Most of my kind have a circle permanently inscribed in their work rooms, but I rent, and my landlord wouldn't let me paint the floor. So a couple of years ago, my mom gave me a rug. She'd woven it herself, and it had a perfect circle done in silver thread. It might not be as nice as the rug we'd used at Paul's house, but it was mine and made with love. Mom's the best!

The work table is where I make potions, and the altar is for rituals. I didn't need either of them right now, so I took my coffee to the rug and settled down in the middle of the circle.

I cast my circle. I wasn't planning a ritual, but a circle was good for blocking outside energies and influences. I was going to go deep into my own mind, and I didn't want distractions.

When the circle was cast, sounds faded, and I felt peace settle over me. I took a few swallows from my coffee, closed my eyes, and began.

Searching your mind for outside influences isn't exactly easy, but it was a straightforward process. Basically, you think of a topic and watch your emotions and where your thoughts wander.

I started with some easy ones in areas where I was

unlikely to have been influenced.

I thought about my dad and grandfather. No flags there.

I thought about my business downline. Again, nothing.

I contemplated the ferrets. Hmm, an image of raisins. Well, ferrets are like cats and seem to have uncanny powers of persuasion.

I smiled, made a mental note to give them some treats later and moved my efforts to topics more likely to have been influenced.

First, I thought about Nicola, carefully examining random thoughts, impressions and emotional reactions. Finally, I got something.

The impressions washing over me included *protect and stay close.*

Ah, that was something. Oh sure, considering what had happened to her, those weren't surprising, but I knew my emotions right now, and those weren't likely to be the first ones to come up. Right now, my feelings around her were conflicted. I liked her. I wanted Paul to be happy to have found his lost lover, but I was just starting to examine my feelings for him, and a part of me wanted her out of the way.

In the quiet of my own mind, however, when I thought about Nicola, all that came through was to protect and stay close.

It may seem subtle to you, but to me, it was a red flag and confirmed my suspicion that someone had influenced my mind.

Anger threatened. Being mind-controlled was akin to rape, and I wanted to find the person who'd done it to me and make sure they could never do it again. But anger wasn't the emotion I needed right now, so I carefully put my feelings into an imaginary box and continued searching for influences.

Stephen was the next person I thought of. If Nicola had been subtle, this one was more obvious. I felt a strong attraction coupled with the desire not to look too closely. I thought about reading him, and my thoughts skittered away from the idea unless I concentrated on it.

This was confirmation. Someone had influenced me to be attracted to him and not to consider reading him. Stephen was involved in some way. As a willing participant or a pawn? I didn't know yet, but reading him might give me the answer. Of course, that was after I eliminated the compulsions on me.

Then I wondered something and turned my thoughts to Paul. I'd been particularly blind to some things about him. Could that have been part of the compulsion as well?

After a moment, I sighed. No, as much as I'd like to blame Malachai, I'd inflicted that blindness on myself.

You might be wondering why I hadn't noticed these influences before, considering how easily I was discovering them now. Let me see if I can explain it.

A friend of mine was studying to be a life coach, and he told me about the work he had to do on his "personal foundation." He described learning about his buttons, values and blind spots. He said to be a good coach, you had to know what could set you off because it was guaranteed that a client would trigger his buttons sometime. The key was recognizing when it happened so he could compartmentalize and deal with his emotions later. To do that, you have to take the time before working with clients to intentionally discover them and learn why and how they could be triggered.

Well, this is kind of the same for me. Remember how I said I'm not much of a meditator? If I were, I might have noticed this earlier. Meditation is all about getting in touch with your true self. Me? I'd rather be doing something active.

Actually, that's kind of a scary thought because it meant Malachai, or whoever set the compulsions, knew that about me.

Anyway, when you're just out doing stuff, how often do you sit down and really think about "why" you're doing it? If you're like most of us, the answer is "Not real often." I'm the same way. Until Paul and I started talking about Stephen, it hadn't occurred to me to read him. It probably should have, but just like it's hard to prove a negative, recognizing that you're *not* doing something is a lot harder than wondering why you are.

At least I knew now, and my dad would be able to help me with the technique to eliminate the influence.

I stretched, careful to not interrupt the circle and stood up. I drew the power I'd used to cast the circle back into myself and felt refreshed and energized. I left my work room and checked the time on my phone. The process had taken about an hour, which meant it was a good time to call my parents.

They live in California, so I'm always careful to remember time zones. While they both tend to get up early, there was that time I forgot and called them at 4 am their time. To say they were "not amused" would be an understatement.

I called home. As usual, Mom answered. She's not magically active, so you might think she handles all the tech stuff. Not true. My dad's as big a geek as you could imagine. You ought to see how he'd tricked out his MacBook. But mom spends more time in the kitchen (she loves to cook), so she's usually the one near the phone.

"Dafydd. Good to hear from you. How's everything? How's that boyfriend? Going to bring him home for Thanksgiving?"

Uh oh. Trust Mom to get to that right away. "Hey, Mom. Everything's fine. Mostly. But it's kind of about the boyfriend that made me call."

Her voice changed. "Oh. Everything okay? Did you guys have a fight?"

"No, nothing like that. Um, it's kind of a magical thing. Can I talk to dad, please?"

Mom's lived around magic enough that she can follow most conversations, but it's always easier to run stuff by dad first, especially anything involving gray or black areas of magic.

"Sure, hon. He's down in his workroom. Let me just make sure he's not doing something he can't get away from." She sounded concerned, but not worried. Yet. Good. I wanted to keep it that way.

A moment later, my dad's voice came on the line. "Dafydd? Something wrong?"

"Kind of, dad. Can we Skype? It'll be easier."

"Sure." His voice was also concerned. "Your grandfather is here too. Want him to sit in?"

My grandfather, whom we all usually call "Pop-Pop," knew even more about magic than my dad. Having his input would be invaluable.

"That's great, dad. I think he'd be a big help."

"It's not something to do with that vampire, is it?"

I knew he'd ask that. Well, do you really think your dad would be thrilled to have you hanging out with a vampire?

"Yeah, sort of, but it's not like you're probably thinking. Let me explain to both of you, okay?"

"All right, son. My computer's booted up, so go ahead and ping me."

"Uh, give me a minute. Mine's not on yet."

I heard him chuckle. "Late night, again?"

I grinned. "Yeah, it's part of being young, right?"

"I guess so. Talk to you in a few minutes."

I hurried to turn on my aging HP laptop. I'd like to be able to afford a shiny MacBook like my dad, but my business wasn't making that much money yet. So I made do.

A few minutes later, we were connected on Skype.

Dad's face appeared on my screen. He was dressed casually, for him, in a polo shirt. I guessed it had been a gift from Mom since he usually wore button-down Oxford shirts, even at home. He's kind of old-fashioned that way. His black hair, liberally streaked with gray, was neatly trimmed, and his blue eyes were grave.

My grandfather stood behind him. You'd know they were related just by looking at them. Same hair (more gray in my grandfather's). Same eyes. The real difference was dress. PopPop was wearing a "Dark Side of the Moon" t-shirt. He's old, but not old-fashioned.

"Hey, PopPop! Great shirt."

He smiled. "Thanks. I just found it in the bottom of my drawer. Forgot I had it."

I nodded. "Behind on laundry again, eh?"

He chuckled but didn't admit or deny. "Your father seems to think you're in a spot of trouble. Why don't you tell us about it?"

I filled them in quickly on Malachai, Nicola and my findings about how my mind had been influenced. I avoided the bit about memory projection. No need to complicate the discussion.

They asked a few questions during my narration, most of them about Nicola and her reincarnation, but basically they let me tell it uninterrupted. Both were frowning at the end, which didn't surprise me. As I've said, mind magic is forbidden in their coven and most of the ones they deal with. Rogue vampires would be a concern to anyone, and the forced recall of past memories was just weird.

"That's quite a story, son," my dad finally said.

"And that's one of your biggest understatements, Randal," my grandfather added. Randal's my dad's name in case I'd forgotten to mention it before. "What do you all plan to do?" he asked.

"Well, to start with, I need to get rid of the compulsion against reading Stephen and find out if he's a willing participant or another pawn."

I saw the sympathetic look on both their faces, and it made me feel a little bit better. Great thing about family. They're always in your corner. At least, that's true with my family.

"And any other influences you might not have already discovered," my father said.

PopPop's expression was grave. "That might be difficult. If he doesn't know what's been altered, he might not find everything. The spell needs something specific to target."

I smiled.

"What, Dafydd?"

"I asked Paul about how vampires do their mind trick thing. He says they have to be in physical proximity and that Malachai probably wiped my memory of it. If I can get the memory back…"

"You'll know exactly what he did," my dad finished.

I nodded. "Exactly. I've got a couple of memory enhancement potions already brewed. I thought if I used one, I might be able to recover the memory. I wondered if either of you had an idea to add to that. Make it more likely to work."

They exchanged glances. PopPop didn't look happy, but he nodded.

"What?" I asked.

My dad sighed. "I'm hesitant to suggest this, but your vampire might be able to help."

I blinked. "How? Like I said, he's not strong in that area."

"That may be, but he does have the ability to make someone more vulnerable to suggestion. If you take the potion and have him use his power to encourage you to remember, that might work."

I thought it through. Obviously, I liked the idea of Paul helping to undo his former master's work. "I can see where that might work."

"Especially if you do it at sunrise or sunset," my grandfather suggested. "I'd imagine the extra power boost would help Paul as well."

Did anyone else find it interesting that my grandfather called Paul by his name while my dad only ever called him "the vampire?" But he was probably right about when to do the ritual. I draw my power both from within myself and from the energy that is always available around us. Certain times, however, have inherently more power available. The full moon is one time, as are solstices and equinoxes. Why do you think many cultures perform major rituals at those times? Even non-talented practioners of magic can make things happen when that much power is flowing around them.

Sunrise and sunset are lesser times, but there's still more energy available than at other times of day. Times of change are particularly potent, and those two happen every day.

I'd never thought about Paul being able to take advantage of the boost, but it made sense. Even if he usually only used his personal strength, he should be able to draw on an external power source. I'd have to run it past him.

And if he couldn't, I had already been planning to take advantage of them myself.

I nodded. "That makes sense. I can talk to him about it. I'm sure he'd be willing to help." Assuming he didn't get weird about using his vampiric power on me. But I decided not to mention that.

"Anything else you need from us?" my dad asked.

"Yeah. Can you send me the ritual to get rid of mental influences? I know we talked about it, but that as a long time ago, and I'm a little hazy on the details."

He nodded. "That's easy. I'll track it down and upload it as soon as we're done."

Dad and I share a Dropbox account, and we use it for exchanging files. Easier than email somehow.

I wasn't sure how to ask this next question, but PopPop snorted and said, "Out with it, youngster."

I sighed. "Well, it's like this. Obviously, you two know a lot about vampires and stuff…"

"Why didn't we tell you more about them when you were a kid?" my father finished.

"Yeah. That."

They exchanged glances again. "You might not like the answer," my dad said.

"You always taught me that the liking wasn't important. It was what I did with the information."

PopPop chuckled. "He's got you there, Randal."

My dad smiled. "Yes, you were correct. It is odd to have your son feed back your teachings."

Get the impression they've had this conversation before?

"All right, son. I can't give you the full answer right now. Come home for the holidays, and we'll talk more. But the short answer is that we, as in the coven, want children to focus on learning their powers first. If we overload you with too much magical knowledge and dance visions of all the supernatural creatures in front of you, you don't focus as much on the learning."

I didn't believe that was all of it. "Yeah, right, dad. If you'd told me more about vampires and werewolves, I wouldn't have studied. I would have totally run off to find them."

More glances. I was starting to get tired of those.

"That's not as far off as you might like to think," PopPop said. "You said yourself that this Malachai has some talent. You don't think other vampires would like to have talented offspring?"

I hadn't thought about that.

My father continued. "Children are vulnerable until they learn to control their abilities. You're old enough to both make an informed decision about becoming a vampire and strong enough that you aren't easy prey. I don't like you hanging out with one, but I'm not concerned you'll be turned against your will."

I wasn't so sure about that with someone like Malachai around, but then I live more in the real world than my dad does. In some ways, he's still sheltered in the coven.

"So you're saying if you don't tell us until we're trained, you can protect us and keep us safer."

They nodded. "It's not the perfect solution, but it's the best one we've come up with. If we don't focus on vampires and other things, you're less likely to head out looking for something you're not prepared to handle."

"But you told me all about demons and ghosts," I said.

"You could potentially summon a demon," Pop-Pop said. "We have to teach you about them, so you don't accidentally do something stupid. Same with fairies and elementals. Anything you can call up through magic we talk about in detail. As for ghosts, with your sensitivity to energies, you were likely to discover them on your own. Better that you knew what to do about it."

I guessed that sort of made sense. "But what about when I left home? You never told me then."

Dad shrugged. "You weren't part of a coven. Usually they are the ones who do the teaching."

I sensed that wasn't all, and I gave them both a hard look, as well as I could over Skype and thousands of miles.

PopPop shrugged. "We knew from your description of your dreams about Paul that he was probably something non-human. We didn't know he would turn out to be a vampire, of course. When we meditated on what to do, the clear answer we both received was to do nothing. To let you meet him with no preconceived notions."

My father nodded. "Anything else seemed to have a bad outcome, both at that moment and further in the future. I don't know what role he's going to play, but it's more than just patrolling for werewolves and defeating rogues. You two are meant to work together in the future."

I blinked. I'd never have guessed that, although considering the strength and persistence of the dreams I'd had about Paul as a kid, I probably should have. Only one other dream has ever been so overwhelming and constant. That one still gives me shivers to think about it and several sleepless nights afterwards. Fortunately, I haven't had it in a while.

"Okay," I said. "I won't say I'm entirely happy about it, but I can see why you didn't tell me. And I know now, so in the end, I guess that's what's important."

They both looked relieved.

I smiled. "Guess that's it for now. Send me that ritual, and I'll let you know how it works."

They smiled, and my dad nodded. "Will do, son."

We exchanged pleasantries, and I hung up. Time to call Paul, check out his new voicemail message and arrange a time to meet. I just hoped he'd agree to help me.

I DIALED PAUL'S number, expecting voicemail since it was much too early for him to be up. I wasn't disappointed. After four rings, I heard the vampire's voice say, "You know the drill. If I know you, leave a message. If I don't, hang up now 'cause I won't call you back anyway."

I blinked. That was different. Yes, Paul has a sense of humor, but in his speech he's usually precise and even slightly old fashioned. That message was a departure.

Just then Paul's voice came on the line. I could hear the smile in it. "Well, were you going to leave a message or just make me guess it was you."

"Uh, sorry. You mean you were there the whole time, just waiting through the message."

"Yes. It's not what you expected, was it?"

"Not exactly, no. But I kind of like it."

"So do you have something, or did you just call to hear the message?"

I shook my head, realizing I'd probably never really learn Paul, no matter how long I knew him. "Yeah, I was definitely influenced by Malachai, or at least I assume it was him."

His voice turned serious. "That's what we'd expected, but I'd hoped to be wrong."

"Me too. I called my dad, and he's sending me the

ritual to banish the influences. And, he kind of had an idea I wanted to run past you."

"Go ahead."

I swallowed hard, not sure how he'd take this. "He thinks you can help me recover the memory of what Malachai did."

"How? I've told you. I'm not good with mind magic." He paused and then added, "And your dad was actually okay with me helping you with something?"

I grinned. "Well, okay might be a bit of a stretch, but he's the practical type. If help from a vampire makes it more likely to work, he'll go with it."

"All right. So what did he have in mind?"

I explained briefly.

When I finished, he said, "I see what he's thinking."

"Would it work?"

"I think so."

That was hardly a ringing endorsement, but I figured it was the best I'd get.

"Willing to try?" I held my breath.

"Willing, yes. Happy about it, not really," was the answer.

I let out my breath. "Can't say I'm thrilled either. I've had my mind messed with once already. I'm not eager to allow it again, but I trust you not to do anything weird."

"Thank you. When did you want to try it?"

My preference was for sunset, but it wouldn't be easy to get Paul over here until sundown. I hated to delay, but I didn't see any options beyond waiting until tomorrow at sunrise. Too bad something was telling me we didn't have that much time to waste.

"I guess sunrise tomorrow. I want the extra boost. My dad thinks you'll be able to take advantage of it to make your ability stronger."

I could hear the surprise in his voice. "Really? I'd never thought to try that. Of course, I don't use that power much."

I snorted. "Guess not since you keep telling me how much you suck at it."

"Thanks."

"What are friends for? Anyway, I want us to try to take advantage of anything we can. So tomorrow sunrise'll have to do."

"But you'd rather do it this evening?"

"Sure. Something is telling me we don't have time to waste. But I don't know how to get you over here in the daytime. I'm all out of shrinking potions."

He chuckled. "Let me call Runner. I think we can make something work."

I glanced out the window at the bright, early fall sunlight. "Okay." I knew he'd hear the doubt in my voice.

"One of Runner's people has an old panel van. No windows. And I've got a long cloak I keep around for these occasions."

"You mean I didn't have to shrink you down a couple of months ago?"

He laughed. "Well, technically, no. But I wasn't

ready to introduce you to all my friends that soon. Or all my options."

That made sense. "All right. When do you think you can be here?"

"Call it 7:30 or so? I could use a few more hours of sleep if that's all right."

Sunset was at 8:03 this evening. I could have everything set up before he arrived, and that would give us time for any final preparations. "I think that'll work."

His mentioning the werewolves made me think of something. "Did Runner know anything about Malachai?"

"Not much. He and his people are aware of the vampire killings, but they haven't seen anything."

"I guess it wouldn't be too hard for a vampire to keep out of the way of werewolves."

"Not hard at all. They have a distinctive scent."

Well, it would have been nice to get more information, but we'd done more with less in the past.

"Well, okay. See you around sunset then?"

"Until then."

We hung up, and I decided to contact Stephen. I was confident enough that what we had planned would work, and I wanted to schedule a time to read him as soon as possible. I really hoped he was an unwilling pawn in all this, but either way I needed to know.

I sent him a text:

Any chance we could get together tomorrow? Miss you. XOX

I puttered around, checking email and the status of my downline's orders. They were actually looking pretty good for this early in the week. Maybe I'd get two nice commission checks in a row. My bank account could use them.

About half an hour later, my phone beeped, and I grabbed it. There was a return text:

Sure. Coffee @ 2? I've got time between appointments. Miss u 2

Stephen's in the same business as I am, so I assumed those were business meetings with new customers or associates, but of course now I was suspicious of everything. I told myself he probably wasn't meeting with Malachai in the middle of the day. *But you're meeting with Paul in the middle of the day* came the suspicious part of my brain.

I told it to shut up and sent my own text in return:

Sounds good. Usual spot?

A minute later came the response:

Works 4 me. See u then

After that, I just sat on my couch and moped. I hadn't always had the best luck in boyfriends, and I'd really thought Stephen would work out. But I was a big boy, and I had other things to do.

I called Laura to run an idea past her. Plus she'd been checking out Paul's place for bugs, and I wondered if she'd found anything. She picked up right away. "Hey, Dafydd. I was just going to call you. I checked out Paul's house like you asked."

"Oh, good. Find anything?"

"What's wrong?" She always was good at reading me.

I filled her in.

"Really sorry, Dafydd."

That's what's great about Laura. She always has my back, emotionally speaking.

"Yeah, well, it happens."

"Not always like that, though. Maybe you'll read him and find out he's cool?"

"Maybe."

"But you don't think so?"

I sighed. "I don't know what to think. Everything's been turned upside down the last couple days. Stephen. Paul and Nicola. I just don't know."

She was silent for a moment. "You know, Paul's probably pretty messed up about Nicola right now. He'll need a friend."

I wasn't sure where she was coming from. "What?"

"Think about it, Dafydd. You said he's killed Nicholas a couple of times. And it sounds like that first time they were really in love. And then he stopped killing after the last time he killed Nicholas. Right?"

"Yeah." I guess I was just being a typically dense male because I had no idea where she was going with this.

"Think about it. Paul's obviously not as straight as

you'd thought. And by the way, I always got a different vibe off him."

As she'd told me routinely. Guess she was right, and I'd been totally wrong. "Okay, yeah."

"Snap out of it, Dafydd." She rarely took that tone with me, so I forced myself out of my funk and concentrated.

"Okay. I'm listening."

"If Paul loved Nicholas as Nicholas and loved him enough to stop killing for him, how do you think he feels now that Nicholas is Nicola?"

I finally got it. If Laura was right, the Universe had just pulled a huge cosmic fast one. But...

"Okay, I see where you're going with that, but he's been with girls before. I mean, he was married and had kids, I think."

"And you think someone can't change in about 150 years."

She might have a point. Even if Paul liked both guys and girls, having your former lover show up in a different body would have to be a big adjustment.

"Okay, I see what you mean. You're right. He probably does need support." I knew what she'd say next, and I hurried to get it in first. "And yes, helping someone else will make me feel better about everything too."

"That's my Dafydd."

"So what do you have for me about bugs at Paul's house?"

Her tone turned business-like. "Looks like he's

clean. Want me to go into the technical details?"

"Not really. I'll take your word for it. Can you check out Nicola's house too?"

"Sure. Give me the address."

One of the advantages of using magic is that I've had to develop a good memory for facts and stuff. Memorizing Nicola's address this morning when she'd given it to Paul had been a snap. I gave it to Laura.

"No problem. I should have something later today. I've got a client project I need to finish up, but I'll get to it after that. Unless it's urgent?"

"Nah. Runner's got his people watching her. I think she'll keep for a few hours."

"Okay. Was that it?"

"No, I had an idea I wanted to run past you."

"Go."

I debated how much to tell her about vampires and what I'd learned. I finally decided she needed a lot of it.

"Um, Paul was telling me that the vampire community has folks inside the police and city government. Maybe farther up than that even."

"Yeah? I guess that makes sense. Easier to cover weird stuff up if someone knows what's real and what isn't."

Which is what I'd decided when Paul had told me. "Well, then it makes sense that there might be some records. Maybe buried deep, but that's not too much of a problem for you, right?"

"What kind of records?" I could hear confusion in her voice.

"Records about vampire kills."

"Oh."

We were silent for a minute. "Any information might give us clues as to what Malachai is really up to. And maybe where he is. Or how many rogues he has working for him."

"Can't Paul get them? I mean, if the vampires have contacts there."

I shook my head. "I don't think so. Paul doesn't always see eye to eye with the other vampires. And even if they did give him stuff, I'd be worried they'd edit it somehow."

"I see." She was silent a moment. "Let me see what I can find. It's been a while since I penetrated the police. I'd enjoy the challenge."

I snorted. "You hack into major government stuff, and you want to convince me that the D.C. police will be a challenge."

Don't get the wrong idea. Laura's a white hat hacker. Organizations hire her all the time to make test runs against their security. You see, Laura's a quadriplegic, and the world of computers is the only place she doesn't feel crippled. So when I say she's been up against some real security, it's not to do anything illegal. But it does mean she's a whiz at research. And she's cleaned up a few of my messes on video, for which I've been very grateful.

"It's all relative."

I laughed. "Okay. When you get a chance, I'd appreciate it. But take care of your client first."

"Will do. Talk later."

"Later. Love you, Laura."

"Love you too, Dafydd."

I hung up, feeling better. Laura's probably my oldest friend. We met when she was in high school, a couple of years before the car accident that crippled her. She moved out here when I did. She said it was to be closer to the government, and that was probably true, but I knew it was also to be closer to me. I wonder if I've ever properly thanked her for that.

But for now, a nap was in order. I'd been running short on sleep a couple of days, and I could always use more. I figured we still had some long days ahead of us.

Chapter 9

Monday, May 3, 2010.
Late Afternoon

S
O MUCH FOR sleep. I tossed, turned and managed little more than a doze. I finally gave it up as a bad cause and got up. It took me only a few minutes to get together everything Paul and I would need for the memory recovery, and I still had a little over an hour to kill.

I grabbed *Storm Front*, the first Harry Dresden book by Jim Butcher. I loved the series and hoped that Harry could distract me.

It must have worked because I jumped when someone knocked at the door. The knock was loud and sounded urgent. I checked the time on my phone. 7:30. Paul, as usual, was punctual. I put aside the book and went to the door, checking at the peephole before unfastening the chain. Couldn't be too careful these days.

Runner and someone wrapped in a long cloak stood outside. Quickly, I opened the door and let them in.

Paul unwrapped himself from his cloak and shook himself. "I always hate that. I can feel the sun, even through the cloth."

I shook hands with Runner. "Good to see you again, man."

Runner was a tall man, about Paul's height but more obviously muscled. His brown hair was unre-markable, if a bit thick and long, drawn into a neat ponytail over one shoulder. His clothes, as always, were simple: jeans, t-shirt and Doc Martin boots. What made him stand out were his eyes. They were mostly brown but they had an odd gold tint to them which flashed when he turned his head in the right light. You might not notice it if you weren't looking for it, but once you've seen it, you know they aren't quite human.

The werewolf's large hand engulfed mine. "And you too. Bloodsucker tells me someone's been messin' with your brain."

"Something like that, yeah." I turned to Paul, who was neatly folding the cloak and putting it on a nearby chair. "You okay?"

He nodded. "Yes. I'm old enough to stand a few seconds of sun exposure. Which does not mean it's comfortable."

Runner was looking around my apartment, and he wandered over to the ferret cage. "These the little sisters I've heard so much about?"

I glanced at Paul, who shrugged. "I like them, so yes, I mentioned them once or twice."

I grinned and walked over to let the ferrets out. I was curious how they'd react to a full-grown werewolf. They'd thought the puppy version had been great fun.

Apparently, they liked Runner too. Gyre danced at

his feet while Gimble raced back and forth between Paul and the werewolf.

Paul laughed and picked her up. "Can't decide, little one?"

She gave him a love nip and wiggled to be let down.

Runner tussled with them for a couple of minutes before standing up. "Guess I ought to go. I don't know much about mind magic, and I'm not in a rush to learn. You gonna be okay to get home?"

Paul nodded. "It'll be full dark by the time we're done. Thanks, man."

The big werewolf shook his head. "Any time. Later, Dafydd."

He left, and Paul faced me. "So what now?"

"Help me get these two back in their cage."

Gyre was easy, but Gimble had to be coaxed out from under the couch. Finally, however, they were safely locked away with plenty of food, water and a couple of raisins for a bribe.

I assembled the few things we'd need, including the all-important memory enhancement potion in its little sports bottle. "Okay," I said. "Now we start."

Paul nodded. "Just tell me what to do."

"Let me show you my magic room. We'll do it in there."

I opened the door and ushered him in. He glanced around. "I don't know. I guess I was expecting something more impressive."

I shrugged. "I'm a poor mage. I can't afford all the

fancy stuff."

He admired the rug. "This is very nice. Make it yourself?"

I shook my head. "No way. Rug making is not one of my skills. Mom made it for me."

"So where do I sit?"

"Center of the rug. Just like when we did the memory projection, I'll cast a circle to block out energy from outside and help us focus."

Paul cocked his head at me.

"What?"

"If we can pull up the memory, is there any reason not to project it?"

I thought for a moment and couldn't come up with any. "Sure. We can do that. It's not part of my automatic repertoire yet, is all."

I went back to the living room and looked around for a likely surface. No way I was carting my HDTV into the work room, and I'm not big on mirrors. There's one in my bathroom, and that's enough for me. Finally, I settled for a large bowl filled with water.

Paul looked at it curiously when I came back, and I shrugged, careful not to spill the water everywhere. "Yeah, I know. Looks like we're going to make a habit of this, so I'll head out this weekend and pick up a portable mirror. Until then, however…"

Paul smiled. "We'll just call it a scrying pool."

"Yeah, we'll do that." I placed the bowl in the center of the circle and glanced around. "Why don't you sit over there." I pointed, and he moved to where I'd indicated. I sat down opposite him with the bowl between us.

"Okay, I think we'll do it like this. I'll take the potion and then put myself into a light trance. It'll take me about 10 minutes to get to the right stage."

"That long?"

I shrugged. "Self-hypnosis isn't my thing. I'm more of a 'do it' kind of person. Anyway, about that time, the sun will be setting and you can do your whammy thing."

He frowned. "I've never tried using sunset to power up my ability."

Oh, right. Using power is something I've done for so long that I kind of take it for granted. I thought for a minute. I'll bet he's been using granted power for years and never even realized it. So how to explain it to him?

I decided to try this approach. "Okay, think of it like this. You get energy from blood, right?"

He nodded.

"Well, my guess is that you don't actually 'digest' blood the way we do food."

"Not exactly," he agreed.

"Then I think you've been drawing on power without being conscious of it. Blood magic is very potent, and I'm thinking that's what you vampires use to maintain yourselves."

His eyes widened. "I'd never thought of that."

"'Course not. You just take it for granted. I don't think about how digestion breaks down food to give me energy. I just eat and let my body take care of the rest."

"So how do I get control of it?"

I looked him directly in the eye, glad we had a few extra minutes to work on this. "Have you fed recently?"

He nodded. "Right before I came over. I do know that my ability is stronger right after I've fed, and I wanted to give us every advantage."

"Good. Close your eyes and look within yourself."

He gave me a skeptical look but closed his eyes. "I'm not seeing anything."

"Can you feel the blood in you?"

He nodded slowly. "Yes."

"What's it feel like?"

He frowned. "Like...I don't know...potential?"

I nodded. "Good. That's what I thought. When you're fighting, have you ever felt yourself drawing on some reserve? Like when you were alive and running really fast and getting tired and suddenly you found some bit of energy you didn't know you had, but you used it to run some more?"

"Yes." His voice sounded uncertain. "I hadn't thought about it like that before, but I think I do that."

"All right. Now all you have to do is control it." How to test this out? There weren't any bad guys nearby, and I didn't want him to rearrange the walls. "Okay, try this. Open your eyes and look at me."

Paul did so. "Now what?"

"Try to make me do something, using your mind control power."

"I told you…"

I waved a hand. "I know. You suck at it. But I bet you are better than you think you are, and I'm not asking you to make me do something weird. Just think of something I might not normally do but won't totally fight you on. Then feel the energy within you. Draw on it and use it."

He thought for a moment. "All right. I'm not sure this is going to work, but here goes."

I shook my head. "No, don't think that it won't work. Believe that it will. Visualize what you want first and then just do it."

The vampire's expression was still doubtful, but he shrugged, closed his eyes for a moment and finally opened them and said, "I'm ready."

I relaxed, wanting to give him an easy target. He met my gaze, and his eyes glowed for a moment.

I left the circle, opened the door, left the room and went to the kitchen, where I opened the cupboard to get out the box of raisins. I shook a couple into my hand and went back to the living room to toss them into the ferret cage. Then I went back to the work room.

Paul was smiling.

I shot him a grin. "That was it? You made me give the ferrets a treat?"

He shrugged. "Well, it didn't seem like something you'd be likely to do just then, but it also wasn't something you'd mind doing."

I nodded. "Good choice. Did you draw on the

power within you?"

"I did, and you're right. I have done it before in a fight. I've just never realized what I was doing."

"Good. Draw on it when you try to bring back my memory. But now I need you to find power outside yourself." I checked my mental clock. Sunset was about 20 minutes away. That wasn't long for Paul to get the hang of it, but since sunset was so close, the power outside was starting to coalesce, and there was a good chance he'd be able to sense it.

"How do I do that?"

I sat down opposite him again. "Close your eyes again."

He did so.

"Okay, sense the power within yourself."

After a moment, he nodded.

"Now move your awareness outside yourself. Can you sense anything?"

He frowned, but a moment later jerked. "Yes. I do feel something."

I winced. "Right. That's me."

His eyes popped open. "What?"

"I'm a source of power. You just 'touched' me, for lack of a better word."

"It hurt?"

I shook my head. "Not exactly. You just touched me. You didn't try to do anything with it. And I wasn't ready for it. When we do work within the coven, we often draw on each other, and there's a way to prepare for it, which I didn't think about doing." I had a thought. "But, that is interesting. If you can learn to draw on my personal power, we might be able to do something with it."

"Is that a good idea?"

I shrugged. "Depends on what we do with it, but it could be useful. Besides, I like learning new things. For now, though, we've established that you can feel power sources outside yourself. Now, we just have to get you reaching for the right one. Sunset is close. You should be able to sense it."

He closed his eyes again. After a moment, he said, "Yes, I think I feel something."

I reached out my own senses. I could feel the blood inside Paul. Interesting. I might be able to draw on him. We had some stuff to experiment with later. I could feel the approaching sunset, and I took a moment to bask in it.

There were other, smaller sources of power nearby, but I had to strain to find them. I doubted Paul on his first time would even notice them.

"My guess is you've found it. Does it feel kind of like a fading shadow?" That was the best way I could describe it.

"I think so."

I nodded. "Good. Then that's likely to be it. Other than you and me, the sunset is the only substantial power source nearby. Now that you've found it, you'll want to grab on and use it just like you did the blood inside you. Think you can do that?"

There was a long pause, long enough to make me

wonder if we were going to be able to make the sunset deadline. Finally, he opened his eyes, his expression full of both doubt and wonder.

I grinned at him. "Yeah, I know how you feel. That's kind of what I felt the first time I touched power."

His voice was solemn. "I think I can use it."

I nodded. "I'm sure you can. Now let me cast my circle and get into the right frame of mind."

It only took me a minute to cast the circle and block out the sounds and impressions from the world around us.

"Won't that block out the power of the sunset?" Paul asked.

I shook my head. "Good question, but no, it doesn't."

"Why not? I thought the point of the circle was to block outside energies and influence."

I couldn't help smiling. I'd asked PopPop the same question when he taught me to create a circle. I could still hear his voice in my head.

"Well, lad. It's simple. If you attune the circle to the power source you want to draw on, it won't be blocked."

I said as much to Paul, who grinned. "That's so obvious, now that you say it."

I nodded. "Yeah. I felt foolish for a while after I realized that."

I closed my eyes. Sunset was close. No more than ten minutes away. "I need to get into my trance. We'll be ready in just a few minutes. Can you feel the approach of sunset?"

"Of course. That's part of being a vampire." Paul's voice held a mixture of confusion and condescension.

I scowled at him. "Not feel it that way. Can you feel the surge of power?"

He blinked. "Oh, that. Sorry." He closed his eyes and nodded a moment later.

"Good. Keep your attention on that. I'll take the potion. As soon as you feel the power at the peak of its surge, do your thing."

"All right."

I opened the small water bottle that contained my potion and drank it down. Memories threatened to overwhelm me.

Learning my first spell
Creating my first potion (and the dramatic explosion that ensued)
My first time having sex
Meeting Paul in the alley, his fangs sunk deep into the throat of a killer

I took a deep breath and relaxed, allowing the memories to flow over me but not touch me. I'd never tried to achieve a trance state while under the influence of this particular potion, but I was confident I'd succeed.

The flow of memories slowed, and I felt my body relax. I let my thoughts drift, without focus, letting them go where they willed. A part of my awareness noted the approach of sunset, and the cells in my body seemed to reach toward the oncoming power. I felt warm, safe and completely in control of myself. Paul's presence was a solid reassurance in front of me. I didn't have my aura sight active, but I could still feel him and the balance between good and evil that teetered within him.

The sun dipped lower, touching the horizon. Power surged. I grabbed it and concentrated on the memories locked within me.

At that moment, I felt a touch on my mind. My first instinct was to pull away, but I recognized the taste of Paul, and I relaxed. I thought I heard his voice, warm and welcome in my mind.

"Open your eyes." His voice was gentle and soothing.

I did so, and his gaze filled mine. His eyes glowed amber, but there was no threat in it. I felt safe and protected.

Remember...

Even though my eyes were open, I plunged deeper within myself. Images flickered. Glowing yellow eyes. Long dark hair pulled back in a tail. A tailored dark suit.

I started to strain, to pull the memories and suddenly Paul's voice was there again, deep inside my mind, enfolding my soul in warmth.

Relax. Let it flow.

I obeyed, and a moment later, I had them. It was like a veil pulled back from my eyes, and I could see everything.

I smiled. "Got them. Now let me project."

The glow in Paul's eyes flickered, faded and their color returned to their usual gray.

I closed my eyes to gather power. I embraced the memories, held them close and then gently tossed them into the bowl.

I opened my eyes and nodded to the bowl. Paul looked, and we watched together.

Roughly Ten Months Earlier

I WAS AT the Dupont Circle Metro station, waiting for a train. A man, whom I now recognized as Malachai, approached me.

"Do you have the time?" he asked.

I pulled out my phone. "Just a few minutes before two."

I thought I remembered when this was, maybe after Paul and I had helped the ghost move on. I think it was probably a month before the werewolf puppy appeared on my doorstep.

I winced, and the projection faltered and stuttered to a halt. Paul's hand squeezed my shoulder. "You all right?"

I gathered my will and nodded. "Yeah. It's a lot to keep track of. Projecting the memory, remembering what I felt at the time and analyzing what was happening."

"Just let it flow. Don't worry about it. You've got this."

Paul's voice soothed me back into the projection, which started again in the still water.

The man nodded and stood to one side, apparently also waiting for a train.

"Pardon me again," he said after a moment.

I turned to him. "Yes?" I said politely. When you ride the train as often as I do, you get used to random strangers asking for help.

His eyes glowed amber in the dim light of the station. "Perhaps you'll come with me." He started to walk towards the escalators. I followed, unable to help myself. I should have been panicked, but my thoughts moved slowly, like honey dripping on bread.

When we reached the top of the escalator, Malachai moved toward the gate allowing us to exit without going through the turnstiles. I didn't seem him do anything, but the attendant opened the gate and motioned us through.

He led me to one side of the station, away from the fare card purchasing machines.

"Let's chat for a moment, and then you can be on your way. You'll only miss one train, so don't worry about being late."

I wasn't worried. I found myself unable to look away from his eyes. Orange heat flickered in their depths.

"Are you involved with the vampire, Paul?"

"We work together, yes."

"That's not what I meant. Are you romantically or sexually involved?" His voice was impatient, and I remembered desperately wanting to please him.

"No, we just work together."

He nodded, and his expression went back to neutral. I felt relief that I'd given the right answer.

"Then you are between boyfriends right now?"

I nodded.

"Excellent. In a few weeks, you'll meet a young man. Stephen will be his name. He'll be exactly your type, and you'll be eager to go out with him. Understood?"

"Of course." My voice sounded slow and dream-like, but that didn't strike me as strange at all.

"No need to read him. He's perfect for you."

I nodded. Why would I want to read him? He'd be exactly what I was looking for.

"You'll like him, of course, but don't move too quickly. Love needs time to grow."

Of course.

"Not long after you meet Stephen, you'll meet a young lady named Nicola. Stay near her. If you meet her without Paul, make sure you introduce them. Paul will very much like her. She'd be perfect for him."

I heard myself whimper. But I wanted Paul to like me.

Malachai smiled. "Enough time for that later, perhaps. For now, concentrate on Stephen. Nicola won't be around long enough to be a permanent rival."

That made me feel better.

"All right then. That's all for now. Date Stephen. Don't read him. Stay close to Nicola and make sure

Paul meets her. Understood."

"Yes."

"Good. Let me take you back to the platform. As soon as we pass beyond the turnstiles, you'll forget this conversation ever took place."

I nodded. No need to remember such an unimportant conversation. Who remembers helping out total strangers on the Metro anyway?

We passed through the gate again, and I took the elevator back to my platform. Darn. Just missed a train. And at this time of day, I'd have to wait another 12 minutes. Oh well, I'd given myself plenty of time to get to my appointment.

The memory faded from the bowl.

I SHOOK MY head. "Hard to believe I could forget that."

Paul nodded. "He's very good. At least now we know what he told you."

"Yeah, it's what I thought from my examination this morning. All he did was send me to Stephen and make sure I'd stay close to Nicola."

"He wasn't taking chances, though. He wanted to be certain she and I met."

I pondered what we'd seen. "I didn't like that part about her not being around long, though."

Paul rolled his shoulders. "I agree." His voice was grave. "I don't know why killing her is part of his plan, but I intend to stop that."

"Agreed."

Paul gave me an odd look. "But what was that part about her being a rival? A rival to what, I wonder."

I blushed. Of course. He'd only seen and heard what happened. He hadn't been privy to my internal thoughts through that. I sighed. This wasn't the time I would have chosen to have this conversation, but maybe there wasn't a good time.

"Um. You can't have been totally unaware that I'm attracted to you."

Paul smiled. "No. Of course not." His eyes widened. "Oh."

The heat wasn't leaving my face anytime soon. "Right. Oh."

Paul's expression grew sad. "I'm sorry, Dafydd. I should have told you a long time ago about Nicholas."

"Yeah, and the fact that you have been interested in guys. I think that might have been relevant." I didn't like the tone in my voice, but I couldn't help it. "Why did you lie to me about Nicholas and Natalie?"

He looked down, not meeting my eyes. "It seemed easier to let you think I was straight. I wasn't looking for complications then. It hadn't occurred to me that we'd start working together."

"And when we did? You still didn't tell me."

His voice was quiet. "No, I didn't."

I waited.

Finally, he sighed. "I don't have a good answer for you, Dafydd. I've indicated that relationships between vampires and humans are complicated. Maybe it wasn't fair to you, but I didn't want it to be an issue. I wanted us to be able to be friends and work together. Without the complication of a potential relationship."

Did that mean what I thought it did? Was a relationship possible between us? Something told me this wasn't the time to push it. "Fair enough, and now isn't the time to worry about it. I still don't know where things stand with Stephen."

He looked relieved. "When do you plan to see him and read him?"

"We're meeting tomorrow afternoon for coffee. I'll do it then."

His eyes softened. "I hope he's a pawn in all this."

I sighed. "Yeah, me too."

I think. Did I really? If Stephen were a willing ally of Malachai, that did make some things simpler. But that wasn't fair either. I owed it to him to free him if he were under the master vampire's control.

But something told me we weren't going to be dating much longer, either way. Would I still like him once I'd rid myself of Malachai's influence?

Paul cocked his head and looked at me. "You all right?"

I shook my head. "Not really. I've been mind-controlled. My boyfriend's working with your enemy, and we've got no idea right now how to stop him. And the reincarnation of your former lover's in the hospital."

"When you put it that way, you're right. Recipe for a pretty lousy day. But, I've got a small bit of good news."

I raised an eyebrow. "Yeah?"

"Nicola's out of the hospital."

"That's good news. Runner's people are keeping an eye on her?"

He nodded. "Round the clock. They're not going to leave her unguarded until we've sorted all this out."

"Glad to hear that."

"Want me to ask them to keep an eye on you as well?"

I hadn't thought of that, but I shook my head. "Not right now. Let me read Stephen first. That'll give us a better idea of what we're up against. As long as I hang close to you at night, I think I'll be fine."

"As long as you're sure. Runner volunteered, you know."

I smiled. "I'll thank him the next time I see him, but now that I'm on my guard, I don't think Malachai will find it as easy to get close to me."

"Did you get what you needed to break his influence over you?"

"I think so. The memory showed me what he messed with. Dad emailed me the ritual. It's pretty straightforward. I've got all the components I'll need. I'll do it at dawn."

Paul got up. "Guess I'd better go then. You'll need some sleep."

I put out a hand to stop him. "Hang on. Let me break the circle first."

He stopped and waited while I pulled the energies

back into me. As always, it made me feel energized, and I knew it'd be several hours before I could sleep.

"There. It's broken. You can step out now." I stood up, feeling like I'd never sleep again. It was an illusion, of course, but there was no way I could sleep for a few hours.

Paul stood up and stretched. I took a moment to enjoy the view.

As he started to leave the room, I said, "I'm wired now. Anything I can help with?"

Paul paused and turned. "I was going to go see Nicola and then visit Damien. I haven't had a chance to talk to him since yesterday evening."

"Want company?" I held my breath while I waited for his answer. I figured he wouldn't mind me being along to see Damien, but I wasn't as certain about Nicola.

He didn't hesitate. "Sure, if you're up to it. I'd like for you to know Damien better. If he hangs around town, he's a decent sort. Not a bad one in a pinch if something happens to me."

A chill went down my back. "Nothing's going to happen to you."

He shrugged. "I've been around a while. I've beaten the odds so far. No guarantee I'll continue to do so."

What had him thinking about mortality all of a sudden? I picked up the bowl of water and stood up. "Let me put this away and grab a couple things." I frowned.

"What?"

"I'm going to run out of potions if this keeps up. I'd just managed to replace everything we used up against the werewolves last month, but I haven't had time to make many more."

Paul followed me into the kitchen. "You know. I've been thinking. Can you use your memory projection spell in combat?"

I poured out the water and put the bowl in the dishwasher. "How do you mean?" I grabbed my daypack and went back to my magic room to rummage through my potion selection. Damn! Only two speed enhancers left. Three strength and two reflexes, though. I tossed one of each in my pack.

"Well, I was thinking about how you told me the first time you did it and having to stop at the kitchen scene in *Jurassic Park*."

I turned to face him. "Yeah?"

"Well, in that scene, don't the raptors get confused by seeing a mirror image of one of the kids in the shiny surface of the kitchen counters?"

I'd seen that movie more times than I could count, and I knew the exact moment he was describing. "Sure. Lex was hiding in a cabinet, trying to pull down the door. It was stuck, and the raptor charged her, only to run into another cabinet. But what's that got to do with me?"

"Can't you project a memory into a reflective surface, to distract someone?"

I stopped. I'd never thought about using the ability

that way. I leaned against the wall and considered it. "Well, first I'd need a reflective surface, so it would be somewhat situational."

"Puddles of water on the ground. Large windows on buildings. Shiny cars. There's probably more around than you'd think."

I nodded, working it out. "Yeah. It would probably help if I came up with some memories in advance. To pull out when I needed them."

"Werewolves make some good ones."

I smiled. "Yeah, and I have some good ones from that last fight. Assuming you aren't around, you'd be good too."

He nodded. "You don't actually need to fool any-one into thinking they are real. You just need to catch someone's attention at a crucial moment."

"Made you look."

"Huh?"

I shook my head. "Sorry. Just something we did as kids. We'd point behind someone and say we saw something. If they turned around, we'd yell 'Made you look.'"

"Exactly. What do you think?"

I kind of liked it. "I'll need to work out some things. I'm not used to doing stuff that fast. In a fight, I won't have much prep time."

"You seem to pull out memories pretty fast."

"Sure, but you've only seen me do it when I was prepared. This would need to be done on the fly." But I thought I could, and I wanted to give it a try. "I think

I can work it out, though. I like it."

He smiled. "Good."

"It'd be easier though if we could have big boss fights in industrial kitchens."

"I'll keep that in mind. What about fun houses?"

I grinned. "Oh, that would be perfect. They're already creepy."

We left my apartment, and headed for the Metro. As we walked, I thought about what I'd need. First, the memories. Those were easy. I could go back through all the fights I'd been in, plus my favorite movies. Paul was right. I didn't have to do more than distract. I'd never convince anyone that a T. Rex was walking down the street, but a glimpse of jaws and teeth out of the corner of your eye would catch your attention, especially if I did it at the right time.

Dogs. Big dogs. I needed to go to a nearby dog park and watch them play. I'd get some good ones there. More realistic than dinosaurs, but just as scary in their own way. Or perhaps a guy with a gun. Even cartoon images would be good. I didn't always have to scare. Startle and distract. That was what I was looking for.

I blinked and realized we'd made the walk to the station and were about to walk onto a train.

Paul smiled at me. "You're back now?" he asked.

I felt heat rise in my face. "Yeah. Sorry about that. I was thinking how to make this idea of yours work." I fixed an image in my mind. As the train pulled away from the station, I concentrated for a moment. "Look to your left a second."

Paul turned his head and whistled. I'd reproduced Runner, loping in wolf form, in the window beside us. He nodded. "Pretty good. I think that would work."

I grinned and let the image fade away.

"How hard was it?" he asked.

I shrugged. "Not bad. From the time I had the idea until I projected the image was just a few seconds."

Paul frowned. "Not bad, but a bit slow for a real combat."

"Hey, give me a break. It was a first try."

He smiled. "Sorry."

"No problem. I think the idea works. Just a matter of refinement."

I sat back, pleased. Conventional wisdom said that magic couldn't be used in combat. I can't call down fire or do any of the things you think about fantasy wizards doing. And I'm not going to do anything close to what Malachai has been using. But this? As long as I pull my own memories, I'm not doing anything to a person's mind. That keeps it out of the black. I think Dad might even agree this wasn't even gray. It's just a clever use of illusions.

"Anyone you know of use the power this way?"

I shook my head. "I don't know anyone else who can project as easily as I do, assuming they'd even be willing to try. Some of us have an odd ability like that. Something we can do very easily that would require preparation by anyone else."

He glanced over at me. "What can your dad do?"

"Actually, as far as I know, he doesn't have anything like that. PopPop, however, can veil on the fly."

Paul whistled. "You mean like you did against the werewolves? Hide yourself so they couldn't see you?"

I nodded. "Yes. One minute he's there. The next he's not. That's why he's so good against other warlocks and the occasional demon someone calls up and can't control."

"I'd imagine."

"He assures me he's only used it for the good, but I know my PopPop. Wouldn't surprise me at all if he used it to perform a bit of larceny when he was a kid. Dad's hinted a couple of times that he had an 'interesting' youth."

"I bet I'd like him."

"I know you would. He's great."

The train pulled into our station, and we got out and walked the few blocks to Nicola's house.

As Paul knocked, I glanced around, trying to spot the werewolves. A large man stepped out from behind a nearby garbage can and nodded at me. I nodded back.

"That's David," Paul said.

"Huh?"

"The werewolf David. Spelled the normal way."

Too bad for him. As a kid I would have killed to change the spelling of my name. Now, I like it.

The door opened a few inches, stopped by the chain. I could see about a quarter of Nicola's face, backlit by the lights inside.

"It's just us," Paul said.

"Hi. Come on in."

"Thanks."

We stepped inside, and she motioned us to a small living room. I paused for a moment to admire the painting of a dragon hanging in the entryway. The red of its hide shimmered, making it appear ready to leap off the canvas.

She must have noticed my gaze because she said, "My sister painted that for me."

"It's great. Her color work is very good."

I admired it for another moment, noticing the sinuous tail and ivory claws on the five-toed feet, which made it an Imperial dragon, if I remembered correctly.

Her living room reminded me of mine, with a worn black leather sofa and a rocking chair by the fireplace. Bookshelves lined every inch of wall space, except for the place of honor reserved for the enormous television. Candles burned on the end tables by the sofa, lending a faint hint of apple and cinnamon to the cozy space.

Paul settled on the couch, moving aside a fluffy blanket, and I sat beside him, leaving plenty of room between us. I didn't want to start this out by making Nicola feel threatened, but I've never liked rocking chairs. They always make me feel faintly sick to my stomach.

Still in the entryway, Nicola asked, "Can I get you anything?"

We both shook our heads, and she sat down in the rocking chair. Great. Watching people rock has a similar effect on me. I hoped we wouldn't need to stay long.

"Have you learned anything?" Nicola asked.

Paul glanced at me, and got it. He wanted me to tell this part.

I nodded. "Yes, a little bit. We think we know the identity of the man who sent you to Lounge 201."

Her eyes widened a bit. "Is he the one you suspected? Your boyfriend?"

I nodded.

"I'm sorry." Considering the circumstances, her voice held a surprising amount of empathy.

I shrugged. "It is what it is. Right now keeping you safe and stopping Malachai is what's important."

Nicola looked at Paul, and I winced at the naked love in her eyes. She rocked harder, and I had to look away, figuring she'd probably misinterpret the gesture but deciding that was preferable to throwing up in her living room.

"Is that all that's important?" she asked. "Paul, what about you and me?"

Oh, shit. I'd put my foot in it there. I wondered if I should leave the room. The anguish in Paul's eyes was obvious. I guessed that, as usual, Laura had seen what was really going on. I had to wonder why Paul had wanted me along. Surely they needed time alone to work this out?

"It's okay, Dafydd. Please stay." Paul's voice was absolutely steady, at odds with the pain in his eyes. I could only imagine what this was costing him.

I turned back to look at Nicola, just in time to see the anger flash in her eyes.

"Is that how it is, Paul? You're with him?" she asked.

The vampire shook his head. "No, it's not like that at all. I just..." He paused. "I wasn't expecting this, Nicholas."

She winced at the name, and embarrassment crossed the vampire's features. "Nicola. I'm sorry. I can't help it. You've been Nicholas to me for decades."

Nicola sighed. "I know. And that's the problem, isn't it? You loved me as a man, and now—" She pointed to her body. "Now, I'm like this."

"No, that's not it." His voice was firm, but I knew him well enough to sense he wasn't being totally honest. "It's more the timing. And what's going on. When we returned the ring, I assumed you hadn't been reborn yet. I thought it would be years before I saw you again. Not months. And with Malachai. I don't want you in any more danger than you already are. If we can figure out what he wants and stop him, then, maybe." He trailed off.

He didn't sound convincing to me, and I doubted Nicola believed him either, but all she said was, "I understand. What can I do?"

Paul sighed. "Right now, probably nothing. The werewolves will keep you safe and warn me if anyone comes looking for you. Dafydd's going to talk to Stephen tomorrow. We should know more by then."

She stopped rocking and sat forward, her expression confused. "How will that help? If he's working with Malachai, he won't tell you anything."

"He won't have to," I said. "I'm going to read his aura. That will tell me if he's working for him willingly, or if he's been mind-controlled. If he's controlled, I can break the spell and get him to tell me more."

"And if he's willing?"

I hadn't let myself think that far ahead, and I had no answer for it.

Paul answered for me. "We'll deal with that when we know it. I can probably get information from him, if that's needed."

From his tone and expression, I knew he didn't like the idea any more than I did. An odd mixture of fear and pity came across Nicola's face, and I wished I were anywhere but here.

However, since I was here, I hurried to say, "And we have a few more leads to track down. The white hat hacker I mentioned is checking some things for me."

Paul glanced at me, the question in his eyes, and I waved him to silence. I'd fill him in later on my conversation with Laura.

"We've stopped other bad guys before. I'm sure we'll figure it out and stop him too. Then you and Paul can...well, figure out the other stuff."

There. I'd said it. I'd let Paul know that, my attraction for him aside, I was willing to let him resume what he had with Nicola. My stomach clenched as I said the words, but I knew it was the right thing. I'd deal with my own emotions later.

She looked at me and then at Paul. I wasn't sure she was convinced, but I kept my gaze steady, determined not to mess up anything between them. "All right. I'll stay here. I guess you'd rather I didn't go to work for a couple of days."

Paul nodded. "Can you manage that?"

She shrugged. "I get paid as an independent consultant. So if I miss work, I don't get paid, but, yeah, I can manage for a few days. Find him quickly though. I can't go without a paycheck forever."

"I might be able to help with that, if needed." Paul's voice was hesitant.

Nicola's eyes flashed anger. "No. I'm not going to accept your charity! That's not how I work."

Paul's voice was soothing. "I didn't mean it like that. I got you into this, didn't I? I think I owe you something for that."

Her expression softened a bit. "We'll see."

Again, I wanted to be anywhere else right then, but Paul had stuck with me through some tough times, and I couldn't leave him now.

Paul got up. "Dafydd and I need to check something else out tonight. The werewolves will stay as long as they need to. I don't expect trouble during the day, but Malachai's got at least one human working for him, and there might be others."

"Won't they be helpless during the day? I mean, won't they change back to humans?"

Paul laughed. "First, these don't work that way. They can take wolf form at any time of day. And second, they're hardly helpless even when they are in human form. No, they can't take on a vampire, but I don't think there are many pure humans who can stand up to an angry were, even when he's not in wolf form. They're pretty tough."

"Oh, sorry." Suddenly, she got up and went to Paul. She looked at him, and he sighed and pulled her into a hug.

"No, I'm the one who's sorry. I got you into this." He kissed the top of her head and held her tight. "I'm so sorry. I never meant for you to be hurt."

She pulled back. "You should have thought of that the last few times you killed me."

He winced. "You're right. I just wanted this time to be different."

"You got that part." Her tone was wry.

He pulled her close again and held her for a long moment before letting her go with a gentle kiss on her lips. I could see she wanted more, but he stepped away.

"Dafydd? Shall we go? I still want to talk to Damien."

I stood up. Nicola stepped over and searched my face. I don't know what she was looking for or if she found it, but she finally said, "Take care of him for me?"

I nodded. "Always."

She smiled, small and brave, and saw us to the door. As we walked away, she remained in the doorway, watching us go.

I didn't turn to look at her. The thought of watching her watch us leave was more than I could stand right then.

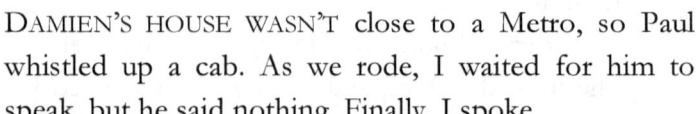

DAMIEN'S HOUSE WASN'T close to a Metro, so Paul whistled up a cab. As we rode, I waited for him to speak, but he said nothing. Finally, I spoke.

"What was that about back there?"

Paul glanced over at me. "What do you mean?"

"She loves you like crazy. You just put her off."

He sighed. "I know, and I hated myself for it, but I don't know what to do."

"Talk to me."

He paused for a moment before saying, his voice low enough that the cabbie couldn't hear, "Nicholas is the only human I've been with since I've been a vampire."

I hadn't expected that. Sure he said that vampires didn't often associate with humans, but as long as he'd lived, I'd just assumed he'd had others. "Really? No one else?"

He shook his head. "Well, technically, I suppose there was one other, but it didn't last long. Or end well."

I wanted to ask more, but his voice told me to leave it for now. I figured he'd tell me when he was ready.

"So the last human woman I was with was my wife, before I became a vampire. I find…." He trailed off, and I waited. "I find that I've lost my taste for human women."

"But not vampires?"

"No, although I haven't been with many of them either." He looked at me, searching my eyes, for what I couldn't tell. Finally, he looked back at the road and said, "I've been alone most of my time as a vampire. So many years with Malachai and his games soured me for company." A slight smile. "Well, until recently. After hooking up with Runner and his people, I find I do enjoy company sometimes."

He glanced at me again. "Present company included."

Ever had both warm and cold run through your body at the same time? The fact that he liked being with me made me warm. Nicola and the complications of her presence chilled it though. I still didn't know what to say, so I just waited.

Finally, he said, "I stopped killing for him, and he comes back as a woman. There must be a message in there somewhere."

Laura had been right.

After a pause, he added, "You must think ill of me, Dafydd."

I glanced to the front of the cab. The radio was tuned to some horrible country station, but the driver was obviously focused on it and not the conversation going on in the back seat. "No," I said. "I think you're conflicted, which makes perfect sense. There's no clear right answer here. She loves you. You want to love her, but as a him, which she's not."

I wondered if that made sense to anyone but me.

However, Paul nodded and said, "That's it. And I'm afraid that anything I do will make her upset. Which I do not ever want to do. Not again. I've hurt that soul too many times. I can't afford to do it again."

Relationship issues aren't really my thing, but I did my best. "I don't know that you can help hurting her. She wants you. That's obvious. It's also pretty clear that you don't want her. No way that can end well."

"I know. I'm trying to find another way, but so far it's not happening."

"Are you sure you won't find it in yourself to love her back, biology aside?" I tried hard to keep my feelings out of that question.

From the wry look he gave me, I figured I hadn't been as successful as I'd hoped. "I suppose anything is possible. But I doubt it. I look at her and I can't help remembering who she used to be. And you saw. I called her Nicholas. I expect I'll do it again. Every time I do…"

"She'll know why." I nodded. "I don't know what to tell you."

"Thank you for trying."

I shrugged. "What are friends for?" Time to change the topic. "Where's Damien live again?"

We had just left the District by way of the Roosevelt Bridge and were looping on I66 around into Virginia. I didn't come this way very often. Metro is my usual way to get around town.

"Vienna."

I whistled. "You vampires know how to live." Vienna is one of the nicer areas in Virginia. Lots of money, nice houses, the works.

He shrugged as we exited the highway, merging on some big road I didn't recognize. "I don't know. I still prefer the District."

We didn't speak for the rest of the trip. I kind of sensed that Paul needed time to think, and since I didn't have any great revelations or ideas for him, I gave him the silence.

Finally, we pulled up outside a nice, but not extravagant, house. Paul paid the cabbie and asked if he could wait. The extra $20 he slipped him sweetened the deal, and the driver settled back into his seat, eyes closing.

As we walked to the front door, he said, "I haven't talked to him, so I don't know what kind of shape he'll be in. I think I told you that he and Darlene were close."

"Brother and sister turned together. Yeah, you said. Anything I should or shouldn't say?"

"I'm not sure. Play it by ear."

I nodded. "That's what I usually do."

I won't lie and say I wasn't nervous. I've never seen a vampire really upset, and I've gotten the impression that Paul is, not exactly tame, but definitely well in control of his emotions. Plus he's sworn off killing humans, so that makes him safer to be around.

Paul put a hand on my shoulder. "Don't worry. Damien's okay."

I glanced at him, and he smiled. "Your heart rate shot up at least 20 beats per minute. I figured you were nervous about Damien."

"Yeah, right. I forget sometimes how easily you hear that."

We walked up to the door, and Paul knocked. A moment later, the door opened to reveal Damien. The vampire looked better than he had yesterday evening at Lounge 201. He had some color in his face, which I assumed meant he had fed. For a vampire, he was dressed casually in jeans and a plain Oxford shirt, half-unbuttoned. His chest looked every bit as good as I'd assumed.

His expression, however, wasn't welcoming. "What are you doing here?" He nodded at me. "And why did you bring him?"

Paul's voice was even. "I came by to see how you are doing." He nodded to me. "As for him? Malachai's been using him too. I figure he has the right to hear whatever you tell me."

"He's a human." The disdain in his voice was clear, and it confused me. I'd met Damien before, and he'd never reacted this strongly to my presence before. Indifference, yes. Outright hostility? No.

My turn to stand up for myself, angry vampire or no. "Yes, I am," I said. "And Malachai isn't hesitating to use my kind against you."

He started to speak, but I didn't hesitate to cut him off. "I'm sorry about everything that's happened, but I can help. And I want to." As I spoke, I looked him directly in the eye. When we first went to Lounge 201, Paul had warned me against meeting a vampire's gaze, but sometimes it's the only way to convince someone you mean business.

It must have worked because Damien's shoulders relaxed slightly, and he said. "All right. Come in."

Paul gave me an approving look, and we entered the house.

Damien led us to a well-appointed living room, decorated in furniture I thought would have looked right in the Roaring Twenties. A cherry ladder-back chair sat by a matching table. A couch covered in odd designs I couldn't quite identify sat across the room from two matching chairs. They looked comfortable enough. Lighting came from two lamps with fringed lamp shades.

Paul and I both took chairs, and Damien sat on the couch. "Do you want to talk about it?" Paul asked, his voice soft.

Damien stiffened again, but this time I thought it was to avoid breaking down. He closed his eyes for a moment, and I saw him swallow, hard. When he opened his eyes again, I could see pain reflected in them. "I guess. You're the only one so far to ask. Lucius and his people have grilled me over and over again, but all they wanted were the facts. They didn't care how I felt."

I didn't know what to say to that, and apparently neither did Paul. We just waited, and after a moment, Damien took a deep breath and said, "We were supposed to meet that evening. It was the anniversary of our being turned, and I was taking her out. Nothing fancy. We were going to hit a couple of clubs, maybe do some dancing. She loved to dance, you know."

Paul smiled, a distant memory playing in his eyes. "I remember. There was that night at Dreamland Cafe. I thought she'd never stop."

A faint smile played on Damien's face. "Yeah. I think she fell in love with you a little that night. You always were a better dancer than I."

"Nonsense."

Damien shook his head. "No, it's true. You were better. And she always had a place in her heart for you after that."

This was weird. I was sitting listening to two vampires talk about love and reminisce about the past, just like two old guys on a bench in the park.

Damien's wistful expression hardened. "But that was then. It's not like I was trying to recapture the past or anything, but we were getting close to a hundred years as vampires. It seemed like we should do something. I had a couple of things I needed to track down for Lucius." He glanced at me and then at Paul, who nodded. "Dafydd knows about our contacts in the force."

Damien snorted. "I hope you know what you're doing."

"I do." Paul's voice was full of confidence.

"All right, then. I needed to talk with one of the lieutenants. Make sure the story about the bodies on Lucius' lawn was being handled properly."

"Is it?"

Damien nodded. "Yeah, looks like. We can't contain it much longer, though. If Malachai wants to blow everything for us, he's doing a good job."

"We'll stop him," I said, before I'd even consciously decided to speak.

"What's it to you, human?"

I shrugged. "I might be human, but I'm still part of the supernatural world. I don't want mundane humans to know any more about us than you do. Plus, Malachai is messing with my friend. I want to put a stop to that."

Damien seemed surprised at the heat in my voice. He nodded, just a slight incline of his head, but I saw the hint of respect in his eyes.

"I work with him for a reason," Paul said.

"Yeah, I guess you do. All right, then, warlock. Maybe I'd turn up my nose at your help before, but after what that beast did to Darlene." He shook his head. "Guess I can't be picky about who's willing to help. All Lucius wants is to keep things quiet, his noble words last night aside."

Paul nodded. "I think he might care, in his own way, but yes, he's more concerned about the challenge to his authority than what happened to Darlene. So what did happen? You gave us a stark version at the club, but what else can you tell us?"

Damien shrugged. "What else is there to tell? I'd called her after I left the station to apologize for taking longer and wanting to let her know to meet me at Twins."

Twins is one of the premier jazz clubs in D.C. I'd

never been, jazz not being my thing, but I have friends who swear by it.

"She didn't pick up, which was odd," he continued. "I didn't really think anything was wrong, but I went home to pick her up. When I got there, the door was open, which wasn't like her at all." His eyes darted to the door, and I noticed the gleam of a new lockset and dead bolt.

"I went upstairs, calling her name. She didn't answer, and I started to get worried. Then I smelled the blood. Darlene's blood."

The weird thing about vampires is that they do bleed. I have no idea how that works. Does the blood they consume run through their body somehow? Is it something other than blood? Some magical substance that keeps them animated? I've wondered, but there are certain questions I've never quite been able to ask Paul.

Damien continued. "I went into the bedroom, by now fearing the worst. And I was right. She lay on our bed, throat slit, stake coming out of the middle of her chest. And he'd…" He shook his head before continuing. "It was pretty stupid, but he'd stuck a dildo inside her. I guess he was trying to send me the message that he'd raped her too."

He sounded more disgusted and resentful than angry and appalled, and I glanced at Paul, who was shaking his head. You know the expression you get when you hear a kid is cutting up and being stupid? Yeah, that was the look Paul had.

"I don't get it. I mean, if she was raped, you ought

to be angry, right? Not looking like a kid had just pulled a stupid prank."

Paul's lips quirked in a small smile. "But that's pretty much what happened here."

"What?" Yeah, vampires are weird sometimes.

Damien nodded, the motion slow and reluctant. "It was obviously a young one, but even so the message was pretty clear."

"I don't think I follow," I said.

"Physical rape doesn't mean as much to us as it does to humans," Paul said. "We've got other ways of dominating and demonstrating power over each other. Only a young vampire would still have enough human belief to think showing he'd raped Darlene would mean something. An older vampire wouldn't bother."

"It's not just that," Damien added. "Sure, we have other ways of establishing dominance and generally being pains in the ass. But vampire females aren't inherently weaker the same way human women are. Only an old vampire would be strong enough to overpower her, and again, he probably wouldn't use force. Old ones have other means."

I wondered what "means" he was referring to, and I made a mental note to talk to Paul about that later.

Damien considered, and a note of pride entered his voice. "Darlene was old enough and strong enough to knock a young male on his ass if he did something stupid. I doubt he actually raped her at all. Or if he did, it was after she was already…dead."

Paul got out of his chair and sat down beside Damien. I expected the younger vampire to move aside, but instead, he leaned closer as Paul put an arm around him. "He must have gotten her by surprise. Otherwise she'd have killed him."

"That's what I still can't figure," Damien said. "Getting into the house? Okay. We never invested much in security. Why would we? But sneaking up on her and killing her? I can't imagine how he could do that."

"Anyone can be taken by surprise," Paul said.

"I can think how he might have done it," I said. Ever since I learned about Malachai, I'd been thinking about how I could take one down, without force since a vampire could take me physically without breaking a sweat.

Both of them looked at me. "How?" Paul asked.

"Magic," I said.

Damien snorted. "I doubt the youngster can do magic."

I nodded. "You're probably right. But we know Malachai can."

Paul's eyes widened. "You're right. Malachai can make potions."

"Exactly. I can think of several potions right off that he could have used."

"Like what?" Damien said. His voice was challenging.

I shrugged. "There's my basic speed and strength enhancing potions for a start. I've heard of potions being created for disguise. I've never used them that way, so I don't know exactly what can be done, but from what you've said about Malachai, I'll bet he's researched them."

Damien shook his head. "I don't know. I guess you'd know more about it than I would."

Paul's voice was firm. "If Dafydd thinks it's possible, then I'd believe him."

Another thought had occurred to me, and I hesitated, not sure how they'd take it. Nothing for it, though. "There's another possibility,"

Paul shot me a sharp look, obviously picking up something from my tone of voice.

I continued. "Maybe it wasn't one of the young ones. Maybe Malachai did this one himself and made it look like his rogue did it. I'm guessing he's strong enough to overpower Darlene, or use one of those other methods you referred to."

Paul and Damien glanced at each other.

"What?" I asked.

Paul cleared his throat. "For him it wouldn't just be a matter of strength."

Damien's expression was crestfallen. "I hadn't thought of that. He's worked through pawns for so many years that it never occurred to me he'd do his own dirty work."

Paul nodded slowly. "That makes more sense even than potions."

"What am I missing?" I asked.

Paul looked at Damien, who nodded. "Go ahead. I guess it doesn't matter now."

Paul's eyes held sympathy. "Malachai created both Damien and Darlene. But that's not common knowledge."

Okay, if Malachai had been her creator, that explained why he might have influence over her. But I was still confused. Why hide the fact? "I don't understand."

Paul sighed. "As you can imagine, Malachai has a bit of a reputation in our community. As do his creations. I was ostracized for decades. That's why I accepted Lucius' patronage. His acceptance of me did much to change perceptions."

That made sense. Insane, crazed fledglings would hardly be welcome even in the vampire version of "polite society."

"Okay, I can see that. But who does everyone think sired Damien and Darlene?"

"Me." The single word fell into absolute silence.

After a moment, while I digested that, Damien finally spoke. "Darlene and I got away from Malachai early on. He'd never sired siblings before. She and I were so close that we were able to shake off his influence early. We fled to Chicago. He'd not been in America much, and we figured we'd be able to avoid him there. Soon after we arrived, we met Paul."

Paul took up the story. "My sire was common knowledge, and they took the chance to come to me to ask for my help." He looked at Damien with fondness. "Which told me how young you really were."

The younger vampire snorted. "Yeah, we didn't

know any better. We were scared and barely knew what had happened to us."

Paul smiled and continued. "It seemed easiest to let people think they were mine. It helped them to not be tarred with Malachai's reputation, and it helped mine too."

"How's that work?" I asked.

Damien answered. "Malachai doesn't lose track of his children often. And even when they do get away, they are scarred and often turn out to be just as bad as their sire. They and their offspring often have to be put down for the good of the community. We hadn't been scarred too badly, so letting people think Paul had sired us made everyone more comfortable that he wasn't a monster creating other monsters."

Paul nodded. "We've maintained the fiction for so long that it's become second nature."

I got most of that, but I still wondered about one thing. "Okay, that makes sense, but you said, Paul, that master vampires don't have much influence over their children after the first decade or so. Darlene was way older than that. So I can see he'd be older and stronger, but you both implied that he'd have special influence over her."

Damien answered, seeming more relaxed and accepting of my presence. "It's true that he couldn't control her very much. But he could definitely use his influence to get her to open the door and let him in. From there, he'd be able to use his superior strength to do the rest."

"That's the way I see it too," Paul said. "Assuming of course that he really did attack her himself, which would be out of character for him."

"And he can't change over time either?" Damien asked. "I think it holds together." He looked at me, a bit of respect in his eyes. "I don't like it, but it was a good thought."

I inclined my head in thanks. "So what, if anything, does this tell us? And does it help?"

"I think so," Paul said. "If he's doing his own work, that probably means one of two things."

Damien nodded. "Yes, either he doesn't have as much control as usual over his current offspring, or he's planning something really big. Something he can't turn over completely to his minions."

Paul shook his head. "I doubt it's the former. It's likely to be the latter, but there's another possibility."

Damien cocked his head. "Like?"

I thought I knew where Paul was going. "Like he's decided to get rid of all his rebellious children all at once. You haven't been in D.C. long, have you, Damien?"

His eyes widened. "No, just a few months. Lucius had asked us to come. He wanted me to work with him on security issues. It's a niche I've been developing in the community."

That led to an ugly thought. "You don't suppose Malachai influenced Lucius to ask for you? Or is somehow involved?"

They shook their heads in unison. "Not a chance,"

Paul said. "Lucius detests Malachai with a passion. While we certainly will work with those we don't like, if we can use it to increase our power, Lucius would never work with Malachai."

"If it got out that they were working together, Lucius would lose his position in an instant. He'd never do anything to jeopardize that," Damien added.

"All right," I said. "Then we'll assume you all being in the same town is exactly the thing Malachai's been waiting for."

Paul nodded. "Yes. It's been a long time. Other than Chicago, we haven't all been in the same place for more than a few weeks at a time. Hardly long enough for him to pull something together."

"That explains why and why now," I said. "And I guess we know what."

Damien nodded, the motion grave. "To kill all his wayward children at once."

"Are there any others of you?"

Paul shook his head. "Not that I know of. Damien?"

The younger vampire shook his head also. "No, he's pretty good about keeping us in line. As far as I know, the three of us are the only ones who got away."

Something told me there was more to that story, but it didn't seem the time to ask.

"So what do we do about it?" I asked. "He's messing with people in my town, and I want to stop him."

"I think you've got the right idea, Dafydd," Paul said. "Read Stephen and see what we can learn from that."

"Who's Stephen?" Damien asked.

"Until yesterday I thought he was my boyfriend. Now it looks like he's Malachai's catspaw."

Was that a hint of sympathy in Damien's eyes?

"What we don't know yet is if he's a willing or un-willing minion. I intend to read his aura tomorrow and find out."

Damien frowned. "Is that a good idea? I mean, I understand you wanting to find out which it is, but won't that warn Malachai that we're on to him?"

Paul answered. "Possibly. But I'm not sure we have much choice right now. Stephen is the only link we know about."

I nodded. "And after tomorrow, we'll have more than knowledge. We should have a physical link as well that I can use to trace him."

Paul raised his eyebrows. "Planning to take a hair from him?"

I grinned. "Or whatever I can get."

"If he's your boyfriend, surely you already have something," Damien said.

I shook my head. "No, he's been careful, although I didn't recognize it at the time. Mostly we've met in public places. The times we've had sex, it's been at odd places. Like a friend who was out of town and had 'a great bed' or outdoors in romantic spots. That sort of thing."

Paul winced at that, but I ignored him. "In fact, now that I think about it, he's never been to my place.

And I'm really disturbed that, even with the spell, I never noticed anything odd about that."

"So he's never left anything of himself behind," Damien said, nodding. "Clever."

"Yeah. I hadn't clued in on it. Every time, it just seemed convenient."

"What makes you think you'll be able to get something off him tomorrow?" Paul asked.

I shrugged. "His hair is long. Unless he suddenly decided to shave it all off, I should be able to get something. Not like I need much."

"Be careful," Damien said. "Malachai's clever. Especially if this Stephen guy is willing, he probably knows what to look for."

"I know. I'm going to try to get the hair before I read his aura. Once I've got it safe, it shouldn't matter."

"Unless he tries to hurt you," Paul said.

"I've thought about that. We're meeting in a public place where both of us are well-known. He shouldn't be able to pull anything there."

Paul still didn't look happy about it. "What time are you meeting him?"

"Two o'clock in the afternoon. During the day, so Malachai shouldn't be able to do anything."

Paul nodded. "True, though Stephen is still a wild card. Come by my place when you're done. Stay in public. I'll feel better that way."

His concern warmed me. "Sure. I can do that, but I'm not too worried. I think he's only using me and Nicola to keep you off balance. He seems focused on killing you, not us."

Damien shook his head. "Don't count on that. He won't hesitate to eliminate you if it will serve his purposes."

Paul nodded, the motion slow and thoughtful. "True, but I think Dafydd is right, at least for the moment. I think he'll see the need to keep them both alive to keep me off balance."

"Maybe, but still, be careful."

"I plan to," I said. "And I think having me come by your place is a good precaution."

"So we're agreed then," Paul said. "Dafydd reads Stephen to see what we can learn. Then we regroup and make plans based on that?"

Damien and I nodded. "I've got Laura working on some stuff too." I looked at Damien. "Laura's a computer whiz friend of mine. She's checking Nicola's house for bugs and doing some other research. With any luck, she'll turn something up by the time I've met with Stephen."

"I'll keep my ears open too," Damien said.

"Stay with others," Paul told him. "I don't think Malachai has gotten to the point of attacking any of us while we're surrounded."

"I can do that, but what about you? You've got a reputation as a loner. Not sure how many people will hang out with you."

Paul shrugged. "I'll get the werewolves to keep an eye on my place. They should be able to give me enough warning if it's needed."

Paul struck me as unusually unconcerned, and I resolved to ask him about it later.

We said our goodbyes, and left. Damien accompanied us and headed for his own car to find other vampires to be around.

Paul and I walked back to the cab.

As the cab pulled away from the curb, I said, "You don't seem worried enough."

He gave me an odd look. "You want me to be more paranoid?"

I shook my head, again checking that the driver was distracted by his music. "No, but when Damien suggested you also stay surrounded, you were pretty casual about suggesting the werewolves. I kind of doubt you're really going to ask them."

Paul sighed. "I was going to call Runner when I got home, but no, I'm not worried about Malachai attacking me."

"Why not?"

"Because I suspect he's leaving me for last. He'll want to take out everyone I'm close to so I suffer before the end."

"Then you think Nicola and I are in danger?"

"Oh, you're in danger. But I think he'll kill Damien before he goes after the two of you. As long as we can keep Damien alive, we can buy some time to figure out the plan and stop it." His voice became almost a growl. "I don't intend to lose anyone else I'm close to."

"I'll still be careful."

"Definitely. I've already asked Runner to send a

couple of his people to your apartment. They should be there by now."

I looked at him in surprise. "When did you do that?"

He shrugged. "When Runner brought me to your apartment. Actually, he volunteered before I could ask. He's quite fond of you and doesn't want to see anything bad happen to you." He looked at me directly. "If anything should happen to me, call Runner. I'll make sure you have his number. We've stirred up stuff in this town, and I want you to have someone to help you out."

I'd never seen Paul like this before, and I didn't know how to react. Sure, I knew he could be killed, but he'd been around so long that I couldn't really imagine him being gone. "Sure. I will. But nothing's going to happen to you. We'll figure out what Malachai is up to, and we'll stop him. Then you can figure out what you want to do about Nicola." I paused and then added. "And I'll see what I can do about finding a new boyfriend who isn't part of an evil master vampire plot."

He gave me another odd look. "As long as you're safe."

His concern both warmed and confused me. We still hadn't really talked about my attraction to him, and I wasn't sure what he felt for me. Friendship was a definite. But might there be more? I shook my head. Wrong time for that. No certainty we'd both be alive this time tomorrow.

And isn't that the best time to figure it out? a little voice in my head said. *While you still can.*

"What?" Paul asked.

"Nothing," I said. "Just wondering what I'll find out tomorrow."

A few minutes later, we up to my apartment. Again, Paul paid the driver and insisted on coming up with me. On our way to my door, a large wolf briefly showed itself and then vanished back into the shadows. My guardians were in place.

Paul quickly checked my apartment. When no bad guys jumped out at us, he nodded and said, "Call me when you finish up with Stephen tomorrow. I'll be awake."

I nodded. "How are you going to get home?"

He shrugged. "I'll walk. It's no big deal."

"Oh, okay. Good night then."

"Good night, Dafydd."

And he was gone. Time to get a few hours of sleep. I had a ritual to perform at sunrise, and that wasn't too far away.

Chapter 10

Tuesday May 4, 2010.
Just Before Sunrise

I HAD SET my alarm for about an hour before sunrise, which meant I hadn't had much sleep. Nor did I have a lot of time to get ready.

Purification is an important part of a ritual, and usually I take a long bath, but my father always insisted showers worked just as well, so this time I hopped into the shower and turned on the water full blast and cold. That woke me up.

I skipped breakfast. Fasting wasn't strictly necessary, but I do it sometimes before a particularly difficult ritual. Leaving the body free to deal with energy instead of being distracted by digestion can help.

Booting up my computer to review the ritual took longer than I'd wanted. It really was time to buy a newer, faster machine. I should have printed it out last night, but I'd forgotten. While I waited for the printer to do its thing, I checked my work room for all the normal elements of a ritual. I placed candles on the rug, positioned the cauldron just so on the altar and placed my ritual knives within easy reach.

Finally, my computer finished pre-loading every program on the planet, and I was able to print out the particulars. Ah. Good thing I'd reviewed. I'd forgotten about the angelica. Dad's a traditionalist and usually recommends Western herbs, but since I get most of my ingredients from a Chinese herb shop, I sometimes have to substitute. Fortunately, bamboo is as good as angelica at banishing hexes and spells, and I had plenty of it on hand. It's also good for luck, and I use it in most of my combat potions. A little extra luck is always good to have.

I gathered up all my ingredients and arranged everything in my circle. Sunrise was close, and I was going to have to hurry to take advantage of the power while still being careful not to miss any steps.

I started placing white candles at the four compass points. Sure, I can close a circle with just my will, but for this kind of working, I like to follow the full procedure. Rituals are a lot like recipes. You follow a basic outline, but the specifics might change from time to time.

I lit a smaller, white candle and took a moment before the altar, calming my thoughts. Then I leaned to the eastern candle, lit it with the small candle and said, "Here I call forth the power of air that I may be unclouded and unbound."

Next, I lit the southern candle and said, "Here I call forth the power of fire, that I may overcome all challenges."

Moving to the western candle, I invoked more power and said, "Here I call forth the power of water to support and protect me."

Finally, the northern candle. "Here I call forth the power of Earth, that I may be grounded at all times."

All the candles burned with a soft light, and I was ready to complete the circle. I closed my eyes, gathering my will and visualizing a soft light around me. As I concentrated, the light of the candles melted together, forming an actual light around me. The circle was almost closed. I sent my will into the aura surrounding me and said, "Welcome Air, Fire, Water, Earth. Shine your light and lend your strength to this my circle tonight. Now is my circle cast, unbreakable and without harm. Thus is sacred space decreed, and no act goes unnoticed. So mote it be."

Circle cast, I could feel a soft thrumming of power around me. Outside sounds were muted, and the thrum seemed to settle in my bones, soothing away distractions. I was ready to move on to the actual ritual.

I lit two more candles on the altar, one blue (for harmony) and one purple (for transformation). I put the rosemary and star anise on a small plate and set a piece of bamboo beside them.

Rosemary and star anise are both good for rituals involving mental powers. In this particular ritual, I was going to use the rosemary to strengthen my mind while burning the bamboo and star anise to weaken Malachai's spell. The bamboo would protect me while the star anise gave focus to exactly what I want protection against.

I rubbed the rosemary against my forehead and set the other ingredients to burning in the cauldron. I arranged the three candles to form a triangle. Then I slowly chanted:

Spirits of protection, I call upon thee,
To protect from those who wish to harm me
Keep them from using the gift of magic to harm me

If you've even seen a Wiccan rite, everything may have been familiar so far. Now was when the actual "magic" came in. First, I reached out with my senses to feel the approaching sunrise. I'd timed it a little tight, and the surge of power was closer than I'd anticipated. I reached for the power and drew it in, mixing it with the energy within me. Suddenly, I felt energized and ready. The power gathered and came under my control. Now to use it.

Focusing my will on the flames of the three candles, I visualized a blue ball of light supported by the tiny flames. When I had the image firmly fixed in my mind, I imagined the ball exploding into lines of blue. I concentrated and saw the lines surrounding me, wrapping me in warm blue, protective energy. The rosemary on my forehead tingled, and I knew the shield was set. I poured more of the energy from the sunrise into the lines, and they tightened around me, though not uncomfortably so.

I felt the strength of the shield and knew it could not be broken. I closed my eyes and focused within, taking some of the strands surrounding me and readying them. One strand at a time, I touched each of the compulsions Malachai had set on me. At the touch of blue light, the compulsions faded. By the time I had extinguished the last one, my mind felt clear and sharp. I was ready for whatever was to come.

I opened my eyes and watched the candles burn for a moment. Their pure light soothed me, and I felt the final traces of his influence leave me.

I nodded and took a deep breath, preparing to release the circle.

Suddenly, I felt a pressure against my mind. With an effort of will, I brought back the blue lines and wrapped them closely around me. I could feel blackness creeping closer, covering me, pressing in, trying to invade every part of me.

The blue lines flickered, sputtering, started to fade. I gasped and fought back. No! I wouldn't let him back inside me. I closed my eyes and relaxed. Fear wouldn't serve me now. I needed to stay calm and focused. Opening my eyes, I saw the blue lines strengthen. Hope started to rise within me but then I saw them falter again. It wasn't working!

I took several deep breaths and felt my muscles relax. The blackness oozed around me. Even though it hadn't yet reached inside my circle, I still felt my skin crawl, as if a swarm of insects skittered over me. Closing my eyes, going deep within to find strength, I repeated my chant from earlier.

Spirits of protection, I call upon thee,
To protect from those who wish to harm me
Keep them from using the gift of magic to harm me

All four candle flames at the cardinal points of my circle flared high. The black cloud retreated and the pressure on my mind faded.

I drew a deep breath. That had been close. Malachai was good. He had reacted quickly to the banishing, and it had almost worked. Fortunately, I cast a good circle, and it had held his power at bay just long enough. I made a mental note not to underestimate him if we met in the future. A powerful warlock linked to vampiric power was a formidable opponent.

Now that he knew the compulsions had been banished, would Stephen still show up for our meeting? Did Malachai have a way to contact his agent during the day? I guessed I'd find out.

I started to release the circle but decided to wait a few more minutes in case the black cloud returned.

It didn't.

Good. Hoping he wasn't just waiting to strike, I extinguished the candles on the altar and prepared to dismantle the circle. Picking up my *athame*, the black handled knife, I used it to draw in the power of the circle. Then I thanked the guardians for their service. I pinched out the candles in the reverse order of lighting them.

North. "I release the power of Earth and thank you for the grounding you gave this working."

West. "I release the power of Water and thank you for your support and protection in this working."

South. "I release the power of Fire and thank you for the strength and endurance you granted this working."

East. "I release the power of Air and thank you for the purity you brought to this working.

I felt the power settle in me, took a deep breath and concluded with, "Farewell Earth, Water, Fire and Air. Your light shone on this working, and protected my circle. Thus is sacred space released and no act went unnoticed. So mote it be."

No blackness appeared, and I let myself hope Malachai had given up, for the moment.

Slowly, I put the knife down on the altar and sat back, resting on my hands. You know how sometimes you're carrying a burden, but you don't recognize it until it's gone? That's how I felt. I hadn't realized my thoughts had been clouded, but now they were clear and completely my own again. It felt good.

I enjoyed the clarity for a moment, but I wasn't certain Malachai wouldn't try again. Fortunately, there was something I could do about that. A candle protection spell.

This one is kind of cool. As long as the candle burns, I'm protected. I use long-lasting emergency candles for spells like this. They'll burn safely for as long as week, so I can leave them behind without worrying that they'll burn down the place or fade out after a few hours. It only takes me a few moments to cast the spell and leave the candle burning in my work room. I felt all the muscles in my shoulders relax as soon as the smoke started curling for the ceiling. I'm good at protective spells. Nothing short of a demi-god should be able to break this one.

I left my work room. Time to call Paul and then get a few more hours of sleep. I needed to be at my best for the meeting with Stephen.

He didn't even bother with a greeting, starting with, "Hey? How'd it go?"

"I banished the spell. My mind is all my own again."

I heard his sigh on the other end, followed by, "How's that feel?"

I smiled. "Good. Not that I'd realized how clouded I'd been until it was gone. But there's something you should know about."

His voice turned guarded. "What?"

"Malachai knows what I've done."

A sharp intake of breath. "How?"

"Well, remember that I haven't done this kind of magic much, okay?"

"Okay."

I tried to explain it, still not entirely certain what had happened. "It looks like the backlash of the banishing warned him in some way. Right as I was finishing the spell, a black cloud appeared, and I felt pressure on my mind, like someone was trying to reassert control."

"Did you know that would happen?"

I shook my head. "No. I've never really studied mind magic. I didn't realize there'd be that backlash. And I guess my dad forgot or didn't know either. Most of this is theoretical to us."

There was silence on the other end for a moment. Finally, Paul said, "They may not have known. Remember that what Malachai used was a vampire thing, not true magic. This isn't exactly my area either, but I think a vampire would know if someone escaped his control."

"But the black cloud was definitely magic, my kind of magic."

"Right. Malachai can use both. You wriggled out of his vampiric control, and he tried to get you back using magic."

I hadn't thought of that. It made me feel a bit better. I'd been starting to wonder if we'd made an obvious blunder.

Paul continued. "You're sure he didn't manage to influence you again?" He didn't say it, but his tone clearly said, "And how would you know if he had?"

I projected confidence in my tone. "I'm sure. His timing was bad. I still had the protections up, and my circle. If he'd waited another ten minutes, all that would have been gone."

"Think he can try again?"

I thought about that for a moment. "Anything's possible, I suppose. I don't know what he can or can't do, but I'm guessing he won't try again. Just to be sure, though, I did a quick candle protection spell. He won't be able to break through that, and it will warn me if he tries again."

A pause. I think he wanted to ask me if I was sure.

"Paul, I'm really good with protection spells. If I

say it'll work, it'll work."

A faint sigh on the other end. "Okay. That sounds sensible. Are you sure you want to meet with Stephen?"

I smiled to myself, sensing how much that had cost him. "I still think I need to. I'll be in a public place. Malachai knows I banished his influence, but he doesn't know what I know. He'll need Stephen to meet with me to figure that out."

"Good point. Expect some pointed questions. Malachai doesn't have many weaknesses, but overconfidence is one of them. He won't pass up an opportunity to learn more. Just be careful and come straight to my place afterwards. I'll be awake."

"Will do." I was nervous, but I'd dealt with demons, werewolves and ghosts. Stephen was only human, and I figured I could handle him, even if things got dicey. "I need some more sleep, so I'll talk to you later."

"Good luck."

"Thanks. I guess I'll need it."

We hung up, and I went back to bed.

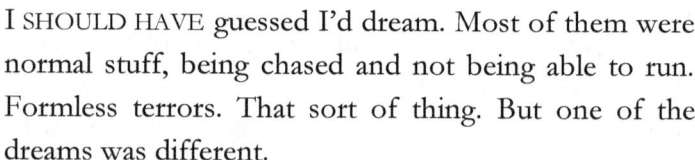

I SHOULD HAVE guessed I'd dream. Most of them were normal stuff, being chased and not being able to run. Formless terrors. That sort of thing. But one of the dreams was different.

You know the old wives' tale of if you die in a dream, you die in real life? I can assure you it's just a tale. Because this dream is one I've had before, and I always die in it.

At first there's not much to it. I'm walking along a dirt road. I'm barefoot, and I can feel the warm earth between my toes. It should feel good, but it doesn't. It's like there's something slimy and disgusting in the dirt. Somehow I know I'm older, at least in middle age. My joints ache, and I don't feel as energetic. When I look down at my hands, they are wrinkled, with slight age-spotting.

I pass a tree. It looks completely normal, but I know it's not. Something about it screams menace, and I go wide, keeping plenty of room between me and it.

Huge thunderclouds move fast above me, though there's no wind. Lightning flashes in the distance, but there's no thunder.

A crow hops by and caws at me, three times. It's always three times. And then I feel a horrible pain in my back, like something is trying to disembowel me from behind.

I fall, blood pooling around me, gasping with the pain. And then everything goes black.

I wake up, shaking. Late morning sun streams in my window, dispelling the darkness that had surrounded me. When my hands are steady again, I reach for my phone and open up a note. I typed in "59" under the note for "Death Dream."

The first time I ever had that dream was when I was about a year old. Really freaky stuff. It was my first prophetic dream, and we still have no idea what it means. My grandfather grilled me on that one as soon as I was old enough to talk, but we've never been able to figure it out.

All I know is that I hope I'll never have it again.

There was no way I'd ever go back to sleep after that, and it was probably time to get up anyway, so I rolled out of bed, had lunch and puttered around for a while. I checked my candle spell. It was still burning away. Nothing more I could do there. I cleaned up my work room and ran a vacuum over the whole apartment. The ferrets looked at me hopefully, but I didn't feel up to playing with them at the moment.

Finally, I ran out of make work, and it was time to go meet Stephen. I had no idea how this would go. I wasn't even sure I knew how I wanted it to go. I just knew this would probably be the end of us as a couple. And that hurt, even more than I'd expected.

Chapter 11

Tuesday, May 4, 2010.
Early Afternoon

I ARRIVED FIRST at Annie's. Sonya, my favorite waitress, was working. She frowned when she saw me. "What's wrong?"

It's good to have friends who can read you. Except when you don't want them to. I shook my head. "Not now, Sonya. Maybe later."

She glanced out the window as she seated me. Stephen was just walking up. He looked so damn good. It wasn't fair. His long hair hung down his back, and I couldn't help remembering all the times I'd held that weight in my hands during lovemaking. He was dressed in his usual tight t-shirt and ripped jeans. I couldn't help a smile. I'd been responsible for one of those rips.

"You're not breaking up with him, are you?" Sonya asked.

I shook my head. "Honestly, I don't know what's about to happen." I hated to ask, but Sonya does know about the weird stuff in my life. "Sonya, if anything happens, call Paul, okay?" I gave her his number, knowing she'd be able to memorize it.

"Dafydd?" Her voice was soft and worried.

I gave her as reassuring a smile as I could muster.

"I'm sure everything will be fine. I'd just feel better, if, you know…"

She nodded, the worry never leaving her eyes. "I'll call. No problem."

The door opened, and Stephen walked in.

"Look normal, okay?" I said.

She definitely should have been an actress. When she turned to greet Stephen, the smile looked natural. "Stephen? And how are my two favorite boys today? I gave you the usual seat." She glanced at me. "Iced tea, Dafydd?"

I nodded. "That'll be good." I don't think I did as well with my voice.

"And one for me too," Stephen said.

She smiled and headed back to the kitchen to get our drinks. She shot me a worried glance over her shoulder, but I couldn't react because Stephen was staring straight at me.

"So, I understand you've been doing some magic."

That was how this was going to play, was it? So much for my plan to try to get something for a tracking spell before I read him.

I didn't say anything as I shifted my vision. It was as bad as I'd feared. Stephen's aura was riddled with black, red and orange streaks. There was just the faintest hint of blue, but it was overpowered by one of the ugliest greens I'd ever seen.

I did a quick analysis. Black is bad, as you could probably guess. It indicates evil. So do certain shades of red, although his particular red was one I'd seen in vampires before, and I suspected it meant Malachai had been feeding off of him. Orange isn't something I'd seen very often, until Paul took me to read the crowd last year at Lounge 201. It wasn't a color I saw in many vampires, but a significant number of humans had exhibited the color. When I'd mentioned it to Paul, he'd told me how vampires frequently own, or possess, their humans. That's what the orange meant.

The blue was the slight remnant of good and humanity that still existed in him. And the green was odd. That particular shade of green meant jealousy. Of what was Stephen jealous?

Taken together, the picture was clear. Stephen was working for Malachai. And he was doing it willingly.

He was grinning at me, not the casual, having fun with life grin I'd started to love, but a "Yes, I am doing something wicked, and now we both know about it" grin. "Like what you see?"

I shook my head. "You know I didn't. Stephen, why?"

He cocked his head and didn't answer my question. "Curious. What did you see?"

Did I really want to tell him? Did it matter? I shrugged. "Probably nothing that'll be new to you. Evil, of course. I can see Malachai's been feeding on you."

He flashed me the grin again and rolled up his shirt to show me the puncture marks in the crease of his elbow. "You never asked why I always wanted to make love with the lights off."

True. I never had.

"What else?"

The grin still hadn't left his face, and looking at it was making me slightly ill. I wasn't enjoying the game, but I was determined to play it well, since I had few other options. "There was something there that makes me curious."

He raised an eyebrow and looked to the side. I followed his gaze and didn't speak until Sonya had put down our drinks. Her eyes asked the question, and I gave a slight nod to let her know everything was still okay.

She sighed and left. Stephen watched her go, a smirk spreading across his face. "You let her know something was up, I guess. And she's all worried about you. Pathetic."

As he spoke, I realized I had an opportunity. Stephen's hair is long, and although he keeps it neatly contained in a ponytail, he's forever leaving strands behind. When he turned his head to watch Sonya walk away, one fluttered down to the table. I quickly reached out, snatched it and put my hand in my pocket.

He turned back to me. "What? You look guilty about something."

I shook my head, letting disgust cross my face. "The only thing I'm feeling guilty about it letting you fool me for so long."

He laughed, again nothing like the rich expression of mirth that had always made me laugh with him. This was ugly and harsh. "Yeah, you were right there with me and my 'oh, I think I'm falling in love with you.' act.

I think I deserve an Oscar for that one." He frowned. "But you said you were curious about something in my aura. What?"

For once his tone was honest. He really did want to know.

"All right. There's this particularly vile shade of green in your aura. Green usually indicates jealousy. I was just wondering what you're so jealous of. Malachai getting it on with someone else on the side? Or are you just envious of his power as a vampire?"

I let a hint of mocking enter my voice. This game was painful, but I needed information. Stephen had never liked to back down from a challenge, and I assumed this was an essential part of his personality, not just the act he'd put on for my benefit.

He snorted. "Goes to show what you know. No, nothing like that." His expression grew sly. "I'm not sure I should tell you."

I took a swallow of my tea. "Suit yourself. I got what I came for today, anyway, so as far as I'm concerned, we're done."

He frowned. "What'd you come for?"

I smiled. "To tell you we're through. And to ask why you did it, but I'm guessing you're not going to tell me that anyway, so I might as well save myself the time."

I started to get up.

"Wait."

I sat down, carefully keeping my face expressionless. Inwardly, I was cheering. Got him!

"It was nothing personal, you know. Malachai needed to keep an eye on Paul, and he noticed he'd started hanging out with you." He shrugged. "You were easier to watch than his vampire buddies."

"Vampire buddies" wasn't quite how I would have described the rest of the community, but I let that go.

"What's in it for you?"

He grinned. "What'd'ya think? Malachai will turn me when this is all over."

No surprise there. I'd already guessed that from what I saw in his aura. "Why? Why do you want to be a vampire?"

Stephen's eyebrows went up in mock-surprise. "Why wouldn't I? Live forever. Be young forever. Be powerful enough to take what I want, whenever I want it. Who wouldn't want that?"

Me for one, but I didn't say it. "He's a vampire, Stephen. He's evil. You know what he makes his fledglings do. You can't want that."

He laughed again. "Oh, so Paul's been filling your head with his 'oh poor me, Malachai made me do it' story. That's crap, you know. Paul enjoyed his years under Malachai. Don't believe him if he tells you anything different."

I didn't see any reason to tell him that I'd seen it, not been told it. "You mean you want to indiscriminately kill people, just because?"

"Why not? They're just prey. It's what they deserve. I mean, seriously. Pitiful creature like that Nicola chick. She'd be better off, and happier, dead. Paul's killed her so many times now it's probably what gets her off."

I didn't need to listen to any more of this. I had his hair. I'd read his aura. I had what I came for. Time to go. I put some bills on the table and stood up. "Good bye, Stephen. I really thought we'd had something, but now I know there was nothing there."

I turned and started to go.

"Wait."

Again? Seriously? I was getting tired of him spoiling my attempts at a dramatic exit, and this time I ignored him.

I felt movement behind me, and I whirled, ready to stop Stephen from doing anything. But all he'd done was gently grab my arm. "He's not done with that chick, you know."

I shook off his hand. "I know. We've got her protected."

He chuckled. "You think werewolves will stop us. Think again."

"Why are you telling me this?"

He looked honestly puzzled. "You know, I'm not sure. Maybe there was more to our relationship than I thought." For a moment, he seemed sad. "You asked me about the jealousy?"

"Yeah."

Stephen looked me straight in the eye. "Maybe I am jealous. Maybe I'm jealous that you had a family and something to live for and a reason to make something of yourself. I never had that."

He pushed past me and started for the door.

"Good bye, Dafydd," he said on his way by.

I stood for a moment, not sure exactly what had just happened.

Sonya hurried up to me and asked, "Are you all right? Nothing really happened, right?"

I nodded. "It's okay. That wasn't exactly what I'd expected, but it was better than I'd feared."

"You hadn't really expected him to hurt you, had you?"

"I didn't know." I'd been answering her mostly on autopilot, and I forced myself to pay attention. "Stephen's not who either of us thought. I don't think you'll see him here again."

Which made me think of something. When Stephen and I had planned our first "date" here, he'd said he'd known Sonya.

"How long had you known Stephen before we started dating?"

She looked up from clearing our table, her expression puzzled. "I don't know. Not long. Maybe a couple weeks. Why?"

I shrugged. "No big deal, I guess. I was just wondering if he'd always come here, or if he'd just been coming to check me out."

"Dafydd, what's going on?"

I didn't want Sonya involved with this. One young woman had already been hurt. I didn't want to add her to the list. "I can't really talk about it now. I have to go meet Paul."

I pulled some bills from my wallet and handed

them to her to cover the check.

She didn't even look at them as she said, "But it's still day."

I grinned. "He just has to stay out of the sun. He doesn't hibernate."

I knew that wasn't quite the right word, but she seemed to get it.

"Oh," was all she said as I turned to go. Followed by, "Be careful."

"Always," I said as I walked out.

I did glance around as I left Annie's. I didn't really think Stephen would jump me on the street, but I had said I would be careful, right? I didn't see him, or anyone who looked dangerous, and I started for the Metro. On the way, I pulled out my phone to call Paul.

He answered on the first ring. "Are you okay?"

I felt my shoulders relax. I hadn't realized until now how much safer I felt with Paul, even when we were just talking on the phone. "Yeah, I'm okay."

"And?"

"It's what I was afraid of. He's working willingly with Malachai."

I could almost feel Paul's sympathy through the phone line. "I'm sorry."

I shrugged and stepped around a jogger with two large dogs on leashes. One of the dogs sniffed me in passing, and I was reminded of Jimmy, the werewolf puppy I'd helped last year. Evil took many forms, and yet, so did good. Who'd have thought werewolves could be the good guys? But my friends are good, and a couple of them died to help me and the kid. I squared my shoulders. "Yeah, it sucks. Umm, no pun intended."

I heard him chuckle, as I'd intended. "But," I continued. "That's done. Now it's time to move on. We've got to keep Nicola safe and stop Malachai's plan to eliminate you guys."

"Are you on your way over?"

"I am. Heading for the Metro now."

"Good. I think you being alone right now is a bad idea."

"I agree." I glanced up at the sky. The sun was still high, but still. Malachai was using at least one human as a minion. There might be more.

"I'll see you soon then."

"Definitely."

If this were a movie, I'd have been jumped by several creepy mind-controlled zombie-like minions in the Metro station, and there'd have been a pulse-pounding fight scene that almost ended with me electrocuted on the third rail, saved by my agility at the last minute.

Fortunately, this isn't a movie, and I made the trip to Paul's house without incident. Well, mostly without incident. I did spend too much time looking over my shoulder, and I did almost trip and fall on to the rail. It would have been nicer to blame it on minions instead of sheer clumsiness.

I was still looking over my shoulder, however, when I knocked on his door. It opened to reveal Paul, wearing nothing but a pair of loose gray sweat pants, artfully draped on his narrow hips. He was standing back from the doorway to avoid the sun. His shirtless, ripped chest completely distracted me from worrying about zombie minions, and I hastily cast about for something to say that was more intelligent than "Guh, you look amazing."

What came out was, "I've been meaning to ask you. Do you explode instantly when the sun hits you, or do you have a few seconds before disaster hits?"

I know. Not the smoothest, but hey, any conversational topic in a storm.

He blinked. "And good afternoon to you too."

I grinned at him. "Well?"

He shrugged. "I don't so much explode as go up in a column of flame. And it takes at least half a minute. But it hurts like hell until then."

"You sound like you're speaking from experience."

"I've been caught out a time or two, yes." He frowned and motioned me inside. "You can't be too worried if you're plotting my demise."

I headed into his living room and flopped onto his couch. "Not yours. Malachai's. I've got a heck of a mad on right now, and I want to burn some vampire butt. Present company excluded, of course."

He followed me and sat down on the couch. Where I "flop," he slouches artfully. "So you're sure he's working willingly for Malachai."

I nodded. "Definitely. Apparently Malachai's promised him vampiric conversion when all this is over."

He rolled his eyes. "Another one of those kids who

thinks it's all romantic."

I shook my head. "No. More like living forever and taking what he wants when he wants it."

"He'll learn there's more to it than that."

I stood up and started pacing. "Not if I can do anything about it. We foil the plan, and he never gets turned. That's what I'm thinking needs to happen right about now."

Paul's head followed my progress back and forth across his living room. "Did you get anything to do a tracking ritual?"

I stopped moving pulled a folded napkin from my pocket. I'd swiped the napkin on my way out of the restaurant and put the hair in it while I was on the Metro. "Right here. If you'll accompany me home when the sun sets, I'll do some magic and find out where they are."

Paul nodded. "Sounds like a plan. I need to shower and get dressed. Make yourself at home. There's tea and, I think, a couple of Cokes in the fridge. I won't be long."

I cocked a curious eyebrow at him, and he smiled. "Yes, I do shower. Hold over from my mortal days, I guess. In my time, you didn't bathe often. I kind of like your obsession with hygiene, and I adopted it about a half century ago."

"Oh. Makes sense, I guess." It didn't really. He didn't sweat or have any bodily functions. I've never seen him grubbing in the dirt. Even while camping, he stayed magically clean.

"Besides," he added with a grin, "I like the smell of soap and shampoo."

Now that made sense.

When he left to go upstairs, I wandered into the kitchen in search of something to drink. I wasn't in the mood for tea, so I opened the fridge. And stopped before I put my hand in.

The two cans of Coke looked like anxious sheep surrounded by wolves, or in this case bag upon bag of blood.

"What do you do? Rob blood banks? Hand over the O positive and no one gets hurt."

It made for an image, and I forced a smile as I reached for a can.

"Saved you," I said to it. Then I popped the top. "Well, maybe not so much."

Great. I was talking to inanimate objects now. But his fridge did make me wonder. How did Paul get his supply of blood? I resolved to ask him later. Much later.

I went back to the living room and sprawled out on the couch. I must have been more tired than I thought because I fell asleep.

Chapter 12

Tuesday, May 4, 2010.
Early Evening

I AWAKENED TO the feeling of someone watching me. I opened my eyes to see Paul sitting in the chair opposite the couch. At least this time I hadn't been dreaming.

"Tired?" he asked.

I blinked, trying to force my tired brain to function. "Yeah, guess I was. I hadn't realized."

"Lots going on."

Something wasn't right here, but I couldn't convince my brain to process it. "What time is it?"

"Just after sunset."

Trust a vampire to tell time based on the sun. Fortunately I have a well-developed time sense, and I figured that meant it was probably a little after eight o'clock.

A phone started ringing, and both Paul and I fumbled for ours, he on his belt, me in my pocket.

Turned out to be his.

"What's up, Damien?" he asked.

I sat up. All sleepiness vanished when I heard the change in Paul's voice.

"All right. Stay put. We'll be there as soon as we

can. You know what to do. Stay in a crowd. He's less likely to do anything with witnesses around."

He paused, and I stood up, ready to move. I didn't know exactly what was happening, but I could guess.

Paul continued. "I know. Yes, he's started doing things he hasn't before, but you are still safer around others. Get to Lounge 201 if you can. Lucius will offer you protection."

He hung up and started for the door, pausing just long enough to turn and ask, "You heard?"

I was already following him. "Enough. Damien's in trouble?"

He grabbed his keys off the hook by the door. "Yes. There's a strange vampire hanging around his house. He thinks he's given him the slip, but he can't be sure. Something about him invoked the impression of Malachi. We can usually sense something about our vampiric siblings. They give off an aura."

"If he's right, it sounds like Malachi is making his move."

"I agree."

By now we were out of his house and at his car. I was just opening the passenger door when Paul's phone rang again. He answered without looking at the display.

"We're on our way…"

I glanced at him when he stopped speaking suddenly. A bad feeling crawled down my spine at his expression. Yes, vampires are naturally pale, and Paul is no exception to that, but as I watched, even the slight hint of color he gets after feeding washed away. I tensed, suddenly suspecting who was on the other end of the line.

Paul confirmed it when he said, "Malachai."

I suddenly understood the cliche, "my blood ran cold." My mind flashed back to the memory he'd tried to erase. The memory of our meeting. His cold voice saying, "Paul will very much like her. She'd be perfect for him."

Suddenly I thought I knew why Malachai had called. And what his plan was.

I watched Paul's face as he shook his head. His eyes started burning a cold amber that I'd only seen a couple of times. "No, Malachai. This is between you and me. Keep them out of it."

He glanced down at his watch and motioned urgently at me. I frowned, not sure what he wanted. He tossed me his keys, and started moving for the passenger side of the car. I nodded, still confused but figuring out that he wanted me to drive.

I ran to the other side of the car and slid into the passenger seat. I barely had time to settle and fasten my seatbelt before Paul was waving me to start the car and drive.

"Where?" I mouthed at him.

"Yes, I'm still listening. I understand," Paul said into the phone before mouthing "Lounge 201" back at me.

I nodded and started the car, pulling out of Paul's parking space with close to the vampire's flair.

"This isn't over, Malachai," Paul said before hanging up. He tossed the phone onto the dash and swore. "Damn him!"

"He's got Nicola too. He's splitting his efforts, isn't he?"

Paul nodded, his expression grim. "Yes, how'd you know?"

I shrugged and made the left turn onto Massachusetts Avenue, barely missing a white panel van going through the intersection. "I suddenly heard his voice in my head saying that Nicola would be perfect for you. You'd already talked to Damien, and we were heading to help him, so I knew it couldn't be him. It had to be Nicola."

"You're right."

I settled my back further into my seat and concentrated on my driving. Paul wanted me to get to Lounge 201, so I set myself to getting there as quickly as possible. "What's the plan? How do you want to play this?"

His voice came out as a growl. "He's finally miscalculated."

"How so?"

I glanced quickly to the side to see the fierce grin he was giving me. "He's underestimated you."

"Huh?"

Paul motioned just ahead. "Drop me off at the next intersection. I'm going to save Nicola while you help Damien."

I found myself giving him back the same grin.

"Yeah, that will work."

"Damien's shaken up by Darlene's death, and he's not thinking clearly. He can handle any of Malachai's offspring. You heard me send him to the Lounge. As long as he can get there, he'll be safe."

"But won't Malachai anticipate he'll go there and have someone waiting for him?"

"Probably. Which is why you have to get there first. Do you have any potions on you?"

"Yeah. In my pack." Ever since I started hanging out with Paul, I'd been carrying a fanny pack with a couple of potions, usually one speed potion for Paul, and a reflex-enhancing one for me. "I've got your usual in there."

He shook his head. "Save it for Damien. He might need it worse than me. I'm older than anything Malachai can throw at me. I can handle this with my own abilities."

I screeched to a halt at the intersection Paul had indicated. "Unless Malachai's taking care of Nicola by himself."

Paul grabbed his phone as he jumped out of the car. "Never happen. It's not his way."

And with that, he was off at a dead run down the street. If you've ever seen a determined vampire in motion before, you'll know just how fast that is.

I pulled back into traffic, an uneasy feeling in the pit of my stomach. Perhaps Malachai's used minions all the time in the past, but Damien and Paul had already said Malachai was doing things out of character this time. What was to stop him continuing the trend?

I put it out of my mind. Right now I needed to focus on my task, helping Damien. I frowned. Which would be a lot easier if I had some way of getting in contact with him. Paul had sent him to the Lounge, but what if Damien had been waylaid before he got there? I had no way of contacting him.

Just then my phone beeped, and I pulled it out of my pocket, checking it at the next red light. I grinned. Trust Paul to think of most everything.

There was a text in the middle of my display:

Damien's number is 202-555-1891

I fumbled to plug in my headset, and I called the number. It rang a couple of times before I heard Damien's voice. "Yeah. Who is it?"

"Damien, it's Dafydd."

"Look, kid, I don't have time…"

I cut him off. "Paul sent me. Malachai is pulling a two-front assault. You and Nicola at the same time. He's going to save Nicola, and he sent me to help you."

I held my breath, half-afraid he'd blow off the offer of help. But apparently Paul was right about Damien being spooked. "All right. Not sure what you can do, but right now, I'll take the help."

"Where are you?"

"About a mile from Lounge 201. Where are you?"

"About the same. I'm in a car." I listened to the sounds on the other end of the phone. "You're on foot?"

"Yeah."

I thought quickly. "Are you being followed?"

"I think so, but he's keeping his distance. Seems like he's getting off on the cat-and-mouse game."

Sounded about right for one of Malachai's minions. "You coming from the Union Station side?"

"Yeah." His voice faltered. "I think he's done playing."

Shit! "Okay, I'll be there in a minute. Hang in there, Damien. Find someplace defensible."

I really needed a course in driving like they give cops and CIA agents. Or maybe that's just on TV. Anyway, I sped up. It's a good thing there weren't any cops around because I counted at least four laws I broke, but soon, I was near Lounge 201, and I slowed down, glancing around for Damien.

I heard a loud crash in the next block and took the chance that was where they were. Luckily a car was just pulling out of a nearby parking spot, and I pulled in. None of Paul's style, but it was a big spot, and I managed.

I leaped out of the car and headed in the direction of the sound of the commotion. A few passersby were glancing curiously in the direction of the noise, but I ignored them.

I heard a loud cry of pain just as I turned the corner to see two vampires locked in deadly combat. Damien was down on one knee. Blood streamed from several wounds, and he was holding one arm stiffly. With the other, he held off his opponent, who was pressing close, fangs extended, trying to get to Damien's neck.

My turn. I grabbed my reflex enhancing potion, popped the cap and gulped it down. Immediately, everything around me seemed to slow, and I felt like I had plenty of time to consider options.

Remembering Paul's words from earlier, "You know, you could use that in combat," I noticed a long window in a nearby building. The street lights shone on it at the right angle to convert the glass into a mirror.

I felt a slow smile spread across my face. I concentrated for a moment, pulling forth the right memory. When I had it clear in my mind, I yelled,

"Hey! Look out!"

It always works. The enemy vampire started to turn. Under the effect of my potion, I could clearly see his eyes widen, and he let go of Damien.

That was my cue to toss my speed enhancing potion to Damien, who neatly caught it. His expression was puzzled, but he gulped down the potion, digging his fangs into the bottle like Paul does. I sighed. So much for that sport bottle. Good thing I used old Deer Park water bottles. They were cheap.

Damien stood up, quickly adjusting to the potion, and his eyes widened as he saw the image I had placed in the window. His brow furrowed, and he glanced at me.

I shrugged and motioned toward the other vampire, who was just recovering from his momentary surprise. I hadn't expected the ploy to work for more than a couple of seconds, just long enough to get the potion to Damien.

Oh, you want to know what they saw? Well, imagine for a moment an eight-foot tall…thing. And by "thing" I mean something that's mostly mouth and tentacles. Paul and I had fought one a couple months ago. He called it a "shuggoleth demon." I called it ugly.

I let the image fade away as I ducked behind a nearby dumpster. My role here was surprise. Damien was going to have to do the rest of the fighting.

The other vampire started to move toward me, but Damien intercepted him. Vampires are naturally fast and strong. Under the influence of one of my potions, they move fast enough that it's hard for the eye to follow them. Thanks to my potion, I was able to see each move.

Damien's wounds were still slowing him, but he was able to hold his own. They slashed, tripped and punched at each other. I had a mental count down in my head.

25, 24, 23

Damn! My potion was about to wear off. I've never been able to make them last more than a minute or two. Damien's would last a bit longer, but it didn't look like it would be long enough to enable him to finish off his opponent.

Time to throw out another distraction. I hoped the other vampire hadn't figured out what I was capable of yet. I also hoped that the distraction wouldn't backfire on Damien.

19, 18, 17

I formed another image in my mind and waited until Damien's back was to the big window while the other vampire was positioned sideways to it. Catching stuff out of the corner of your eye is the most distracting.

As soon as they were positioned properly, I tossed the image of Paul, muscles rippling, in a full run toward the fight.

9, 8, 7

The enemy vampire jerked and started to turn. At the same moment, Damien whipped his head around, his fangs ripping at his enemy's throat. The other vampire collapsed, eyes wide open, stolen blood pooling around him.

2, 1

Time came crashing to a halt.

A few seconds later, Damien slumped to the ground, barely catching himself with a hand.

Neither of us took our gaze off the other vampire, who lay, motionless, in front of us.

Words fell out of my mouth. "So that's how you kill a vampire."

Damien's eyes flicked in my direction, and he nodded. "It's one way. Not the one I recommend, by the way. If you're close enough to slash his throat, you're close enough for him to do the same to you."

"Makes sense," I said. "What do we do with him now?"

Damien struggled to his feet, and I hurried over to support him with a shoulder. His blood smeared my clothes, but I didn't care.

"You got a car nearby?"

I nodded. "Yeah. Paul lent me his."

"Good. Help me with him."

Between the two of us, we hauled the vampire to his feet and dragged him to the car. A couple of people on the street watched us, and I said, "He was attacked. We're getting him to the hospital."

That was enough, and everyone went back to their business. In big cities, no one wants to get involved.

We tossed the body into the back seat, and I got in the driver's seat. Damien climbed slowly into the passenger seat.

"Drive the rest of the way to the Lounge. They'll take care of him there."

He got out his cell phone and made a call while I drove the few blocks to Lounge 201.

Three vampires met us on the street and took the body from the car. It was that simple. We let them have him, and we drove away.

"Aren't you guys supposed to turn into dust, or something, when you die?"

Damien gave me a weak chuckle. "You've been watching too many movies."

"Well, it does make sense."

"Yeah, it does, and actually the old ones do just

that. Young ones like him just rot quickly. His body'll be gone in a couple of days."

"Convenient."

He lay back in his seat and closed his eyes.

I glanced into the back seat. Yep. The cooler was there.

"Reach into the cooler behind you. I think there's a bag of blood in there."

Damien opened his eyes, looked at me in surprise but reached back to open the cooler. He pulled out a bag filled with blood, ripped into it with his fangs and sucked it down in seconds.

"Thanks."

I thought I detected a note of respect in his voice.

"No problem."

I thought for a minute, trying to remember how to get to Nicola's house. Ah, right. This way. I made a turn.

"Where's Paul?" Damien paused for a moment and then added. "Not that I wasn't grateful for your help."

I nodded. "He's with Nicola. Just as we were mounting up to come after you, he got a call from Malachai."

He sighed. "Divide and conquer."

"Exactly. Paul sent me to help you while he raced off to save Nicola. I'm guessing it's all over now, but I wanted to get over there as quickly as possible, just in case."

"Right."

My thoughts raced. Had Paul been in time? Was

Nicola okay? Was Paul up against another minion, or was he fighting Malachai himself? I knew my friend could handle himself in most situations, but I didn't know how he'd fare against a vampire who was so much older. And his creator and former master.

"What was in that potion?" Damien asked.

I was glad of the distraction. "Some stuff to boost speed. I make them for Paul for when we're fighting bad stuff."

"It worked. Thanks."

"You're welcome. It looked like he was giving you some trouble."

"Yeah. He got me by surprise." He chuckled, a rueful sound. "There I was being so alert for danger that when it actually hit me, I was looking the wrong way. He knocked me off my feet and was practically biting my head off before I knew it."

"Glad he didn't kill you before I got there."

Damien nodded. "About that. What was with the thing in the window?"

I swore instead of answering.

"What?"

"I think I turned the wrong way."

Damien glanced out of his window and nodded. "Yes, you did. Hmm…" He paused for a moment before saying, "Take a right up here. Then a left on 2nd. That'll get you going the right way again."

"Thanks." I followed his instructions and a few minutes later was back on familiar ground. I know my parts of the city well, but even after all these years, I can still get lost in certain areas. Like this one.

Damien spoke as soon as I was back on a street I knew. "About that window thing."

I shrugged. "Yeah, it worked pretty well didn't it?"

"It did. But what was it?"

I'd suppressed that ability for so long that it was hard to talk about it, even now. I sighed. "It's a spell, sort of."

"Sort of?"

"Yeah, well, most spells require a lengthy set-up time, but I can pop this one right off."

He chuffed. "Okay, it's a spell, and you can pop it right off, unlike most spells. But what is it?"

"I basically pull up a memory and project it somewhere."

He was silent for a moment. "Any memory?"

"Pretty much. If I can remember it well enough to form a picture, I can use it."

"I've worked with a few warlocks over the years." His voice sounded dubious. "Don't take this the wrong way, but I don't remember any of them doing that."

I turned down the street that led to Nicola's house. My stomach was clenching in worry, but I forced my voice to stay calm. "It seems to be a particular talent of mine."

A hand touched my arm, and I jerked. It remained, and I glanced over to see Damien, his eyes full of sympathy. "He'll be fine. He's tougher than I am. If the one I fought was any indication, Malachai's not making them like he used to."

I gave him a small smile. "Yeah. He'll be fine."

I pulled up outside Nicola's house, and my anxiety doubled. All the lights were on. The front door was lying in the front yard, and several bodies lay crumpled near it.

I fumbled with the seatbelt, my hands clumsy in my hurry. Damn! I couldn't get it.

Damien's hand reached over and popped the latch. I gave him a quick, grateful smile and hopped out of the car.

I dashed to the house, pausing just long enough by the bodies to determine that none of them were Paul's. Then I rushed for the open doorway.

No, I didn't rush in without looking. I've learned that much recently. I paused just before going in, forming an image in my mind. I was pretty sure I remembered a big mirror in Nicola's front hall, and I was ready to use it if I needed a distraction.

My mind calm, and the image steady, I took a deep breath and peered around the smashed doorway.

Paul knelt on the floor, cradling Nicola in his arms. His head was bowed, and I heard a shrill keening coming from him.

Blood pooled around him, and I stepped closer. That's when I saw the deep slash on her throat. Ominously, I noticed that blood wasn't flowing, just dripping from the wound. As I watched in horror, one droplet hung, falling in slow motion to land with a tiny splash in the pool beneath her.

I'd watched enough TV crime shows to know what

it means when the blood is no longer spurting. Nicola was dead. We hadn't been in time.

I had an idea and shifted my vision to the magical spectrum, trying to "read" the scene the way the witch had. Colors overwhelmed me, and I took a step back from the red, black and green that swirled through the room. For just a moment, I thought I saw a vampire standing over Nicola, fangs ripping at her throat. In my vision, the vampire looked up, and his eyes locked with mine.

I quickly shut down my aura vision and bent over, trying to keep my stomach from rebelling. I never wanted to do that again, but if I was going to stay in this line of work, I figured I'd need to learn the skill.

Hearing motion behind me, I whirled to see Damien standing in the doorway. His eyes were sad. He motioned me to Paul and jerked his head in the direction of the lawn. I took that to mean that he'd check the bodies outside.

I turned back to the grim tableau and took a hesitant step forward. Paul hadn't moved or in any way acknowledged my presence. He just rocked her body, back and forth, the odd keening rising and fading in an eerie kind of rhythm.

"Paul," I said, my voice soft. Some irrational part of me wanted to be quiet, to not awaken her.

Nothing. Just that broken back and forth motion.

I took another step and knelt down. I started to reach out a hand.

Paul snarled, and whipped his head around, fangs

extended and eyes glowing. I snatched my hand back, but otherwise didn't move. I trusted my friend not to hurt me.

Still, facing down a furious vampire wasn't easy.

As soon as he finished his turn, his eyes cleared, and I think he finally realized it was me. Fangs receded, and his eyes shifted back to their usual gray.

"Dafydd?"

I nodded. "I'm here. Damien's all right. I got to him in time."

He looked down at the body in his arms. "I didn't."

I reached out and put a hand on his shoulder. "Are you all right? It's a lot of blood."

He shook his head. "None of it is mine." His voice broke. "I was too late. By the time I got here, she was already…" His voice trailed off, but I knew what he had been going to say. She was already dead.

"I'm so sorry." It wasn't enough, but I didn't know what else to say. What can you say at a time like this?

Motion behind us again. This time both Paul and I turned and relaxed when we saw it was Damien.

He was shaking his head. "They're all dead out there. I assume they were werewolves?"

Paul nodded, his expression still broken, but a bit of life, if you can call it that in a vampire, coming back to his eyes. "Yes. I'd asked them to guard her house."

"Was it Malachai himself, then?"

Paul looked down at the body in his arms before answering. "Yes." His tone turned bitter. "I'd say he was too strong for me, but the truth was he'd already finished with her and was just waiting to taunt me, to make sure I knew it was him. He ran as soon as I arrived, and I was left with a choice."

I didn't follow him, but Damien obviously did because he knelt, not seeming to notice the blood staining his clothes. The other vampire put a hand on Paul's shoulder and squeezed, hard. "You made the right choice. She wouldn't have wanted it any other way. You know that."

I was still confused, but Paul nodded, the motion slow and reluctant. "I know." His voice was almost too quiet to be heard.

Damien stood up and spoke, his voice firm. "I'll take care of the werewolves outside. You and Dafydd take care of her." He moved past me, giving me a stern look, but I couldn't read it. I knew there was something significant I was missing, but I guessed I'd learn it later. For now, of course, I'd help my friend.

"Paul," I said, not sure what to ask.

He sighed and got to his feet, still clutching Nicola's body. "He's right. Come on."

I followed him outside, noting that he moved past the bodies without even a glance. Damien had neatly stacked them and was on the phone. I assumed he was calling the vampires to perform the same clean-up they had done earlier on the vampire who had attacked him. It seemed odd that there was a body disposal service in my city I'd never heard about.

Paul glanced up and down the street and walked toward his car. I hurried to follow him. "Want me to drive?" I asked.

"Please."

I guessed he was going to ride, still holding her, so I opened the passenger side door for him. He nodded his thanks and climbed in, adjusting her to drape comfortably in his lap. Were it not for the blood, she would have looked like she was just sleeping.

I got in and started the car. "Where to?"

"Fort Totten."

I frowned, wondering what was there, but I shrugged and started driving.

"We don't usually bury vampire kills. We burn them. There's a landfill over there I've used this way before."

Oh.

We drove in silence. I desperately wanted to say something, but I was out of my depth here. Sure, I'd been to family funerals and the like, but this was different, more personal somehow. I'd barely known her, so I didn't feel sad, exactly, but I could feel Paul's pain, and I wished I knew the right thing to ease it, even a tiny bit.

We were almost there when he finally spoke. "I guess you're wondering what Damien and I had been talking about back there."

Actually, I'd forgotten about it, but now that he mentioned it, yeah, I was curious.

"Yes."

He sighed and shifted Nicola. "When I arrived, Malachai was standing over her, blood dripping down his face."

That surprised me. From what I've seen, a limited sample to be sure, but still, vampires seemed to be neat eaters.

Paul echoed my thoughts. "He's usually very neat, but this time he wanted to make the statement. He wanted me to know, without any doubt, that it was he who had killed her. Not one of his minions."

I nodded. That made sense.

"He didn't say anything. He nodded at me and left."

"Why didn't you follow him? Attack him?" I winced at my words. They sounded so harsh, so unfeeling.

But Paul didn't seem to take them that way. He just nodded. "You're right. I should have done just that. But…" His voice broke, and I glanced over to watch him take a deep breath before continuing. "She was still alive."

I gasped, glancing again at the body in his lap. With a wound that huge in her throat, Malachai must have done it just moments before Paul arrived. She would have bled out almost immediately.

"Just barely, but there was still life there. Enough to…" He trailed off again, and I suddenly got it.

"Enough to still turn her into a vampire." I was surprised at the flat sound of my voice. It sounded like I was judging him and his kind. I didn't want him to think that.

"Exactly." He seemed to be accepting my judgment.

"No, I didn't mean it the way it sounded."

"Didn't you?"

I shook my head. "No, really. I didn't. You loved her. You had a chance to save her."

He laughed, the sound bitter. "Save her? Is that what you think I would have done? Turn down the next street."

I blinked at the seeming non sequitur but made the turn. "I didn't mean... I guess... Oh, I don't know. You've told me you don't regret being a vampire. So wouldn't it have made sense for you to have turned her?"

He sighed. "I think you may be a better friend than I'd realized, Dafydd."

I glanced at him, surprised by the warmth and gratitude in his voice. "What? You thought I despised you for what you are?"

He shrugged. "The thought had crossed my mind, yes."

As we neared a large landfill, Paul indicated I should stop. I found a spot nearby and parked.

"No, I don't despise you. I never have. Right after we met, I guess I was a bit scared of you, but I've always accepted what you are. You're my friend. How could I judge you? And now that I've seen how you were turned, well, it wasn't exactly like you asked for it, was it? And with everything you've done, you're still basically a good person."

"Thank you for that. I never expected that level of

acceptance from a human." He glanced down at the body in his lap.

"She…or he, rather, never accepted you?"

He shook his head. "No, he loved me, but he always hated what I was. And as much as I didn't want to lose him again, I couldn't do that to him."

I reached out to grasp his hand. "Come on. Let's send him on his way."

He nodded and opened the door, managing to get himself and Nicola's body out of the car in one smooth motion. I got out and this time remembered to lock the doors.

We walked over to a chain-link fence. I looked at it and then at him. "Not sure how we're going to get over that."

"Stay with him a moment." He carefully put the body down on the ground, arranging limbs into a comfortable position.

It probably should have seemed strange to keep referring to Nicola as "him," but I knew that Paul had known the soul as male for a very long time. And when they had been together, even when Nicola had been aware of herself, there was something not quite female about her. Weird or not, it fit. I just wished I'd had more time to get to know her.

I knelt down and took Nicola's hand. There was still a faint warmth there, felt even through the cooling of death. I watched Paul stride up to the fence, reach out with both hands and casually rip a hole in the chain links, plenty large enough for us to pass through. I wondered what the workers would think when they saw it in the morning.

Paul came back to us. "It won't be the first time. Small, valuable gifts seem to appear occasionally. They stopped reporting 'vandalism' to the police a while ago." He crouched down to pick up the body. "This way. There's a good spot over here."

Good spot was relative, unless you really think burned out car hulks are a good place for a cremation. But I didn't say anything. This was Paul's show.

He reverently placed the body on top of one of the cars and then moved around, gathering flammable materials. It was an odd assortment that finally ended up surrounding Nicola's body: an old tire, part of a seat back, some scrap wood and, no kidding, a small pile of pine air fresheners, you know, the ones that hang on the rear view mirror. I shook my head hoped his spirit didn't mind. Of course, as well as he knew Paul, he was probably more amused than anything else.

Paul adjusted a few items and stood back to survey his work. "That will work." He reached into a pocket and pulled out a lighter.

"Hang on," I said.

He turned to look at me.

"Start a small fire over there. I think I can help with this." I pointed to a pile of junk over to one side. Most of it was paper, and I thought it would burn easily and hot, which was what I needed.

"What are you going to do?"

I gave him a small smile. "Wait and see. I'm not

terribly good at this, but I think I can make it work."

He quickly built a small fire. As I thought, it burned bright and hot, lighting up the immediate area. I knelt by the fire, feeling the heat caress my face. I stared into the flames and watched them dance, seemingly alive. I concentrated and sent out a silent call.

A moment later, I was rewarded. The dancing flames resolved into a small ball of fire, points of fire crackling around it.

Paul chuckled behind me. "A fire elemental?"

I nodded absently, most of my attention on what I had summoned. Elementals don't speak human languages, but they are attuned to their summoners, and I knew I could get my message across. A moment later, the ball lengthened into an oval and seemed to bow. Then it moved to the junk surrounding Nicola. It took a few minutes (it was a very small elemental), but finally flames leaped around the body and began to burn, far hotter and faster than anything Paul could have set.

I stepped to one side to avoid the greasy smoke, smelling disturbingly like barbecued pork. Paul stood beside me, and we watched as the fire reduced Nicola's body to ash. What should have taken hours took less than half an hour.

As soon as it was finished, the fire elemental danced across the ground to hover near me.

"Thank you. That was well done. You may go."

It lengthened and bowed one more time and then slowly faded from view. A single coal remained behind, which guttered and went out.

"I didn't know you could summon elementals," Paul said.

I shrugged. "I'm not very good at it. I can only summon small ones like that. PopPop can whistle up big ones, large enough to be effective in a fight. It's why he was such a good warrior for the coven. Demons quickly learned to avoid him and anyplace he was protecting."

"There's level of skill involved? I thought summoning was summoning."

A wave of fatigue washed over me, and I swayed. Paul caught and steadied me. "Not with elementals. It's different with extra-planar beings like demons, but the size and strength of an elemental depends on the ability of the summoner."

He pointed me in the direction of the car, and we started walking, his arm keeping me from falling on my face. Magic can be very draining, especially when a warlock is working out of his comfort zone. Summoning isn't something I do very often. While popular fiction has most magic wrong, it's actually pretty close in this area, as I explained to Paul.

"Anyone with a hint of talent, or a mundane with the right ingredients and right magical time of year, can summon a demon. They are happy to have an opportunity to come to our plane, so they use their powers to aid the summons."

"I'm guessing most people don't know that."

We got to the car, and I handed Paul the keys. No

way I was going to be able to drive in my current condition. He unlocked the car and helped me into the passenger seat. I sat back and closed my eyes. The advantage of youth? I was already starting to get my strength back.

He climbed in and started the car.

"You're right," I continued. "Most people who dabble in summoning don't know exactly what they are doing. It's extremely dangerous."

"Of course. We're talking demons after all."

I nodded. "Sure. But there's always someone who is stupid, or arrogant enough to think they can control one."

Paul frowned as he drove. "So the demons make it easy to bring them across. And hard to control once they get here?"

"Pretty much."

"But elementals are different?"

I opened my eyes. The movement of the car was making colors swirl nauseatingly behind my eyelids. "Yes. The warlock provides all the energy to bring an elemental across. More energy equals a bigger, stronger elemental."

I glanced over to see Paul staring at me. "What?"

"Well, you've said it's a matter of strength. You're strong. You've said so, and I've seen you in action, so I believe it."

I smiled, absurdly glad he thought well of my magical ability. "Yeah, I'm pretty strong, especially considering my age. I'll get stronger and better as I get older. But remember how I've said some warlocks have certain talents?"

He nodded.

"It's not just raw strength. It's also how you apply that strength. My talent lies in divination." I paused, trying to figure out how to put it. "Think of it as efficiency. When I'm doing a divination, or projecting an image, every bit of my strength is used in the spell. Nothing is wasted."

Paul's eyes brightened, and I thought he'd just gotten it. "But when you're summoning an elemental, you can't use all your energy as efficiently." He paused and then added, "More like two to one?"

I nodded. "Pretty much, but call it more like five to one. I'm probably only applying about 20 percent of my ability to the summons. And it tires me out more than other magic because I'm working damned hard to get even that much into the spell."

He stopped at a light. "We really are more alike than I'd thought."

"Sure. You're good at the physical stuff while Malachai is wiz at the mental manipulation." I grinned at him. "I hope you won't mind, but I prefer your abilities to his."

He chuckled. "I don't mind." Then his expression grew serious, and his eyes glowed faintly. "Speaking of which."

"Yeah. Malachai needs to go down. Hard."

The light dimmed in Paul's eyes, and he gave me a curious look.

I rolled my eyes. "Oh. come on. Yes, I'm as interested in taking him down as you are. No, I didn't know Nicola the way you did, but there's a bad dude killing people in my town. I want to stop it. I thought you got that by now."

He looked abashed. "Sorry. I'm so used to doing things alone, and being at odds with my supposed allies. I forget that you're different."

I smiled. "It's okay. I'm patient. I'll get it through your thick skull some time. Anyway, now that we are agreed Malachai needs to do down, what's the plan?"

Paul pulled up outside his house. "We stay together. Malachai's used the divide and conquer trick once. I don't intend to let him do it again."

I gasped at a sudden thought. Paul must have had the same idea because he was pulling his phone out of his pocket and dialing. A moment later, his shoulders relaxed, and I realized I'd been holding my breath.

Paul nodded as Damien said something. "Good. That's good. You're with the others now? Excellent. Don't be alone for a while. Dafydd and I are planning what to do about Malachai." He paused. "All right. We'll save some part of the plan for you. But until then—" He chuckled. "Okay, yes, you've got it, and I'll stop playing mother hen. Goodbye."

He hung up. "He called the clean-up squad, and they've dealt with the werewolf bodies."

"Were any of them people I knew?"

Paul shook his head. "No, Runner and Mack had just gone off patrol when Malachai showed up. I don't think you've met any of the others."

I thought for a moment. "Think that was part of his plan?"

"What?"

"Waiting for Runner and Mack to leave? Were they stronger than the other wolves?"

Paul opened his door, and I started to follow him out of the car. He motioned me to stay put, and I froze.

Slowly, he made a circuit of the car, walked up to the door of his house and then came back. His body was tense and alert, and he held his head high, sniffing the air.

"It's okay. You can get out."

I opened the door and got out, the hair prickling on the back of my neck. Without thinking, my vision slipped into aura sight, and I yelled, "Paul!"

A shot rang out, and time stopped for a moment.

Objects and people have auras. Buildings sometimes have auras. And occasionally, the very air can reflect the emotions of nearby people.

When my eyes slipped into my other form of sight, I saw blackness: deep, inky black shot through with green and red.

An instant after I heard the shot, I felt a heavy weight slam into me. My first thought was that I'd been hit by a humongous bullet, but then I realized it was Paul, knocking me to the ground and protecting me with his body. Warm, sticky blood flowed over my arm, but none of it was mine.

Then the weight left me, and Paul moved. His aura crackled with rage, and something I realized, with a queasy feeling in my stomach, was hunger. The air around us hung silent, heavy and dark.

I scrambled back to the car, hoping it provided cover from the right direction.

Paul started running in the direction of his house. I desperately wished I had another potion on me at the same moment I realized Paul was running in the direction of the shooter, which meant I was on the wrong side of the car.

As fast as I could, I crawled around to the other side, and then poked my head around to take a look. Yeah, I know, probably a bad idea, but I couldn't resist.

I wished I hadn't.

Just as my head cleared the side of the car, Paul reached the shooter, who was just emerging from behind a nearby car, gun extended. He never had time to get off another shot. The vampire was on him immediately. Paul didn't hesitate. He grabbed the shooter, wrenched his neck to one side and buried his fangs in his neck.

I'd only seen Paul kill once before, when we first met and I came upon him in a similar pose, fangs in a guy's neck. This was different. I hadn't known the other guy, but I knew this one.

Paul had just killed Stephen.

He dropped the body and stood over it for a moment, his eyes still burning with rage but no longer hunger. Don't ask me how I knew the difference, but I did. He looked down at the body, as if seeing it for the first time, and he stiffened before turning to me.

"Dafydd. I didn't—"

I wasn't sure what to feel. My best friend had just killed my boyfriend. Okay, ex-boyfriend, but you know what I mean. I thought I'd loved Stephen. Sure, he'd betrayed us, and I was furious with him for deceiving me, but emotions don't just vanish immediately.

Paul took a step toward me, his body language hesitant.

I shook myself and forced my shocked brain into action. Stephen had lied to me and just tried to kill me. No matter what I thought I'd felt for him, those two outweighed everything. I slowly got to my feet. "It's okay. You did what you had to do."

"But, it was Stephen."

I nodded. "Yeah, I know. And he tried to kill me." I essayed a small smile. "Thanks for getting to him first."

Paul's body relaxed, although his eyes moved in all directions, obviously searching for more danger. "Let's get in the house."

"What about him?" I motioned to Stephen's body, lying so still and somehow forlorn in the diffuse street light.

"We could take him back to where we cremated Nicola."

My head jerked in fierce denial. "No! That was special, for her. She deserved it. He doesn't."

Paul tossed me his keys and glanced around one

more time. "You head into the house. I think we're safe for a bit. I'll take the body around back and call Damien when I get in."

We were keeping the vampire clean-up squad busy this evening, but I didn't know what else to do, so I took the keys and headed into his house.

I went straight for his fridge and this time didn't hesitate when I grabbed the remaining can of Coke. It looked even lonelier than last time, or maybe it was just my morbid state of mind. I popped the top and took a long swallow before going to the living room and sitting down on the sofa. I collapsed into its welcoming softness and closed my eyes.

Chapter 13

Wednesday, May 5, 2010:
Dawn

GAIN, I DREAMED. This was a dream I'd had for many years as a warning of what was to come. But even as I dreamed, I knew there was something wrong. This event had already happened.

I was walking along a dark alleyway, faint light from nearby apartments providing just enough light for me to place my feet.

I look up at a sudden sound and draw back in alarm. In front of me stands a man, tall and imposing. Although I should be frightened, something about him is strong, safe and reassuring. Which is odd because he's drinking the blood of someone, long fangs gleaming redly. I take a closer look at the face of the man he's feeding from. I'm not surprised to see that it's Stephen.

I glance around, looking for the figure I knew would be lurking behind him. Sure enough, she's there. Only this time it's Nicola, transparent but still clearly visible. She's smiling and nodding at me. Her mouth moves, and I can just read the words on her lips.

"He's not lying anymore."

Then I wake up.

Again, Paul was sitting in a chair opposite me. He smiled. "Welcome back."

I blinked and glanced around. Faint light tinged the sky outside, and my inner sense told me it was about 45 minutes or so to sunrise.

"You were dreaming."

I nodded. "Yeah, and it was weird."

Suddenly, I realized the approaching dawn meant something, and I leaped off the couch.

"What?"

"We need to get to my place. Dawn is almost here. I need to do the finding ritual."

Paul's expression softened. "Dafydd. Stephen's dead."

"I know that."

His expression grew curious. "Then what's to find?"

I huffed out an impatient breath. "Come on. I'll explain in the car."

I started for the door, but he stopped me before I could open it. I nodded and let him go first. This close to dawn, Malachai was unlikely to be waiting for us, and I thought he was out of minions, but we couldn't be sure. I figured I'd be letting Paul go out a lot of doors ahead of me for the next couple of days.

He glanced around and nodded. We hurried for his car, and drove off in the direction of my apartment. I quickly ran down what I'd need for the ritual and nodded to myself. I'd just restocked all my supplies a few days earlier, and I had everything I needed. My eyes flicked to the sky and the growing light. It would be close, but I thought we'd make it in time. The ritual I was planning could be done with minimal preparation.

"So, what are you planning?"

"I can look for more than just where someone is. As you said, we know where Stephen is now." I paused. "Did you call Damien?"

He nodded. "While you slept. He said he'd take care of it, and he sends his apologies."

I smiled. "I'll thank him the next time I see him. Anyway, finding rituals can be used to discover where someone is. But they can also be used to find where someone has been."

Paul's expression brightened. "Of course, which you need because you don't know where he lives"

I grinned. "Exactly."

"So you think there might be something at his place that will give us a clue where to find Malachai."

"Exactly. If we're lucky, we might get two locations out of the spell. Stephen's house and maybe somewhere else he spends a lot of time."

It's like this. We leave impressions behind us. Every place you've ever been has a trace of your aura. If you've only been there once, like a restaurant you tried but didn't like, the trace is faint and fades quickly. But if it's a place you go to frequently, that trace is renewed each time. If you're there often enough, you leave enough behind for me to find with my spell.

Paul seemed to follow my thinking. "You're hoping to find where Stephen met Malachai."

I nodded. "Yes. He had to give Stephen his instructions, and Malachai doesn't strike me as the phone type."

"Probably not. It's hard to maintain any kind of control over distance, and even though Stephen was working for him willingly, he would have wanted to reinforce his influence as often as possible. So you're right. They probably met in person."

"Then let's just hope they were sloppy and met in the same place each time."

Luckily, rush hour traffic wasn't bad yet, and we made good time to my house. I reached to open the car door, but stopped at the last second to glance at Paul. The vampire was out of the car and looking around, nostrils flaring and eyes wide. After a moment he looked at me through the car window and nodded. I got out and started for my apartment.

"The ferrets are going to be pissed. Can you feed them while I get set up?"

"Sure. Do you need me for the ritual?"

I unlocked my apartment door. As I'd expected, two sets of bright eyes were looking our way. "Need you? No. But I wouldn't mind you being there."

I glanced at my phone and consulted my inner time sense. We were close, but I thought I had just enough time to set up.

Paul moved to the ferret cage while I hurried to my work room. I heard him talking quietly as I closed the door to make my preparations.

Magic isn't something that should be performed in a rush, but finding rituals are the ones I work the most often, so I can afford to be hasty with them.

I quickly ran a vacuum cleaner around the room. It was still clean from my last ritual, so it only took a moment. I set up my ritual materials on my altar and checked the time again. Barely enough time to cast the circle.

I opened the door a crack and peered into the living room. The ferrets were dashing across the floor, delighted to have their favorite plaything. I grinned as Gimble leaped from the couch to launch herself at Paul, who was distracted by Gyre dancing at his feet. Without missing a beat, he turned to catch the white ferret and spin her around, once, twice.

I could have watched them longer, but there wasn't time. "Paul," I said. "It's time."

Without a word, he gathered up the ferrets and put them in their cage, settling each of them with a quick stroke along the back. Then he followed me.

I stripped off my shirt and shrugged into my ritual robe. If I'd been alone, I would have removed my jeans as well, but with him here? No way!

"Where do you want me?"

I considered a moment. "Inside the circle, with me. Over there." I pointed to the west side of the carpeted circle, comfortably away from the altar, leaving me plenty of room to maneuver. He settled where I'd indicated, and I glanced over the room one more time, ensuring everything was ready. I was grateful once more to Mom for the circle on the carpet. No way I could have done this in time if I'd had to draw it by hand.

I turned to the altar and concentrated for a moment, preparing to close the circle. It was pretty much like last time, with me placing the candles, lighting them and saying the appropriate chants. Nothing new this time. Although when I got to the part about decreeing the space sacred, my heart did skip a beat. If you're thinking that it's odd to have a vampire in a "sacred space," don't think you're the only one.

Circle cast, I felt the usual soft thrumming of power around me. Outside sounds were muted, but I found myself even more aware of what was inside, which meant Paul's presence was like a physical thing, and I closed my eyes again to focus my attention on the spell I was ready to cast.

I lit two more candles on the altar, one black (for solving mysteries) and one orange (for luck, useful since I was doing something a bit more complicated than a traditional finding.).

I placed some ritual components in the cauldron, lit them, and left them to smolder.

"Will asking questions disturb you?" Paul asked, his voice low.

I shook my head. "No. During my training, my dad often made me explain along with doing a ritual. Helped reinforce the learning and was great for teaching multi-tasking. Ask away."

"What did you just put in the cauldron?"

"Acacia leaf and sandalwood. Burned together, they enhance psychic powers. I'm going to need all the enhancing I can get since this is kind of an odd way to do a finding."

I had already placed some buds and flowers on a plate, and now I took out the hair I had taken from Stephen and slowly mixed them all together before crushing them and rubbing them on a small magnet.

"The buds from a Balm of Gilead tree and Crown Vetch flowers. The buds are used to ease the pain of a broken heart." I smiled ruefully at the vampire. "Stephen's name means 'crown,' so the flowers symbolically represent him. I've got his hair, but I wanted to strengthen the link for this spell."

"I see." His tone was full of sympathy, but I ignored both my emotional pain and his implied offer to ease it. Right now, I could use the strong emotions to fuel my spell.

Everything was ready, and sunrise was almost upon us, so I took a deep breath and gathered in all the energy nearby. Automatically, I included some of Paul's in my gathering. Distantly, I heard him suck in a quick breath, but he didn't say anything, and I concentrated on my chanting.

Bound and Binding
Binding Bound
See the Sight
Hear the Sound
Where Stephen once resided

Now is found
Bound and Binding
Binding Bound

Focusing my will on the flame of the black candle, I visualized Stephen, just as I had most loved him, his eyes sparking with humor and his mouth curved in the smile I'd thought was just for me. I'd never seen his home, but I imagined him in a living room, filled with generic furniture. It wasn't perfect, but it would have to do. I felt tears threaten in the corner of my eye, but I blinked them away and continued.

Placing the magnet between the two candles, I stroked it towards me as I recited,

By the wavering flame of this black light,
Grant to me of lost love a sight.
By the power of this orange flame,
Give me luck to find the same.
On this map, his home I see
Make the magnet draw it to me.

I put down the magnet, and, still concentrating on my vision of Stephen and his room, I took the orange candle and held it over the map, moving it back and forth slowly. I shaped the power within me and concentrated on the link created between me and (hopefully) where Stephen had once lived. After a moment, I felt a burst of energy as I made the link. If I had been searching for a living person, the energy would have been colored, but since Stephen was dead, it was a blast of gray light in my vision. As I blinked to clear it, the candle dropped a blob of wax onto the map.

I carefully marked the location on the map with a grease pencil.

Paul looked down. "That's it?"

I nodded, feeling drained from the magic. "Should be. The spell felt right."

"It's not far from here."

"No, let me shut this down, and we'll decide what to do next."

I extinguished the smoldering sandalwood and acacia. Then I pinched the orange and black candles with my fingers to put them out.

Finally, I turned my attention to the circle. I raised my *athame* and drew in the power. Then I thanked the guardians for their service. I pinched out the candles in the reverse order of lighting them, and when the last of them was extinguished, I felt the power settle in me, recharging my energy. You know you've done a ritual correctly when you feel more energized than when you started. I took a deep breath and concluded with, "Farewell Earth, Water, Fire and Air. Your light shone on this working, and protected my circle. Thus is sacred space released and no act went unnoticed. So mote it be."

I took a deep breath and closed my eyes for a moment, just aware of myself, the power within and Paul beside me.

Finally, I sighed and spoke. "Well, it was partially

successful. I know where Stephen lived, but I didn't get anything about where he's been meeting Malachai."

He shrugged. "Half is better than nothing, I guess."

I nodded. "Yeah, but I was hoping for more."

"That close by, he was probably he watching you."

"Probably." Which was just creepy to think about. My abilities are supposed to give me a warning if I am being watched regularly. It doesn't trigger if someone just glances at me on the street, but if someone were following me for weeks or months, I should have known about it. Malachai's spell had been very thorough.

"We need to get over there and take a look," Paul said.

"Yeah. How are you at breaking and entering?"

He grinned. "I've developed numerous skills over the years."

I suddenly had an idea. "Let me call Laura for a minute. She might be able to help us."

"How?"

I waved him off and quickly gathered up my materials, putting them back with reverence.

"It's been interesting to watch you work," Paul commented as I finished up.

"Really?"

"Yes. Malachai let me watch a few rituals, but they weren't the kind you'd enjoy."

I shuddered. "I suppose he used blood magic."

"Of course."

No, those wouldn't have been fun to watch. Blood

magic generally requires the death of something. The larger or more intelligent the creature, the more power is available for the spell. Sacrificing humans is particularly potent.

"Until you, I'd never seen white magic at work. The energy feels…good."

I smiled. "That's the part I like."

He cocked his head at me, and I shrugged. "Well, yeah, I like what I can do with the power, sure, but the way it makes me feel? Who needs drugs with that kind of high?"

I folded my robe and stood up. Paul remained sitting, still cross-legged on the floor, and I shot him a curious glance. He shook his head and stood up. "Something wrong?" I asked.

"Not exactly." He hesitated, which was odd enough that I stopped.

"What?"

He shook his head. "When you gathered energy. You took from me."

With an effort, I stopped my mouth from dropping open. He was right. I'd guessed earlier that I could draw on him as a source of power, but I'd not intended to do it. Then, during the rush of this ritual, I just … did it.

"I'm really sorry," I said. "I didn't mean to. It just—"

Paul shook his head. "No, don't worry. It's not a problem. If you needed it, and it helped, then I'm glad you did. I just didn't know you could."

I relaxed a bit, glad he wasn't pissed. "When I showed you how to gather power from outside sources, I'd guessed I probably could. I'd sort of meant to test it later, but then when we were in there, well, I was kind of in a rush, and I just grabbed everything nearby."

"Which included me."

"Which included you." He was taking it calmly, but I still felt bad. I was trained better than that, and my dad would be pissed it he ever found out. I took a deep breath. "Look, I shouldn't have done that. It's not right to take without asking first, and I didn't. It won't happen again."

He smiled. "Don't worry." His voice grew strangely formal. "You have my permission to draw upon my power whenever you need."

I blinked, taken aback at that. Energy stirred between us, and as his eyes widened, I guessed he'd felt it too.

"I didn't expect that," he said.

I shook my head. "Neither did I. But thanks."

I really wasn't sure what that meant, but I knew I'd need to figure it out later. For now, though, we had things to do.

I opened the door, and we left the work room. My phone was on the table, and I picked it up to call Laura. Paul followed me, his expression curious.

Laura picked up right away. "Hey, Dafydd. It's early."

"Yeah, sorry. I didn't wake you?"

"No. I was just about to kick some butt in World

of Warcraft before heading to bed. But what's up?"

I chuckled at the game reference—yes, I do know what World of Warcraft is—and gave her the address of Stephen's house. "Can you see if there's any cameras near there? See if you can find where Stephen went when he left home."

Her voice was puzzled. "Sure, I can do that, but why are you checking up on your boyfriend?"

Right. She wasn't all up to speed yet. I filled her in on Nicola's death and Stephen's involvement.

When I was done, she said, "I'm really sorry, Dafydd."

My eyes started to water. Damn! Wrong emotion here. Paul gave me an encouraging look, and I rubbed my eyes and said, "Yeah, thanks. We'll talk later, but for right now I need to know more about where Malachai was meeting him. I'm hoping you'll come up with something."

"Right." Her tone became business-like. "Of course. I'll get on it right away."

My heart swelled with gratitude toward her. "Thanks. You know how much I appreciate you, right?"

I heard her chuckle. "Yes, but you're always welcome to show it in tangible ways."

I nodded. "Of course. Ruth's Chris after all this is done."

I smiled at her sudden intake of breath. "Yeah, okay. So when I say 'right on it,' I mean like this instant." She paused for a moment, and I started to say "goodbye," but then she added. "And Dafydd. About that other thing you wanted me to check out—"

Oh, right. Vampire penetration of the police department. I resisted the impulse to look at Paul as I said, my voice smooth, casual. "Yeah, thanks. We'll talk about it later."

I knew she got it when she just said, "Sure. I'll call you as soon as I have anything. And tell your boyfriend I said 'hi.'" I could hear the laughter in her voice.

"Yeah, I'm on that. Thanks." And I hung up.

I stood, sad, for a moment. Laura really has been amazing, and I just wish there was some way magic could heal her. But it doesn't work that way.

I turned to Paul, who was giving me an odd expression. "What?"

He shook his head. "Nothing." He walked over to the window.

Okay, that was weird. I know Paul well enough to guess that something was wrong. Then it hit me. I always forget about his hearing. He heard everything Laura had said.

Hastily, I said. "She's just teasing me, you know. She's been calling you my boyfriend almost from the first minute we met." I really hoped that was all he was thinking about. I didn't want to explain right now why I was checking up on the vampire community.

He faced me. "Really?" His voice was too casually dry.

"Yeah, really." His expression was still weird. I sighed and added, "So what's wrong?"

Paul turned away before saying, "It's been obvious to me for a while now that you're ... well ... attracted to me."

Damn! Did he have to bring that up right now? Sure, we probably needed to deal with it, but there was a lot going on. "Yeah, of course. You're one of the hottest guys I've ever known. And we're friends, and we work well together. Kind of inevitable, really."

I tried to be casual about it, but he demonstrated how well he could see through me.

"It's more than that. Something changed recently."

I spoke without thinking. "Yeah, I finally found out that you aren't straight."

Oops. That came out with more heat than I'd intended.

He was still facing away from me, and I really wished I could see his expression. "I'm sorry. I probably should have told you earlier. But, well—"

I nodded, even though he couldn't see it. "You're a vampire, and you like to keep things close to the vest. I shouldn't have expected anything else, but, I thought we were better friends than that."

"We are. That's part of why I didn't say anything."

Twisted logic, but I thought I followed it. "You didn't want sexual attraction to mess anything up."

Suddenly, I realized something. "Is that why you lied to me months ago, when we first met? You let me think Natalie had been your lover. Not Nicholas."

He turned around, embarrassment on his face. "That was part of it."

I thought for a moment and then said, "But not all of it. Not like I'd moved far from 'gee he's hot but God he's a vampire.' at that point. You knew I was gay. Not like I was going to judge you for loving a guy."

"No."

Gods above! I'd been dense. I'd been so worried about my own feelings and trying so hard not to be attracted to him that I'd missed the obvious.

"You were attracted to me, too. And that was the complication you didn't want."

It made sense. It wasn't like relationships between vampires and humans tended to be healthy. Look at Nicola.

Paul's eyes widened. "You mean you really didn't figure it out until now?"

I shook my head. "No, I didn't. I mean, in hindsight, it's obvious. Laura's probably been laughing at me the whole time now. But, well, I'd just gotten dumped by a boyfriend, and then Stephen came along, and it wasn't something I guess I wanted to deal with."

His eyes brightened. "There was Malachai's spell."

I hated to disappoint him. "No, I checked for that. My blindness about you was completely self-inflicted."

There really wasn't any good way to deal with this now, and I wanted to head it off. "Look, now isn't the time. We need to deal with Malachai, and, spell or no spell, I thought I was in love with Stephen. I'm not in a place to deal with this right now."

Paul's tone was brisk. "Of course. Sorry."

I recognized the wall going up, and I didn't want

that either. I reached out and touched his arm. "I'm not putting you off. Some good stuff came out right now, and I'm glad. I think I'd like to see if there's relationship possibility between us, but I don't want to share it with blood and death." I paused. "Okay, with you being a vampire and all, I guess sharing with blood is part of the package."

He smiled, and the humor reached his eyes. He put his hand over mine and squeezed. "Yes, it is. But I know what you meant, and I agree."

I nodded. "So you heard my conversation with Laura. She'll check cameras. Not sure what it'll tell us, but knowing the directions he went might help."

"It might. Especially if we can find something in his apartment to give us a clue."

"Right." I glanced out the window. "Speaking of that, it's not like we can do much about it now. The sun's up."

"Let me call Runner. He can bring the van."

"Still won't let you break in."

"No, but Runner's also got some special skills." He winked at me.

"Ah. In that case, why don't you just stay here, out of the sun. Let Runner and me snoop around."

"You'd be okay with me staying here?"

I snorted. "I just let you share a ritual with me. Snoozing on my couch is nothing compared to that."

He laughed and called the werewolf to arrange things.

RUNNER SHOWED UP soon after and of course had to take a moment to jibe Paul for his sun issues. "Yep, leave it to the werewolves to take care of stuff during the day."

Paul punched him in the shoulder. "You're just jealous of my superior abilities."

Runner rolled his eyes.

"I'm sorry about your people last night," Paul said, changing the subject and growing serious.

Runner nodded. "Yeah. That was bad. I'm sorry we couldn't protect her, though." He cocked his head. "She was pretty special to you somehow?"

Paul nodded. "Yes. I'll fill you in later, when things slow down, and when I can talk about it." His voice started to break, and he cleared his throat.

"Got it, man." The werewolf turned to me. "Okay, warlock, what's the plan?"

"A bit of breaking and entering. Paul says you're up to it?"

A slow grin spread across his face. "Sure thing. Well, the breaking is easy. Entering's up to you."

I glanced at Paul. "I was under the impression that we could be bit more subtle than that."

The werewolf chuckled. "Don't worry, kid. I was just having you on. One of my roles in the community is to verify the 'arrangements' of the infected werewolves who want to be locked up. I've had to learn how to get around locks and security, so I can make sure they can't, if you get my drift."

"Ah. That makes sense. I never knew about vampire clean-up crews. Adding were-burglars to the list was starting to be a bit much."

"Let's go. You can fill me in on the way." He glanced at Paul. "You're staying here?"

The vampire shrugged. "Doesn't seem like my services are needed, and the run out to the van is never my favorite thing."

As we left, I heard him opening the cage to let the ferrets out. They'd never want him to leave.

As we walked to his vehicle, Runner asked, "So who are we breaking into? Paul was short on details when he called."

We climbed into his simple white panel van, and I filled him in. He nodded when I was through. "Good. I want to get this guy off our streets. Vampire killing's always bad news, but this one is a real mess."

"Yeah. And it's kind of personal to Paul."

He looked at me, his expression shrewd. "And so that makes it personal to you, right?"

I blushed. "Yeah. That obvious, is it?"

Runner shrugged. "I've had to learn to read people, so I noticed. Doesn't mean the whole world knows you've got it on for a vampire." He paused. "He's a good one. You could do worse, you know."

"Think so?"

Anyone else think it was weird to be having this conversation?

"Yeah. I'm not big on my kind or his kind mixing it

up with humans. It goes bad most of the time. But Paul? He's more than okay." He grinned at me. "And I've seen you in a fight. You've got big ones. You'd do okay, if you guys decided to make a go of it."

I tended to agree with him, but I couldn't get the image of Nicola and the slow drip, drip of her blood out of my head.

We arrived at the address, and Runner found a (relatively) nearby parking spot. I was absurdly pleased to see that he didn't parallel park quite as well as Paul.

As we climbed out of the van, he said, "All right. We're here. This is your show. I'm just here to get you in."

I pointed to the apartment buildings. They were just a couple of stories, much like mine, with the exterior entrances to the individual units. My spell had given me the approximate area, but not the exact apartment number. That's why I had brought the magnet with me. "Give me a sec." I closed my eyes and attuned myself to the energies which still remained on the magnet. When I opened my eyes, I had shifted to aura sight and could see what I needed.

To aura sight, the magnet glowed a deep maroon, and when I looked at the apartment buildings, one of the units glowed a matching shade. I nodded. "Right. That one." I shifted my sight back to normal.

Runner glanced at the magnet in my hand. "How can you tell?"

"My ritual sets up a resonance between the magnet—" I held it up. "And the place I'd tried to find."

"And you can see that somehow?"

"Yeah. I can shift my sight to see magical auras."

He looked at me, his face full of curiosity. "So you can view my aura?"

"Of course." I'd actually viewed him a while ago, soon after we first met. I liked to know the character of the people I was working with.

"What did you see?"

I smiled. "That you're a good-hearted person, that you like to hunt, but not for evil or cruel purposes." My smile widened into a full grin. "And that you like dark ales."

He snorted. "You did not see that in my aura!" But his expression looked pleased at the rest.

I laughed. "Nope, you're right. I figured that last one out from observation. But the others are clear in your aura."

"Okay. Suppose that does come in handy sometimes."

"Sometimes, yes." I glanced at the apartment building. "But let's get in and do more of that old fashioned observation thing."

"Right."

We walked up to the door, and I stood a bit back, keeping an eye on the street. Runner took a small pick out of his pocket, and in just moments, he had the door open. "Not much to that. I hope your lock is better."

"Probably not." I'd never given it much thought, but with everything going on, maybe I should.

"I'll stop by later today with some better lock hardware. Ideally, we'd reinforce your door, but I'm guessing your landlord would have issues with that, so we'll settle for some good locks."

"Thanks."

I eased open the door and peered in. I shifted my vision.

"Can't stand around here too long," Runner said.

"I know, but I wanted to check for magical residue." Magic can't be used to set traps, per se, but it is possible to set up a sort of warning system. If Malachai was as powerful as I thought, it'd be simple for him to have left behind a spell to let him know if anyone unauthorized entered the apartment. If he were really good, he could have set up a channel for remote viewing.

And, no, in case you were wondering, I don't have stuff like that set up in my own place either. But I intended to correct that soon.

I briefly filled in Runner on what I was looking for as I surveyed the entryway. Nothing visible to my magical eye. It's possible Malachai could have veiled it somehow, but I didn't think he'd have wasted time or energy on that. A veil like that would need regular renewing, and even though Stephen had been working willingly with Malachai, I doubt either of them would have wanted Malachai coming by his apartment often enough to renew veils.

"Entryway looks clear." I motioned him in far enough to close the door.

From where we stood, we could see the kitchen and a bit of the living room. I held up a hand to stop Runner from moving farther. He waited for me. Nothing in the kitchen. Good. I took a few steps and moved to where I could see all the living room.

Ah! Something at last. The floor glowed a sickly yellow. "Stay right where you are. Don't enter the living room until I say it's safe."

"You see something?"

"Yeah, the floor is covered by a spell." I took a closer look, picking it apart in my mind. "I think it's intended to warn Malachai if someone enters the room. It's probably keyed to ignore Stephen and maybe one or two others. But if anyone else steps on the floor, Malachai will know about it."

"Why not cast it on the entryway?"

"How often do you need to invite a stranger in for a moment? Maybe someone doing a survey, or a neighbor stopping by to ask for a favor? It's too much bother to cast it on the entryway. But anyone who really shouldn't belong would head for the living room first. Looks like the door to the bedroom is this way as well. That's where we were planning on going, so that's what he covered."

"Any sign of remote viewing?"

I was looking for that even as he asked. Then I saw it. "Clever!"

"What?"

"He's got it cast on the TV. It's always easier to cast a spell on an object whose function has relevance to the spell. He probably watches the image on his own TV." I chuckled. "For an old vampire, he's surprisingly modern."

"That makes him more dangerous."

I sobered instantly. "Good point."

"Can you do something about it? Like break the spell or something?"

I thought for a moment. "Not exactly, but I think I can do something. The only catch is you'll have to do the searching. I'll be kind of occupied."

He frowned, the expression drawing his heavy eyebrows together. "What am I looking for?"

I shrugged. "I'm not sure. That's the problem. Paul and I figured we'd recognize it when we saw it, but—"

Runner rolled his eyes. "Amateurs! Okay. So if I've got this straight, there's a master vampire in town, messing with everyone. He used some human patsy to do his dirty work and get close to you. You want to know how to find the master, so you're hoping there's some clue here. Does that about sum it up?"

I nodded. "Pretty much. We were thinking we might find ... I don't know ... something about where he spent time, which might be a clue to where he met Malachai." As soon as I said it, the whole thing sounded lame and unlikely to work.

"Okay," Runner said. "Not much to go on, but I'll see what I can find. So how're you going to make it safe for me to go looking?"

I grinned. "Well, you're going to trigger the spell. He'll know someone's here, and then he'll check the

TV. Only thing, is he's not going to see anything useful."

"How's that?"

"I can cast a sort of illusion. He'll see only that and nothing else."

Runner shrugged. "Okay. That's magic stuff, and it's your area. I'll take your word on it. But I'll still look fast. I don't think it'd be a good idea to hang around too long."

"Agreed. It's daylight, so he can't come himself, but he's probably got more human minions."

"Right. So when can I go in?"

"Give me a minute to prepare."

I'd never done the spell quite like this before, but I was pretty sure it'd work. Remote viewing spells require line of sight from the object used as a focus. If I projected my image just in front of the TV, Malachai would see it and not anything else. Most warlocks wouldn't think to make their spell adjust for illusions because they're just not that common.

I thought about what I wanted him to see. Then I grinned. Perfect!

"Okay. Just another minute or so. You'll know when it's okay to move."

"How?"

"Watch the TV."

I concentrated, drew in energy and focused on the image. Then I placed it just in front of the TV.

Runner immediately started laughing. "Oh, nice! And reversed too."

Before I could respond, he moved into the living room, and started quickly, but efficiently tearing it apart. I wanted to pay attention to what he was doing, but maintaining this required too much of my attention. This was more than making Malachai see something out of the corner of his eye. This needed to be good enough to confuse him and keep his attention for long enough to let Runner do his search.

What was I projecting? Why, Roadrunner cartoons. Reversed, so they'd view properly from Malachai's point of view. He seemed to be a modern vampire, so I hoped he'd get the reference. I kind of liked envisioning the master vampire as Wile E. Coyote and us as the clever Roadrunner.

I felt Runner trigger the warning spell when he moved into the living room, and I thought we had only seconds before Malachai would activate the remote viewing spell. I wished I could spare the attention to shift to aura view and check out the spell. It's always enlightening to see the work of another warlock, but I didn't dare split my efforts.

Sure enough, in less than a minute, I felt the remote view spell activate. How can I tell? Remember how I've said magic is just manipulation of energies? Well, I've been working long enough with magic to sense when it's being used nearby, especially divination-type magic since it's my area of specialty.

"He's viewing now," I said.

Runner grunted but didn't stop his search. "Keep him entertained as long as you can."

Wile E. Coyote ran off a cliff, his legs pumping hard to try to keep from falling. No luck.

"Will do."

Two minutes. Three. Runner finished in the living room and darted for the bedroom.

Four minutes. I started to sweat. Plenty of time for Malachai to have called on his minions. He wouldn't know exactly who was here, but the spell would certainly give him a clue, and if I were him, I'd send someone over to grab us.

"Runner..." I started to speak, but just then he came out of the bedroom.

"I think I've got what you were looking for. Come on. Let's get out of here. We've been here too long."

He did spare a second to glance over his shoulder, just in time to see Wile E. Coyote blow himself up with some Acme explosives. "Appropriate."

We hustled out of the apartment. I let my spell fade as soon as we were outside. Runner ran for his van, me close on his heels. Moments later, we were away from the area. Runner drove in a random pattern, both of us frequently looking around, searching for followers. After about ten minutes, he relaxed. "I don't think we were followed."

I nodded. "Agreed. Good thing. Not like it wouldn't have been smart for him to have minions watching the apartment."

Runner shook his head. "Oh, I think he actually didn't care if you found it. In fact, I think he might have counted on it."

"What do you mean?"

He handed over a small brochure. I looked at it and groaned. "Oh, that's too obvious."

"Yep."

The brochure he'd handed me was for a bar. The Meeting Place. I vaguely knew the place. It wasn't too far from my home, and it was certainly an easy walk from where Stephen had lived.

"He had to know we'd find the apartment and check it out. So he planted the brochure."

"Looks like it." He turned at the next intersection and started back for my apartment. "Look on the bright side. You provided him with some entertainment."

PAUL WASN'T REALLY happy when we got back and showed him what we'd found. He agreed the brochure was planted, but that's not what upset him.

"That was clever and all, using your ability to mask his spell, but now he knows you can do it. Would have been nice to keep that in reserve. When we confront him, we'll need every advantage."

I nodded, knowing he was right. I'd been too interested in being clever and not focused enough on long-term strategy.

Paul's shoulders relaxed, and the corner of his mouth quirked. "On the other hand, using Wile E. Coyote. That was sheer brilliance."

I grinned back at him. "So the moral of this story is

that if I'm going to be stupid, I should at least do it with style."

Humor still tinged the vampire's voice. "Something like that, yeah."

Runner tapped the brochure. "Okay, enough with the bromance. This isn't a story with rabid fans looking for a ship. Let's get back to what's important."

Both Paul and I shot him looks. Shipping? Really? Well, then again, he had kind of guessed about the attraction between us. But the point was well taken.

The werewolf continued, ignoring our unspoken communication. "It's an incredibly obvious trap, but that doesn't mean we can avoid it."

Paul was nodding. "I agree. It's the vampire way to posture and play before the kill. Usually it works. But that doesn't mean we can't turn it to our advantage."

"Tonight, I guess?" Runner asked.

I was nodding along with Paul. "I think so. It's pretty obvious we can't avoid the confrontation, and the longer we wait, the more people will likely die. Besides…" I glanced at Paul. "Just because he knows some of what I can do doesn't mean he knows all the ways I can use it."

The vampire shook his head. "Have you been inside? I have. Looks like a cafeteria in a basement."

In other words, not many mirrors, windows or other reflective surfaces. My new favorite method of fighting wouldn't be useful. I shrugged. "There's always potions."

Runner snorted. "Let's try to avoid fighting in a

karaoke bar. It's too cliche. I'll round up a few of my people. If there's enough of us there, I doubt he'll try anything. You guys posture, threaten, find out what's up, and try to move the main event to another location."

"Works for me," I said.

Paul clearly didn't like it. "I could go alone to this one, you know. I have been taking care of myself for a number of years now."

Gently, Dafydd, I told myself. "I don't think that's a good idea. It's possible that the trap isn't at the bar. What if Malachai wants you to go alone? Divide and conquer. You said we'd better stay together until this is all over, and I think that's still the best idea."

"Agreed," Runner said.

Paul glanced back and forth between the two of us. "All right. Tonight then. As soon as it's dark. That'll give him less time to set something up."

Unless it's already set up. He's already proven himself to be at least one step ahead of us. But I didn't say it. Instead, I just yawned. "I need a bit of sleep. All these late nights are wearing me down. You're welcome to stay, Paul. Just don't make too much noise."

Runner started for the door. "I'll meet you there at sunset." He glanced at me with a small grin. "What time is that today?"

Runner loved my parlor trick. "Eight oh-five."

"Right. See you then." He left, closing the door behind him.

I yawned again and started for my bedroom. "Help

yourself to the TV. And if you want to let the weasels out, go for it. Wake me around four, if I'm not already up, okay?"

"Dafydd…" His voice was soft, almost pleading.

I turned to look at him. The half-conversation from earlier hung between us. I shook my head. "Not now. I'm tired, and there's too much going on."

I walked into the bedroom before he had a chance to say anything.

Chapter 14

Wednesday, May 5, 2010:
Late Afternoon

I SIGHED AND rolled over in bed. I'd like to say I slept well, but I'd be lying. Mostly I tossed and turned, moving from one lousy dream to another. None of them prophetic. Just bad. Right now I wouldn't have minded some sort of dream clue as to what was to come, but apparently the Universe wasn't in the mood to come clean. Sucks to be a diviner and not have a clue what was coming.

As I sat up and stretched, I heard a soft knock at the door. I picked up my phone and squinted at the time. Just after four o'clock. As usual, Paul was on time.

"Yeah, I'm up," I said. "Thanks. I'll be out in a minute, after I shower."

"I've got food ready."

I couldn't help the grin that spread across my face. I could get used to having someone cook for me. I rushed the shower and dressed in club gear, tight purple T-shirt (Dark Side of the Moon—yeah, I'm like PopPop) and tight, ripped jeans. Black Chucks completed the image.

I hustled into my tiny kitchen where Paul had the

table set and food spread out. "That smells good."

The vampire shrugged. "It's just rice and beans." He mock-scowled at me. "You don't leave me much to work with."

"Most of the time I'm not much of a cook."

"Obviously. The spices are pretty old."

I sat down and took a bite. Ouch! Hot! But good. I swallowed carefully and blew on the next one. "Mom sent them with me when I moved here."

Paul sat down opposite me. "Most of them haven't even been opened."

I ate a bit more before responding. "Then they should still be good, right?"

He chuckled. "Doesn't work that way."

"Oh, well. Whatever." And then I dug in and refused to say anything else until I'd finished.

Finally, I sat back, my stomach content. "If Runner's going to meet us right at sunset, I guess that means you want me to drive."

"Yes. I'll use the blanket."

Since we still had plenty of time, I took my time gathering my stuff. I was low on potions and desperately needed to brew some more. Assuming I had time, I'd work on that during the day tomorrow. All I had was a sense enhancer and one strength boost.

"That's not much," Paul said when I held them up.

"I know. Been using them up faster than I can make them. Hopefully Malachai will give me some time to brew some new ones tomorrow."

"I'll be sure to impress on him the urgency." His

tone was dry, but amused, and I shot him a quick grin.

"Yeah, you do that."

I packed my mace and a few other things that I thought might come in handy and tossed the strength potion to Paul. "It's not much, but you'll probably make better use of it than I will."

He took it, double-checked the label and pocketed it in the inside pocket of his blazer. It made an odd-looking bulge, but he shifted his stance, and it nearly vanished. Paul had a gift of making anything work with clothing. "What's yours?"

"Sense enhancer. Probably not useful, but better to have it than not. I really need another reflex boost, but I used the last one saving Damien's butt."

"Worthwhile cause."

I grinned. "You bet. He's got a great ass."

Paul snorted and motioned to the door. "If you're done lusting after my friends, perhaps we can go."

I was glad to be back to our usual banter. I'd been concerned my not wanting to talk last night had messed stuff up between us, but he seemed willing to let it go until a better time.

"Sure thing. Let's go spring a too-obvious trap."

He opened the door and glanced outside before motioning me on, handing me his keys as I passed him. I hurried to his car, trying to look in every direction at once. Sure, I trusted Paul's senses, but it's just not easy going out when you know someone's gunning for you. Or maybe it's "fanging" under the circumstances, but that doesn't flow as well off the tongue.

I unlocked the Prius and grabbed the blanket from the back. Paul used it to get to the car without blowing up, and we started for The Meeting Place.

We pulled up just as the sun dipped below the horizon. It surprised me how easily I was adapting to his schedule. He was definitely getting too far into me, my thoughts and my feelings. I shook myself. Wrong time to worry about that.

"What?" Paul said, coming out from under his blanket.

"Nothing. Just a sudden chill."

"Do you sense something?" His eyes were intense, his voice concerned.

Oops. I hadn't meant to hint that my divinations might have revealed something.

"No, sorry. Just a stray thought. Nothing to worry about."

"If you're sure—"

I took the keys from the ignition and handed them to him. "No, really. Nothing. I mean, we're about to walk into a trap, but other than that, everything's peachy."

He chuckled. "All right then. Let me get out first. I'll signal when I think it's safe."

I nodded, glancing around the street myself. Nothing drew my attention. Well, nothing other than the woman biking down the street towards us. Not an ounce of body fat, multiple piercings and horrible color sense. Tight, purple lycra pants coupled with a neon green wife beater (do they even make them in that color?) is hard to pull off no matter what your body type. Well, that's Dupont Circle for you.

Paul must have noticed my gaze because he grinned at me through the window. I rolled my eyes back at him, and he resumed his scan of the area.

My turn. He's not the only one who can look for danger. I shifted my vision and opened myself up to the riot of auras surrounding us. Mostly the usual. Love, anxiety, jealousy, happiness. A hint of anger in the woman marching down the street, speaking intently into her cell phone. Wait. Stop. Arousal. Two attractive young men hanging off each other, on the verge of a public kiss. Okay, that was fun for a moment. Back to business.

I finished my scan at the same moment Paul signaled me. One quick look back at the two men. Hmm. Nice kiss. Paul tapped the window. Busted!

I shifted my vision back to normal and climbed out of the car. "Anything noteworthy?"

He shook his head, glancing down the street one more time. "No." He shot me a look. "Beyond the obvious." A slight smile danced at the corner of his mouth.

"You should have seen it in aura sight." Amazingly, I kept my tone even and slightly dry.

He held up one finger. Touche!

I grinned and stepped in behind him as he started for the bar. A bit of humor to ease the mood was good, but now it was time to concentrate.

We entered, and I glanced around. It was pretty

much as I'd heard it described. A bit dingy with concrete floors and beat-up tables. Karaoke equipment was set up near one end, and I hoped we'd be long gone before any of that started up. No, not a fan. Thank you for asking.

Paul stopped just inside the door. His eyes were alert. I suspected he was seeing far more than the sad decor. His nostrils flared. It always kind of creeped me out when I remembered he learned almost as much about the world around him through his nose as his eyes. I'm just as glad most of the time to have a human nose. How he can stand some of the smells is beyond me. Or is he like a dog and does really stinky stuff smell good to him?

"He's been here, but I can't sense him now. And no, I find most of the same odors offensive that you do."

My head shot around. "How'd—"

He shrugged. "You always give me a funny look when I sniff the air, and I figured it's the question I'd ask me if I were you."

I scowled at him but said, "Right. Okay, about Malachai. You say he's been here?"

"Definitely."

A host wandered over right then and asked if we wanted a seat. Paul nodded, and the host grabbed some menus and showed us to a table. I glanced over the offerings and decided to just order iced tea. Most of the menu didn't appeal.

Paul didn't even glance at the menu, his eyes moving over the room. "Can you take a look and see what you see?"

I knew what he meant and shifted my vision. Like before, not much to remark on, until my gaze ran over the bar. I hissed.

"What?" Paul's hand touched my shoulder.

I covered his with mine and squeezed briefly. "It's okay. Well, not really, but it's not like we're in immediate danger."

"Want to be more specific?"

I examined the aura again. The bartender's aura had orange in it. Lots of orange. His eyes briefly met mine, and he smiled, a thin expression that didn't reach his eyes. Under aura sight, it was particularly unpleasant, and I shuddered. I thought I understood what a mouse must feel, right before the hawk struck.

"I think we're about to have company." I nodded toward the bartender, who finished filling an order and started toward us.

Paul's eyes narrowed. "Orange?"

"Oh yeah."

The man was almost to our table.

"Let me handle this," Paul said.

"All yours."

A thrill ran through me. Paul and I were a team again. We'd been ... well ... sort of off-kilter for a day or two, but we were back, and it felt good.

The man was still smiling as he approached, but his lips were pressed together, and there was nothing of humor in the expression. The hair on the back of my neck rose, and I caught myself fingering the potion bottle through the cloth of my fanny pack. The orange in his aura swirled into a sickly red.

Paul glanced at me, and I nodded fractionally, hoping he got the message that this guy was dangerous and that I'd back whatever move Paul wanted to make.

"Paul, I presume," the man said.

Paul nodded.

"I have a message for you."

"So I gathered."

I remained alert, watching for shifts in his aura. As he spoke, the orange became more prominent. I wondered if Malachai was somehow influencing him at a distance. If so, that level of power and ability terrified me.

The bartender turned to me. The smile broadened. His eyebrows, which had been even when he spoke to Paul, lifted, giving him a coldly whimsical look. I suppressed the shiver.

"And this must be the boy toy with the funny name. I've heard about you. About how ... easy ... you were to control."

Paul stiffened beside me, but I managed to remain calm and relaxed. "Sticks and stones and all that. I'm the one who broke it in the end."

"Not without help."

I shrugged, making the gesture as insolent as possible. "With the figuring out of the spell, yes. But the breaking?" I allowed a slow grin to cross my face. "That was child's play to break. I would have thought your … Master … could do better than that."

I didn't need to look at Paul to feel his approval washing over me. I was starting to make a habit of baiting big, bad vampires. Still not sure if that was a good or bad thing.

His expression faltered just slightly as his eyes shot to the floor and then back to look at me directly. I was on guard for tricks, and Malachai didn't disappoint me. Some sort of power crackled between us, but with my aura sight active, I saw it coming and turned to Paul.

"Incoming."

One second Paul was sitting beside me. The next he had the bartender in a headlock, with his eyes turned away from me. Several patrons and waiters started toward us, but a growl from the vampire gave them second thoughts.

"We don't have long," I said quietly.

"I know." Paul dragged the bartender's head around to face him. "Give me the message before I kill the messenger."

The other man suddenly relaxed, and I felt the power fade. The black which had invaded his aura dissipated, to be replaced by the familiar orange. I nodded in satisfaction. "You can let him go now, Paul. He's stopped whatever he was trying."

Paul let go, wiping his palms on his trouser legs. "The message."

The bartender smiled again, eyes wide and guileless. "Oh, it's simple. Come back to me or they all die. Every one of them." His eyes darted to me. "Ending with this one. I'll especially enjoy breaking and then turning him."

Paul growled deep in his throat. I put my hand on his arm. "I think you'll find me more difficult prey than Nicola."

He laughed abruptly. "But of course." His voice hardened with grim humor. "That's why I found it so easy to take control of you earlier."

I smiled, knowing it wasn't pretty and not caring. "You'll have to do better than that. I'm ready for that one."

Out of the corner of my eye, I noticed patrons hastily leaving the restaurant. Magical show downs weren't good for business apparently.

"Oh, you mean that pathetic candle you have burning to 'protect' you. Good luck with that one."

I didn't let my smile falter. "That's the one you know about." Okay, I didn't really have any other protections up, but no reason to let him know that.

His expression faltered again, and his eyes turned to Paul. "You're drawing attention to yourself. I suggest you leave before someone calls the quaint excuse this town has for law enforcement. No challenge in coming to get you if you're behind bars. I'd rather you had room to run."

Paul glanced around and obviously noticed the hasty retreat that had gone on around us.

"This isn't over, Malachai."

"Of course not. I've still got lots of playing to do." The bartender tipped an imaginary hat. "This has been fun. Until next time."

Suddenly the bartender collapsed to the ground, a discarded plaything tossed by the side of the road.

"I think that's our clue to make tracks."

"Agreed," Paul said as he took my arm and guided me to the door.

We didn't exactly run for the car, not wanting to draw more attention to ourselves, but we didn't waste any time either.

"Well, that was interesting," I said as I got into the car. Paul pulled away from the curb as soon as my door was closed. "You know. Projected memory didn't do his creepiness justice."

Paul gave me a small smile. "I believe I did say he was crazy."

I nodded. "Yes, you did, with your usual penchant for understatement. He's not just crazy. He's completely bug-fuck mental. And how did he do that 'talk through someone else' trick? That's got to be a vampire thing. I've never heard of a warlock doing it."

Paul shot me a frown. "Really? I always thought it was a warlock thing. I don't know of any other vampires who can do it. I'd only seen him do it one other time." He shuddered, and I didn't ask.

I pondered. Could I think of a way to do it? Unfortunately, the more I thought about it, I could. Paul gave me time to work it through, and I finally figured it.

He must have noticed the look on my face because he said, "It is a warlock thing, then."

"I think so. Well, in part. I bet he needs your vampire mind whammy thing to really pull it off. And maybe the vampire/human bond you've described. I don't think much about mind magic since it's black, but I kind of put together what I know about memory projection and what you've told me about vampires and their human bonds, and yeah, I think I can see how to do it." I shook my head. "But if it's all the same to you, I think I'd rather not go into details."

"Fine by me." His expression was grave. "Can you block it?"

I'd kind of guessed that would be where he'd go next, and I'd already worked that out too. "I think so, but it's not something I can do on the fly. I'd have to prepare in advance."

Paul's fingers had been tapping the steering wheel as he drove. Suddenly they stopped.

"What?"

"You said you put together what you know about memory projection. Does that mean Malachai can do what you do?"

An excellent question, but I didn't think so, and I told him as much. "Oh, he probably can do a basic memory projection, like I did with you to see your past. But that doesn't mean he can do it on the fly like I can. It's likely that he needs a circle, ritual and the whole nine yards."

"Are you sure?"

I frowned at him. "Are you saying you've seen him do it before?"

"No. You were the first time I'd seen that."

I relaxed muscles I hadn't realized had tensed up. "That should be okay then. You know how I said that warlocks generally have a talent, at least the good ones do. Something they can do fast where others would need to do it the slow way?"

"Yes. I think I remember that."

Think, hell! So far I've never caught Paul forgetting anything, but I let it go. "Okay, projection's my thing. It's not completely impossible for two warlocks to have the same talent, but I think the odds are against it here. Some sort of mind control is probably his talent. When I said I used what I knew of memory projection, I was figuring out how *I'd* do it. Which doesn't mean it's exactly how he'd do it."

Paul's fingers resumed their tapping. "All right. That's good. I've enough to worry about in a fight with him. I'm just as glad not to have to add something else."

I realized just then that he was driving to his house, and I cocked an eyebrow at him. "I know you'd said we should stay together until this is all over, but don't you think this is just asking for trouble? Maybe staying in a hotel would be less like putting out a target?"

"My place is safer."

He said it with such finality I didn't feel like arguing with him. A few minutes later, we pulled up outside his house, and Paul opened his car door to do his now-familiar scan of our surroundings. I did the same with my aura sight from inside the Prius. "Looks clear from my end."

"And from mine as well, but don't dawdle."

I got out and followed him. "Dawdle? Really? I thought only my mom said that."

"It's a perfectly good word," he said over his shoulder as he opened his door.

"Yeah, if you're as old as the hills."

"Well, I am pretty old, as you well know."

"True." Just to be safe, I glanced around his interior with aura sight. No spells that I could see. He waited, probably figuring out what I was doing.

"All clear?"

"Yeah." I flopped down on his couch while he went to the kitchen, probably to get some blood.

"By the way, before you say you're going to leave me behind when you go up against Malachai, just forget about it."

He wandered back, bag of blood in one hand and a Coke in the other (when had he found time to restock with everything else going on?). He handed me the can, and I nodded my thanks before taking a cautious sip. Considering what he kept in his fridge, I figured it paid to be careful.

He didn't sit down, instead leaning against the door jamb. "I can't let you come. This is between him and me."

"Nope. This is between all of us." I frowned. "Does that work grammatically?"

"Not really. And no, I can't let you come."

I decided to let it go for now in favor of a more important question. "Confrontation? Where and when?"

Paul started to answer and then froze. His eyes went dead for a moment, and his body was completely still. Again, I was reminded that he had no need to breathe, so when he went still, it was startling.

The seconds passed, and I wasn't sure what to do. Then a series of emotions crossed his face, almost too quickly to track. Pain, anger and was that resignation?

His body relaxed, and life returned to his eyes, though they remained gray, no hint of blue visible.

"What just happened?"

"It will be tomorrow night." His voice was lifeless. "I'll know where at the time."

"But how?"

A bit of animation returned to his face, and his voice developed some tone and timbre. "I'm too old for him to control, but he still has enough of a hold to send a message."

That explained the resignation I'd seen in his face. I got off the couch and went to him. Hesitantly (I was never sure how he'd react to being touched), I put an arm around him. He didn't react, and I pulled him close, drawing his head down to my shoulder. With the other arm, I ran my hand up and down over his back.

He relaxed just enough to let me move his head, but the rest of his body remained rigid.

"It'll be all right. Okay, maybe he can send you a message. But he can't control you. Your mind and will are your own. If you let him get to you, he'll win. But you're better than that."

No response for a minute. I let my hand continue to roam over his back. Muscles relaxed minutely at my passage, and I figured I was doing him some kind of good.

Finally, he took a deep breath, lifted his head and pulled away, but not so far away that I couldn't keep my hand on his back.

"Thank you. You're correct. It was just … for a moment, the touch on my mind. It was familiar, horrible, and yet—"

Now he pulled away and stumbled across the room to the fireplace. He leaned heavily on the mantelpiece, face turned from me.

"And yet what?"

I took a step forward but respected his obvious need for some space.

He turned to look at me, his eyes lost. I'd seen him grieve, but I'd never seen quite that expression before, and it chilled me.

"And yet for a moment, though it was horrible, and I denied his touch, a part of me craved it. Still."

He looked on the verge of some kind of breakdown, but I smiled slightly. I knew I had the answer to this one. I shifted my vision and examined his aura closely.

Agitation? Yes. Fear? Oh yeah. And I'd never seen that before in his aura, so it was unsettling. Grief? Yep, that was still there. Plus a blue green tinge that made my heart pound and my stomach clench. Not unpleasantly. Put that aside for the moment. I looked again.

Nope, not a hint of what he feared.

My smile broadened, and I let my vision return to normal. Paul was frowning at me.

"What?"

"No orange. You're clear."

His shoulders relaxed. "You're certain?"

"Oh yeah. And nothing else to make me worry about him having a hold on you. Habit can be a powerful thing, and Malachai's counting on it. He sent you a bit of something to shake you up and make you doubt yourself, but it didn't stick."

Paul turned back to the fireplace, but not before I saw relief wash over his features.

"You're completely certain?"

My instincts guided me to him. I placed both my hands on his shoulders. "I'm completely certain. The only hold he has on you is the one you let him have. Continue to deny him, and he's got nothing. Your mind is your own."

"I want to believe you."

My hands tightened. "Believe me. I know what I saw."

"But he's fooled you before."

"True, but I didn't know what to look for back then. If someone had looked at my aura, it would have been obvious. But because I don't hang with other warlocks, he knew there was no one here to read me." A sudden thought. "Might be a good idea to change that."

"It might."

I pulled him close for a quick hug. "You're okay. But…"

He turned, eyebrow raising. "I'm not going to like this, am I?"

"Probably not."

"But what?"

"This is why you need me to come along."

He shook his head, and all the walls went back up. He pulled away from me and crossed back to the doorway. "Absolutely not. And that's not negotiable. You will stay someplace safe, so I don't have to worry and be distracted by your safety."

I can see when there's no point in continuing a conversation. Of course, I wasn't going to stay behind, and if he hadn't just been rattled by Malachai, he'd know it too. I'd be able to find him with ease. I've cleaned him up after enough fights to have swiped a couple of blood samples.

"All right then. It's your fight. I'll leave you to it."

He shot me a look filled with suspicion, but I gazed back at him levelly, enough anger and frustration in my eyes to convince him. It was damn tough to keep smug off my face, but I must have managed it because he turned to look out the window.

"That's that then. I'll take you home and call Runner to have one of his people keep an eye on your place." He turned, his expression stern. "And to keep you put. Don't think for a minute that I've forgotten you can find me."

"Never dream of it."

He snorted. I just smiled to myself. Runner would be a piece of cake. He'd see my side of it and probably could be convinced to give me a lift where ever it was that we needed to go.

"I've been meaning to brew some more potions, so if it's not too much trouble, you might want to stop by tomorrow evening and pick up a few."

Gratitude. And just the tiniest bit of shame. Yep. This would work nicely. I really should stop with the aggravating of vampires. It's not a good survival trait. But their stiff pride makes it so darned easy!

"Ready to go?"

I decided not to mention that ten minutes earlier he'd declared that his place was safer. This was not the time to argue. "Sure. I'm ready." I yawned. Not an act. I really was tired. "I can use some sleep."

He looked at me with suspicion, but I smiled blandly back at him, and he let it go. Pulling out his phone, he said, "Let me call Runner first, and we'll go."

"Sure thing."

I waited while he made the arrangements for my jailing ... I mean guarding, of course, and when he finished, he motioned me to the door.

Have I mentioned that I really hate it when he goes all "aloof creature of the night" on me?

Chapter 15

Thursday, May 6, 2010:
Just After Sunrise

PAUL TOOK ME home, and we saw one of Runner's people lurking around my apartment. Fine. I didn't mind the company.

I took the opportunity to get some sleep. We had a big night ahead of us, which was going to follow a long day brewing potions.

Like most of my magic, potion-making is more of an art than a science, although it looks more like science than most of what I do. I'd stocked up on materials before the trip to see the fairy ring. Wow! Was that really just a few days ago?

Anyway, while the extra magic of sunrise and sunset is helpful to rituals, I don't need it for potions, so I treated myself to sleeping in until almost nine o'clock. I kind of figured I deserved it by now.

After a quick breakfast, I got started.

If you've ever made tea, and I'm guessing most of you have, you've made a potion using the "infusion" method. Pretty simple, really. You assemble your herbs, boil some water, toss in the herbs and wait for them to steep. When they've steeped enough, you have your tea. It didn't have magical properties, unless you also happen to be a warlock, but the herbs probably had some specific property to be soothing, energizing, or the like. That's a basic potion, and I use that method for quick and dirty stuff.

But infusions make fairly weak potions, so most of the time I use the "decoction" method. That's where you add your ingredients to cool water, bring the whole thing to a boil and wait until about two thirds of the water is gone. Then you strain the whole mess. That makes a much stronger concoction and is what I use for most of my utility potions.

So what's the difference between you making tea and me making a potion? Well, same as the difference between a non-talented wiccan ritual and one of mine. Magic. Real magic.

I let the ferrets run around for this. They don't mess up the energies for potion making, and they'd been cooped up for too long. Tossing a couple of raisins in the living room bought me enough time to get my materials ready. I didn't have time to make a lot of potions, but I needed something for tonight. I'd already given Paul a strength enhancing potion, and he hadn't needed to use it. I sent him a quick text.

> Don't forget the potion I gave you last night. I'm making another special one for you, and I won't have time to make a strength one too.

I didn't get a response back, and I hadn't expected one. Paul was most likely sleeping, or doing whatever it is that vampires do in lieu of sleep. I'd never actually asked him about that. But I knew he'd check his messages before going out, so I was sure he'd see it.

Tradition-minded warlocks and witches use cauldrons, just like the one I use for my rituals. But I'm lazy, and I like my potions to be easy to pour into sports bottles (also definitely a modern warlock thing), so I use a big cast-iron tea kettle. It's a pain to keep seasoned and clean between each use, but I've made this little mesh thing that fits in the spout part, so I can strain and pour in one go. Easy and neat!

So, just like in a ritual, I needed my ingredients. The first potion I wanted to make was a reflex enhancing one for me. I already had a sense enhancer, so I didn't need another one of those.

Okay, so if you are an expert of herbs, you're going to question this one, but trust me, it works. Also, remember what I said about mostly using decoctions? Well, this one works best as an infusion.

I mixed an assortment of buchu, echinacea root and horehound, until I had the right balance. How could I tell? By smell. Once you've got the hang of rituals and potion making, you can kind of tell if something's right by the odor. This one needs to smell sharp, and I tossed things together until it smelled right.

When I started making potions, I was all about the measurements. I thought everything had to be just right, but the more precisely I measured, the less well it worked. Then one day I was in the kitchen watching my mom cook spaghetti sauce. She grabbed bottles of spices and just shook them into the pot. She didn't measure a thing. I asked her how she knew it was right, and she shrugged and said she just did. When it smelled right, she stopped.

Mom's an awesome cook. And you know, I realized then that nothing she made ever tasted quite the same way each time, but it was always perfect. I think she actually has a bit of magic in her. She just uses it in cooking instead of for spells.

Once I saw her cook, I knew what I'd been doing wrong with potions, and I threw away all my measuring cups, spoons and the like and mixed them by feel and smell.

By the way, my dad knew all the time that I'd been doing it wrong, but he wanted me to figure it out on my own, and he was right. I'd never have believed him if he'd told me. I was stubborn that way. Still am, I guess.

Anyway, making potions always makes me think of Mom.

I dumped the herbal mixture in a measuring cup (okay, yeah, I still use them sometimes). The water had been boiling in my kettle, and I poured about a cup of water over the herbs. This one needs to infuse for about five minutes before it's ready to be activated magically, so I set a timer and dumped the boiling water out of the kettle to get it ready for the next potion, which was to be a decoction.

Remember how I said I was lazy? If you do potions in the right order, you can minimize clean-up time.

Infusions don't make a mess in my kettle, so they're the ones to do first. It's all about planning ahead.

I carefully cleaned out the kettle. Sure, it wasn't that dirty, having just had boiling water in it, but purification is an important part of magic, and I don't skip that step unless I have a reason to be in a hurry.

By the time the kettle was clean, my timer was going off, and it was time to enchant the potion. At that moment, it was no more than a funny smelling (and kind of nasty tasting) tea. It'd make you gag, but it wouldn't do a thing for your reflexes. That's where the magic came in. The herbs set the stage. Use the correct herbs, and the energies come into alignment, making the enchantment a breeze.

I've heard of witches who can enchant just about anything, regardless of magical property, but I'm not that good. If I tried to enchant, say horseradish (good for exorcism), in my reflex potion, it wouldn't work. I might be able to get rid of a magical influence really quickly, but that's not what I was going for.

So I make sure to use ingredients with the right properties. What are the properties of buchu, echinacea and horehound, you ask? Well, it's simple. Buchu is used to enhance psychic powers and to foretell the future. Okay, you might be thinking that reflexes aren't foretelling the future, but really, what's acting quickly except, in some way, being able to anticipate what's coming and react appropriately? Makes sense when I put it that way, doesn't it?

An infusion of horehound clears your mind and

promotes quick thinking. Couple that with the ability to foretell the future, and you're going to react wicked fast.

What about the echinacea? You might think of it as something to take to fend off a cold, but magically, it just strengthens spells and generally makes things work better. I use it in a lot my potions for that, and who knows? Maybe it's why I don't get sick often.

I took a sip of the tea. Yep, tasted pretty bad, but the tingle on my tongue told me the mixture was just right and ready to be enchanted. If you were hoping for a lot of chanting and waving about of incense at this point, I'll have to disappoint you. I just focused my will, visualized the exact effect I wanted and sent my magical energy into the potion.

Presto! Done. I added a bit of hazelnut syrup (for taste) and poured the completed potion into a sports bottle. Grabbing a black Sharpie, I labeled the bottle and put it aside.

Note for you budding potion brewers. Always. Always label them. It's not cool to be in the middle of a fight, grab what you think is a strength enhancer and discover you've accidentally swilled a lust enhancer.

Why no. I've never done that. What made you think I had?

Now to the new potion for Paul. I'd never made this one before, but I'd been pondering it ever since I'd learned about Malachai and his ability to influence minds. Dad had told me it was possible to create potions to could counteract mental influence, but I'd never had need to brew one. I had a pretty good idea of where to start, though, and I assembled the ingredients.

This one needed to be a decoction, for the greater strength. I rummaged around in my herb cabinet until I found alyssum and agrimony. I also pulled out a package of dried huckleberries. Huckleberries are tasty, by the way, and I absently munched a few while I tried to decide on roughly the correct proportions. In addition to tasting good, they are also one of the best hex-breakers I know of, and as such, made the ideal base for a protective potion. I could probably have gotten away with a pure huckleberry decoction. The berries are that good.

But I didn't want to take any chances. Hence the alyssum, an all-purpose protective herb which can also dispel glamours and veils. One usually fashions alyssum into an amulet, not a potion, but I've used alyssum this way before. (It's not just good for dispelling glamours. It can also banish charms, and I've found it terribly useful before meeting with people I thought might con me.) I wasn't exactly sure how Malachai did his mental whammy, but I figured protecting Paul against a glamour couldn't hurt.

And then for my final ingredient. Agrimony is another hex-breaker. Not as good, in my experience, as huckleberries, but agrimony has another useful property. It can bounce a hex back to the caster. I didn't know if it would work on a vampire, and I wasn't sure how much use Paul could make of it, but even if it did no more than distract Malachai, that could give a key second or two in a pinch.

Because my dad didn't raise a fool, I planned to make two of these. My protection candle was effective at a distance, and it might protect me at close range, but I didn't want to take the chance. The second I thought Malachai was nearby, I planned to take this one.

Unlike enhancement potions, protective potions last a while, upward of 20 to 30 minutes if I brewed them strong enough.

I finally decided that four huckleberries and roughly a teaspoon of alyssum and about half that of agrimony would be right, per potion. I tossed two potions worth of ingredients into my cauldron and took a sniff. Nope, not quite right. Too bitter. Another pinch of agrimony and an extra huckleberry made it perfect. I could feel the energies snap into place, and I knew this one would work. Perhaps not exactly as I planned, but it would be effective.

I added enough water to fill the cauldron and set it to boil, figuring it would take at least an hour to make a strong decoction.

I'd planned to spend the time going over "battle kit," but my phone rang when I was half-way to my bedroom. I glanced at the display and saw that it was Laura. Damn! I was supposed to call her back.

"Laura. Sorry. Got busy."

"Everything okay?"

I sighed. "Not really." And I filled her in on the latest.

When I finished, she said, "So of course you're going to ignore him and tag along anyway."

She knew me too well. "Of course. And not because of any macho crap either."

I heard her laughter on the line. "Of course not. It's how you are. And—" He voice trailed off before she finally said, "... And you've figured out he's important to you."

What could I say? "Yeah."

"Good for you." I could hear the pride and satisfaction in her tone.

"Gotta get through this first, though."

"Yeah."

I was about to say goodbye and get back to my preparations when I remembered that she'd called me. "So I'm guessing you didn't call to ask about my love life."

"Nope." Her tone was merry but changed quickly at her next words. "I tracked down that stuff you'd asked about."

"You mean how far vampires have infiltrated the police?"

"Yes."

I sensed I wasn't going to like what she found. "And?"

"A long way, Dafydd. Oh, they are doing their job. Well, as well as the D.C. police ever do, but the vampires are pretty deep inside."

"You mean actual vampires on the force?"

She laughed. "No, there's no Nick Knight, vampire

cop, working there."

I grinned at the reference to a favorite show. Laura and I had binge-watched the entire series on Netflix one weekend.

She continued. "But I was able to track down cases that went cold and other signs that the vampires are able to get away with just about anything they need."

Great. Another thing to deal with one day.

"Thanks. Not sure right now what I'll do about it. Or if I can do anything, but at least I know."

"Anytime. And, Dafydd—"

"Yeah, I know. I'll be careful. Call you when it's all over?"

"You'd better!"

I laughed and hung up. I itched to do something about this latest revelation, but now really wasn't the time. Right now I had a badass vampire to deal with, and I wanted to be sure I was prepared.

Before I met Paul, most of my magical efforts had been in the area of divinations and the occasional exorcism. Of course, there had been that minor demon who'd gotten away from a particularly stupid coven of Satanists. They'd thought the spell was just a joke, and it would have been if they hadn't performed it on Mabon (autumnal equinox to you non-pagans). Remember how I've said certain times of the month or year have power? At those times even non-talented practitioners can create real effects. So don't use that Ouija Board on a solstice or equinox, and, just to be safe, avoid full moons as well.

Fortunately the demon had been more in mind to make mischief than mayhem, and I was able to distract it by throwing sunflower seeds in its path. Minor demons have this weird compulsion to collect and count small items, and it's useful for buying some time to whip up a quick and dirty exorcism. Wheat grains would have been better (smaller), but sunflower seeds were what I had in my pocket at the time. I generally carry a small kit of seeds and exorcism herbs around during potent times of the month and year. Just in case.

Anyway, once I met Paul, I discovered a need to be a bit more offensive in my repertoire, and I developed a kit of useful items, which I carry around in an over-size fanny pack. The contents go something like this:

1. Potions (in the water bottle pockets)

2. Mace container. I use the industrial strength kind that combines pepper spray and a dye. If the pepper spray doesn't work (and Paul tells me it doesn't work on vampires), being covered in blue dye might embarrass Malachai enough to put him off his game. Actually, I was planning to use the mace on any human flunkies. I also learned earlier this year that it's effective against werewolves.

3. Whistle. Useful for calling for help.

4. An assortment of healing herbs for quick first aid, along with bandages and antiseptic cream. I added baby wipes after the last time I had to clean caustic demon gunk off of Paul. He wasn't really happy about it, but he put up with it well.

5. Holy water. Good against demons and vampires.

And that was where I hit a snag. I was down to just one vial. Paul and I had tracked down and banished a small shuggoleth demon about two weeks ago. Same variety as the one we'd fought near the Washington Monument a while back but only a quarter the size. I'd used the holy water to keep it at bay while Paul wrapped it up in a big sheet. Then he was able to hold it while I worked the exorcism. It's always neater to banish rather than kill them and generally keeps one on better terms with the denizens of the lower planes.

Unfortunately, I'd used almost all of my holy water, and I'd forgotten to restock.

Bad timing. I really didn't want to go into a fight with a vampire without it. I knew it worked because I'd accidentally splashed a bit on Paul during the fight with the shuggoleth, and it had burned a neat dime-sized hole in his arm. As with the baby wipes, he was pretty stoic about it.

Paul would pitch a fit if he found out I'd gone out. So, I'd just have to make sure he didn't find out. I walked to my front door, opened it and glanced around. My aura sight was active. I'm not stupid. Reckless maybe, but not stupid.

Someone I recognized stepped around the corner. "Hey, Mack!"

He was one of the werewolves I'd fought with during the business with Jimmy, the werewolf puppy, whom he'd adopted. "How's Jimmy?"

Mack smiled. "He's good. Growing like crazy. You'd hardly recognize him now."

"Bring him over sometime."

"I will." His expression grew stern. "You know you're not supposed to be out here."

I nodded, trying to keep my expression the very picture of obedience.

Obviously, I failed because Mack added, "And don't think you're fooling me with that look."

I gave up the weak attempt at subterfuge. "All right. Here's the deal. You and I both know I'm going to fight with Paul tonight. I bet Runner's on the night shift, right?"

He chuckled, the sound deep in his chest. "Yeah. He made a point of it, in fact."

"Right. Which means he knows what I'm planning, and he's going to back me up."

"Probably," Mack said agreeably.

"Well, then, I need to be prepared, and I'm almost out of holy water. If you could accompany me to St Patrick's, I'd be most grateful. Quick trip there and back again, and I'll stay inside until Runner's shift. I promise."

He grinned and took out his phone. "Let me check in, just so my ass is covered."

I waved him on.

He made a call. "Yeah, the kid's going tonight. Good thing I didn't take that bet."

I hid a smile at that.

The werewolf continued. "He says he needs more holy water."

A pause as Mack looked at me. "Can one of the

pack pick it up for you?"

I shook my head. "If I sent a note, Father Eyler would probably let you have it, but I need to ask him something."

He nodded and went back to the phone. "No dice, man."

Another pause, and then Mack said, "Right," and hung up. He motioned to me. "Runner says okay, as long as we make it quick."

We both glanced up at the sky. The sun was still high. Should be perfectly safe. Assuming Malachai didn't have minions out looking for me.

"Let me get a couple things. I'll be just a minute."

"Fine by me. I'll take a stroll around the block and make sure no one's around who shouldn't be."

I dashed back into my apartment and grabbed my bag. Mace might not work against vampires, but it was fine versus minions. Between it, my illusions and Mack, we'd be fine. It wasn't far.

Mack was waiting for me when I got back out and locked my door. "Anything?" I asked him.

He shook his head. "All clear for now. No one saw anything last night either." He cocked his head at me. "This vampire's a pretty mean critter, Runner tells us."

We started walking. St. Patrick's almost a mile away and it would have made sense to take Metro, but just then I felt safer on the street. Better sight lines. Both of us maintained a watch while we talked. My nerves felt tight, but it was good. I thought I'd sense it if anyone attacked.

"He is. He's the one who made Paul."

Mack frowned. "Vampires don't stay close with the ones who make them?"

I snorted. "Do infected werewolves?"

He grinned. "Okay, good point. Vampires are weird anyway."

I thought about "pot" and "kettle" but considering what I could do, it didn't seem appropriate.

The trip was uneventful, and just entering holy ground made me relax. Vampires are perfectly capable of entering churches and killing there, but there's just something about holy ground that makes you feel like nothing bad can ever happen there.

"Stay sharp," Mack said.

He was right. Safety was just as much an illusion here as anywhere else. I let my vision drift into aura sight, and I glanced around.

Places can have auras just like people, but most don't. Generally it takes strong emotion to leave an aura in a place. The more the emotion, the brighter the aura. That's why certain places feel safe or give you the creeps. Even though normal people can't see auras the way I can, they can still sense something, just at the edge of perception.

This was a good church. The members defended Mary Surratt, a parish member who was convicted of aiding Lincoln's assassination. They opened their doors to soldiers during the riots following another assassination, that of Martin Luther King, Jr. You could still see echoes of those events in the mingling of red and deep blue that surrounded the church and its grounds. Plenty of yellow to show its connection to the community as well.

Nothing disturbed the usual colors. Oh, there was a bit of dark green hovering near the confessionals, and I guessed someone had just been seeking advice about a relationship, probably one involving adultery, but that wasn't any concern of mine. My relationship problems were tricky enough. I didn't need to involve myself in anyone else's.

Father Eyler approached as I finished my scan. He frowned. "Dafydd? Something wrong? You don't usually scan the church."

He's got a touch of power in him, not enough to be a full warlock but enough to tell when I'm using aura sight. Out of habit, I checked his. Plenty of deep blue for honor and purple for spirituality. Lots of yellow. Father Eyler was connected to his church and his flock.

His eyes darted to Mack. "And who is this?" He reached, as if by reflex, to the crucifix around his neck.

"It's okay," I said, wanting to reassure him. "This is Mack, and he's a friend."

He relaxed slightly, but his blue eyes didn't stop scanning the area around us. The father might be a priest, but he's also fit and keeps strong. Most people wouldn't mess with him, but I couldn't say his caution was misplaced this time.

"How about we go to your office?" I glanced over my shoulder to Mack. "You stay here?"

The werewolf looked like he was about to protest,

but he must have changed his mind because he asked, "Where's the office?"

I nodded to a small hallway leading off the transept. "Just over there. I'll be within earshot the entire time."

Father Eyler watched our exchange, alarm growing across his rugged face.

I took his arm and led him off. "Come on. Yes, there's trouble, but it shouldn't affect the church."

He allowed himself to be led. "And you'd tell me if it did?"

"Of course."

We entered his office, and I closed the door partway, far enough for privacy but not too far to block Mack's voice if he needed to attract our attention.

The priest sat at his desk, which was completely neat and organized, much like the man himself. Not a sheet of paper was out of place.

"What's going on?"

I sat in the chair for visitors. "The main reason I'm here is that I need more holy water."

He steepled his fingers. "What are you facing this time?"

"Vampires."

His eyes widened. "Not Paul?"

I shook my head. "No. His maker."

"I take it then that they are not close." Father Eyler had made a study of supernatural creatures, and he sometimes knew more about them than I did.

"Not hardly." I gave him the quick version of the story, including Stephen's betrayal, the murder of

Nicola and who she had been. He said nothing while I spoke, but I watched his eyes, and I knew he was taking it all in and drawing his own conclusions.

"I'm sorry to hear about the young man you had been dating. I know you had hoped that would go somewhere."

I blinked back sudden tears. Yeah, even though he had betrayed me, it still hurt to lose that relationship.

He continued, "But I think what you really wanted me to know is that Paul is also attracted to men."

I drew back in my chair. That was not the next thing I had expected him to say. "Uh, yeah. But that's not the most important thing here."

Father Eyler smiled, his eyes kind. "No, it's not. But it's the thing most on your mind, isn't it? That's really why you came. You could have sent your friend to pick up the holy water."

Damn. He was good. Some people think priests don't understand affairs of the heart, them being celibate and all. I don't know about most priests, but Father Eyler was sharp about just about anything involving people and emotions.

I slumped in my chair. "Yeah, I guess it was."

He looked at me over his hands, still in front of his face. "You know it doesn't mean anything to our friendship, correct? I've known what you are from the moment I met you. I may follow the laws of my church, but you're not an official member of my congregation."

Father Eyler had pegged me as gay from the start,

and he was right. I'd never noticed that it affected our relationship at all. But that was when I was in love with humans. A vampire, though?

He seemed to follow my thoughts. "Dafydd, I trust you and your instincts. Remember that ghost I wanted to exorcise, and you convinced me to wait, that you thought you knew how to help him move on?"

That had been an odd case. A parishioner's home had been haunted by a poltergeist. Usually you want to exorcise those bad boys right off, but something about this one had given me pause. I did some research and discovered the ghost was just a kid and still mourning the loss of a beloved puppy. The ferrets helped me with this one. I brought them to the house and let them make their usual mayhem. We heard the ghost start laughing, and then both of us felt him move on. Mission accomplished. I still get periodic care packages of raisins and other treats from the owners of the house.

"Yeah, I remember."

"Well, you were right, and I was wrong. You may be young, but after that I learned to listen to you. You've known Paul long enough to have a feel for him, and it's been obvious to me for months that you are strongly attracted to him. I'm not sure I'd ever precisely advise anyone to fall in love with a vampire, but I think you should trust your heart in this matter."

My shoulders relaxed, and I felt immediately better. I wasn't fooling myself about the potential difficulties in this, and I was aware that it was still awfully soon after Stephen, but, well—Yeah, I wanted it, and having Father Eyler's blessing (so to speak) on it, made it easier.

"Thanks."

He smiled. "Happy to help." Then his expression went grave. "But you indicated there's trouble. Anything I need to be concerned about?"

I shook my head. "I don't think so, well, other than the fact that I'm going to be facing a master vampire tonight. Mack and I were kind of on edge because we don't know if Malachai has human minions lurking in wait for us."

"Do you think it likely?"

Shrugging, I answered, "Really don't know enough yet about this dude to say, but I'm not underestimating him."

The corners of his mouth twitched. "I'm fairly certain that calling him a 'dude' isn't going to go over well."

I grinned back at him. "You know me. I deal with danger by laughing in its face and calling it names."

The padre rolled his eyes. "I suppose there are worse strategies. Just be careful."

"I will."

He stood up. "Now, about that holy water. I'd suggest several vials. You're unlikely to know exactly what you're facing until you get there." He gave me a sharp look. "I assume Paul told you to stay out of it, and you're planning to disobey him."

"Of course."

He grinned, the expression incongruous with his stark black outfit. "Good." The lines in his face sobered, and he added, "I think you're right, and that he'll need you. This is more than just facing a difficult foe. Paul is going to have to face his past here. And he'll need assistance with that."

The priest was right. I think I knew that on an instinctive level, but my conscious mind hadn't processed it yet. Paul was comfortable with who and what he was now. But my memory tap had told me he still had issues with what he had been and what his master had made him do. I'd need to be on my guard.

We went back to the nave. Mack's eyes showed his relief at seeing us alive and well. Father Eyler dipped out several vials of holy water. I carefully packed them in my bag and thanked him.

"Let me know how it all turns out."

"Of course. I'll try to stop by tomorrow or the next day."

We said our goodbyes, and Mack and I left for the trip back to my apartment.

Chapter 16

Thursday, May 6, 2010.
Late Afternoon

"GET WHAT YOU needed from him?" Mack asked as we walked back to my apartment.

I held up my pack with the holy water. "Yeah. You saw it."

"Didn't mean that. I meant the other thing you wanted to talk to him about."

I nodded, the motion slow. "Yeah, I did. It wasn't quite what I expected, but yes, everything's cool."

"Good." His head suddenly shot up, and his nostrils widened.

"What?" I shifted my vision. This was becoming a habit I could learn to live without.

Scanning my surroundings.

Green
Yellow
Deep blue
More green
Aquamarine
Shaded yellow and green
Purple

Orange!

"Mack! To your right."

As I spoke, I ducked down behind a car. A heart-beat later, a shot whizzed past me, close enough that I felt the heat on my face.

Another shot. Mack grunted, and I heard him stumble. Damn. I think he was hit. My fault. My fault. If I had only listened to Paul.

Enough, came the quiet voice in my head. The one that came out under stress. I took a deep breath. Right. Recrimination later. Action now.

I peeked out from behind the car, aura sight still active. Few auras. Most of the people on the street had done the sensible thing and ducked for cover as soon as they heard shots. Good. That bought me time.

I drew a potion out of my pack. I'd been saving it for this evening, but it wouldn't do me any good if I were dead. Checking the label (Reflex), I unscrewed the cap and downed it in one gulp.

Immediately, the world around me slowed, and I felt like I had plenty of time to analyze and react. It was illusory, of course. The effects would last no more than two minutes, but I intended to make the most of them.

I started the mental countdown.

120
119
118

There were three auras I needed to concern myself

with. Well, four if you counted Mack, who was lying down, groaning, behind a nearby car.

"You okay?" I asked, still scanning and planning.

113

112

111

"I'll live. There's three of them."

"I know." Based on information in their auras, I saw which one needed to be dealt with first.

"Are you able to fight at all?" I needed more information for the tactical situation.

"Yes."

105

104

103

"Good. Shift and take the guy on the left. I'll distract the one on the right to buy you time."

"What about the guy in the middle?"

I was surprised at how cold my voice sounded. "We'll just have to hope his aim is lousy."

98

97

96

"Right."

I heard flesh tear and fur grow, and I knew Mack had changed. Claws scrabbled on concrete, and it was time to go.

My mace container was in my right hand, but it wasn't important right now. Briefly I wished for a gun, but I didn't have time to think about it. I'd had my illusion ready before I'd moved. The guy on the right (red hair, orange, brick red and hunter green in his aura, jeans, t-shirt—totally ordinary) was crouched next to a huge plate glass window. I focused my talent and threw the memory of Runner in full leap, fangs bared.

He did what I expected. He turned to look, which bought me just enough time to scramble for the other side of the street.

A shot rang out. I felt no pain, so it must have missed.

77

76

75

A scream ripped from my left. Mack's work, I hoped.

I ducked behind a battered green Ford Focus. Why couldn't there be bigger, sturdier cars on the street?

Listening, I heard someone moving nearby. Behind the purple Chevy Malibu.

Colors threatened to overwhelm me, but I forced awareness down. Nothing mattered but my target.

Time slowed again.

69

68

67

Another scream. This one sounded canine. Coldly, I ignored it. Time to move.

I burst up from behind my car, mace canister extended. My target was right where I'd expected him to be. I blasted him full in the face. He screamed and fell, clawing at his face (blinding red of pain in his aura, overwhelming the orange).

One down.

Ducking down behind the Malibu, my eyes roamed over the scene. Mack growling over his target (black hair, shorts—in this weather?—red polo shirt, orange, blue and yellow in his aura—all the colors fading fast).

Two down.

59

58

57

The third man stood up from behind a white Nissan X-Terra. Finally, a decent sized vehicle. Too bad I wasn't the one behind it.

His gun extended, he carefully took aim at Mack, who was still growling over his target, oblivious.

54

53

52

Windows? Glass? Water on the road? Anything reflective?

There! An approaching white panel van, the driver obviously not aware of what he was driving into.

Wait for it.

50

49

48

The man still hadn't fired. Mack was moving, not presenting a good target. Keep it up! I needed just two more seconds.

45

44

Now!

I cast my illusion while I ran, hoping I could get it off in the right place. Magic wasn't intended to work this way.

A police officer, riot gun extended.

The man turned away from Mack, and I ran faster, head and shoulders down. Tackling him with my head in his stomach, we both went down.

He struggled to raise his gun. I went for his throat with fingers and teeth, all I had since I'd dropped my mace container in my charge.

We rolled, over and over, into the street. Praying for no more cars, I bit him in the shoulder while clawing at his eyes.

(More red—loud—stabbing all my senses.)

He screamed and dropped the gun.

Blood in my mouth. Horrible!

I scrambled to my feet, kicked him solidly in the kidney and ran like hell.

(Explosion of red. Orange snapping back.)

Mack caught up with me a block later, limping heavily but still moving faster on four feet than I could on two.

15
14
13

And we were gone.

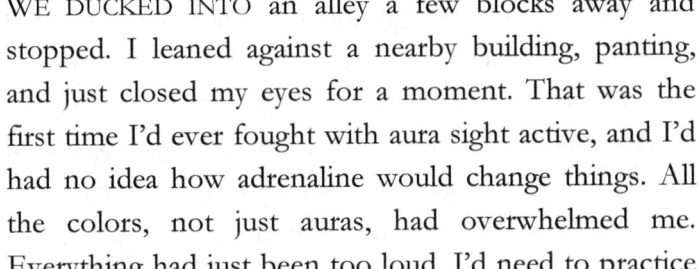

WE DUCKED INTO an alley a few blocks away and stopped. I leaned against a nearby building, panting, and just closed my eyes for a moment. That was the first time I'd ever fought with aura sight active, and I'd had no idea how adrenaline would change things. All the colors, not just auras, had overwhelmed me. Everything had just been too loud. I'd need to practice because it was a useful tool.

I opened my eyes and looked at Mack, still in wolf form next to me. "You okay?"

All right. It was kind of a dumb question. Blood streamed from a bullet hole in his side, but he nodded anyway. Lycanthropes were tough like that.

I pulled out my cell phone and called Runner. I figured he'd be pissed, and I wasn't wrong, but he said he'd meet us at my apartment.

"Can you make it that far?" I asked Mack.

He nodded again. The heaving in his sides was slowing.

I pulled out some of my first aid stuff and patched him up as best I could. He gave me a canine grin of thanks, and we started back to my apartment.

You'd think that walking down Connecticut Avenue in the middle of the day with a huge wolf would attract more attention. Sure, some people gave me odd looks, and one lady yelled something about "leash laws" at me, but no one stopped us or even seemed terribly concerned. It's amazing what people will do to avoid seeing the supernatural around them.

We made it back to my apartment with no further incidents, other than frightening the piss out of a couple of lap dogs. I've never liked lap dogs, so that didn't worry me too much.

Runner met us at the door, a grocery bag full of clothes in his hands. "Inside. Both of you." He snapped off his words, and I found myself obeying.

We got inside. Mack collapsed on the floor and changed back to human. Runner was intimidating enough that I didn't remember to sneak a peek at the naked werewolf.

The pack leader tossed over the bag of clothes, and Mack pulled out jeans and a shirt, slowly and with obvious discomfort.

"Let me check your wound," I said, moving over to him.

He shook his head. "I'll be fine. It's already healing."

Runner stood nearby, arms folded tight across his chest, foot tapping in what I recognized as the beat to "Another One Bites the Dust." I stifled a chuckle.

When he didn't add to the conversation, I pushed Mack onto the chair. It's seen worse than werewolf blood. "I don't think the bullet went through. I'm guessing you don't want to heal with it inside you."

He glanced at Runner, who nodded, once. "All right then." Mack wiggled around in the chair to finish pulling on his jeans, but he remained bare-chested.

A very nice chest, if you don't mind me mentioning it. Werewolves stay in good shape.

As I said, I've developed some experience over the past year with patching up Paul, and that's included digging out a couple of bullets. No one would hire me to work in an Emergency Room, but it works, especially since supernatural creatures heal up faster than humans.

He winced a couple of times at my clumsiness but remained silent. When I finished, he took a look at my work and nodded. "That's better."

I bandaged the wound and sat back on my heels, looking up at Runner. "Okay. Have at us."

The lead werewolf shook his head. "No. I knew you were going. I could have said something then." He snorted. "Unlike your blood-sucking boyfriend, I don't see much need to wrap you up in cotton wool."

"He's not my boyfriend," I said automatically.

He just gave me a look that said "you're not fooling

anyone, so stop trying," and I shrugged.

"Well not officially anyway." A moment later, I added, "And thanks. I know I'll hear from him later. Nice to not have to sit through it twice."

I stood up and went to the kitchen. "Coffee anyone?"

Both werewolves said "Yes," and I started brewing enough for all of us.

"What happened?" Runner asked when I returned to the living room.

"Human minions," I said. "Mack spotted them before they could act. I don't think they were expecting that. Malachai must not properly appreciate werewolf senses."

"Good thing that."

I nodded. "Yeah. Too bad I can't take a couple of you along this evening."

Runner cocked his head. "Why not? We'd be willing to help."

"I know you would, but it's going to be tough enough to get Paul to accept my help. He'd never go for you guys too."

Runner growled, low in his throat. "That's what he thinks. At the very least, I plan to be there."

I shook my head. "No. Get me to the rendezvous point definitely, but then leave it to the two of us."

Both Mack and Runner shouted "Why?" at the same time. I had to cover my ears.

"Hey, calm down," I said, putting out my hands to stop them. "I'm not being stupidly overconfident or anything. I actually have a good reason."

"Out with it, warlock," Runner said, a snarl in his voice.

I kept my tone even. "Warlock is why. Malachai can do more than a typical vampire mind whammy thing. He's got magical power backing him up. Now I've got a potion that should protect Paul, and I've got ways of protecting myself. If we had a couple of days, I'd brew up potions for all of you as well, but we don't have time."

I pulled out my phone and glanced at the time. "I have barely enough time to brew another reflex potion. I can't manage anything else."

Runner's shoulders relaxed, and Mack slumped in my chair. They glanced at each other, and I'm not sure what passed between them. Finally, Runner said, "All right. I don't like it, but I see your point. We've got no innate protections against vampire mind control." He paused and took a deep breath before continuing. "Odds are he could turn us against you, and that would just make things worse."

I nodded. "Exactly."

"Still don't like it," Mack said.

"Like I'm happy about it?" I said.

Runner shook his head at Mack. "No, he's right. We need to stay out of it."

I had an idea. "Yes, but that doesn't mean we can't use your help."

Both of them straightened. "How?" Runner asked.

"Well," I said, drawing the word out to buy me a

bit of time to put the idea together. "My guess is that Malachai isn't the 'fair fight' kind of guy."

Mack snorted. "Vampires rarely are."

I grinned at him. "Hey, Paul does okay."

"Most of the time," Runner added, but he was smiling to take the heat out of it.

"Right," I said. "So, if I were Malachai and could make mind-controlled puppets, I'd keep some of them off stage, ready to spring an ambush at the worst possible time."

Runner nodded. "So you want us to patrol the fringes and take them down first."

"Yep. Then all we have to worry about are the ones we can see. Not having to watch our backs will be a big help. Think you can do that without Malachai knowing you're there?"

They both nodded. "Werewolves stalk better than vampires," Mack said, his tone confident.

Runner's nod was less certain. "But won't he know when his puppets are dispatched?"

I grinned a wicked grin. "Oh, I'm counting on it. All that power snapping back at him will be a terrible distraction."

Both werewolves grinned at that. Mack turned to Runner. "Nice having a warlock about the place, isn't it?"

I smiled at the approval in his voice. Good thing the werewolves approved of me. I wasn't so sure Paul would still be speaking to me after this evening, and it was nice to have supernatural muscle to call on when I needed it.

Runner must have seen something on my face because he said, "Oh, he'll be pissed, but he'll get over it. He's not letting you go anytime soon."

I shook my head. "After losing Nicola, I'm not sure he's going to be in a forgiving mood."

He walked over to me and put a heavy hand on my shoulder. "After losing Nicola, he's not going to chance losing you too."

I accepted the comfort gratefully. Following Paul was the right thing to do. No question. But would he see it that way? I could only hope so. After he'd had a chance to calm down.

"Anyway," Runner said, his voice back to business. "I'll round up a couple of pack members to give you a hand today." He shot a glare at Mack. "But not you. You go home and rest."

Mack looked like he was going to object, but then he sat back, lowered his head and was silent. Pack hierarchy was a big thing to werewolves.

"Thank you, Runner." I turned to Mack. "And thank you for today. I don't think I would have survived without your help."

Mack gave me a measured nod, but I could tell he was pleased. He got up and limped to the door. "Let me know how it turns out."

"Of course."

He left, and Runner sighed. "That could have been a bigger mess."

I nodded. "Yeah. He's good, you know."

"I know. That's why I had him on guard. You and Paul are hard on my people, you know."

I turned away from him, my shame washing over me. A rough hand gripped and turned me. "No! I didn't mean it that way."

I pulled away. "But it's true. Last year you lost five of your people, another four at Nicola's house, and you almost lost Mack today." And to think that earlier I'd been taking their continued backup for granted. Was I really becoming that callous?

"Sit down." His voice wasn't loud, but I responded automatically to the tone of command.

When I was sitting, he continued. "Yes, we've lost some people. But it's also good for them."

"How?"

He smiled. "Because it pushes us to be better. Something is coming. We can feel it."

A chill ran down my spine. My dreams had been telling me that for several years now. "How do you know?"

His gaze was sharp. "You know something of what's coming?"

I shrugged. "Yes and no. Tell me what you know, and I'll tell you what little I do."

"It's little enough. More of a smell in the wind. I can't explain it any better than that. One minute, everything is as it should be. Then the next, a rotten stench blows across our noses. Most of us have smelled it. None of us know what it means. Just that it's trouble and it's coming soon."

"How soon do you think?" If the werewolves had a sense of that, it might confirm some of what I'd been dreaming.

He shook his head. "Soon. No more specific than that."

"Soon as in next week, next year, next decade?"

"Not next week, maybe next year, maybe farther out. We don't know. We just know we need to be ready, and you and Paul are giving us something to hone our skills on."

Great. We're training and assembling a supernatural army. We might just need it.

"I think what's coming is in 2012."

His eyebrows shot up. "You're kidding. Isn't that just fear mongering and hype?"

"I don't think so. I've been dreaming about something coming for years, almost as long as I've been alive, and my dad and grandfather both believe it's something to do with 2012."

His expression was stunned, and I couldn't blame him. I've been dreaming about it for years, and I still don't always believe it.

"So what is it?"

I frowned in frustration. "That's what I don't know. The dreams don't make any sense. It scares the pants off me, but I don't know exactly what I'm scared of."

He sat down heavily in the other chair. "That's interesting. I was hoping we were wrong about what we were sensing, but you seem to be saying we're not."

"I don't think so. Like you, though, I'm hoping it's nothing." But I knew better. That particular dream was just too strong. And I've had it too many times.

I shook myself. "But that's enough. It's still a couple years away, so I think we can safely ignore it for now. I'm sorry Paul and I have been hard on your people, but if you're getting ready, that's a good thing. Let's just see if we can't cut down on the number of deaths."

Runner nodded. "I can get behind that. But don't beat yourself up. Paul has saved so many people with his efforts, and you're adding to that number. We need both of you." He paused and then added, "Actually, I think we need more of you."

"I've been thinking the same thing. Malachai couldn't have worked his will on me if I were in regular contact with other warlocks and witches. I'm starting to think it's time for me to establish a D.C. coven."

His eyes widened. "There isn't one already?"

"Nope. As far as I know, I'm the only practitioner of any significance in this town. Time to change that."

He shook his head. "Another day."

"Oh, yeah." I stood up and started for the kitchen. "I've got just enough time to brew a potion to replace the one I just used. I'd better get it finished before Paul gets here."

"He's stopping by?" Runner sounded surprised.

"He'd better be. I told him I had a potion for him."

He grinned. "Good thinking. Following him makes it easier to figure out where this showdown is happening."

I shot him an answering grin over my shoulder. "I thought so. And the potion really will help, so he'd better show up. But I've got a Plan B just in case he doesn't."

"With Paul, that's always a good idea."

"Don't I know it!"

"May I watch?" Runner asked. "I've haven't seen much magic before."

I shrugged. "Knock yourself out. Potion brewing isn't like ritual magic. It's not very exciting to watch, but you can't really distract me either."

I bustled about the kitchen, assembling all the same ingredients as before. Fortunately infusions don't take as much time as decoctions, and I thought I had just long enough to finish it before Paul would likely be over.

Runner asked a few questions but mostly just watched. Just as I started the herbs steeping, my phone beeped. I had it on the counter beside me, and I glanced at it quickly.

Thanks. On my way

"That him?" Runner asked.

I nodded as I set my phone timer for five minutes. "Yeah. He should be here about the time I get this bottled up."

"How do you want me to play this?"

I thought for a minute. "Don't want to overdo it. He'll pick up on that right away. You'd better be outside. He'd expect that. If he asks, I'm pretty pissed about staying behind, but you'll make sure I don't slip off. I'll make a stab at changing his mind, but I won't push it."

"Sounds like a plan."

"Then as soon as he's out the door, I'll do a tracking ritual, and we'll follow him."

"I can put one of my people on him?"

I shook my head. "I thought about that earlier, but I don't think it's a good idea. He'll be on edge and especially alert. If he sees the tail, he'll either overreact and hurt someone, or he'll be tipped off about me. I can't think of how he'd stop me tracking him, but he might surprise me. Rather not take that chance."

Runner nodded. "Makes sense. Even if he can't stop you, he'll be so distracted Malachai might be able to get the drop on him."

"Agreed. You can stay in touch with your people to follow us and get into position?"

"Absolutely." He held up his phone. "I texted a couple folks while you were making your potion. They're ready to move when I give the word."

I clapped him on his shoulder. "Good. You get outside then. Let's get this started."

My phone timer went off right then, and I moved to finish up my potion while he slipped out the door. I poured it back into the same bottle I'd used earlier. No use wasting it when it was already labeled.

Then I made a quick sandwich and waited for Paul to arrive. Let's see how I do at "fool the vampire."

Chapter 17

Thursday, May 6, 2010.
Late Evening

P AUL ARRIVED A few minutes later. I examined
him carefully. He didn't give much away, but
I'd known him a while now, and I saw more
than most people.

He was anxious but controlling it well. Malachai
hadn't told him where yet then. His eyes flicked from
my sandwich to the potion brewing mess on the
counter. His shoulders relaxed fractionally, and I hid an
inward smile. So far so good. I looked like I was
planning to stay put. Now to shake him up a bit. He'd
suspect something if I didn't put up something of a
fight.

I reached for a potion bottle, checking the label as I
did so—Mind Control Block—and handed it over.
"This is for you."

He read the label and raised his eyebrows at me.
"Are you serious?"

I smiled and took another bite of sandwich, chew-
ing slowly before answering. I made it look good, but I
didn't taste it at all. "I can't guarantee it. Not like I have
tons of mind-controlling vampires to test it on, but I
think it will work."

"What exactly is it supposed to do?" He sat down in the chair Runner had recently vacated. I held my breath. Would he pick up on the residual body heat?

He said nothing, just waiting for me to answer. Apparently not. Okay then.

"It should protect you against any attempt to mind control you. I combined huckleberries for general hex-breaking, coupled with alyssum. It's an all-purpose protective herb which can also dispel veils and glamours. I don't know how Malachai does his thing, but I figured it couldn't hurt." Then I grinned. "But that's not the best part."

He nodded at me to continue.

"Agrimony. Also a good protective herb, but it has an added property. It can bounce hexes back to the caster."

The eyebrows went up again, and he inhaled sharply, heightening his cheekbones. "Does that mean what I think it does?"

"Yep. If it works right, anything Malachai tries should bounce right back at him. Oh, I don't think he'll suddenly be under your control or anything like that, but it should be a hell of a distraction."

"I'd imagine." His shoulders relaxed more, and he looked about as happy as could be expected under the circumstances. His eyes glowed blue, and the look he gave me was warm. "That's very good. Thank you."

Damn. I wrestled recalcitrant parts of my body under control. That look was just ... hot!

His nostrils flared, and I swore to myself. A pox on

vampires and their senses! I wondered exactly what arousal smelled like to him. A slow smile spread across his face, but he didn't say anything. Somehow that made it more embarrassing.

"Did you remember the strength potion?" I asked, desperate for something to distract him from ... whatever he was thinking right then.

The smile didn't go away, but he said, "Yes. I did. It's all right to take them together?"

"Yes. And the protection one will last 20-30 minutes, so don't wait to take it."

"That's good." Something flashed across his face. Shame? Regret? "I do appreciate you making them for me."

Here was my chance. He'd suspect if I didn't take it. "Potions are one thing. But I still think I'd be useful."

There went the walls. "No. Absolutely not. It'll be hard enough for me to deal with him without needing to worry about you."

I hoped he never found out about this afternoon. "You know I can take care of myself in a fight. We've done it before."

His expression softened a bit. "I know. And I don't want you to think that I don't have confidence in you. It's just—It's just that Malachai is well beyond anything we've ever fought together. I'm not convinced I can take him."

All the more reason to have me along, I didn't say. Instead, I sighed and took another bite of sandwich. "All right. I don't like it, but all right." Because he'd expect it of me, I added, "Do you know where yet?"

He shook his head. "Not yet. He'll want to prolong the anticipation."

Right. Sure he would. "If I don't hear back from you by sunrise, what should I do?"

I hated even saying it. Just thinking that he might not come back was enough to bring a catch to my voice. Losing Paul? No, I didn't know how I'd face that.

He took two quick steps to close the distance between us, and long arms surrounded me. I relaxed into the hug. Vampires aren't exactly as cold as the grave, but they aren't warm either. His body held just enough heat to tell me he had fed, and fed well. I wondered if it had been animal blood this time, or something else. He hadn't said, but I suspected he was stronger after feeding on a human.

"I'll be fine," he said, lips moving in my hair.

"I know," I said into his chest. "But just in case."

"Call Damien. He'll know what to do."

"Assuming Malachai doesn't get him, too?"

He froze, and I hated causing him more pain. "Good point. I think I'm the one he really wants, but I can't assume that." He paused, and I held him, willing strength into him through my arms. "Go to the Lounge. Ask for Lucius. He'll need to know and take precautions."

Paul pulled back and looked me in the eyes. His had shifted to gray, and I didn't like what I saw there.

"Then get out of town as quickly as you can. Go back to your parents. You'll be safe enough tonight. Killing me will sate his lusts for that long. But by tomorrow night, I can't guarantee anything."

I shivered at the thought of Malachai on my trail. I thought my dad's coven could stand up to a single vampire, but I'd rather we didn't have to put it to the test.

"I'll do that. But, hey, just beat the guy tonight, and then we don't have to worry about it."

He gave me a small smile. "Of course. We'll do that."

He started to pull away from me, but suddenly he stiffened in my arms. I held on tight, not sure for a moment what was happening. Then I got it. Malachai was sending him the location.

Paul's eyes were dark and unseeing. His face twisted in pain, and as I watched, his fangs dropped. His head slowly lowered to my neck, and I knew what Malchai was trying to do.

The smart thing would have been to let go, but this wasn't the time for the smart thing. Instead I started talking, low and soothing, with absolutely no fear. It wasn't an act. Paul would have seen through that. I was cold and confident.

"No, Paul. Don't do this. He can't make you do this. I know you don't want to. I trust you, Paul. Always have. Always will. He doesn't have a hold over you anymore. Fight him. Fight him now, and you'll be able to fight him later."

I could feel the tension thrumming through his body as he fought the compulsion to rip into my throat and drink. His eyes flickered, black to glowing yellow. His head dropped lower, but I didn't stop my low patter. I wasn't even sure what I was saying anymore. I just knew I needed him to hear my voice. My not-prey voice.

His motion slowed, and I turned, slowly, carefully, to watch the struggle on his face. His eyes glowed a brighter yellow, and I felt his claws prick the skin on my back. But I held on, still talking.

Finally, the glow faded, first to a dark gray and slowly, so slowly, back to blue. His body relaxed, and he raised his head.

I let myself take one deep breath. No change. Another. Still no change. I gently squeezed his arms, and he tightened his muscles in response. I let myself smile, gentle, affectionate.

"Welcome back."

He took one of his rare deep breaths, and he smiled back at me. "That was … well done. Exactly correct. How did you know?"

I gave him a quick hug and then stepped back. "Instinct, I guess. I didn't want to look like prey in any way. The slightest bit of fear, and I think you wouldn't have been able to resist. But I wanted you to hear my voice. To give you something else to focus on besides him in your head."

Paul closed his eyes and took another deep breath. "Thank you. It worked. I was able to let your voice drown him out." He opened his eyes, expression grave. "To say he's not pleased would be an understatement."

A quick laugh barked out of me. "Yeah, I'd guess so. Does that make it harder or easier?"

He shook his head. "I don't know. Guess I'll figure it out when I get there."

I desperately wanted to ask him one more time to let me come, but after that, I knew I had no chance. He'd nearly killed me, and there was no way he'd put himself into that position again.

"Too bad I hadn't already taken the potion."

I nodded. "Yeah, that could have been interesting. You know where now, right?"

"Of course." He said nothing else, which was what I expected.

"Well, I guess you'd better get on then."

He closed his eyes again and nodded. I stepped forward and crushed him against me, not wanting to let go. Not now. Not ever. He held me back like I was the only thing in his world at that moment.

It couldn't last of course, and I let him go after a minute. His arms slipped away slowly, but he finally let go.

"You come back to me, you hear?" I forced the words out past the tightness in my throat.

"I'll do my best." His voice sounded equally choked.

I shook my head. "Not good enough. I will see you again."

He nodded, and his eyes glowed briefly, yellow, but

not threateningly. "I promise I will be back."

I sighed. Paul didn't break promises, so it would have to be enough. "All right," I said. "Off with you then. Don't keep me waiting too long."

Did that sound too much like a heroine in a bad romance novel? If it did, too bad. I wanted him at that moment. I could see myself slamming him against the wall, ripping his clothes off, and ... well, you can probably imagine what would come after that.

His nostrils flared again, but this time it didn't embarrass me. He smiled, but didn't say anything. He just took the potion, turned and left.

As soon as the door closed, I slumped against the counter for a moment before gathering myself. I had work to do.

I didn't waste any time. Earlier, I'd set up everything in my ritual room. It was a risk, but I'd thought I could sufficiently distract Paul that he wouldn't think to check. I hadn't expected Malachai to give me so much help.

I ran to my work room and threw open the door. All was ready. The candles just needed to be lit, and the incense was already in position on its holder. I made the final preparations, closed the circle and began.

This sort of thing is my bread and butter, and while I usually liked to go through the entire procedure, I could do it on the run when I needed. This time I needed to do it fast.

My magnet was ready, as was the vial of Paul's blood. I chanted my focusing spell, tossed my will and energy into it, rubbing the blood over the magnet while I chanted. Moments later, it began to glow, and I felt the link to Paul snap into place. I could find him anywhere now.

I opened the circle, releasing the bound energies, and dashed back to my living room, where I grabbed the new potion and an ADC Street Map of Washington D.C.

I reviewed everything else in my bag. Yes. I had what I needed. I glanced at my phone. Not bad. Only fifteen minutes. Dad would have been proud of me.

I was certain Paul was long gone by now, but to be sure, I sent Runner a text.

He gone?

My phone beeped almost immediately.

Yes. Now?

I sent back:

On my way out

This was it. I hoped I was ready.

I dashed outside and saw Runner's truck, already running. I hopped in the passenger seat, and he took off, almost before I had closed my door. I stuffed the seat belt catch in place and took out my map.

I heard the intake of breath, and felt my face turn red. "God Damn it! You too?"

"What?" His voice was entirely too innocent.

Curse me for hanging out with people with a supernatural sense of smell.

"Where?" There was no humor in his voice now.

"Give me a minute," I said as I struggled to find the right page in the book. "And by the way, nothing happened."

"Oh, I know that." No innocence now, just amusement. "How's this work anyway?" His voice was back to business as he merged into traffic on Massachusetts Avenue.

I held up the magnet. "This has a connection to Paul." I nodded at the map. Finally! The correct page. "I can follow along on this." I held the magnet close to the map page, and it thrummed in my fingers. Moments later, it found its place. "Damn! He's moving fast. We'll have to hurry."

"He was burning rubber when he turned off your street."

The magnet moved, almost of its own will, across the map. "Okay, he's heading south-east on Pennsylvania Avenue."

A chill ran down my spine, and I knew where they were going. "Runner, head for where we fought the werewolves last year."

He glanced away from the road long enough to shoot me a look. "You sure?"

The magnet felt alive in my hand, and certainty ran through my entire body. "Absolutely. Damn him!"

"What?" Runner took a left turn down a little-used street, but I didn't say anything, figuring the werewolf knew his territory well enough to find the quickest route.

"He was watching us last year."

"You sure?"

"It makes sense. The rogue was active then, so Malachai was in town. I doubt he does much of anything by accident, so he'd want to see what Paul's allies could do."

Runner shook his head. "No, he wanted to see what *you* could do. He'd know about werewolves, but you're the wild card here."

I nodded. He was right.

"So what'd you do then?" Runner continued. "What does he know?"

I thought back. That was my first big fight, and it was embedded in my memory. "Veils. I did one of those. Protection circle." Tension flowed out of my body as I realized he actually didn't know much.

"What?" He made another turn. He was good. We were making good time.

"He doesn't know much of anything. The veil was moderately advanced magic, but well within the capabilities of most warlocks. The protection circle was common. I keyed it to just werewolves, so that tells him I'm no slouch, but still, he doesn't know much."

"What about your illusion thing?"

"Yeah, Paul gave me hell for that, but he doesn't know I can pop that off with a thought, so I think it's okay. He'll know I carry mace, but he won't be worried about that. And I think my protection potion will be an eye-opener for him."

"Good." Runner fumbled in his pocket with one hand, the other gripping the wheel. "Here. Send a text to Charley. Tell him where we're going. He'll get the word to the others."

I swiped the screen and was relieved to see it was Android. Good. Familiar. I opened the messaging app, found the right number and sent the text. "Done," I said as I handed back the phone.

"Thanks. We'll be there in ten."

I paged through the map book, found the right page and checked the magnet. Yes. I'd been correct. Paul was pulling into the parking lot of the old warehouse.

"He's there now. Make it snappy."

Runner's phone beeped, and I glanced down. "They're just a couple of minutes away. How'd they get there so fast?"

The werewolf gave me a feral grin. "I do know something of strategy. I had four teams out, covering what I thought were likely parts of town. I didn't think he'd actually use the same place, but it was a likely area, so I had Charley set up near there."

Wait a minute. Runner had sent out four teams? "How good are they?"

He grimaced and ran a red light. My head snapped around. No cops. Good. "They're okay. As you've obviously guessed, I had to spread my people thin. Everyone is competent, but there's only one of Mack's quality in Charley's group."

"Charley himself?" I guessed.

"Right. The rest can handle themselves in a fight, but don't expect anything fancy."

I was glad Runner had taken the chance, but I couldn't help worrying.

"I figured it'd be okay. You only wanted them going after minions, right?"

I nodded. "Yeah. You think they're up for that?"

"Wouldn't have sent them otherwise." His voice was confident.

"Okay, then. You help your people. Leave Malachai to me." Right. I couldn't quite believe I'd just said that, but it was the only thing that made sense.

"Almost there. If you need any preparations, better make 'em now."

I took out my protection potion, unscrewed the cap and gulped it down. I felt it settle over me like a warm blanket on a fall day. I ran over some possible illusions. It's not easy to come up with things that might scare or startle a vampire, but I thought I had a few. Minions were much easier. Humans have a good startle reflex, especially if we catch something just out of the corner of our eyes.

Runner pulled to a stop about a block away. "I'm thinking we shouldn't just charge in there."

"Sounds good." I held the magnet in my hand. Yes, Paul was very close by. I could feel his presence like a physical pull against me. Unfortunately, this particular spell only gave me location, not frame of mind. Can't have everything.

I glanced over at Runner, who was texting, his fingers flashing over the tiny keyboard. "Your people in place?"

He shook his head. "Not quite. They got hung up by an accident. Still two minutes away."

I considered. "Can you make a quick sweep and give me the tactical situation?"

He finished sending his text. "Yes. Hold my phone? Charley'll let us know if they run into anything else."

"Sure."

He opened the door, being careful to not let it "thunk" closed. He stripped off his clothes, and a moment later a shaggy wolf stood by the car. He nodded and loped off.

I shifted my vision and did my own survey of the area. Trees blocked my view of the building and parking lot, but I wasn't worried about that yet. I figured I knew who was there. I was more concerned about the minions. I picked up three orange auras right away, each about 200 yards away. They were spread around, in what looked like good positions to observe and move in quickly. Darn. Just once I'd like to go up against a master villain with a lousy sense of tactics.

I measured distances and considered. I was pretty sure I hadn't seen them all, so I hesitated to take too overt of an action, but two of them were positioned nicely to send into a trap, assuming I had some werewolves to sic on them.

Just then another car pulled up, tires crunching on

the road. Doors opened, and three men and one woman got out, moving with the casual grace I'd learned to associate with werewolves. I was always surprised to see their auras looked pretty much like humans, with the usual mix of colors.

One stepped forward. "You Dafydd?"

"Yeah. Charley?"

He nodded and introduced the rest of them. I actually made an effort to remember their names, using a technique I'd learned from Bob. This time if any of them died, I never wanted to forget them.

"What's the situation?" Charley asked after finishing the introductions.

"Three bad guys there, there, and there," I said, pointing each of them out in turn. None had moved. "Runner's doing a quick recon. Paul's over there," I waved in the general direction of the parking lot. "Assume Malachai is with him, but there's too many trees in the way. I can't get a read on any auras."

Charley's head shot around to look behind us. I followed his gaze and saw Runner returning. The big wolf stopped, and a moment later shifted back to human form.

Have I mentioned Runner has a particularly nice form?

Completely unconcerned about his nudity, Runner greeted his pack and hunkered down to draw something in the dirt. I knelt down to get a better view.

"There's five minions." He drew them in on his rough diagram. He noted the three I'd seen and two more who were on the other side of the building.

"That's one for each of us," Charley said, his tone smooth and confident.

Runner nodded. "Exactly. But we need to be careful. They all have guns."

One of the other wolves, Billy, snorted. "Like they can even see in the dark?"

Runner's teeth flashed white in the dim light. "Don't underestimate them. Dafydd can do some unexpected stuff with potions. Assume they can do the same."

He glanced at me, as if for confirmation. I nodded. "Malachai's a warlock. I don't know exactly what he can do, but assume he can brew sense enhancing potions. He can't confer true dark vision, but my sense enhancing potions would let me see well enough to shoot you. Assume the minions can do the same."

Billy's shoulders slumped. "Okay then."

"Is that a big puddle of water I see over there?" I pointed between two of the minions.

"Yes." Runner frowned at my question, but then his face brightened. "Think you can distract them?"

I grinned. "I think I can do better than that. I think I can send them exactly where I want them to go. But first, what about Paul and Malachai?"

He shrugged. "They're in the parking lot, like we'd thought. Talking, for now. It's hard to tell with vampires—their smell is off—but it didn't seem like things were going to come to blows for another couple of minutes. Paul's angry. Malachai's amused."

I nodded. "Good. Let's hope that buys us a couple of minutes to deal with some minions." I quickly outlined my plan, and all the werewolves grinned. Picking off outlying members of a herd appealed to them for some reason.

A moment later five big wolves surrounded me, pressing against my legs. Then they were off. I gave them about 30 seconds to get into position. I didn't want to move until I had to. Moving silently isn't one of my skills, though Paul keeps meaning to teach me.

As soon as I thought they were ready, I concentrated and tossed an image into the puddle. One slight warlock, crouched down, obviously trying to move quietly. I hoped the dim lighting would make up for the perspective, which wasn't quite right.

Apparently it worked. One of the orange auras started moving, right into the path of a wolf. One orange aura winked out. Good. The other started to move toward his fellow, and another wolf aura appeared to come out of the ground. Another orange aura winked out.

Excellent. Two down, which just happened to open up a path for me to get to the parking lot. Time to figure out what was happening with Paul and Malachai. I hoped killing his minions had given the master vampire at least a tiny bit of heartburn.

I moved quickly but quietly, watching as best I could where I put my feet. I would have preferred to have had aura sight active, but that would have made it much harder to see the myriad things that could have tripped me up, so I went for normal vision.

Arriving near the parking lot, I heard voices, at first low, then rising in tone and volume. A shiver passed through me as I recognized the smooth tones. Malachai! It was hypnotic and pulled at me, even through the glow of my potion. I hoped Paul had already taken his.

I moved closer, watching my steps. I peered out from behind a tree. At first, it didn't look too bad. Malachai was talking, and Paul appeared to be listening. Then I saw my friend's face. Damn! His expression was tight, his hands clenched at his side. I could almost feel the thrum of tension in all his muscles.

I glanced at Malachai. Even at this distance I could see his eyes glowing a deep amber, tingeing more toward orange. Right. He was trying to influence Paul through the master/child bond. Had he taken the potion? I shifted my vision and looked deep into Paul.

Deep blue
Hints of red and black
Purple
Yellow

And creeping like a sickly fog over all of them, the same amber orange as Malachai's eyes. The blue fought back, but it was succumbing. Only a matter of time.

However, there was no sign of my potion in his aura. That was good and bad. Good because we still had a chance. Bad because I wasn't sure how to break this to give him a moment to take it.

Well, I'm not a warlock for nothing. The building behind them did have large windows, and the security lights gave enough illumination for one of my images. Only one problem. Malachai was facing the wrong way, away from the windows.

Time to improvise. I created an image of me, waving frantically. I tossed it into the window and willed Paul to see it, recognize it and know what to do.

Seconds passed. Malachai spoke. Paul's face mirrored his internal struggle.

I made my image wave faster.

Finally Paul shifted a few inches to his right. I could see how hard he'd worked for it, and I silently cheered him on.

Malachai stepped to follow him, and I moved my illusion toward me, out of the range of his peripheral vision.

Okay, Paul had made him move. It wasn't quite enough, but I thought I could make it work.

I let the illusion of me drop, and I concentrated. This was going to be tricky. Malchai wasn't quite positioned correctly, and my usual casting of an image into the window wasn't going to work. So I decided to find out if I could make an illusion extend out from the surface. *No reason it shouldn't work,* I told myself and proceeded to make it happen.

So what would startle a master vampire, you ask? Good question. I hadn't been able to ask the obvious sources, so I'd improvised.

I tossed an image of Father Eyler, cross and holy

water outstretched. I focused my will as tightly as I could, and, slowly, one inch at a time, I made his arm extend from the window.

Paul's expression changed, just slightly, and it was enough to make Malachai turn, just another inch or two.

Enough! He saw the image and took a step back.

I yelled as loud as I could. "Paul! The potion!"

At the same moment, I gulped down my own reflex enhancer. I thought I was going to need it.

As usual, everything around me seemed to slow. Well, everything except the furious vampire coming my way.

I dodged behind a tree and scrambled several feet to my right. I couldn't fight him, and I knew it, but I hoped I could keep him off balance enough to give Paul time.

I fumbled in my pack for a vial of holy water, praying it worked on older vampires, and cautiously peeked out from behind my tree.

Malachai was right there, smiling. Nope, not a nice, "how ya doing, glad to see you" smile. More of an "I'm going to rip you limb from limb and enjoy every minute of it" smile.

Without thinking, I threw the vial at his face. My potion should have allowed me to place it exactly where I'd wanted it, but his natural reflexes were faster than my enhanced ones, and he moved his head a couple inches to the side. My vial sailed past him and shattered uselessly on the ground behind the vampire.

I darted to the right, and he followed. Good. The vial had landed close enough to a pool of light to create a tiny reflective surface. Just enough for me to project a claw-tipped hand, moving fast.

Malachai flinched back, and I ran as fast as my enhanced reflexes would let me, dodging trees, fallen branches that might have tripped me and anything else in my way.

The smart thing might have been to run back to the werewolves, but I knew Malachai would destroy them with little effort. So instead I ran to the building, closer to Paul.

Did I mention that vampires are fast?

Malachai caught me before I'd gone more than 50 yards. I felt a heavy hand grip my shoulder and whirl me around.

I faced glowing amber eyes and extended fangs. I went completely still, feigning utter terror. Only my left hand moved, slowly, inch by inch, toward my bag. If I could only get another vial, just maybe I could get out of this.

"So, little warlock. You think to face me?" His tone was conversational but dripping with menace. By all rights, I should have been pissing my pants, but I was too stubborn to let fear get the better of me. I could feel his will pressing in on me, no specific instruction yet, just moving in to take over. For the moment, my potion held, and I saw confusion cross his features.

"What's this?" he asked.

Another inch.

Suddenly, I realized I'd been too distracted when I took my potion to start my usual countdown. How long had it been? 30 seconds? Longer. Damn! I had no idea. Better make every second count.

Something rushed past us, grabbed me and threw me toward the surrounding trees. I managed to get my shoulder under me and rolled instead of skidded, my arms cradling my pack with its precious vials.

I finished my roll on my feet and blinked to get my bearings.

Paul!

He had turned after tossing me and faced Malachai, who recovered quickly from his surprise. I'd expected them to go at it physically, you know, a sort of "Battle of the Titans" thing. Instead, Malachai retreated several steps, chanted something in Latin and stood, grinning.

Paul took a cautious step forward, testing in front of him with his hands. Three steps, and he hit something.

Double damn! That's Malachai's trick. Not mind control after all, or at least not *just* mind control. He could cast protective circles on the fly. What I wouldn't give to have that ability!

"Paul! Protective circle!" I shifted my vision and swore. "Back away. *Do not* touch it."

I didn't know what else he'd added to the circle, but that particular shade of green mixed with muddy brown wasn't good.

Paul backed up several steps. "What now, Malachai? Looks like an impasse."

I'd been using the temporary calm to move into position. I didn't know exactly what I could do about the circle, but I had several ideas. Well, a couple. Well, okay, only one. But it was a really good one.

"Dafydd, stay back!" Paul's voice oozed tension.

"Yeah, we've seen how well that's worked for you. Two are better than one."

Malachai just grinned.

"It's over, you know." Baiting vampires was becoming almost a life calling for me. "Your minions are down. It's two against one now, and even you know those aren't good odds."

The master vampire's grin widened. "Yes, my minions are down. Didn't they provide an excellent distraction?" His expression grew almost sorrowful. "And if you were hoping for some sort of backlash when they died, so sorry to disappoint. It doesn't work that way."

Drat! It had been a long shot anyway. Wait a minute. Distraction? I shot a glance at Paul, who looked back at me, expression troubled.

"Don't you just wonder what else I have up my sleeve?"

Actually I did, but I wasn't going to let on to him.

Malachai laughed, the sound evil and rich. Then he said, "I believe one of your potions is ending. Right. About. Now."

His timing was perfect. My reflexes snapped back to human normal. Shit!

"Time for me to bring in my real reinforcements.

Damien, if you don't mind."

Paul's face fell, and my heart plummeted somewhere near my feet as a familiar shape lurched out from behind several parked trucks. It was Damien, his face contorted with effort, but still moving, one painful step at a time, our way.

Paul reached out a hand, then let it fall. "I'm so sorry," I heard him whisper.

This was so not good. What to do? Sure, Paul was stronger than Damien and could probably take him, but being forced to kill his vampire brother would break his heart. And while he was dealing with Damien, Malachai would be making shish kebob out of me.

We needed reinforcements of our own.

At that moment, I saw movement in the nearby trees, low and fast. Werewolves! Of course. We did have reinforcements. As inexperienced as they were, I thought five werewolves could take on one vampire of Damien's power. And as long as Runner was with them, he'd know not to kill the younger vampire.

Paul's eyes flickered, and a frown passed across his face so quickly I almost missed it. He'd seen them too. Now how to make this work for us?

"Don't think I've missed your little friends," Malachai said from the protection of his circle. His voice had lost none of its confidence. Or insane edge. "I'm quite sure you want more blood on your hands."

I ignored him. He was just trying to bait me. Damien moved closer, his struggles growing less with each step. It was now or never. I didn't think I could distract

Damien, not mind-controlled. And Malachai was facing away from the big windows, obviously wise to my tricks by now. That left just one use for my illusions. How nice of Malachai to be facing the wrong way.

"Paul! Break left!" I yelled as I tossed my illusion. Paul's eyes flicked toward the window as he followed my directions. A faint smile played about his lips as he charged Malachai.

Five werewolves glided across the parking lot towards Damien, following my illusory directions.

Malachai's eyes widened, and he glanced behind him to see an image of a wolf pack taking down a deer. I'd figured Runner would figure out what I meant.

I hadn't actually expected to distract Malachai, but it was a nice bonus. Paul took that moment to lean down, pick up a rock and throw it at Malachai. It should have hit the barrier and dropped down, useless, but my mouth dropped open as it passed through the barrier and hit him, hard, in the forehead. Stupid! He'd forgotten to make his protection circle effective against inanimate objects. That's what happens when you get overconfident.

Malachai staggered back, just outside the circle of his magic, and Paul charged, following up the rock with his own body. Both vampires went down in a snarling, clawing heap. Malachai's talent was for magic and mind control. Paul's was physical ability. I hoped that in a reasonably fair fight, Paul could take him.

Now for my part. I hated to do it, but I knew Paul could take care of himself for a few seconds. I needed to aid the werewolves. I didn't have the effects of my potion anymore, but I was young and in pretty good shape, which meant I could move when I needed to. I ran toward Damien, pulling out a vial of holy water.

I skidded to a halt in front of him and a few feet away, just out of easy reach. The werewolves were coming, and I only had a few seconds.

"Sorry," I said as I tossed the vial. I watched him struggle harder, not to avoid the holy water but to move into its path. I had to admire that kind of determination.

Gratitude flickered in his eyes as the vial hit him, broke and splashed holy water all over him. Skin immediately started bubbling, and his face screwed up in pain.

A second later the wolves were on him.

"Try not to kill him," I said as I left them to their work. Runner shot a look over his shoulder, and I knew he'd understood.

All right. I hoped that was the end of Malachai's reinforcements. Now to see if I could help Paul.

As I turned, compulsion flowed over me, warm honey over all my nerve endings. My steps faltered as I fought the urge to return to the battle with the werewolves. No! I wasn't going to give in to that. I refused to pull out my mace and start attacking my allies.

I focused my will and concentrated on the effects of my potion. Two steps toward the werewolves, silently battling a wounded Damien. One step toward Malachai. Magical energy flared within me, and I closed my eyes, concentrating on moving away. One more step. Slipping a bit. One step back.

A tiny part of my mind wondered what had happened to Paul. If Malachai was controlling me, did that mean he'd killed Paul?

That sharp stab of fear gave me enough of a boost to throw off his influence. My aura flared blue, overwhelming the slow creep of orange, and I staggered.

A quick glance behind me. Runner and his pack had Damien well in hand. Two wolves were down, but the remaining three had him surrounded. He was bleeding freely, but I knew vampires well enough by now. He was weakened, but nowhere near dead.

Good. I turned in the direction of Malachai, fearing what I'd see.

It was every bit as bad as I'd thought. Paul was lying slumped twenty or so feet away. He was completely still, which in a vampire wasn't necessarily a bad thing, but his body had a boneless stillness I'd seen before. My memory flashed back to two homeless people, still and discarded in a filthy alley. Paul's body looked just like that.

Okay. I thought I'd been angry before. That emotion had been a mere burning ember in an almost-dead fire in comparison to what blazed within me now. Sure, I had nothing useful. Illusions, holy water and mace. None of those were worth anything in a fight against something of Malachai's power, but right then, I didn't care. He'd killed my friend, the man I'd wanted to be my lover. No chance of that now.

At that moment, I didn't care if I lived or died. I just cared about taking Malachai down with me.

The master vampire grinned at me, his posture relaxed and confident. He'd moved back into his protective circle, which limited my options even further. His eyes flicked dismissively at the remains of the battle behind me.

"They can't help you now, you know."

Then his eyes flicked to Paul's still body. "Nor can he. I just love it when a plan comes together."

Involuntarily, I winced. Really? Quoting bad 80's TV shows at a moment like this?

I took a step forward, gathering energy around me. Honestly, I had no idea what to do with it. I couldn't cast anything offensive. Magic didn't work that way. I'd never studied mind magic, so I had no hope of matching Malachai in a battle of wills.

Suddenly, I felt several furry bodies press against me. I glanced down. Runner and two others. I thought one of them was Casi, but I couldn't be sure. Then I had an idea. I couldn't stop the grin that started across my face.

"Can you guys buy me a few seconds?"

Runner growled in assent, and they charged Malachai. I wasted one of my precious seconds in pride that they trusted me. They had no idea what I was planning. I had no idea if it would even work, but they trusted me enough to give me the chance.

I didn't plan to waste it. Out of the corner of my eye, I saw Malachai position himself outside his circle to meet the charge. His insane grin never left his face, and I knew he'd enjoy killing the wolves. It was my job to be sure that didn't happen.

I threw all but one of my remaining vials of holy water on the ground.

Malachai's laugh rang across the parking lot. "Throwing away your last defense, warlock? Foolish!"

I ignored him, disturbed that he could fight and jeer at the same time, but not letting it distract me. I'd already gathered every bit of will and magical energy I could bleed from my surroundings. I had it. Now I need to shape and use it.

I sent out a silent call, resolutely ignoring the sounds of combat near me. A moment later, my call was answered, and the spilled water formed into a small whirlpool, spinning endlessly in front of me. I gave it instructions and sent it to do my bidding.

The whirlpool moved away from me, changing form until a tiny silvery angel flew, just inches above the ground. Huh. Hadn't expected that, but it fit. Sometimes magic has a mind of its own.

I followed its path, wincing when I saw all but one of the werewolves on the ground. Only Runner remained, and he was staggering, one leg broken and limp. He gathered himself for one more leap. Malachai was barely scratched. Three determined werewolves had managed to inflict only one deep gash across his chest, marring his expensive suit coat.

Malachai danced back, a cat enjoying his play with a mouse. Fortunately, he wasn't looking at my elemental, which closed the gap in seconds.

"Back!" I yelled, and Runner staggered backwards. The vampire followed, stepping closer to the elemental, which ignored the werewolf and engulfed Malachai's foot.

The scream was gratifying. Damn fool had stepped out of his protection circle to "play" with the werewolves. My plan wouldn't have worked otherwise, but thank goodness for overconfident boss villains.

My elemental slithered up Malachai's leg, burning its way higher and higher. The vampire continued to scream, the sound high and agonized. I hadn't been certain holy water would affect a vampire so powerful, but my plan was working beyond my wildest expectations.

I scrambled over to the werewolves, checking for pulses. They were both alive and conscious. Good. "Get out of here. You've done enough."

Runner nudged me, and I looked up. Malachai had managed to extricate himself from my elemental. Blood and flesh bubbled down his legs, but he was still up.

Die already, damn it!

I was out of ideas. I still had one more vial of holy water, but it wasn't nearly enough. Runner stood by me, only on three legs, but still obviously determined to stand with me as long as I stayed.

Malachai took one halting step toward us. And another. Each step was more fluid than the last. He was healing faster than I'd expected, and I hadn't the faintest idea what to do.

Something moved fast and hit Malachai from behind. Runner gave a delighted sounding yip, and a slow grin broke across my face.

Paul wrestled his master to the ground, and they rolled, clawing and biting at each other.

Runner pressed close to me, and I reached down to ruffle his fur. My heart felt light enough to float right out of my body. Paul was alive! I hadn't felt this good in a long time.

But I couldn't let joy get in the way of sound tactics. As I watched them fight, I was already planning what I could do to help. My elemental was still pulsing gently nearby, and I called it back to me. I couldn't send it into the melee because it would hurt Paul as much as Malachai, but I wanted it close by in case Malachai got free. I clutched my remaining vial. Again, not sure how to use it, but it was handy if I saw an opening.

The fighting was fierce. Malachai had managed to get to his feet, but Paul wasn't letting him get away, staggering him with repeated body blows. He was breaking bones with each strike, and I was pretty sure he was using my strength potion. Malachai had his arms up, trying to block blows to his face, but Paul was weaving back and forth, finding places Malachai couldn't defend.

Runner growled softly. It sounded like approval.

"Yeah, about time," I agreed.

Malachai finally got his feet under him, dodged two of Paul's strikes, landed a solid one of his own and staggered backwards, putting a few feet between them. His eyes glowed the sickly orange of a leprous pumpkin, and Paul stopped, still as death.

No! Malachai was trying to control him.

"Fight it, Paul. Fight it! He can't control you if you don't let him. He's not your master anymore."

Paul didn't move, and Malachai's grin returned.

"Well played, my child," Malachai said, his tone sneering. "I'd thought you dead, but I should have known my get would be hard to kill." His voice lowered to a perversion of intimacy. "You always did know how to take your punishment like a real man."

Runner growled beside me, and I felt an answering sound try to claw its way out of my throat.

Malachai's amber eyes flashed, and Paul's body started to turn.

"No." I almost didn't recognize the sound as coming from my own throat. I glanced down at my elemental, ready for my bidding. Could I do it? Could I send it against Paul? How strong was the hold Malachai had on him? Could I use it to break his concentration?

"Kill the human, my child. Lose this ridiculous sentiment and become again the perfect killing machine."

I screamed. "No! Don't make him do this!"

Malachai turned his attention back to me. Even injured, he managed to look cool and unruffled. His fine clothes were tattered, allowing me to watch his injuries close over and heal.

"And why not, warlock? Unless you are offering to work for me?" His voice lowered to a purr. "Yes. That could work nicely. Imagine what I could do with someone like you."

The thought revolted me, but I didn't say no. Was there a way I could use this? Pretend to yield? Give Paul a chance to recover, and we could take him later?

Malachai laughed. "Oh, warlock. Your thoughts are so plain. No, I won't let your … lover go." He made the word sound vile and perverted. "Agree to work with me, and I'll just have him kill the werewolves. But I'll let him spare you."

Paul had stopped moving while Malachai spoke. His eyes were blank, nothing that made him "Paul" visible in those dilated, all black orbs.

I shook my head. "No. I couldn't ever work with you."

"Then die, human. Paul, finish him."

Runner moved to stand in front of me, but I pushed him aside. I'd face this alone. "Run. Save as many of your people as you can."

Paul took another step closer, and I saw something flicker in those dead eyes. A sudden hope leaped in my chest, and I fought to keep it off my face, not wanting to give Malachai any warning. Compulsion was a tricky thing. It was hard to make someone do something against their nature, and I was pretty sure Paul felt something for me. Maybe not love, but something. Perhaps that was enough to give my potion room to work.

I stepped forward, dropping my hands to my side, putting up no defense at all. "It's all right, Paul. I understand. You can't help this, and I forgive you in advance."

Another flicker. Deep black started to melt away into gray. Was I getting through to him?

He stepped closer. I could have reached out and touched him. Another step. I could feel the chill of his body. He'd burned through all the reserves of his last feeding. Hope faltered in me. Did he still have the energy to resist?

Just then, his eyes widened, and I suppressed the joy that shot through me. He stepped closer and bent his head over me. I closed my eyes, doing my best impression of someone too terrified to move.

His lips touched my throat, and I felt the gentle prick of sharp teeth.

"That's right, Paul. Very good. Make it slow. I want to see it last."

"What now?" I felt the words against my skin, his voice so low I could barely hear it. "There's something. Pushing at me. What do I do with it?"

I moaned, deep in my throat, hoping it sounded like fear. Ever tried to talk and moan at the same time? Not recommending it, but I managed. "Use it. Turn it on him."

I opened my eyes and looked at him. His eyes glowed yellow, no hint of orange. His lips curved into a smile, and he turned around.

I shifted my vision as he turned, wanting to see this. Paul's aura glowed deep blue, almost enough to blind me. Then, to my other sight, a shaft of orange shot from Paul, straight for Malachai.

The master vampire's expression went from gloating to puzzled to alarmed. His own aura flared, but Paul's orange went straight through him.

"Leave us!" Paul's voice was commanding, and I caught myself taking a step back before I got my legs under control. I nodded in approval. Good move. Paul's vampire mind whammy wasn't good enough to make Malachai do anything even remotely self-destructive, but with the potion backing him up, Paul might be able to get him to run.

And I still had my elemental, which I commanded to move forward.

Malachai took one step back, but he managed to get himself under control. However, I noticed with great satisfaction that his expression held more than a hint of confusion, and just a bit of fear.

"How?"

Paul growled, deep in his chest and took several steps forward. "Leave here. Never come back."

The orange light still shone between them, fading but still strong. Malachai's eyes flicked toward the parking lot, then back to Paul, but the confident, insane glow was gone.

I stepped forward now. I didn't really think I could do anything to threaten him, but I wanted to make it clear that I was supporting Paul. If he wanted to continue the fight, he'd still have to deal with both of us.

I felt a presence beside me, and I risked a quick

look and smiled.

Damien stood beside us. His knees looked like they might collapse any minute, and blood still flowed from a dozen wounds, but his aura was clear and his expression determined.

The three of us stared at Malachai, daring him to make a move. My elemental was almost to his feet.

Malachai eyes flashed back and forth, resting on each of us in turn. Guess he didn't like what he saw because he drew himself up to his full height and said, "Don't think you've won, Paulus. I will be back."

Damien and Paul both growled, and I caught myself making a noise that sounded suspiciously growl-like. Too much time hanging out with vampires and werewolves, I guess.

"If you come back, we'll just beat you again," I said.

His eyes shone amber. "You have not beaten me today."

"Nope," I agreed. "That's why you're still over there, and the three of us are all together over here."

Runner howled from somewhere behind me. A moment later, answering howls surrounded from all around us, still at a distance but coming closer.

"And if you really want to keep this going, come right on." I made a "come here fool" gesture, and watched him grind his teeth. I hoped it was in frustration.

Wolves howled again, closer still.

With great dignity, Malachai straightened his ruined suit jacket and turned, walking to the parked cars, his step slow. The message was clear. This was just a strategic retreat, not a rout, but right then I didn't care.

He was gone.

I released the water elemental with a little bow just before Paul and Damien both slumped, on either side of me, and suddenly I had both arms full of exhausted vampires.

I spotted Paul's Prius in the parking lot. "Come on, guys. Let's get out of here."

No one disagreed, and the four of us, including Runner, made our slow, careful way to the car.

We'd won.

Chapter 18

Thursday, May 6, 2010.
Just Before Midnight

I WAS THE only one in any condition to drive. It seemed odd. The only human in the fight, the one most easily injured, and I didn't have a scratch on me. Both vampires, however, were in terrible shape, healing, but still weak.

I'd helped Damien and Paul to the car and left them there for a few minutes while I helped Runner gather up the werewolves. All of them were alive, which was a huge relief. I hated losing people. Casi was the least injured of their number, and she drove off, still complaining bitterly that one of her high heels had been lost in all the confusion.

"I just bought that pair yesterday," came her voice as Runner's truck pulled onto the street. I grinned, glad that someone's priorities were still in order.

"What?" Paul asked as I settled myself in the driver's seat. He was beside me, and Damien was sprawled out in back. Two empty blood bags lay limp on the passenger floor well, and I knew they'd taken care of replenishing themselves. Good.

"Nothing," I said as I buckled my seatbelt. "One of the werewolves was complaining about losing a shoe."

Paul smiled, a contrast to his obvious exhaustion. "Casi?"

"Of course."

I started the car and tried to remember the way to Damien's house. "You think it's safe to take him home?" I indicated the back seat with my chin.

"Yes," Paul answered. "Malachai's packing up to leave town. He'll be back, but not for a while."

"How long is 'a while?'"

"Good question." Paul leaned back in his seat and closed his eyes. "I don't know."

At the next light, I took the opportunity to give him a thorough look over. Tired and injured, definitely. His clothes were ripped up. I wondered why he still bothered with the shirt. It was barely hanging on his right shoulder, and his pants weren't much better. Long gashes still marred his chest and left leg. A long slash, healing, but still prominent, went across his throat. Looked like Malachai had tried, and almost succeeded at, ripping his head off.

"Yes, it was bad. Yes, I'll be fine. No need to mother hen me."

I grinned and turned my attention back to the road. "Damien? You okay back there?"

A weak voice answered me. "No, but I'll recover." A pause. "I'd gladly accept some 'mother henning,' though."

A low growl came from the seat beside me. I glanced over. Paul hadn't even opened his eyes, so I knew he wasn't really serious.

"I think you'll have to look for that somewhere else," I said, my voice mild.

Damien chuckled. "Yeah, I'll fight him for you later."

A small smile lifted the corners of Paul's lips.

I was relieved to see him in such a good mood. Maybe he wouldn't make me pay too badly for following him to the fight.

"How'd he get you, anyway, Damien? I thought we'd agree that you'd lie low."

A low groan from the back seat. "Yeah, that was the plan. But remember how we thought from the beginning there might be an inside man?"

That had totally slipped my mind. I pummeled my tired brain into shape and remembered our viewing of the first killing. How we'd thought it was odd that someone had been able to get in and out without being seen.

"Yeah," I said.

"Well, turns out we were right."

Paul finally spoke. "And he got you?"

Damien chuckled, the sound tired. "Not a 'him.' Her. And yeah, she got me. She said Lucius had sent her as extra protection, and like a fool, I bought it."

"Who was it?" Paul asked.

"Lola."

I'd never heard of her, but from the way Paul was shaking his head, I guessed he knew her. "Right. Assume you'll let Lucius know?"

"Of course, but she's long gone now."

"Yeah, but at least she won't be able to come back without most of the community gunning for her."

"True."

We dropped Damien at his house, and I hung around to make sure he got into his house safely. He stumbled a few times on the walk but finally managed the stairs and the doors.

"Fighting off mental influence can take it out of you," Paul said from beside me. His eyes were open now.

I pulled away from the curb. "I should have thought about him. I could have made one more potion and had a werewolf run it over to him." I shook my head. "Totally didn't think about him still being in danger."

"Don't feel too bad. I didn't think of it either."

Damien's door closed, and I started off down the street. "Your place or mine?"

I assumed it was a rhetorical question, so I was surprised when he said, "Yours."

Okay, then. Not sure what that meant, but I headed in the direction of my apartment.

"Speaking of werewolves running errands for you—" he began.

Uh, oh. Here it comes.

"You seem quite chummy with them."

Chummy? Really? We needed to update his vocabulary.

"They are good friends." I wasn't planning on giving him too much ammunition.

"Yes. Seems so. What part of 'I didn't want you following me' did you and they miss?"

"The part where it applied to me?"

He opened his eyes and sat up in his seat.

Before he could say anything else, I added, "Look, you needed me. The werewolves and I took down Malachai's minion backup, and we saved Damien."

He snorted. "Sure, by beating the crap out of him."

I shrugged. "It worked. He's alive, and Malachai is gone. Sure, we didn't beat him beat him, but he's retreated for now. We can figure out a strategy to take him down for good another day." I glared at him. "You should have figured out I had no intention of staying behind."

He nodded. "Of course. That's why I had Runner guarding you. I figured he'd see the sense in keeping you out of it."

I shook my head. "No, he saw the sense in us being back up." I paused, trying to find the right words. "Look, Paul, you've been the lone vampire for a long time. Saving the world from evil and all that. You've gotten used to doing it on your own. But you don't have to any more. Sure, I'm not able to keep up with you in a fight, but I do have something to offer." I sighed. "I thought we worked through all of this when we took down McDonald and his werewolf gang. You accepted me as a partner then. What's so different now?"

He sighed and closed his eyes again. "The difference was Malachai. He terrified me. I knew he could use me to get to you. And … and I couldn't bear to live with it if he'd made me kill you."

Okay, yeah. That was a pretty good reason, but still not enough.

"He didn't. You fought him off. I had faith in you."

"But what if I hadn't."

"Then I'd be dead. And you'd be Malachai's slave again. But it didn't happen. You fought him off."

"With the help of your potion."

I nodded. "Exactly. With the help of my potion. We're stronger together than we are apart, you know."

His voice was quiet. "I know." I had to strain to hear his next words. "And I think that terrifies me more than my former master does."

I almost crashed the car at those words. What could I say to that?

Paul opened his eyes and looked at me. I could feel the weight of his gaze. Usually that weight felt warm and comforting. Not now.

"You've seen what happens to those who are close to me."

I sighed. Not this again. How long was he going to keep trotting that one out? "Fine," I said. "Then leave. Go back to being the lone vampire. I'll build my business and take care of the odd ghost. I can't keep doing this 'I want your friendship, but only on my terms' crap."

We pulled up in front of my house, and I turned off the car, tossing the keys to him. "Good night, Paul. You know where to find me if you need me."

I grabbed my bag and stalked to my apartment, fumbling with my keys to open the door. It was just being tired. Yeah, that's right. Had nothing to do with the tears filling my eyes.

I closed the door behind me and just stood there a moment, letting the solid wood support me. After a moment, I pushed myself erect and headed for the kitchen, with some vague plan of making some coffee or a snack. Or maybe just drowning my frustration in a pint of Ben and Jerry's.

A soft knock at my door.

"What now!" I thought about ignoring it, but decided that would be childish. So I went back and opened it.

Paul stood there, his clothes hanging off him, but still somehow looking good enough to eat.

"What?" I asked.

"May I come in?"

I stepped back. "Sure, I guess."

He followed me, and I closed the door.

A moment later, my back was against the door. My arms were full of vampire, and his lips were on mine. Hungry and so damned good.

Of course, I'd dreamed of this, and reality was every bit as good as the dream. Paul's tongue darted across my lower lip, and I opened my mouth to let him in. He pressed against me, and I moaned deep in my throat when I felt how hard he was. I moved my hands down to his ass and pressed us close together. If I could have made us one person, I would have.

His arms moved restlessly up and down my back. Fiery tingles followed his fingers, and I stood up on my toes to get better access to his mouth. A vague thought crossed my mind that the bed would be a better place for this. I took a small step back. The small whimper of protest from Paul was … just fantastic. Suddenly, I wanted him on my bed. I wanted him in me, and I wanted to see him come apart.

Reluctantly, I disengaged from his mouth. "Bed. Now."

He followed me willingly enough, although our progress was slowed by heated kisses. Along the way, I toed off my shoes and stripped off shirt, jeans, boxers and socks. Then I ripped off the remains of Paul's clothes, not hard since they were already a mess.

He chuckled at my desperation to get to skin on skin. We hit the bedroom, and I pushed him onto my bed, climbing on top of him and sighing when I finally felt all of him against me.

The coolness of his skin calmed my raging heat, and it was good. I didn't want this to be over too soon. Now that we were in full contact with each other, I could relax into the kissing. Paul's fangs dropped just a bit, enough that I could feel their scrape against my lips, and it was one of the most erotic things I'd ever felt. I ran my tongue against their sharp points, and he growled, deep in his chest. Instinctively, I knew it wasn't a threatening sound, and I pulled back.

"Your fangs are—" How did I put this?

He smiled, eyes glowing faintly amber. "Yes, they

are sensitive. Drinking is a sensual experience for us."

"Will you? I mean, from me?" Did I really just ask that?

His pupils dilated, and he pressed harder against me. "If you'd like. Yes." His voice was deep and husky, and his tone went straight to my cock. His lips nuzzled my neck, and I could feel cool prickles against my skin.

While all I wanted was to drown in the sensations darting all through my body, I forced enough awareness to ask, "Is it safe?" Sure, they call climaxing "the little death," but I didn't want to test that too far tonight.

He nipped lightly near my jugular, and I gasped, jerking my hips against his thigh. "It's safe enough." He tone was like a man only half-awake. I could feel the tension in his body under my hands, and his hips rhythmically moved against me.

Oh hell. This was Paul. I trusted him, and if I was going to go, it might as well be like this. "Do it," I said, my voice little more than a whisper.

Fangs pressed against me for a moment and then were gone. Now it was my turn to whimper in protest.

His hands soothed me as he said, "It's okay. Just not like this. It can be even better."

With his hands, lips and fangs, he inflamed every sense in me, until all rational thought fled and all I wanted was more of him.

When I couldn't stand it any longer, he took me, with both his body and his teeth, and I came apart completely. It was the most amazing thing I'd ever experienced.

When I came back to myself, I rolled over with a huge sigh. "God, Paul. That was amazing." Truly it had been the most incredible sex I'd ever experienced. The hint of danger. Paul's evident skill. All of it combined to leave me breathless. And greedily wanting more. I touched my neck. A bit sore, but not much more than a bad bug bite. I could live with that. I pulled back my hand. No blood, which didn't really surprise me. Paul had been ... quite thorough in cleaning up after himself.

Although my body didn't really feel like moving, I propped myself up on an elbow, wanting to just look at Paul. I'd never really felt I had the right to look. And touch. And everything we'd just done told me I had the right to do both. And perhaps I'd had them for longer than I'd realized.

The vampire's eyes were closed, and his face relaxed. His skin was warm under my hand, which surprised me. He hadn't taken much from me.

"I need less when it's fresh from the source." He didn't even bother to open his eyes, but he did arch into my hand as I continued to stroke his side. No one ever mentioned that vampires were really like big cats. I'm shallow I know, but I couldn't help it. I was completely incapable of halting my eyes from the slow scan, up and down. Sculpted chest with only a scattering of chest hair, ripped abs and still half-hard cock. My own nudged at me, suggesting perhaps a second go was in order.

Maybe later. Curiosity was stronger than arousal. "Could you ... well ... live off me?"

He smiled. "No." He paused, and I suppressed the sudden surge of disappointment that shot through me. "Well, maybe if we never fought anything, but that doesn't seem likely."

No, not the way things had been going.

"I need the extra blood to heal and recharge. But for day-to-day feeding, yes, what we just did would be enough."

I couldn't believe he was being so open and relaxed about this. What happened to the Paul who barely wanted to tell me anything about himself or his kind?

I lifted his arm so I could snuggle under it, my head on his chest. "You're okay with this?"

I felt him nod. "Yes."

"Why?" The word fell out of my mouth before I could stop it.

I felt his body stiffen under me, and I bent my head so I could see his face. Now his eyes were open, and he was frowning at me.

"What do you mean?" He sounded hurt, and I stroked my hand over his chest.

"I mean that it wasn't that long ago that you were telling me how dangerous you are. How you didn't think you could have another relationship with a human, and now, you're curled up with me, practically purring."

A low rumble started in his throat, and the expression in his eyes turned wicked.

My hand stopped its roaming. "Oh, that is so not fair! Awesome at sex, hell on two legs against bad guys, and you can purr."

He grinned. "It's all part of the package." His muscles relaxed against me, and he continued. "I guess I just can't fight it anymore. You're ... something special."

I liked the sound of that, but I also knew when he wasn't being completely honest with me. "There's more to it than that?"

He eyed me, and a bit of red suffused his cheeks. Was that embarrassment?

"You're right."

I waited, but he didn't say anything else. "Go on."

He closed his eyes and shifted under me. "I'm not sure how to say this."

"How about straight up?"

"While vampires have intellect, and mostly we are in control of our actions and reactions, there are a few things that are instinct with us. Feeding for one. Fighting is another. I can plan tactics and strategy, but most of it is instinct."

"Okay. So what's the other thing that's instinct?"

He sighed. "This isn't easy, Dafydd. This has never happened to me before. I never thought it would."

I was getting frustrated. "What?"

He opened his eyes. No trace of amber, just cool blue-gray. "You started it that time at Lounge 201. When you acted like we were bonded. And then a few days ago, when you took command at the crime scene, with the witch."

"Started what?" Yeah, I had an inkling where this was going, but I wanted to be certain.

He didn't answer my question, instead saying, "And then tonight. You ... fought for me. You stood up to my master and fought for me."

"Well, I was kind of pissed. I thought he'd killed you."

"No, I don't think you understand. By fighting another challenger, you ... sealed me to you."

My hand stopped moving. "You mean—"

He nodded. "Yes, you bonded to me."

I blinked. "And that means what, exactly?"

He shifted, trying to sit up, and I moved, sitting up, but keeping my leg in contact with him.

"Probably not as much as a fantasy writer would think, but basically, it means that I can resist draining you when I feed because the bond just won't allow it. And I'll get more from it, because of the strength of what's between us."

I shook my head. That didn't make sense. "Wait. You've said that vampires bond with humans, but you indicated it still wasn't entirely safe. That a vampire could kill its human at any time. The danger was what some humans get off on."

He looked away. "True. But, we don't exactly have that kind of bond."

"Then what do we have, exactly?"

He closed his eyes for a long moment, then opened them and looked at me directly. "You are a warlock, not a normal human. You have magic, and that changes everything. Also, you fought for me." He paused a moment, obviously trying to gather his thoughts. "That means … that means I'm not exactly the one initiating this. Or completely in control of it."

Oh?

Oh!

"You mean, I did this to you. And, I'm the … err … senior partner in this?"

He nodded, his expression hesitant and even, well, a bit fearful. "I wasn't completely certain until you left me in the car, but then I realized I couldn't resist the pull."

I pulled on his arm, and drew him close. So, I just bonded a vampire, and not completely willingly. Oh, not that he seemed to mind too much, but Paul had always been the dominant half of this relationship. He usually called the shots, and he definitely was the one with more knowledge of tactics and the supernatural world. That had made him the logical leader.

And now I had just turned that on its head.

"I love you." Under the circumstances, it seemed the best thing to say.

He relaxed against me. "And I love you."

I closed my eyes. I thought so, but he hadn't said it before. And his voice had no hesitation.

"Will this hurt you with the vampire community?"

He shook his head. "No. As I said before, it's not a common arrangement, but warlocks are both respected and feared. So there's no shame in it. Most of them think we've been bonded for a while. As far as the community is concerned, nothing's changed."

I nodded, satisfied. "Well, all right then. It's good."

"It is?"

"Definitely. I figured you'd go all noble and right-eous after we made love, and you came back to your senses. You'd do the 'right thing' and leave for my safety."

He chuckled. "I can't say you're entirely wrong, but I really can't. Not now." His expression grew thought-ful for a moment, and he said, "There's something I've been wondering about."

I shifted to a more comfortable position on his chest. "What's that?"

"It's been obvious you were attracted to me, and, although I tried to keep my sexuality from you, I know I slipped up a few times. I mean, where I lived should have been a big clue."

Yeah, I had been acting kind of clueless, hadn't I?

Paul continued. "So, I was wondering, why didn't you ever make a move?"

Ah, good question. Well, he'd been honest with me. Guess it was only fair that I shared back. "It's kind of an awkward thing for me."

His arm tightened around me. "If you don't want to—"

I shook my head. "No, it's okay." I took a deep breath. "So, I've known I was gay a long time. I came out early to my parents. They were like 'no big deal' about it. But the first time I was attracted to someone … well, let's just say it didn't work out that well. I was fifteen, and I thought he was as into me as I was to him. We'd kissed and done a bit more than that. I was sure I was in love, and he was the one for me."

Paul made a sympathetic sound deep in his throat. "But something happened."

"You could say that. One day, he just started yelling at me. Calling me a faggot and saying I was sick for being interested in him. Then he hit me and took off. I never saw him again."

The memory of the humiliation and shame I'd felt that day washed over me, and I shivered. Paul kissed the top of my head. "Do you know what had happened to make him change like that?"

I shrugged. "One of my friends hinted later that his parents were really conservative. I'm guessing they found out and, I don't know, made him break it off with me. Anyway, I was pretty gun shy for a while after that, and I've been really careful not to make a move on someone until I'm completely sure."

"That's not quite all, though, is it?" His voice was smooth and warm.

I shook my head. "No, I guess not. You see, I wanted you so badly, it's like I couldn't believe you'd want me back. So I kind of convinced myself that you weren't interested."

"So it wouldn't hurt as bad when you finally discovered the truth."

"Yeah, something like that." I hugged him tighter. "But it didn't work out quite as I'd planned. Once I figured out that what I felt wasn't just 'attraction,' I was figuring out that there was no going back. If you hadn't been interested … well, it would have hurt. A lot."

"Not a problem now." Affection suffused his tone.

I pulled back to look at him directly. "And if I had to bond you to keep you with me, well, then, that's that." I let amusement creep into my expression. "And if I'm the 'senior partner' in this, I promise to keep you more in the loop than you've kept me."

He grinned back at me. "That's more than fair."

I nodded. "All right then. First things first. You're going to make wild passionate love to me again."

His lips quirked, and his eyes glowed amber. "Done. And after that?"

I kissed him before saying, "Then you're going to tell me everything I need to know about vampires. No holding back this time."

He kissed me and pushed me back onto the bed.

"Done. Partner."

The End